Warped 1

A Jo Riskin Mystery: Book 2

Debbie S. TenBrink

Warped Passage
A Jo Riskin™ Mystery
Red Adept Publishing, LLC
104 Bugenfield Court
Garner, NC 27529
http://RedAdeptPublishing.com/

For my family

Every story has a beginning, a middle, and an end.

You are my story.

Chapter 1

Jason watched his girlfriend, Lisa, gyrate to the techno music thumping out of the Bose speakers propped on the stump of a downed oak tree. Her electric-blue ponytail swung wildly as she threw her hands above her head and rocked her hips to the beat.

She held out her hand to him. "Come on, Jason. Dance with me!"

He exhaled a stream of smoke, squinted at her through the haze, and smiled lazily. "How about you dance for me? I'll just chill here and watch."

She tugged on his hand and stuck out her bottom lip in an exaggerated pout. "I want to dance *with* you."

"Come on, babe." He groaned as he pulled her into his lap, then he brought the joint back up to his mouth, inhaled deeply, and held the sweet smoke in his lungs.

"I'll make it worth your time," she said, wrapping her arms around his neck.

Struggling to keep his eyes open, Jason blew a stream of smoke out of the corner of his mouth. He could feel the burnout coming on as the buzz settled in and turned his bones to jelly. "Maybe later. I'm just taking a little smoke break."

Lisa threw her hands in the air. "Fine! I'll find someone else to dance with me."

She slid off his lap, grabbed a beer from the cooler at his feet, then stomped around the bonfire to join a group dancing on the other side. Glaring at him from across the flames, she pressed her tiny frame against a lanky stranger who was all too happy to accommodate.

Kenny whistled. "Damn, she don't mess around."

"Looks like she's about to," Peter chimed in. He held out his fist for a knuckle bump. Kenny shook his head and left him hanging.

Jason rolled his head around to stare Peter down. "Shut the hell up." He chugged the rest of his beer, tossed the bottle into the woods behind him, pulled another one from the cooler, and twisted off the top. "Who's that dickhead she's dancing with?"

"I don't know, man. He came with Trevor. Looks like a jock, though," Kenny said.

Peter snickered. "Don't worry. Chicks never go for the jocks. Especially not the ones that are jacked like that dude."

Jason flipped him the bird with the joint still gripped between his thumb and pointer finger. "Didn't I tell you to shut the hell up?"

"Just messin' with you, bro. Damn, chill out." Peter took a swig of his beer then leaned forward and swung the bottle lazily between his legs.

Jason tossed back his head and powered down his beer. He pounded a fist into his chest and belched then pushed himself out of his canvas camp chair. "I think it's time Dickhead Jock learns just where the bear shits in the woods."

He slammed the beer bottle down onto the top of the cooler then staggered around the fire, stepped between Lisa and the stranger, and stood toe-to-toe with the much taller boy. "How 'bout you get your hands off my girl."

The other boy took a step back. "I was just dancing. Your girl came to me. I can't help it if she's looking for a real man."

Jason sneered as he balled up his fist and pulled his arm back.

Lisa grabbed his wrist and pulled him toward her. "Jason, don't."

He yanked his arm away. "What do you care?"

"You're so stupid sometimes." She wrapped her arms around his waist and rested her chin on his chest, looking up at him with melted-chocolate eyes. "Why would I want him when I have you?"

Relief washed over Jason. He was so baked he could barely stay on his feet. No way could he have taken on some jock. He turned around and cocked his head at the boy. "I guess we know who the real man is here, don't we?"

The boy took a step forward, and Jason jolted, stumbling backward into Lisa. He stuck his hand out to catch her before she fell, but his reflexes were tweaked, and she hit the ground with a thud.

"You son of a bitch!" he growled, glaring at the jock.

Lisa jumped to her feet and grabbed his hand. "Come on. Let's go."

"That prick knocked you over!"

"*You* knocked her over, you clumsy shit," the jock said.

Lisa pulled on his hand. "I want to go home."

Jason flung his arm around his girl, flipped his middle finger at the boy, then turned toward the woods.

Lisa looked over her shoulder. "Where are we going? The path is that way."

"I gotta take a piss."

She rolled her eyes. "Nice."

Ten yards into the dense woods, Lisa stopped and shrugged off his arm. "We don't have to go all the way in there. I'll just wait here."

"You scared?" Jason teased, grabbing her hand and pulling her deeper into the trees.

She yanked her hand free then crossed her arms and leaned against a tree. "Just go. It's really cold now that we're away from the fire."

"Okay, but be careful here all alone. The boogeyman might get you."

Looking around the area, Lisa crinkled her nose and brought her hand to her face. "It smells like something died out here."

"Well, we're in the woods, babe. Animals die, and ain't nobody burying 'em."

She gagged and pulled her coat up to cover her nose. "I'm getting out of here."

"Just give me a minute." Jason stumbled through the overgrowth, forcing his legs, which felt like heated rubber, over the tangle of vines and brush. "Your dumb jock probably took a deuce in the woods!" he yelled over his shoulder then snorted at his own joke.

"Just shut up and hurry!"

He stopped at a large tree, leaned one hand against the trunk to steady himself, and fumbled with his belt buckle with the other hand. Unable to manage the buckle one-handed, he let go of the tree. The odor suddenly hit him like a slap in the face. Vomit pushed at the back of his throat as the world lurched and spun out of control. He took a step to regain his balance and fell to his knees. "Damn it!" he roared as he dropped onto his butt.

"You okay?" Lisa called.

He grabbed his knee where it had banged against a knobby tree root. "I fell. Hurt my damn knee."

He rolled onto his back, holding his knee, and stared up at the sky while the trees spun around him. Dropping his leg back to the ground, he flung his arms out to his sides to stop the spinning. His hand hit something solid and sticky. "What the...?"

Jason sat up and pulled his cell phone out of his pocket. After six tries, he managed to turn on the flashlight. Shining the light on his hand, he stared at the inky substance smeared across his palm. He rubbed his thumb over his fingers. *Did I just stick my hand on a freakin' dead animal?*

He flashed the light on the spot where his hand had been. "Oh my God! Shit! Shit!" His phone slipped from his grip as he desperately scrubbed his hands on his jeans.

"Jason? What's going on?"

"Call the cops!" he cried, frantically feeling around on the ground for his phone.

Lisa crashed through the brush, sticks snapping loudly under her feet. "Are you kidding me? You want all our friends to get arrested?"

Jason's fingers brushed against the cool smoothness of his phone case. He picked it up and blew out a quick breath of relief when the light shined one bright spot in the darkness.

Lisa came around the side of the tree. "What the hell is going on? Can we just get out of here? It stinks worse than back there."

Jason's hands shook. The thumping of the techno music from the party pounded in his chest. He buried his nose in the crook of his elbow, took a deep breath, then slowly raised the light to the tree. The beam first caught work boots and blue jeans.

Lisa threw her hand to her mouth. Jason swallowed hard then moved the light up. Emerald-colored eyes bulged out of a dark, bloated face. A thick tongue, black and swollen, lolled out of the side of a gaping mouth.

Lisa screamed. Jason scrambled away on all fours and vomited up beer and pizza. When there was nothing left in his stomach, he wiped the snot from his face, dragged himself to his feet, and staggered back to find Lisa rocking on her knees, her face in her hands. He dropped down beside her and put an arm around her shoulders. She gripped the front of his coat and buried her face in his chest.

Jason gently rubbed her back. "I think we better call the cops."

Chapter 2

Stroking her dog's head with one hand, Jo Riskin grabbed her cell phone with the other and dialed Jack Riley.

"Hey, Jo." Jack spoke barely above a whisper.

She pressed the phone between her ear and shoulder and picked up her Corona Light from the end table. "Did I catch you at a bad time?"

"Finally got both kids to sleep. I wasn't quite out of the room when the phone rang."

Jo squeezed her eyes shut, mentally berating herself for calling so late. "I didn't wake them up, did I?"

"Nope, I can be quick and quiet at the same time."

Jo chuckled. "That's probably one of the most important parenting skills a person can possess. I saw that you called me a little while ago. What's up?"

"I wanted to let you know I got a call today from Dave Jasma, the prosecutor on Drevin Clayburn's case. The motion to dismiss was thrown out."

She pumped her fist as relief flooded through her. "Yes!" Mojo raised her head and regarded her with sleepy eyes. Jo dropped her hand back to the dog's head and buried her fingers in the silky fur. "How much of a song and dance did he have to do to get around my involvement?"

"Well, the fact that you were near the premises when the gun was found wasn't a consideration and was thrown out immediately. He had to do a little more dancing to get around you having been the one who brought him down."

"What was I supposed to do? Let him run?" Jo huffed then took a swig of her beer. As she had done countless times, she replayed tackling her husband's killer and pulling her gun. Too often, she envisioned herself pulling the trigger. She could almost feel the rush of adrenaline she would get from watching the light go out in the eyes of the man who had destroyed her life. It had been the only time in her career that she wished she weren't a cop. "They should give me a medal for not putting a bullet between his eyes."

"We both know you're not built that way. If anyone believes in the justice system, it's you."

"I have to believe in it in order to sleep at night and to do what I do every day. You know what else I believe in? Heaven and hell."

"Well, then you can entertain yourself with fantasies of Drevin's eternal damnation," Jack said.

"Oh, I already do that more often than I want to admit. Seriously, though, what did the judge think I should've done?"

"Jasma didn't say, but he made the same case you did, that a killer could have run free if you hadn't chased him down. And since we have matching ballistics and the statement of the ex-girlfriend..."

Jo grinned. "The son of a bitch is going to trial."

"Yes, he is. And I promise you he will pay for killing Mike."

Jo dropped her head back on the headrest of her reclining sofa then looked toward the end table and gazed at a picture of her and Mike at the peak of Pictured Rocks. They had hiked that whole day. Her hair was a tangled mess, and Mike had an angry red streak across his right eye where a tree branch had smacked him. But they were grinning from ear to ear, and it was her favorite picture. "What's the going rate these days for killing someone's husband?"

"It will never be enough. I had a long talk with Jasma, and he doesn't think he can get first degree. He can't prove the murder was premeditated."

Jo slammed her beer down on the end table. "So he'll get second degree? Or manslaughter?"

Mojo raised her head and cocked it then stared at Jo with her ears raised in attention. Jo dropped her hand down onto Mojo's head and petted her gently.

Jack answered, "If he can get the evidence he needs, he'll press for first degree, but if the evidence isn't there..."

"Then he skates." If that son of a bitch ended up walking the streets again, she wasn't sure how she would deal with it. The thought of seeing him stroll away from Mike's murder unscathed sent a flood of anger crashing through her body like ocean waves in a hurricane.

"He's not going to skate, Jo. Even if Jasma's forced to settle for second degree, he's adding on charges of intent to distribute, possession of a stolen vehicle, and anything else he can think of. I told him to throw everything but the kitchen sink at this guy."

"Well, I hope he does, because if that guy ever gets outside that cage..."

"He won't."

Jo rubbed her eyes. It was late, and she was exhausted. "Thanks for everything you've put into this, Jack."

"Of course."

She toyed with the frayed end of the blanket on her lap. "I mean it. I appreciate how you've made this a priority."

"It's a priority to me because it's important to you."

Her heart skipped a beat. "Thank you," she said, trying to talk around a yawn.

Jack chuckled. "You better get some sleep."

"You heard that, huh? I'll talk to you soon."

"Good night, Jo."

She laid the phone on the end table, closed her eyes, and indulged in a momentary daydream in which none of the current situation was real. Mike walked in, dropped onto the sofa next to her, and asked about her day. They talked about her cases, about his, about something mundane like what they would have for dinner or how the truck needed new tires—all things that Jo had taken for granted for so long and missed with a dull ache. The times when the lump would close her throat or tears would crop up out of the blue were getting fewer and further between, but the ache in her chest was a constant companion.

Jo groaned when her phone buzzed. She opened one eye and turned her head to read the display. *Shit. Dispatch.*

She sat up, muted the *Ellen Show* she had recorded earlier, and snatched the phone from the end table. "Riskin."

"Lieutenant, this is Jerod in Dispatch. We've got a body found on the ninety-seven hundred block of Baumgard."

"In the park?"

"On the river, ma'am."

"Damn, a floater?" Nothing was worse than what time spent floating in water did to a human body. She would never get used to it.

"I don't know. The caller was a bit hysterical. We dispatched patrol cars to the site, and they called in a suspicious death."

Jo ran her hand through her hair then checked her watch: 11:25. "All right. Thanks, Jerod. Dispatch Detective Parker to the scene."

"Yes, ma'am."

She scrubbed her hands over her face then put the footrest down. Mojo raised her head and gave Jo a sleepy look, her brown eyes barely open.

Jo took Mojo's face in her hands and kissed the top of her head. "Sorry, old friend. Duty calls."

When she slid off the sofa, Mojo flopped her head back down.

Jo smiled and scratched behind the dog's ear. "Stay comfy. I'll be home as soon as I can."

She put on warm boots, wrapped a scarf around her neck, pulled on a stocking cap, and slipped into her heavy winter coat. After clipping on her credentials, she grabbed her bag, slipped on warm gloves, and headed out into the frigid November night.

JO PARKED ALONG THE side of the highway behind a myriad of emergency vehicles. Red and blue lights pierced the darkness. Traffic droned by, with drivers slowing slightly for the flashing lights or, more likely, hoping to catch a glimpse of the tragedy. She flung her bag over her shoulder and stepped out of the Ranger. A uniformed officer jogged around the front of her vehicle and met her at the door. She held up her badge for his inspection.

"I know who you are, Lieutenant," the officer said, light steam floating from his mouth as his warm breath met the cold air. He pointed toward the thicket down a steep slope from the road. "The body is down in the copse."

Jo raised an eyebrow. "Copse? It's not every day you hear someone use that word to describe the woods."

The officer looked embarrassed. "Sorry. My mom's an English teacher. I know a lot of weird words."

"Don't be sorry. I'm a bit of a word enthusiast myself." She eyed the throng of vehicles vying for position on the narrow gravel strip along the busy highway. "When you call 911, you get the whole kit and caboodle, don't you?"

The officer scoffed. "You sure do, Lieutenant. Everyone's just hanging around down there right now, waiting for you."

"That's good. I'm going to want to keep back any lookie-loos who decide to stop along the highway. And I'm sure the press will be here any minute. So"—Jo leaned close and read the officer's badge—"Officer Shaner, maybe you can help me with that."

"I can do that. I'll show you where they are then head back up here."

Jo took another quick look around. Lynae's car wasn't there. "My partner will be coming along soon. She drives a red Mazda."

"I'll take her down when she gets here."

"Appreciate it." Jo motioned to him with a grin. "Now lead me to the other cops by the body in the copse."

Shaner led the way down an embankment to a clump of trees. Midway down, he turned and pushed through the brush, holding back branches for Jo to duck under. What little light the moon had provided was absorbed by the dense thicket. She pulled her flashlight from her bag, flicked it on, and shined it directly in front of her feet.

Shaner looked over his shoulder. "Sorry, I should have thought of that. I've been through here a couple times already, so I know where I'm going."

"No problem. I just prefer to see what's under my feet so I can stay on them."

Disjointed, mumbling male voices echoed out of the darkness. "So seriously fucked up, it's gotta be a woman." Someone else said, "Fifty bucks says it's the wife. Bet she caught him screwing around. They can only hold out so long before a guy's gonna do what he's gonna do." And a third added, "Well, if it *is* a woman, we should start looking around. I'm sure she's still lost in here somewhere."

A roar of raucous laughter ensued. Jo stepped into a clearing and raised her flashlight, shining it on the group of men gathered around in a semicircle. Six sets of deer-in-the-headlights eyes turned.

"Well, gentlemen, I'm glad we have this case solved. Shall I send out a search party—of men, of course—so I can quickly find and arrest our victim's jealous, frigid wife? Or should I, perhaps, do an investigation first?"

Two firefighters and a paramedic shuffled uncomfortably, shifting from their cross-armed stances to shove their hands in their pockets and look anywhere but at Jo. Two of the three police officers came to full attention, while the last one stepped forward.

Carrot-orange hair was barely visible under his city-issued hat. Freckles danced across his nose and cheeks, deep brown against his pale skin. "Just trying to break the tension, ma'am. We're not used to seeing stuff like this."

Jo regarded the young officer. "Find a better way next time. And if you ever get used to this, it's time to retire." She turned to Shaner. "I can take it from here. Will you please go wait for Detective Parker?"

Shaner scowled at the redheaded officer then shook his head and turned back to follow the path he had forged.

Jo eyed the group of men. "My partner will be here soon. You're not going to want to let her catch you talking like that. I'm the nice one."

The men nodded as a unit. The young redhead looked at the ground. "Yes, ma'am."

"It's Lieutenant Riskin," Jo bit off. She took a deep breath through her nose to level out her anger with the chauvinistic bunch. "Who found the body, and where are they?"

A husky, middle-aged man stepped forward. He wore black pants and a white shirt with a Townline Paramedic logo emblazoned on the left pocket. "It was two teenagers. They're pretty shook up. My partner walked them up to the ambulance. I'm on my way up there now."

Jo pursed her lips. "Teenagers? It's almost midnight in the middle of the week."

The paramedic shrugged. "They can't be more than sixteen, seventeen years old."

Jo shook her head and sighed. "Okay. Keep them comfortable until I can talk to them. I'm sure you know the drill."

The man nodded and hustled to follow Officer Shaner's trail back to the ambulance.

Jo looked back at the group of men. "I'm going to need lights."

"We have portables in the rig," one of the firefighters offered.

"Great. Get them down here." She turned to the redhead, who was still staring at the ground. "You take me to the body."

The officer perked up and pointed at a tree directly behind where they stood. "Right over here, Lieutenant."

Jo followed him to the other side of the tree. The body dangled from the lowest branch. The man's feet were sprawled out in front of him as if he were sitting in a lounge chair, but his rear and upper body didn't touch the ground. The rope knotted around his neck held his head at an impossible angle and pushed the skin up into a grotesque cowl. Jo shined her light up the rope and noted that the branch had cracked at its base.

She exchanged her warm winter gloves with a pair of nitrile ones from her bag. "Thank you, Officer. Please go back up to where the vehicles are parked and help keep the area secure."

He nodded and scuttled away. The chill of late fall had slowed the decomposition process, but the pungent stench of rotting flesh combined with wet leaves tickled the back of Jo's throat. She unzipped an inner pocket in her bag and pulled out a small container of Vicks VapoRub. As she smeared a small amount under her nose, she heard a rustle in the thicket. Lynae's raspy voice said something Jo couldn't make out, then Officer Shaner's low chuckle came through clearly. A light bobbed as the officer led Lynae over.

When Jo could finally see their faces, she pointed her light at the victim. "The man of the hour."

Lynae flinched when she caught sight of the body. "Hanging is the worst."

"Floaters are the worst, but yeah, this is a close second."

Shaner looked over his shoulder into the woods. "Well, I better get back up there."

Lynae smiled up at the handsome officer. "Thanks for the escort, Randy."

He swallowed hard. Jo couldn't see it in the darkness, but she was sure his face flushed. "Anytime."

Lynae watched as he clomped back through the trees. When he disappeared into the darkness, she whistled quietly. "Damn."

"You need another minute, or are you ready to get to work?" Jo asked, smirking.

"You couldn't have found a reason he needed to stay here? Maybe something he had to bend over and pick up for us?"

"If there's any bending or picking up to be done, I'll be sure to call him back down here."

"Sure, you say that *now*."

Jo raised her flashlight and lit up the victim with its beam. "Maybe we should think about this guy for a while."

"I suppose," Lynae mumbled, looking over her shoulder at the path Randy had taken.

"You're going to want this," Jo said, handing the Vicks to her before squatting in front of the body. She tried to ignore the fact that her leather boots were sinking into the muddy earth. "This guy's been here at least a few days."

"Our killer probably didn't expect anyone to find him this quick, if ever. We're not exactly in a high-traffic area."

Jo ran her hand along the prickly surface of the rope around his neck. "Blood on the rope and scratch marks on his neck. He fought against it."

Lynae hunkered down next to her and tucked a stray strand of auburn hair behind her ear. "Probably dug his hands into the rope hard enough to make his fingers bleed."

The victim's arms hung limply at his sides, slightly behind the body. Jo pushed away some debris and picked up the left hand. Two fingernails were torn back, exposing the tender skin underneath. All four fingers were ripped raw, with blood dried on their tips.

"Oh, yeah, he fought." Jo pulled the sleeve of his jacket up and shined the light on raw red marks encircling the wrist. "Rope burns. He was bound at some point and awake enough to fight."

"He couldn't have been bound at the wrists and still have been able to fight against the rope around his neck. So he was held, at least for a little while, before he was brought out here."

"That would be my take, especially based on this bruising," Jo said, pointing at the black-and-purple bands surrounding the burns. She reached for the other hand and got only cloth from the cotton sweatshirt he wore. She gripped the forearm and lifted the whole arm up, exposing the meaty end where the hand should have been. Dried blood, black from time and exposure, caked the sleeve. "What the hell?"

"Shit." Lynae drew the word out until it formed its own complete sentence.

The cut was torn and uneven, as if the killer had sawed with a dull blade or hastily chopped in anger. "That's quite the hack job."

Lynae crinkled her nose. "Yeah. Not exactly surgical precision. Probably done with a hunter's bone saw or even a hacksaw." She gingerly picked her feet up, one at a time, and looked at the soles. "You think the hand will be here?"

Jo stood and shined her light around the body and the base of the tree. Pools of deep crimson stained the leaves that blanketed the ground. The VapoRub provided a welcome sting to her nostrils as she concentrated on breathing through her nose.

"We have to look for it, but no, I don't think it will be here. I think our killer would have kept it for whatever sick motive he had for hacking it off. There's enough blood on the ground that I think it was removed here. I would guess the killer had him bound when he brought him here, then he cut off the hand and strung him up. The victim fought with the one hand he had left, but he wouldn't have had much energy to fight for long with that volume of blood loss."

"Wouldn't he pass out after getting his hand chopped off? Or even *during*?"

"It sure seems like it, but sometimes, when there's no option for flight, the fight instinct pumps enough adrenaline to keep a person going longer than seems possible."

"You think he took the hand for a trophy?"

Jo shrugged. "Don't know. Maybe it's symbolic, like 'you did something terrible with this hand, so I'm cutting it off.'"

"Stole from someone, touched the wrong person, molested a child."

"The possibilities are endless at this point. We need to know more about our victim and what he may have been into."

Lynae looked around the thick woods, her flashlight illuminating one small portion at a time. "I wonder why here."

"I can't imagine. This spot would be a pain to get to with the highway on one side and the river on the other." Jo pointed back the way they had come. "That's too steep of an embankment to drive off from the highway, and there's no accessible path."

"And there's really no time when that stretch of highway doesn't have heavy traffic," Lynae added.

Jo stared in the general direction of the highway. "No, there isn't, so it's not reasonable that he carried or dragged the body from the road." She turned back to the body. "I don't want to touch anything else until Forensics gets here. Let's see what's on the other side of these trees."

Jo walked carefully through the thick underbrush, following the steady babble of the Grand River. She stopped and sniffed the air. "You smell that?"

Lynae drew in a deep breath through her nose. "It smells like a campfire."

"And pot."

Lynae's mouth dropped open. "How would you know what pot smells like?"

"Doesn't everyone?"

"Well, yeah, but I thought you probably wouldn't."

Jo sized up her partner. "I was married to a Narcotics cop for all those years, and you don't think I know what pot smells like?"

"Well, it's not like he brought it home and the two of you smoked it. Wait. Did he?"

Jo shot Lynae a look that she hoped would turn her partner's insides to jelly. After Mike's murder, local news outlets had speculated that his involvement in a drug ring was to blame. It took months to clear his name, and even then, it was done with little fanfare and no apology. That travesty still gnawed at Jo's gut. "Not funny." She turned and walked in the direction she thought the smell was coming from.

Lynae grabbed her arm. "I'm sorry. I wasn't thinking."

"I know. Forget about it."

A few yards away, Jo found a still-smoldering fire pit surrounded by multiple-sized river rocks. "I think we found where the smell is coming from."

Lynae directed her light around the perimeter of the pit. The grass was trampled, and logs had been pulled into a circle around the rocks. Beer cans and cigarette butts littered the ground. "Hopefully, our killer didn't come through here. Any trace evidence we might have had would be obliterated by this mess."

Jo shook her head in disgust. "Not only could the crime scene be jeopardized, but leaving this kind of mess on public property is just wrong on general principle."

Lynae groaned. "I hope we don't have to try to process all this."

Jo walked past the fire pit and scanned the area. "I know this stretch. There's a pretty well-worn footpath between here and the river. Mojo and I run it sometimes when I want to get out of our neighborhood. It's mostly hidden from the highway, other than a few patches where the trees thin out."

Lynae craned her neck to look around. "Then there is accessibility to it somewhere."

Jo flung her hand in the direction of the path. "Way the hell down. We're probably half a mile from the nearest parking lot in that direction, and there's nothing for a few miles the other way."

"Our victim had to be at least six-two and a solid two-forty. No way anyone dragged a body that big very far."

Jo pictured the fishing boats and men in waders who were a daily sight in the Grand from Riverside Park through downtown. Every morning, she saw them lined up as close as they legally could be to the fish ladder, and sometimes, she took a walk along the boardwalk at lunch to watch them haul in their take. November was cold, but the die-hards were still out there most mornings. "Our killer had to have come by boat. It's the only logical way to get someone here." She turned back toward the woods. "We're on a direct line from where our victim was found. Let's walk the riverbank."

They picked their way past the path and to the bank, carefully watching their feet. Jo stopped beside the bank and pointed her flashlight back at the trees. Those on the bank leaned heavily toward the water, their roots exposed and vulnerable from the constant pounding of the river. *Even if they were strong enough, he wouldn't want to leave the body that close to the river.* Willowy saplings and short bushes surrounded the trees and pushed back into the woods. "He would have had to stake this place out first or have prior knowledge of the woods. No way he took the chance that he could find a suitable tree. If he didn't, he would've had to drag the body all over the place, looking for one."

"Someone who lives on the river, maybe?" Lynae suggested.

"That would be my first guess. But it could be someone who does a lot of fishing or runs along this trail. Hell, it could be someone who just got in a boat and started looking." She shook her head. "This may have to wait until morning. With our limited light, we're going to be hard-pressed to find anything."

Lynae stopped and put her hand on Jo's shoulder. She pointed her flashlight beam at the ground. "Drag marks. And looks like a pretty good shoe imprint." She stepped carefully around the spot.

Jo squatted and examined the print. "Heavy rounded-heel imprint. Looks like a boot."

"He probably figured the water would wash away any footprints."

"Or he didn't think about his feet at all. Most people don't." Jo looked over her shoulder into the trees where the body waited. Bright lights illuminated one patch of the dark woods. "Looks like they have the lights set up. We're going to need some of those down here too."

Lynae pulled out her phone. "I'll get someone from Forensics down here to tape this area off and take a mold of the print. They'll bring lights with them."

"I hope Mal's leading the team. She's been pretty busy in the lab, so she may have sent someone else."

Lynae stopped, the phone halfway to her ear. "Ugh, I hope not. Wiseman is the best the county has."

"That's why she's so busy. Apparently, she's made a name for herself with hair and fiber analyses, and she's doing consults on cases outside the county. Leave it to Kent to find the best and mentor her into being even better." Jo had nothing but respect for Kent Alderink, the county coroner. He and his team had worked miracles on more than one case for her, and she had a soft spot for the elderly man who shared her love of unique words. She dreaded the day he decided to hang up his white coat to enjoy the retirement he so deserved. He was a mainstay in her life that she wasn't ready to lose.

Jo stood, hands on hips, and looked out across the river at the quiet neighborhood on the far bank. Street lights radiated yellow in the darkness. Cars lined the side streets in front of the houses that ran parallel to the river. Those people had no idea that directly across the river from their safe suburban homes, someone had been tortured and left to swing from a tree. "Maybe someone across the river saw a boat. It's a long shot, but let's call in some unis to go door-to-door."

Lynae smirked. "I can talk to Randy about that."

"You do that. I'm going to see who's here from Forensics, then I'll head up to talk to the kids who found the body. You know your way back?"

"Oh yeah, I'm actually really good at finding my way through the woods. I was a Girl Scout back in the day."

Jo crossed her arms and cocked a hip. "So that *Thanks for the escort, Randy*, eyelash flutter, giggle-giggle was completely unnecessary."

Lynae raised one eyebrow. "I do *not* giggle."

After a moment of contemplation, Jo said, "No, you're right. It was more of a sexy growl."

"I *do* sexy growl."

Jo rolled her eyes. "Go find Randy. And try to remember why you're there."

Lynae gave a quick salute and headed into the woods. Jo high-stepped through the thick bramble and back to where the forensic team was working in full force. Mallory Wiseman snapped pictures in rapid succession, expertly stepping around the scene without taking her eye from the camera viewfinder. She leaned in and focused on the victim's arm stump.

When the shutter stopped clicking, Jo stepped into the tech's view. "Hey, Mal. I'm glad to see you're on this."

The petite brunette lowered the camera so that it dangled around her neck, and she gave Jo a weary smile. "Hey, Jo. I'm happy to get out in the field. I don't do enough of it these days."

Jo nodded at the body. "Still happy to be here after seeing what we're dealing with?"

Mallory's face scrunched. "What one human is capable of doing to another never ceases to amaze me. But I must admit this is interesting. I've never had a case in which a body part has been intentionally removed. It will be a good one to add to my records."

"Livin' the dream, aren't we?"

Mallory raised one shoulder. "Life can be ugly. Gotta make the most of what we have."

"Good point. Have you seen anything that's jumped out at you yet?"

"Not yet, but I'm just getting pictures right now. Trace will take some time, considering this location."

"That's what I figured, but it can't hurt to ask. Can you give me a preliminary time of death?"

"Because of the cold temps with the dips in the evenings, it's a little hard to get a solid time this quickly. However, I can tell you he's been out here a minimum of three days."

"In my experience, your guesses are as good as science, so I'll run with that."

Mallory fiddled with one of the spotlights the firemen had set up. "I appreciate the confidence."

"I have a secondary location where I'll need your team," Jo said, reaching for the light to help the much shorter woman. "Lynae will take you to it whenever you're ready. If anyone's looking for me, I'm going to go talk to the kids who found the body."

Mallory nodded and went back to snapping pictures. Jo made her way back to the top of the embankment where the two witnesses were waiting. They sat motionless, wrapped in blankets, inside the ambulance. An officer stood outside the open back door.

Jo climbed into the back of the ambulance and sat down across from the pair. She leaned forward and rested her forearms on her legs. "Hi, I'm Lieutenant Riskin. I know this is really rough."

The girl nodded and palmed a tear from her cheek. Mascara melded with eyeliner and formed streaks that ran down her pale face like zebra stripes. "Can we go home soon?"

After pulling her notebook and pen from her bag, Jo settled back on the bench seat. "We'll get you home as soon as possible. I just have a few questions for you. Let's start with your names."

"Lisa Rowden?" the girl answered, lilting the last syllable so it came out like a question. The gum she was chewing didn't hide the smell of beer on her breath.

"And you?" Jo asked, turning to the boy.

He whipped his head to the side, forcing back the bleached hair that had fallen over one bloodshot eye. The hair immediately settled right back over his face. "Jason Benton."

Jo wrote their names in her notebook. "It's a little late to be out on a school night, isn't it?"

Lisa's head dropped. Jason shrugged and gave Jo a look of practiced boredom.

Jo looked from one to the other. "Why don't one of you tell me what happened. Why were you in the woods?"

Jason cleared his throat. "We were having a picnic."

Jo cocked her head. "A picnic?"

"Yeah. Ain't that right, Lisa?"

Lisa's dark eyes flicked to Jason. She nodded without looking at Jo.

"So the fire pit and beer cans down by the river... not yours, huh?"

Jason shook his head. "We were just having a picnic."

So this is how we're going to play it. "And you walked into the woods?"

"We were going home. I had to pee, so I went into the trees." Jason opened his hand and stared at his palm. "I tripped over something, and my hand went right on him."

"Where did you touch him?" Jo asked.

"I don't know. It was dark, and I couldn't see where my hand landed. But there was blood on it."

"Did you touch him besides that? Did you touch anything else, even accidentally?" *Tell me you didn't handle the rope.*

The silver gauge dangling in his left ear glinted as Jason's head shot up. "Hell no! I kinda yelled, maybe freaked out a little." Red crept up his face as he gave Lisa a sideways glance. "I puked in the bushes right next to him."

Lisa pulled her hand out from under her blanket and grabbed Jason's hand.

Jo's fingers itched to push that hair away from his eyes. "That's a terrible thing to see. We have seasoned detectives that still struggle when it's that bad."

"The smell was..." Jason closed his eyes, his mouth contorted as he swallowed hard. "It looked like there was a lot of blood. What happened to him?"

"We don't really know at this point. Anything you can tell us may help."

He looked down at his hands. "Do people always look like that when they're dead? All puffy and black like that?"

"No, they don't. I'm afraid what you saw is as bad as it gets," she said gently.

Jason didn't mention the missing hand. He must not have looked close enough to see it. "Did you take the footpath to get here?"

Jason jerked his head in the general direction of downtown. "Yeah, my car's parked back by the bridge on Broadway."

"Did you see anyone on the way to your picnic that looked out of place?"

Lisa wrapped her arms tightly around her body. "Did that just happen? Is the guy that did it still out there?"

"No, it wasn't recent, and I have no reason to believe the person who did this is still nearby. But sometimes people come back. I'm just covering my bases."

"We didn't see anybody on the path except a couple joggers. And we didn't see anyone in the woods but the dead guy."

Jo closed her notebook and slid it into her bag. "Thank you for talking with me. We may have questions for you later, but you can go home for now. Either we can call your parents to come get you, or I'll have an officer take you home."

"They can just take us back to the lot where my car is," Jason said.

Jo had noticed Lisa swaying slightly every time she raised her head, and Jason struggled to keep his watery, bloodshot eyes open. The sickly-sweet smell of marijuana clung to their clothes and hair and filled the confined area in the back of the ambulance. "I'm not going to bust you for your *picnic*, but I'm also not going to let you get behind the wheel of a car. You've been through enough today, so I'll save my lecture about drugs and alcohol for the next time we talk."

"I don't know what—"

Jo held up her hand. "Save it, Jason. If you want an officer to take you home, we'll make arrangements to get your car home also. Otherwise, we'll call your parents. Either way, you're not driving."

Lisa nudged her boyfriend with her elbow. "We'll take a ride from the police."

Jo stood and handed each of them a card. "I know that what you've seen can be very traumatic, and it may not hit you right away. If you need to talk to someone, at any point, we can set you up with a counselor. Just contact me, and I'll put you in touch with the right person."

"I think I'll be all right," Jason said as he stretched out his long legs and shoved the card into his front pocket. "I'm just never going to get that dead guy out of my head. Ever."

Lisa stared at the card in her shaking hand for a moment, then she looked up at Jo with glassy brown eyes. "I'm pretty sure I'm not going to be okay."

Jo sat down next to the girl and put her arm around her shoulders. Her slim body trembled with each breath. Jo worried that the teen might be on the edge of going into shock. "We'll get you home safely tonight. I know it seems impossible right now, but try to get some sleep. In the morning, I'll get the counselor's contact information to your parents. I'll make sure Dr. Mason fits you in right away."

Lisa covered her face with her hands and sobbed. Jo rubbed her shoulder while Jason stared at her helplessly.

When the girl was wrung out, she leaned against Jo and said, "I'm sorry."

Jo gave her shoulder a squeeze. "There's nothing to be sorry about. Do you think you're okay to go home?"

Lisa nodded and wiped her eyes and nose with the sleeve of her jacket. Jason dropped his blanket, stood, and held out his hand. Lisa drew in a deep breath and took it.

Jo jumped out of the back of the ambulance and turned to help Lisa. *Maybe this will be a wake-up call for both of them.* She turned to the officer standing by the ambulance door. "We need to get these kids and his car home. They are *not* to drive themselves."

The officer nodded. "No problem, Lieutenant."

Jo turned back to the couple. "Thank you for your help. I'll be in touch."

Chapter 3

Working well into the morning hours, Jo and her team searched the woods and the surrounding area. The forensic team, under the hawklike eye of Mallory Wiseman, processed the site, took a mold of the shoe imprint, and removed the body.

Lynae rubbed her eyes with the back of her hand and stifled a yawn. "Are we gonna get a few hours' sleep at some point?"

Jo checked her watch and realized it was later than she'd thought. "Go get some sleep and food. Come in whenever you're ready. We're done here, so I'll follow this back to the station. I'm good for a while."

Lynae closed her eyes and threw her head back. "You're awesome."

"Don't let word get out."

Lynae cocked one eyebrow. "Don't worry. No one would believe me, anyway."

Jo pointed toward the cars. "Go home."

After watching her friend pick her way out of the woods, Jo went back to her team. "All right, let's pack it up." She followed the county van back to the station, confident the adrenaline and caffeine would keep her going long enough to set up her murder board.

Back at the station, Jo grabbed a three-by-four board from the supply closet and set it up on an easel in her office. She sent a close-up of the victim, still strung to the tree, from her phone to her email then printed it off and taped it in the center of the board. She didn't have a name yet as it would take a little time for the fingerprints to be processed.

The adrenaline had worn off, and the thought of driving all the way home for only a few hours of sleep seemed pointless, so she decided her office was as good a place as any to catch a short nap. She shot out a quick text to her neighbor, Myla, asking her to drop in and take care of Mojo, then slid down in her seat, leaned her head back, and propped her feet up on her desk.

A KNOCK ON THE DOOR startled her awake. She grabbed the back of her neck and squeezed at the pain her sudden movement had caused. She checked her watch and was surprised to find she had been sleeping a few hours. "Come in."

Jack Riley stuck his head in the door.

Jo grinned, wondering for the umpteenth time if his tousled hair was an intentional look or if it just refused to be tamed. "Hey. What are you doing here?"

He set a drink carrier on her desk, pulled out a tall cup, and handed it to her. "I heard you caught a case late last night. Knowing you, I figured you skipped sleep and breakfast, so I brought you some strong coffee that doesn't suck."

"MadCap," Jo whispered reverently as she took the cup.

"And..." He pulled a bag out from behind his back, set it on her desk, and removed a bagel.

"If that's cinnamon raisin, I just might kiss you."

Jack wiggled his eyebrows and pulled a handful of peanut butter packets from his coat pocket. "And what's a cinnamon raisin bagel without peanut butter?"

"You're kidding me right now." Jo took the warm bagel in one hand and snatched two peanut butters from his outstretched hand with her other.

He made himself comfortable in her visitor chair, pulled his own bagel from the bag, and slathered it in peanut butter.

Jo took a bite of hers and moaned. "Oh God, this is good." She hadn't realized how hungry she was. *One bagel isn't going to cut it. Did I have dinner last night?*

After licking some peanut butter from his fingers, Jack retrieved the Bagel Beanery bag from next to his chair and tossed in onto Jo's desk. "I brought you two."

Jo's hands froze in midair. "You did not."

"When's the last time you ate?"

Jo squinted at him. "Are you in my head? I was just trying to remember. By the way, my head is a scary place. You do *not* want to spend much time there."

Jack leaned forward and stared intently at her. "You have to take care of yourself. With Mike's case heating up, it won't do you any good to be sick."

"Don't worry about me," Jo said, flopping back in her chair. She pulled off a piece of bagel and popped it in her mouth. Rolling the cinnamon-peanut-butter goodness around in her mouth, she suppressed a moan of satisfaction.

"Well, I do. I'm serious. You can't let it consume you."

Jo waved her bagel at him. "Jack, we're talking about the trial of the man who murdered my husband. This case has consumed me for over two years. And it isn't going to stop consuming me until it's over."

"I get that. I really do. But you have to eat. You have to sleep." He pulled an envelope from his jacket pocket and slid it across her desk. "And sometimes you have to have a little fun."

She furrowed her brow. "What's this?"

"Why don't you open it and find out?"

"Why did you get me something?" She turned the envelope over and examined it, trying to glean something from the innocuous white envelope.

Jack grinned. "You'll know when you see it."

"It isn't my birthday."

He threw up his hands. "I know! Just open the damn envelope."

Her eyebrows shot up. "A little testy for a guy offering a gift."

Jack huffed and pointed at the envelope. Jo slid her finger under the seal and dumped out the contents. She picked up a pair of VanAndel Arena tickets then sucked in a quick breath.

She gaped at him. "Garth Brooks? You got tickets to Garth Brooks? It's this week! How did you manage?"

Jack shrugged. "I have a few connections."

"Oh my God! I love Garth!"

"I gathered that from the fact that *Ropin' the Wind* is the only thing that's ever playing in your truck."

"Not true. I change it up with some *No Fences* or even the occasional *Man Against Machine* once in a while."

"You rebel."

She read over the ticket information a second time, unable to accept that they were real. "I tried to get tickets, but they sold out too fast. I don't know what to say."

Jack gave her one of his lopsided smiles. "How about thanks?"

Jo grinned. "Thanks." She spotted something else still inside the envelope and pulled it out. "Holy shit! These are backstage passes."

He beamed. "I told you I have a few connections."

"This is amazing." She reached into her desk drawer and removed her purse. "How much do I owe you?"

Jack lifted an eyebrow. "Really?"

"Well—"

"I thought we could have dinner at Cygnus first," he blurted.

"Oh, I don't—"

"I'm not much of a country-music guy, but I'll make an exception. Actually, we probably can't go to Cygnus. I don't think we'll be properly dressed. Unless, of course, you want me to wear a suit to the concert."

Jo's mind went blank. He was asking her out on a date. Up to that point, the time they had spent together was over coffee or a beer after work. They talked about cases or sports or lamented the pain of the politics that encompassed their work. A date was completely different. Mike's face popped into her mind, his warm green eyes crinkling up at the corners as he laughed at one of their inside jokes. He had been her only date for so long, she didn't even know if she knew how to go out with anyone else.

"Jo?"

She looked into Jack's questioning eyes, and Mike's face faded. She realized she had been staring at him without responding for a bit too long. *Can I do this? He's such a nice guy, but what about Mike?*

"I mean, if you don't want to go... I just thought, you know..."

Jo made up her mind and slid the tickets back into the envelope. "No."

Jack's face fell. "No?"

"No suits for Garth Brooks. Strictly jeans." She scowled. "You do own jeans, don't you?"

Jack's face lit up. "I'll see if I can scrounge up a pair. I'll try not to embarrass you."

"Good. I don't want to make a bad first impression on Garth."

Jack rolled his eyes then took a bite of bagel and washed it down with some coffee. "So what do you got going on with this new case?"

Jo dug into the Bagel Beanery bag and pulled out her second bagel. "Guy found in the woods by the Grand. Missing his right hand. Hung from a tree there but mostly on the ground by the time he was found. I'm waiting on an ID."

"Who found him?"

Jo slathered all the remaining peanut butter onto her bagel and licked the plastic knife before throwing it into the trash can. "Couple of kids on a picnic."

Jack cocked his head. "A picnic?"

"That's teenager speak for sex and partying," she said around a mouthful of bagel.

He pursed his lips. "Not very creative. What parent is going to believe that?"

"Right? And they were trying to sell it to a cop." When her desk phone rang, she wiped her hands on her pants before answering. "Riskin."

"Lieutenant, this is Kate in the lab. I have an ID on your victim."

"That was quick."

"Isaac asked me to push it to the top of the pile. Your guy's name is Brad Kramer. I have an address, a driver's license picture, and a couple of morgue shots. I'll email them all to you as soon as I get my computer working."

Jo jotted the victim's name on a sticky note. "Computer problems already this morning?"

"It was working. Now it's making some scary whiny noise, and the cursor won't move."

Jo grimaced. "That can't be good."

"I'm jinxed. Computers see me coming and just roll over and give up."

"Maybe you should email the results to Lynae. I don't want your bad computer juju."

Kate snorted. "Smart woman. Oh, wait. What the...?"

"More problems?" Jo pulled off a piece of bagel and popped it in her mouth.

"The noise stopped, but now the screen is completely black, and the power light is red."

Jo looked up at Jack and shook her head. "Red's not good. Maybe you could have someone else in the lab email them to us?"

Kate sighed heavily. "That would probably be best. I'll have to call IT again. I think they play paper-rock-scissors when they see my number come up."

"Maybe you should ask for a new computer. It sounds like that one has some issues."

"Doesn't matter. I've killed more computers than anyone wants to talk about."

"I wish I could help you, but computers and I have an understanding. I use them, but I don't try to fix them. In return, they generally leave me alone."

"Lucky."

Jo checked her watch. "Thanks for the quick turnaround on this. We'll look out for the results coming from someone other than you."

"You should see them in a few minutes from Steve."

Jo hung up and committed Kate's name to memory. She finally knew Isaac's "in" at the lab and fully intended to exploit it at every opportunity. She would have to thank the newest member of her team for being so charming that he managed to get results that the rest of her team could only dream of. She downed the last bite of bagel, wadded up the bag, and two-pointed it into the trash. "We have an ID. Time to get to work."

Jack popped out of his chair and slipped on his coat. "Go get 'em, Lieutenant."

Jo smiled up at the first man since Mike to even make her consider going on a date. "Thanks for breakfast. And of course, for the tickets. I can't wait for that concert."

He pulled his keys out of his coat pocket and swung them absently around his finger. His green eyes danced mischievously. "Maybe we should forget the restaurant and have a picnic instead."

Jo pointed at the door. "Get out of here."

Jack threw back his head and laughed then ducked out of the office before she could find something to throw at him. She could still hear him laughing as he got on the elevator.

Her heart thumped. *Damn. That laugh.* She gathered her notes for the morning meeting to discuss caseloads and make assignments.

JO STOOD AT THE HEAD of the table at the front of the room, case notes laid out next to her. She scanned to the first case on the list. "Evans and Manson, what's going on with your drive-by?"

Luke Evans set down his coffee cup and held up his hands. "Nobody saw anything. The mom gave me some names, and we've interviewed them. Every one of them has a record, and we know they're with the Widow Makers, but we don't have anything to hold them on. No witnesses, no threats. You know the drill."

"Ballistics?"

"Ballistics are still out," Luke said. "That's all we have, Lieutenant. We canvassed the neighborhood, talked to every neighbor. Nobody saw anything."

Jo crossed her arms. "Try to shake down some of the other Widow Makers. They're the biggest gang in Grand Rapids. One of them will have something to gain or lose. Find out who and what and work with it. Other than that, we wait for ballistics. Then get the suspects back and press them a bit. If they're guilty, somebody will crack or brag."

Luke nodded, his second chin almost making contact with his burly chest. He reached across the table to grab another donut. The effort caused his faded blue shirt to stretch dangerously around the buttons. "You got it, boss."

Jo jotted a note on the Evans-Mason file then flipped to the next one. "Breuker and Lainard, what did you guys pick up?"

Charles Lainard leaned his lanky frame back in his chair. "Just a junkie hooker."

She gave him a sharp look. "Just?"

Isaac Breuker cleared his throat and gave his partner a sideways glance. "Got an ID from her belongings. Can't find any family yet. We think the name and ID might be fake. Victim was found in the old Crestwood High School on the north side. What's left of her and her belongings indicates she may have been a prostitute with a heroin habit."

Jo raised one eyebrow. "What's left of her?"

Isaac shifted in his seat. "She'd been there a while. Abandoned building. Vermin. You know the story. The lab's trying to get enough finger to make a print."

Jo felt her stomach lurch. *Left alone in a building to be picked at by rats. No one deserves that.* She made a note on the file then went to the next and continued in that fashion until she had been updated on every active file. "All right, we're pretty loaded up right now. Lynae and I caught a new one last night. ID has been made, thanks to a quick turnaround in the lab." She closed her case notes. "Let's get to it."

Paper was shuffled, and metal chairs slid across the linoleum floor. The din of multiple conversations filled the room.

Jo dropped her notebook into her bag and motioned to Lynae that she would catch up. "Charles, hang back a minute."

Charles stopped at the open door, looked at Jo over his shoulder, then strolled back into the room. "What's up?"

She searched his eyes. "You tell me."

Charles sat on the corner of the table. "I don't know what you're talking about."

"*Just* a junkie hooker? What the hell is that about?"

"I'm just saying nobody's going to care if this gets solved right away. If there's another case that needs our attention, we can back burner this one for a while."

Jo cocked her head. "You think that woman is less important than our other cases?"

"I didn't say she's less important. I just think you live the life, you take your chances."

"So she deserved to die?" Jo asked, searching her detective's eyes for any indication that he actually felt that way. That kind of thinking was out of character for him and absolutely unacceptable in her department.

He held up his hands, palms out. "That's not what I'm saying. I just think they know what they're signing up for when they start walking the streets. It's no surprise to anyone when one ends up dead."

Her brain ping-ponged between the prostitute dying alone in a school and Mike dying alone in a cold warehouse. His killer was going to pay, and that woman deserved the same justice. She jabbed a finger at Charles, anger turning her voice up a notch. "You know nothing about this woman. You don't know why she's on the street. You don't know what drove her there, what happened in her life to put her in that desperate position. You don't know what kind of addictions she had that were so overpowering that she would sell her body for one more hit. Or maybe she had kids to feed, and that was the only way she could do it."

Charles rolled his eyes. "Everyone has a story, but not everyone ends up on the street. People have to take a little responsibility. If she was an addict, she should have gotten help, not started walking the streets."

Jo stared, dumbfounded. *Is he serious?* "We both know it's not that simple. No one lives that life because it's what they always dreamed of. And she wasn't just a prostitute. She was somebody's child or somebody's sister, mother, or friend. She was somebody."

He gave her a smug look. "She was dead in that old school long enough that, thanks to time and vermin, there wasn't much left of her. In all that time, nobody even reported her missing. Still haven't. Nobody cares."

Jo opened the case file and pulled out the victim's picture. Hot-pink hair screamed out from a face gruesomely pulled apart by rats. "If she doesn't matter to anyone else, that's even more reason she should matter to us. What someone does for a living doesn't determine how well we work the case or how much we care."

"They all know that every time they get in some john's car, it could be the last time. And they keep doing it."

Jo raised one eyebrow. "And we know every time we take a call, it could be our last."

"It's different, and you know it."

She slapped the file shut and handed it to Charles. "Every case is as important as every other case. Work it, and work it right. If I need your expertise on my case, I'll ask for it, and you do the same for yours. But you work that case. And don't ever let me hear you say it doesn't matter again, or you'll be looking for a new job. Do we understand each other?"

Charles looked at her blandly. "Perfectly."

Jo softened. "What's going on? I've known you for a long time. This isn't like you."

Charles shrugged and stared at the floor.

Jo perched on the table next to him. "Lisa okay? The kids?"

He heaved a sigh. "Lisa left me last week. Took the kids and went to live with her sister in Kentwood."

Jo laid a hand on his arm. "I'm so sorry, Charles. Have you been able to talk to her about it?"

"What's to say? I'm a lousy husband."

"Charles, that's..." She trailed off. They both knew it was true. Consoling him with platitudes wouldn't help.

He hung his head. "Exactly. There's no denying it. I suck. I wasn't meant to be a husband. Or a father. But man, I love those kids."

"You're a good dad. You just need work in the husband department."

"More work than Lisa is willing to deal with."

"Would you be willing to get counseling? Would she?" Jo wanted to scream at him to not give up without a fight, but she knew his wife was justified in leaving. She had watched him flirt with too many women to doubt that he was a lousy husband.

"I think it's past that. She's put up with too much for too long." He stood and walked to the door. "I won't let it affect me here again. Sorry about the attitude."

Jo smiled sadly. "You're a hell of a detective. I would hate to lose you. I can be flexible on a lot of things, but—"

"But not on working the cases. I know."

"Talk to someone, Charles."

Charles opened the door and looked back over his shoulder. "Thanks, but I'll be fine." He gave her a half smile that never reached his eyes and slipped out of the room.

Jo leaned her head back and stared at the ceiling. *If only people knew what they had before they lost it.* She slid off the table, grabbed her bag and coat, and headed to the bull pen.

Lynae was engrossed in whatever was on her computer monitor. She leaned in close to the screen and jotted notes with one hand while scrolling with the other.

Jo walked up behind her and quickly scanned her screen. "Detective exam?"

Lynae jolted. A small squeal escaped before she slapped her hand over her mouth. She jumped out of her chair, eyes wide. "What the hell?"

The three detectives in the bull pen broke into laughter.

Jo snorted. "I'm sorry. I didn't mean to scare you."

"Don't you people have anything better to do?" Lynae scolded her fellow detectives, giving them her most vicious glare.

The detectives looked at each other and shrugged.

"Nope," one said.

Another added, "I don't."

The third threw in, "I had a couple free minutes."

Lynae pinched the bridge of her nose then grudgingly chuckled. "Thanks for having my back, guys. I'll remember this." She turned to Jo and pointed. "And you—"

Jo held up her hands. "What? I just came to get you. I'm completely innocent."

Lynae propped a hand on her hip. "Innocent? Never. So did you come out here just to make me pee my pants, or are we heading out?"

"I need you to print everything you got from Kate in the lab."

Lynae held up a folder. "Already done."

"Then it's time to make the notification."

"The victim's wife's name is Carla," Lynae said, grabbing her coat from the back of her chair and swinging it on. "She works at a dentist office on the west side. We'll have to make the notification there."

Jo crossed the room and hit the elevator button. "Fantastic."

Chapter 4

Jo followed the GPS instructions through the business district on the west side of town, past Captain Bizzaro's, The Mitten, and Long Road Distillers. She turned into the driveway that the dentist office shared with Arnie's Bakery and realized she hadn't been to Arnie's in months. If she had time, she would swing in on the way home and treat herself to homemade pot pie for dinner and a cupcake for dessert. Across from Arnie's was a one-story redbrick building with a white sign proclaiming Dr. A. Pederson, DDS, the best in the west.

Jo followed the drive around back and eyeballed the building. "Do all dentist offices look the same?"

Lynae nodded. "Absolutely. They have a floor plan that they hand out with degrees at graduation."

"Just the sight of the place makes my mouth hurt. I fear the dentist more than a chainsaw-wielding banger hopped up on crack."

"Right," Lynae scoffed.

Jo gave her a sideways glance. "Do I look like I'm kidding?"

Lynae's mouth dropped open. "All this time, and I've never known you to be afraid of anything."

"Now you know."

They exited the truck and walked through the parking lot to the sidewalk that led to the front entrance of the building.

Jo shoved her hands in the pockets of her black slacks. "I'll take the lead on this."

Lynae pulled open the glass door and motioned for Jo to go ahead. "After you, oh fearless leader."

Jo gave her a steely-eyed glare. "So much for sharing secrets." She stepped into the tiled entryway, tapped her boots on the industrial-grade rug, then strolled into the waiting area.

Wooden chairs with ivy-green padded seats sat back-to-back in the middle of the room and along one wall. A television mounted in the corner aired the morning news. Dull brown carpet showed worn paths to the seats, to the magazine rack hanging beneath the television, and to the one door leading to the back of the office. Lynae plopped into an empty chair next to a heavyset middle-aged woman reading a *Glamour* magazine. After skirting around a toddler pushing a racecar across the floor and waving off the mother when she apologized, Jo approached the counter.

A twentysomething woman greeted her with a smile. "Can I help you?"

Jo leaned on the counter and glanced at the woman's name tag. "Hi, Angie. I'm here to see Carla Kramer."

"Sure, just a minute." Angie swiveled her chair to face her computer. She tapped the screen and scrolled then turned back to Jo with a concerned look. "Carla just took someone back. Do you have an appointment?"

Jo shook her head. "This is a personal matter."

"I'm sorry, but—"

Jo held her badge in the palm of her hand and discreetly flashed it for the woman. "Carla isn't in any trouble, but I'd like to keep this between us until we've had a chance to talk to her."

Angie's eyes turned to blue saucers, oversized for her thin face. "Oh... um... okay. I'll have to get someone to take her patient."

Jo smiled thinly. "I would appreciate that. We can wait a few minutes, but I'm afraid you'll need someone to take her patients for the rest of the day."

Angie nodded, her blond curls bouncing with the motion. She pushed her chair back and stumbled over one of the legs as she tried to stand.

A woman wearing pink scrubs came around the corner, dropped the file she was carrying, and caught Angie mid-stumble. "Geez, Ang. Be careful!"

Angie straightened and looked up into the concerned eyes of the other woman. Her face fell. "Carla... um... this—"

"Carla Kramer?" Jo interrupted.

Tucking a strand of dark hair behind her ear, the woman smiled at Jo. "Yes, I am."

Jo opened her hand to reveal the badge still in it. "Is there someplace private we can talk?"

Carla's shoulders sagged. "There's an office in the back. Just come through that door on your right."

Lynae popped out of her seat and followed Jo through the door to where Carla waited at the far end of the reception area. She led them down a hallway lined with eight cubicles equipped with black leather chairs, gray file cabinets, and silver trays lined with shiny equipment. The moist sucking sound of the Yankaur suction tube, combined with the high-pitched whine of a drill, set Jo's teeth on edge. She pressed her lips together and ran her tongue along her gum line. Lynae snorted and attempted to cover it with a low cough.

Carla stepped into an office with a door nameplate that read Dr. Aaron Pederson. She flipped on the light then moved to the side and waved them in.

Dr. Pederson either had an eye for design or a budget that allowed for a decorator. The space was small but elegant with rich wood, gray walls, and splashes of color added via artwork and meticulously placed knickknacks.

Carla turned to Jo, arms crossed. "Is this about Brad?"

Jo was startled by the abruptness but kept her expression impassive. "Yes, it is."

"What has he done now?"

Jo raised her eyebrows. "Excuse me?"

The woman cocked a hip. "I'm not bailing him out again. He's not my problem anymore."

"We're not here because Brad is in jail," Jo said.

"You're not? Why are you here then?"

Lynae walked around the woman and pulled a dark leather chair to the front of the mahogany desk. "Why don't you have a seat, Mrs. Kramer."

Carla startled then swung her head around and stared at Lynae for a moment before going over and dropping into the chair. Jo and Lynae sat in the two visitor chairs.

Carla folded her hands in her lap, her brow furrowed over her sable-brown eyes. "What's going on?"

Jo inched forward and leaned her elbows on her knees. "I'm sorry to have to tell you that your husband's body was found late last night."

Carla jolted. "Body?" She covered her face with her hands, pressing her fingers over her eyes. "Oh, hell."

"I'm so sorry," Jo said as she reached out and put her hand on Carla's knee. "Can we get you something?"

Carla shook her head then peered at Jo with glistening eyes. "Are you sure it's him?"

"We would like you to make a positive ID when you're ready, but we've identified him through his fingerprints."

Carla wrapped her arms around her body and dropped her head to stare at the floor. "I knew he would end up like this. I just knew it."

"Can you tell me what you mean by that? Was there someone who wanted to hurt your husband?"

The woman raised her head and looked Jo in the eyes. "Pretty much anyone who's ever met him."

Jo snuck a sideways glance at Lynae. *This is a first.*

Carla wiped away a single tear that was sliding down her cheek. "Don't get me wrong. I loved Brad. But most of the time I hated him too."

Jo pulled her notebook from her bag and removed the blue-and-gold GRPD pen from the holder on the side. The tear seemed genuine, and Jo believed what Carla said. What she didn't know was if the woman loved or hated him more. Over the years, she had seen plenty of people kill the ones they loved. "Was someone in particular threatening your husband?"

"Not that I'm aware of."

Jo held the pen poised over the paper. *How do I word this?* "So... just people in general didn't care for him?" she asked carefully.

Carla reached back and pulled a Kleenex from a box on the desk. She dabbed her eyes and wiped her nose. "My husband was a mean bastard that pissed off pretty much every person that he ever encountered. He was a bully who liked to throw his weight around. I feel terrible saying that about him since he's dead, but it's just the truth."

Clenching her hands between her knees, Lynae leaned forward. "Tell us about your relationship."

Carla raised her shoulders in a hopeless, sad gesture. "There's not much to tell. We met in high school. He was a football player. Really good at it." Her lips twitched into a semi-smile. "And so handsome. I thought he was so amazing that I looked past all his faults." Her gaze dropped to her hands, and her fingers tore at the used tissue. "Football and good looks don't last long in a relationship when an unexpected baby comes along. Brad had big plans, and he blamed me for ruining them."

Jo gave her a sympathetic smile. "What plans did he have?"

"He was going to play football in college and get a degree in business. He had already signed with Ferris State University. When I found out I was pregnant, his dad did the 'you made your bed, now lie in it' thing. So we got married, and he got a job. He never went to college."

"What did your husband do for a living?" Lynae asked.

"He worked for the Kent County Road Commission. It's a good job, good pay and benefits. It's just not what he wanted to do."

Jo flipped back a couple pages in her notes. "We found your husband's body last night, and with our preliminary exam, it appears that he may have been killed up to two days prior to that. Did you report him missing?"

Carla shook her head. "I didn't know he was missing. We're separated. Again."

"Again?"

Carla tossed the shredded tissue into the trash and pulled another from the box. "It's pretty much a habit for us. I never filed for divorce. I was going to this time, but I just hadn't done it yet. Money is tight, and lawyers don't come cheap. It was just easier this way."

"Mrs. Kramer, I have to ask: where were you Thursday evening?" Jo asked.

"I was home," she answered quickly.

"Can anyone verify that?"

"My kids were there. It's a school night." Her face crumpled. "How am I going to tell the kids?"

Lynae put her hand on the woman's knee. "I'm sorry. I know that will be hard. We can recommend counselors if they need it."

Carla wiped away a tear with the remains of the tissue she had again been shredding. "Okay, thanks."

"Did Brad have a life insurance policy?" Lynae asked.

"Yes, through his work. I don't know how much it's for. I guess I'll find out now."

Lynae tilted her head. "You have no idea how much your husband's policy is worth?"

She shook her head. "I never really paid attention." Her eyes widened. "You don't think I had something to do with this, do you?"

"We don't think anything at this point. We have to ask these questions in order to find out who did this to your husband."

"Okay. I don't know who killed him, but it wasn't me. Most people didn't really like Brad. They tolerated him, maybe thought he was funny if they were like him, but I honestly don't know anyone who would've actually wanted to kill him."

The statement struck a chord with Jo. "What do you mean by 'if they were like him'?"

Redness crept up Carla's neck. "He wasn't exactly tolerant, if you know what I mean. He liked to make off-color jokes. It was like living in *South Park*. That's part of the reason we separated so often. I didn't like him talking like that around the kids."

Jo tapped her pen against her notebook. "I imagine county road workers would be a pretty diverse group."

Carla nodded. "Yes, they are. The county makes sure of that."

"Do you know anyone in particular that he made one of these off-color jokes to that may not have taken it well?"

"No. I'm sorry, but I don't. He's been out of the house for a while, and before that, our marriage wasn't good, so we didn't really share that much." Her voice caught. "I'm afraid I haven't taken an interest in what's been going on in his life for quite some time."

Jo closed her notebook and slid it into her bag then pulled a card from a side pocket and held it out. "I promise we'll find whoever did this to your husband. If you think of anything, please contact us. We'll be in touch as soon as we have any information for you."

Carla took the card and absently tapped it on her knee as she stared out the office window. "I hope you find whoever did this. He was an asshole, but he didn't deserve to die for it."

Lynae laid a hand on her shoulder. "Is there someone you can call to be with you?"

"My sister lives close by. I'll call her." She pressed her fingers to her eyes. "She can help me talk to the kids. And the girls here will be with me until then."

"Okay, then we'll show ourselves out," Lynae replied.

As they made their way out of the office, every mask-covered face at every station turned to watch.

"Looks like Angie wasn't so great at keeping our visit private," Lynae said after pushing through the front door.

Jo pulled her coat more tightly around her neck and braced against the cold. Even in her heavy winter coat, the frigid November wind cut through and chilled her to the bone. "Gee, I'm shocked."

When they reached the truck, Jo slid into the driver's seat. "I wonder what it would be like to lose a husband and not be devastated."

Lynae paused in buckling her seat belt. "It'll hit her eventually, but it does make the notification a little easier. Do you think she had something to do with the murder?"

"It's a lot easier to collect life insurance money than it is to collect child support."

Lynae rolled her eyes. "Do you buy that she doesn't know how much her husband's life insurance policy is worth?"

Jo shrugged. "I didn't know how much Mike's was worth, so yeah, it's possible."

"Oh, sorry. Wait. Wouldn't Mike have had the same policy as you?"

Jo backed out of the parking lot and pulled into the street. "Mike didn't work for GRPD. He was county."

"Oh yeah, I knew that."

"Anyway, I knew about *that* policy, but he had taken out an additional one that I didn't even know existed. When that came out, I had to answer questions similar to what we just asked."

Lynae's jaw dropped. "Are you shittin' me? Bastards! Who the hell would think you would have anything to do with Mike's death?"

Her indignation made Jo smile. It warmed her heart to have a friend who always had her back. The thought often tickled at the back of her brain that if Lynae had been by her side through Mike's death, she might not have lost the baby.

"They were just doing their job, Nae. They have to ask. You know that."

Slumping in her seat, Lynae crossed her arms. "No, I don't. They could have given you the courtesy of knowing who you are and who you two were together. I wasn't even working here yet, and I know."

Jo slid through a green light and made a quick turn. It still twisted her gut that she'd had to sit with a fellow homicide detective and answer questions about how much she would *gain* from Mike's death. She'd been surprised by the second policy, and her hesitation when the detective asked about it had led to more questions. She answered them calmly, even as her head swam and her hands shook. Though the detective was eventually satisfied, he warned her not to leave the area in case they had more questions. She left the interrogation room, headed straight for the bathroom, and vomited up everything she had forced herself to eat for the baby's sake.

Jo's hands tightened on the steering wheel. She took a deep breath and blew it out slowly. "Water under the bridge."

Lynae stared at her for a few seconds, clearly unconvinced, but she knew Jo well enough to let it go. "All right. Then let's talk about Carla Kramer. What's the over-and-under that she's involved?"

Jo pulled onto the highway on-ramp and gunned the accelerator. "It would be very unusual for a woman to do that kind of damage when killing."

Lynae grabbed the sissy bar and glanced over her shoulder at the oncoming traffic. "Yeah, I thought of that. Women usually use something like poison. *Never* take a bottle of Gatorade from a pissed-off woman."

Jo didn't know why, but her driving made Lynae nervous. Unfortunately for Lynae, Jo thought it was funny and had no intention of slowing down.

"Sound advice." Jo checked her mirrors and crossed two lanes to merge into traffic. Once in the lane she wanted, she adjusted the heating vent to get the full force blowing directly on her cold face. "Even if Carla was capable of the violence, consider his size and hers. The drag marks originated on the beach, so she would have had to lift his body out of a boat and drag him into the woods. Not to mention hoist him into a tree. That would be almost impossible for a woman her size. Also, those boot prints definitely didn't come from her shoes."

"She could have hired someone."

"That's a much more likely scenario. And if it was her, trusting someone else is where her mistake will be."

Lynae held her hands in front of the vent, rotating them homecoming-queen-wave style. "If she was involved, she's one hell of an actress."

Jo's phone rang, and she grabbed it from the console. "Riskin."

"LT, it's Isaac. I just got a call from one of the uniforms that canvassed the houses on the river. He found a woman who saw a fishing boat in that area last Sunday night. She remembered because she thought it was odd how long he sat in that one spot without a fishing pole."

Jo squeezed the phone between her ear and shoulder and turned down the radio. "Could she give a description of the boat or the person in it?"

"The officer didn't get the details. He told her he thought you would want to talk to her."

"He got that part right, at least."

"I've already contacted her. She and her husband would rather come to the station than have you come to them. Apparently, the husband was on the job for, like, forty-some years and wants to see what the station looks like now."

Jo loved it when she had a chance to talk with a retired cop. They always wanted to come back to the station to see what had changed. They would reminisce about the good old days in one breath and in the next, talk about how much harder it was when they were on the beat. She used to have the same kind of talks with her grandpa, so the meetings always left her feeling a little bittersweet. "We'll be back soon. They can come in anytime."

Isaac cleared his throat. "I told them they could come right in. I figured if you weren't back yet, I could give them a little tour and take her statement, if it came down to that."

"Perfect. See you in a few."

She disconnected and dropped the phone into the console. "We've got a potential witness coming in. Why don't you see what you can find out about Mrs. Kramer's finances and our victim's life insurance while I talk to the witness."

"Sounds like a plan. If I dig that up quick enough, I'll look into contacts that might be able to tell us if she had another man or any huge arguments with her ex lately. You know, all the usual reasons people take out a spouse."

"Isn't it sad that there are *usual* reasons?" Jo pulled into the city lot and parked in the first spot she found. "After this interview, I think our next stop should be the County Road Commission. Why don't you find out who our contact should be there."

Lynae hopped out of the truck. "Will do."

Jo hustled around the truck to catch up to Lynae. "By the way, what was the deal with the detective exam? You know you're already a detective, right?"

Lynae snorted. "A friend is going to take it. I was just looking to see if anything has changed."

"Does this friend have a name?"

Lynae pursed her lips. "Yes, I believe he does."

"Not going to make this easy, are you?" Jo huffed.

Lynae gave Jo a sideways glance. "Doug. You know, from the Megan Tillman case?"

Jo smiled. "Of course. I figured it wouldn't be long before he took the exam. I didn't know you were keeping in touch with him."

"I don't know if I would say 'keeping in touch.' He emailed me about the exam, wondering if I had any advice."

"I think he'd make a good detective. He has good instincts."

They hurried into the station and went straight to the elevator. "I agree. He's nervous, but I think he'll be fine."

"Sounds like you've had more than one conversation about this."

"Don't start."

Jo smirked as she stepped into the elevator. "Just sayin'."

Hooking her hands in her back pockets, Lynae rocked back on her heels. "Have you talked to Jack today?"

The elevator dinged, and the doors opened. Jo stepped out and looked over her shoulder at Lynae. "Well played, my friend. Well played."

Lynae grinned. "You've taught me more than detectiving."

Jo raised an eyebrow. "Apparently, I should have worked on teaching you English."

"Can't have everything."

Jo felt her phone vibrate in her pocket before she heard the muffled ring. She pulled it out while she strode toward her office. "Riskin."

"Gerald and MaryEllis Schoen are here to see you," the silky voice of the receptionist said.

"Thanks, Aneace. Go ahead and send them up." She slid the phone back into her pocket. "Looks like my witnesses are here already. I'll check in with you on your search results after their interview."

As she strolled back toward the elevator, the doors opened, and an elderly couple slowly stepped out. The long-limbed man gripped the elbow of a prim, grandmotherly woman who held her chin high and carried her purse in both hands. The man beamed, his head swiveling from side to side, taking in the bustle of the bull pen.

Jo approached the couple with her hand out. "Mr. and Mrs. Schoen?"

The man looked down at Jo from his towering height and grasped her hand in a viselike grip. "Gerald, and this here is my wife, MaryEllis. We're here to see Lieutenant Riskin."

"I'm Lieutenant Riskin," Jo said, giving his hand a brief, firm shake.

The man's eyebrows shot up. "By God, you don't look like any detective that worked here when I was on the job."

Jo ignored the comment and motioned toward the conference rooms. "Why don't we talk in a conference room? My office is a little tight."

The old man smacked his lips. "Well, some things never change."

Jo walked more slowly than normal to keep pace with the elderly couple, who had to be pushing eighty. Mr. Schoen gallantly escorted his wife, though she seemed more able-bodied than her husband, who favored his right leg. In the conference room, the man pulled out a chair for his wife and helped her ease into it before dropping his angular frame into the seat next to her.

Jo asked, "Can I get either of you a cup of coffee or a glass of water before we get started?"

Leaning back in his chair, Gerald pointed a gnarled finger at Jo. "I never turn down a cup of coffee."

Jo smiled. "A man after my own heart."

He turned to his wife. "M'rel?"

"No, thank you," the woman said through pursed lips, settling into her seat and propping her purse on her lap.

Gerald winked at Jo, his weather-worn tan face wrinkled deeply around twinkling hazel eyes. "Looks like it's just me and you."

Suppressing a chuckle, Jo said, "I'll be right back." She hustled to the break room and poured two cups of coffee. After spotting an unopened box of Girl Scout Cookies on the counter, she grabbed them and headed back to the conference room. She set the coffee in front of the man, opened the cookie package, and offered it to him. "I found these in the break room."

"There never was a lack of treats in the break room." Gerald pulled a cookie from the plastic tray, dipped it in his coffee, then tapped it on the edge of the cup. Thick, raised veins snaked across the backs of his hands like a roadmap of his life and disappeared under the cuffs of his winter coat.

Jo sat across the table from them and pulled her notebook out of her bag. "How long were you on the force, Mr. Schoen?"

"Forty-seven years," he said proudly. "'Course, that was before you had to go to college. I started right out of high school."

"That's an impressive amount of time, sir."

The man leaned his arms on the table and spoke conspiratorially. "Loved every damn minute of it."

Jo smiled warmly. "So do I." She turned to the woman, who had been quietly taking in the conversation without attempting to join in. "Mrs. Schoen, I understand you may have some information for us."

MaryEllis gave Jo a curt nod. "That's right." The woman sat bolt upright in her chair, both hands firmly grasping her purse.

Jo couldn't decide if her posture was one of anger or trepidation, but she knew she should tread lightly. "You saw a boat in the area where our victim was found?"

"Yes, I did. It's right where those kids are always making so much noise."

"That area is a known place for parties?" *Did our killer want the body found?*

MaryEllis pursed her lips. "I've called the police to report it. But no one has done anything to stop them."

Ah, and there it is.

Gerald shifted in his seat. "Now, M'rel—"

The woman raised her chin and gave him a glare that Jo imagined had stopped his heart on more than one occasion. "Those kids are there every week and not just on the weekends. The noise carries over the river."

"I imagine it does. I'm Homicide, so I don't really have anything to do with noise complaints, but I will certainly put in a word with the proper division to watch that area." Jo made a show of writing in her notebook, setting her face in a stern expression to show disapproval of the woman's problem not being properly addressed.

The elderly woman's posture relaxed. She reached out and took a cookie from the tray. "Thank you. That would be nice."

Jo took a sip of her coffee and caught Gerald's eye. He gave her a discreet wink.

"I understand you saw this boat on Sunday night," Jo asked MaryEllis.

"That's correct."

"Is that unusual? I've noticed that many of the fishermen are still out on a regular basis. What made you take note?"

MaryEllis said, "I noticed it because it sat in one spot for a very long time, and I couldn't see a fishing pole."

"How far is your house from the river? Would you say you had a good view of the boat and fisherman?" Jo hated to get ahead of herself, but a good defense attorney would rip apart the testimony of an elderly witness who wore glasses if distance was a factor.

"We're across the river, of course, but after he sat there for so long, I took out my binoculars."

Jo felt a small rush of adrenaline. "You saw this person through binoculars? Can you give me a description?"

Mrs. Schoen shook her head. "I saw him, but he was sitting down with his back to me. And he was wearing a hat."

"Stocking cap, baseball hat? Did you notice any hair sticking out from beneath the hat?"

"It was a stocking cap pulled low. I didn't see any hair." The woman glanced at her husband. "I'm afraid I'm not being much help."

The man patted his wife's hand, his tan skin a stark contrast to her almost transparent complexion. "You're doing great. You can't tell her anything you didn't see."

"He's right," Jo added. "I don't want you to embellish, but anything and everything helps. Can you tell me anything about the boat?"

The woman nodded eagerly. "Yes, it was a silver-and-green aluminum Lund fishing boat. I would say fourteen feet. It looked old. It had casting chairs, but he wasn't sitting on one."

Jo raised her eyebrows. "You know your boats."

Smiling proudly, MaryEllis said, "I raised four boys on the river."

"That will do it. What time did you first notice the boat?"

The woman frowned then looked at her husband. "When was that football game on that you were watching? It was during that."

"It started at three."

Jo toyed with her coffee cup. "Michigan, Michigan State. Good game. Although the offensive pass interference non-call with a minute forty to go killed my team." She had watched that game at Ucello's with Jack. Unfortunately, they had never discussed their allegiances. When she got there, she saw him wearing the wrong colors and almost turned around but decided to have fun with it instead. Since she enjoyed smack-talk more than she should, her team's loss was a major blow. He was still sending her in-your-face texts about his win.

The man roared. "By God, you're right! And it helped mine. You know your football."

"You bet I do. That's how my husband and I used to spend every fall weekend."

The older man glanced at the wedding band on her left hand. "Used to?"

"He was killed in the line," Jo said over the sudden lump in her throat.

Mrs. Schoen drew in a quick breath and laid her hand over Jo's. "I'm so sorry, dear. That's the fear of every officer's spouse." The coarse skin and the surprising firmness in her touch reminded Jo that the woman had not only been married to a cop but also raised four boys and taught them about the river. No doubt, she had been a force to be reckoned with.

Mr. Schoen patted his wife's shoulder. "I put this old girl through too many sleepless nights over the years."

Jo smiled thinly. "The sleepless nights worrying seem like a cakewalk compared to the sleepless nights remembering."

"I imagine you're right." Mrs. Schoen's blue eyes softened as she gave Jo's hand a quick squeeze before pulling hers back and again resting it on her purse.

Jo cleared her throat. The conversation had taken a personal turn that she hadn't expected, and she needed to get back to the problem at hand. "So you first noticed the boat around three o'clock?"

The woman straightened. "It was partway through the game. I would say closer to four. I saw it drive into that spot and noticed a bit later that it was still there."

Jo jotted the time in her notebook. "Do you know how long it sat there?"

"It was still there when it was getting quite dark. That's when I looked closer. I noticed it didn't have any running lights on. I was going to report him, but Gerald told me to mind my own business."

Gerald cringed. "If I had let her be a busybody, you might have your killer already."

Jo fought the smirk that tried to play across her lips. "Did you notice what time the boat left?"

"No, I'm afraid I stopped watching. It got dark, and I couldn't see it any longer. I never did see any lights."

It made sense that if the killer was there, he would have waited until dark to get out of his boat so as not to draw any attention to himself. He probably had to get there in the daylight to find his location, but coming early enough to be spotted was a mistake that could be Jo's break. "Is there anything else you noticed?"

The elderly woman cocked her head. "The only other thing I could see in the boat was a gaff."

"What's a gaff?"

"It's a metal pole with a hook on the end." She stretched out her hands to pantomime the shape. "It's used to boat a large fish. I'm afraid that's all I can tell you."

Jo jotted down the term in her book, planning to look it up online later. She closed her notebook and smiled. "Mrs. Schoen, you've been incredibly helpful. Thank you for coming in to speak with me."

"I hope it helps."

Gerald stood and took his wife's arm to help her to her feet. "You know, young lady, when I was on the force, we didn't have any woman detectives. We thought we'd leave the heavy thinking to the men."

Jo bristled. "I'm aware."

The old man held out his hand. "I reckon we were wrong, Lieutenant. And we probably missed out on some damn good detectives."

Jo relaxed and gripped his hand. "I appreciate that, sir."

After giving Jo's hand another shake, he motioned toward the elevator. "We'll show ourselves out."

Jo followed them to the bull pen then veered off to go to Isaac's desk. "I need you to do a search for all registered Lund fishing boats in Kent County."

Isaac groaned, leaned back in his chair, and began his habitual pencil roll, deftly manipulating the utensil between his dark fingers. "No one in this county lives more than five miles from a lake. You know how many boats that's going to amount to?"

"Nope, but I will soon."

"I'm on it," he mumbled, tossing his pencil into the mesh holder on his desk before turning to his computer.

On her way to Lynae's desk, Jo checked the time and decided she could go a few more hours without sleep.

As Jo stepped up behind her, Lynae popped out of her chair and held up a sticky note covered in her neat cursive handwriting. "I have our contact at the County Road Commission."

"I'll get my coat," Jo said. "On the way there, I can fill you in on what I learned."

Chapter 5

Navigating her truck through the Kent County Road Commission parking lot, Jo marveled at the size of the building, which rivaled a professional football stadium. Bright-green snowplows, sand trucks, and various other construction vehicles lined the parking lot.

Lynae gawked at the monstrous vehicles. "These things are incredible up close."

Jo leaned forward and craned her neck to look up at a snowplow. "Yeah, they're cool, but let's hope we don't have a use for them for a while yet." She pulled into a parking spot next to a small section of building that jutted out from the rest of the enormous structure. "This looks like the office end." She grabbed her bag and slipped out of the car.

Lynae jogged around to catch up. "You think they'd let me sit in one of the snowplows?"

Jo sighed as she pulled open a side door on the office building. "Please don't ask that while we're here on duty."

"Don't worry. I won't embarrass you. But... I mean, if they offer..."

"You worry me sometimes."

They stepped into a tiny entryway with a heavy metal door directly in front of them. A glass partition slid open to their right.

"Can I help you?" a middle-aged woman asked, leaning through the opening. She looked up at them over a pair of granny glasses perched on the end of her nose. When she smiled, her dark eyes all but disappeared into her full cheeks. "I didn't mean to startle you."

Jo put her hand on her chest. "A little jolt is good for the ticker once in a while."

Dark curls bobbed as the woman threw her head back and laughed. "Happy to help your heart. What can I do for you?"

Jo held up her badge. "We're with the Grand Rapids Police. We'd like to talk to..." She hesitated when she realized she hadn't asked Lynae for their contact's name.

"Bob Tennison," Lynae chimed in.

The woman's eyes bulged, and her hand dropped to fidget with the collar of her blouse. "Just a moment. I'll call him for you." She slid the window closed, rolled her chair to face away from them, then picked up the handset of her phone.

Lynae slid Jo a sideways glance. "A jolt is good for the heart? There's no way that woman got the jump on you."

"As far as she's concerned, she did."

Lynae smirked. "Can't hurt to break the ice comfortably with the woman who runs the show."

"Precisely."

The heavy door clicked, and a man poked his hard-hat-covered head around the corner. He pushed the door the rest of the way open and stepped into the small space. "I'm Bob Tennison. What can I do for you ladies?"

Jo held up her badge. "Lieutenant Riskin."

Extending her hand, Lynae said, "Detective Parker."

Bob shook Lynae's hand. "Detective." He held his hand out to Jo. "Lieutenant. I apologize if 'ladies' came across wrong. No disrespect intended."

"None taken," Jo said. "We're with Grand Rapids Homicide. We'd like to talk to you about one of your employees."

"Homicide?" Bob ran his hand over the gray stubble on his cheek then looked up at Jo, a light suddenly coming on in his dark eyes. "Brad Kramer?"

Jo cocked her head. "As a matter of fact, yes. How did you know?"

"He hasn't shown up for work or called in since Thursday. Everyone else is here or accounted for."

He took off his hard hat and scratched his bald head. "Son of a..."

Jo glanced toward the slightly cracked-open sliding window of the reception desk. "This may not be the best place for us to talk."

"Why don't we go to my office?" he offered before pushing open the metal door that he had come through and holding it open.

He led them across a tiled hallway at a clipped pace impressive for his small stature then stopped in front of another set of doors and pulled two hard hats from the line of them hanging on pegs. "You'll have to put one of these on to walk through the shop."

Jo took a hat and plunked it on, noting the tight fit of the plastic band on the inside. Lynae fiddled with hers while it wobbled precariously, balancing on the bun she wore loosely on the crown of her head.

"Why don't you just take the bun out?" Jo said under her breath.

"My hair will be a disaster," Lynae mumbled back.

Bob regarded Lynae with an amused look. "Don't worry about it. We have a short distance to go, and you won't be in the danger zones. I'm just following protocol."

Lynae let out a sigh of relief and held the hat in place with her hand.

Bob pushed through the second set of doors, and Jo's senses were immediately assaulted by the odors of motor oil and rock salt. Dust particles floating through the air tickled her nose and made her eyes feel gritty. A gargantuan truck sporting a massive V-shaped plow idled near a vented door, and two men in hard hats and coveralls stood on a raised platform in front of the open hood. Their mouths were moving, but she couldn't hear their voices over the din of the engine and the clanking of metal tools. Bob led them around the perimeter of the workspace, staying on a path marked by green lines. After two quick honks, a hi-lo came through an opening with thick plastic strips hanging in place of a door. It stayed between a pair of yellow lines that zigzagged across the open space.

The green path took them to a set of wooden stairs leading to a window-lined office area that overlooked the facility. Bob took the stairs two at a time and opened the door at the top then motioned for Jo and Lynae to go in ahead of him.

When Jo stepped through the doorway, four pairs of eyes stared at them from the four occupied workstations. She turned to look at Bob and asked, "Is there any place we could talk in private?"

"We have a small meeting room in the back. We could go there."

"I think that would be best."

Bob stepped in front of them again and led the way to the far end of the expansive room. He opened the door and flipped on the light. An oval table with six chairs dominated the small space. Coffee cups and a plastic bowl filled with creamer and packets of Equal sat on a credenza along one wall. A whiteboard, wiped clean, covered the opposite wall. A silver tray along the bottom held dry-erase markers in various colors. Bob flopped heavily into a chair, and Jo and Lynae took chairs facing him.

The stocky man set his hard hat on the table then leaned forward and rested his elbows on his thighs. "It's weird, you know, thinking that one of my guys is dead. I've been the foreman here for over twenty-five years, and this is the first person I've lost."

"I understand this must be very difficult for you," Jo said as she pulled out her notebook and found a blank page. "I hope you'll be able to help us piece together what happened."

"I'll do whatever I can."

"You said the last time you saw Brad was Thursday?" Jo asked.

"Yeah, he was here that day. And that's bowling night. The guys on his team said he was there."

Lynae raised her eyebrows. "He's on a bowling team? So he has a group here that he's pretty good friends with?"

Bob's face scrunched, pushing his thick eyebrows together. "I hate to talk bad about him since he's dead, but no, he didn't have friends. He was a good bowler, and he liked to be a big shot by buying rounds. Basically, they tolerated him for the team and for the drinks."

Lynae leaned back in her chair. "What happened when he didn't show up for work on Friday?"

"I called him a bunch of times. I figured he got drunk at bowling and was just sleeping it off. After I got sick of calling, I left him a message telling him he better show up or call me with a damn good excuse."

Jo jotted that information in her notebook. "Was that something that happened often with him?"

"Once in a while. He was a good worker when he was here, so I didn't want to lose him. But I had to dock him more than once for no show, no call."

"Does he normally work on Saturdays?"

Bob shook his head. "Not unless we have an emergency, like a snowstorm. Then it's all hands on deck."

"So after leaving the message on Friday, you didn't look for him again until Monday?" Jo asked.

"There wasn't a reason to. I planned on giving him hell when I saw him, but I figured it could wait until Monday."

"So what happened when he didn't show up Monday?"

Bob leaned back and crossed his ankle over his knee, tapping his heavy work boot against one of the table legs. "I called his wife and got an 'I don't keep tabs on him' kind of answer. I called his cell again and left him another message."

So the wife knew the vic had been AWOL from work since Thursday. Funny she didn't mention that. "Then on Tuesday?"

"I was getting worried that something might have happened to him, so I sent a couple guys over to his apartment. His truck was there, but nobody answered the door. So I called the cops."

"You filed a report with Missing Persons?" Jo asked.

Bob ran his hand over his bald head. "I felt kind of stupid. I mean he's a grown man. But no one had seen him since they left bowling on Thursday. They said with him being an adult and no family reporting him missing... you know. They said they'd look into it, but I don't know what they did."

Jo made a note to contact Missing Persons. If they had followed up at all, the first thing they should have done was to contact his wife. That could be two strikes against her. "You did the right thing by calling them."

Bob held up his hands. "That's pretty much all I can tell you. I figured he'd show up with some lousy excuse, I'd chew his ass out for the hassle, and we'd forget about it."

"Are any of the men Mr. Kramer bowled with on Thursday here today?" Jo asked.

"Just Jimmy Z. The other two are out on the road. I can call them in if necessary."

"We'll start with Jimmy and let you know if we want to talk with the other two right away."

Bob grabbed his hat from the table and pushed it securely on his head. "I'll get him for you. There's coffee right out here in the office. Would either of you like a cup?"

Jo smiled. "If you don't mind, we'll just help ourselves while you get Jimmy for us."

"You bet." Bob pulled the door closed behind him as he hustled out of the room.

Jo leaned back in her chair and tapped her pen on her notebook. "The wife knew he was missing."

Lynae nodded. "Failed to mention that little tidbit, didn't she?"

"If our vic is in a Thursday-night bowling league, anyone who knows him very well would be aware of that. They'd know where to find him and approximately what time he'd be leaving the bowling alley."

"Maybe it's one of the guys from his team. He could have done something to one of them, or they know something he did that they couldn't forgive him for."

"Hopefully, we'll get something from Jimmy Z—which, by the way, is a cool name." Jo pushed her chair back and stood up. "I'm going to grab a cup of coffee. Want one?"

"I'll come with," Lynae said, getting to her feet. "You never get the sugar-to-cream ratio right."

"It is a delicate balance."

Following Lynae out of the conference room, Jo spotted a small alcove with a ten-cup coffee pot. "Apparently, there aren't a lot of coffee drinkers in the office."

"There are only four desks. Not everyone can drink a couple pots a day like you can."

Jo pulled two paper coffee cups from a stack next to the pot and filled them. "Yeah, it takes a real woman." She handed a cup to Lynae. "Mike and I were on a bowling league once."

"You don't strike me as the bowling-league type." Lynae grabbed five packets of Equal and passed two to Jo before emptying the other three into her cup.

Jo shook enough powdered cream into her cup to give her coffee a cappuccino look then handed the container to Lynae. "Neither of us were. That's why we only did it once. And the schedule of a detective isn't exactly conducive to planned activities."

Lynae huffed. "Tell me about it. I have to bail on my softball team all the time. I don't think they'll have me back next year."

"Even if you're the best one on the team?"

"Awww, thanks."

"Must be you don't spring for enough rounds." Jo stuck a stir stick in her cup and swirled the creamy mixture.

Once they were seated again, Jo wrapped her hands around the warm coffee cup. "Would you keep someone on your team that no one liked?"

Lynae raised one eyebrow. "Oh yeah. We play to win."

"Of course you do. What was I thinking?"

Lynae screwed up her face. "I can't imagine a bowling league being that competitive, though. Aren't most of those just a bunch of guys looking for an excuse to hang out once a week and drink too much?"

"That's pretty much what our league was like, except it was couples. We were just there to have fun." Jo took a sip of her coffee and turned toward the door when she heard voices on the other side.

The door opened, and Bob walked in, followed by a clean-cut man carrying a hard hat. His hazel eyes flicked between Jo and Lynae. The newcomer set his hat on the table then wiped his hands on the legs of his jeans. He held his hand out to Jo. "Jim Zielstra. Everybody calls me Jimmy Z."

Jo gripped his calloused hand. "Lieutenant Riskin. And this is my partner, Detective Parker."

Jimmy nodded then blew out a long breath. "I'm a little shook up."

"Understandably so." Jo motioned toward the chairs across the table. "Have a seat."

The man took the chair across from Jo and nervously ran his hands up and down his thighs.

Bob looked at Jo. "Should I stay, Lieutenant?"

"Why don't you wait for us in your office so you can show us out when we're finished? I have a feeling it would be easy to wander into the wrong area here."

"Yes, it is. And it can be dangerous if you do so."

Jo smiled up at the older man. "We won't go anywhere without you."

Jimmy watched Bob leave the room then turned, wide-eyed, back to Jo. "Was Brad really murdered?"

Jo nodded. "I'm afraid he was."

"Damn. I never really liked the guy, but..."

Jo pulled her chair close to the table and leaned her elbows on it. "I understand you were in a bowling league with Mr. Kramer."

"Yeah, every Thursday at Kegler's Kove."

"But you didn't like him?"

Jimmy shrugged. "Not really. He could be all right sometimes, but no one really likes... um, liked him."

"Was there anyone in particular who had a problem with him, more than the others?"

Jimmy shifted in his chair. "Not enough to kill him, if that's what you're asking. I mean, he was cocky and kind of embarrassing sometimes, but I don't know anyone who would kill him."

Lynae tilted her head. "Embarrassing?"

Jimmy wiped his face with one hand. "He wasn't exactly, you know, politically correct. If he was drinking, which he usually was, he could get pretty bad."

His hands never stopped moving from his hat, to his face, to his jeans. Jo wondered if he knew something he wasn't telling them or if the police just made him nervous. She made a mental note to check his record when she got back to the office.

"Did he have an altercation with anyone Thursday night?" Lynae asked.

Jimmy shook his head. "No, not that I saw. But he didn't leave with us, so I don't know what happened after we left."

"The rest of you left together?" Jo asked.

"Yeah, we always do. We all have to get up and go to work in the morning, so whenever the first person calls it a night, we all bail."

"But that night Brad decided to stay?"

Jimmy rolled his eyes. "He had it in his head that some woman at the bar had been checking him out all night. He was going to see if he could get lucky."

Jo's pen hovered over her notebook. "Do you know who the woman was?"

"I didn't even look. Brad was always trying to get some tail." He squeezed his eyes shut. "Oh man, I'm sorry. That was... sorry."

Jo smiled thinly. "It's okay. We want you to tell it like it is."

"That's all I can tell you. We bowled, we drank a few beers, then me, Mike, and Dave left, and Brad stayed."

"And you haven't seen him since?"

Jimmy shook his head. "He didn't come to work Friday. We figured he got lucky."

Jo flipped her notebook to a blank page then handed it to Jimmy. "Can you write down the names of the other two men in your bowling league?"

Jimmy wrote down two names in neat block print.

When he finished, Jo retrieved the notebook and dropped it into her bag. "We appreciate your help, Jimmy." They weren't going to get anything more from this guy.

"I hope it helps," he said then grabbed his hard hat and strode out of the room.

After he was gone, Jo said, "Gee, I wonder why Brad had trouble in his marriage?"

"Wives can be so difficult when their husbands are always trying to *get some tail*." Lynae glanced at her notebook. "If all these guys left together, I'm not sure we'll even need to talk to them."

"We'll keep them on the list just to tie up the loose ends. They may have seen something Jimmy didn't. We do need to talk to the bartender at the bowling alley. Maybe he remembers seeing our guy with a woman."

Tapping her notebook, Lynae said, "Already in my notes."

"That's why you're my partner. Nothing but the best for me."

Lynae winked at her. "And don't you forget it."

They made their way back to Bob's desk and got contact information for the other two bowlers. He then escorted them out of the building.

Jo pulled her coat tight against the cold wind, put her head down, and jogged to her truck.

Lynae beat her there and was waiting by the passenger door. She jumped in as soon as Jo hit the locks. "When the hell did it get so cold?"

"This is Michigan. The weather can go from summer to winter while you're getting dressed in the morning."

Jo cranked up the heat and pulled out of the lot. When she felt her phone vibrate in her pocket, she tried to keep her eye on the road while fumbling for it, all the while cursing herself for forgetting to drop it into the console. By the time she pulled it out, it was too late to catch the call, so she pressed the last number on her Recent Calls list without bothering to see who it was.

"Jack Riley." The smooth tenor of his voice made her heart jump.

"Jack, it's Jo. I couldn't get my damn phone out of my pocket." She chuckled. "What's up?"

"Where are you?"

"On my way back to the station. Should be there in about ten."

"I'll meet you there."

Jo's heart dropped to her gut. It wasn't a friendly call. Something was wrong. "What's going on?"

"I'd rather not talk to you while you're driving. I'll be in your office when you get there."

"What the hell's going on, Jack?"

"I'll talk to you when you get back to the station, Jo." His agitation came through loud and clear. Jack didn't get agitated easily.

"All right, I'm almost there." The line went dead.

Lynae grabbed the sissy bar when Jo gunned the engine. "That sounded serious."

"Jack wants to talk to me, and he didn't sound happy." She felt the tension creep into her neck as she ran her hand through her hair. "I hope it's not bad news about Mike's case."

Chapter 6

When Jo marched into her office, Jack was staring out the window with his back to the door. The tension emanating from his stance was palpable.

She halted in the doorway, her fight-or-flight instinct screaming at her to run. "What's going on that you couldn't tell me over the phone?"

Jack turned around, his face drawn in concern. "Have a seat, Jo."

"No. Tell me what the hell is going on."

"I got a call from Captain Brody at the jail," he said, his eyes boring into hers. "Drevin Clayburn killed himself in his cell last night."

Jo's vision blurred. "No," she whispered as the air was sucked from her lungs. When her ears started ringing, she leaned on the edge of her desk. She wasn't sure her legs would stay under her.

Jack rushed across the room and wrapped his arms around her. "I'm sorry."

"This can't be happening." She swallowed hard, forcing down the bile snaking up her throat.

He tightened his hug. "We know he's guilty. We have the evidence. This doesn't change anything."

She pushed away from him and took a ragged breath. "I wanted to hear him say it. I wanted to *hear* the guilty verdict. Damn it, Jack, I wanted him to pay."

"He's dead, Jo. He *is* paying."

"I didn't want him to get to choose his own way out. I wanted him to lose his freedom, his dignity. I wanted him to suffer for the rest of his damn life, locked in a box."

"I know. I—"

Anger surged through her like a lightning bolt. She grabbed the first thing her hand touched and fired it across the room. Her coffee mug shattered against the filing cabinet. "I want to know who else was there. I want to know why the hell they went in without backup. I wanted that son of a bitch to die in that cage, but I wanted to know all the *whys* first!"

Jack grabbed her by the shoulders. "Drevin Clayburn wasn't going to be able to give you all the answers you need."

Isaac appeared in the doorway. "Everything all right, LT?"

Jo clenched her jaw, the pressure in her back teeth radiating through her temples. "No, everything is not all right."

"Anything I can do?" he asked, stepping into the room and leveling Jack with a cold glare.

Jack let go of Jo and pointed at the door. "Yeah, shut the damn door when you leave, and don't let anyone else in."

Isaac studied Jo's face. His eyes darted to Jack then back to Jo.

Jo pinched the bridge of her nose. "It's not him, Isaac. Please, just go."

Isaac backed out of the office and closed the door behind him.

Jo folded her arms. "How could this happen? After all it took to find the bastard, he doesn't deserve to die before I get my day in court." The pounding behind her eyes was relentless. Her mind was reeling with the idea that she would never know the whole story behind Mike's death. For the first time since his death—his *murder*—she had felt as if her life was getting back on track. But Clayburn's suicide had stolen that from her.

"I'm sorry, Jo," Jack said quietly. "I don't know what else to say."

Jo hit the desk with her fist. "He had a cellmate. How the hell does someone off himself in an eight-by-eight cell with another person in there with him?"

Jack shoved his hands in his pockets. "He was involved in a fight in the yard. He got sent to solitary to cool off for the night."

Jo paced the small office. She felt trapped, like a grizzly at the zoo, looking for an escape route. There had to be a way out. "And suddenly he decides to kill himself? No. These things don't happen with guys like him. He was cocky, arrogant. He had a high-priced lawyer and was sure he was going to get off. Why would he suddenly decide to end it?"

"The motion to dismiss had just been thrown out. That might have knocked the cocky out of him. He was only in County and already getting the shit beat out of him. He had to know he was looking at life in maximum security. Maybe he couldn't handle the idea."

"And how the hell does someone kill himself in solitary? Don't they pat them down before they go in? Did he hang himself with the bedsheets?"

"I don't know. I don't have all the answers. I just wanted to tell you before you heard it from anyone else."

"Our case is dead. Literally." Jo's feet continued the motion of pacing, but her strength waned as the last of the air left her balloon.

Jack crossed the room in two long strides. He stood in her path and stopped her pacing. "Maybe that's not a bad thing, Jo. You found the guy who killed Mike, and you put him in jail. Now he's dead. There's nothing more you can do. Maybe this is your sign that it's time to move on."

"I would if I thought that was all there was to it. I just don't believe it is."

"So I take it this means you're not going to let it go."

A grim frown tightened her lips. "I can't yet."

Jack laid his hands on her shoulders and squeezed gently. "What's next?"

"I don't know. I'm still trying to process. I guess I talk to the guards or inmates. I need to find out what happened in the yard, who he was fighting with, and how the hell he managed to kill himself in solitary."

Jack ran his hands down her arms and took her hands. "I'm not sure they'll let you do that."

"Well, I have to try," Jo said through gritted teeth.

"What can I do to help?"

Her mind stopped racing long enough for her to recognize that he wasn't trying to talk her out of taking the next step. Not only was he asking what she was going to do, but he was also supporting it. She looked up into his concern-filled eyes. "I don't know. I can't think right now."

He smiled warmly. "I want to help in any way I can."

Jo dropped her head and rested it on his shoulder. "I know you do. It helps to know that."

Jack gently pulled her closer. She knew he would listen to any theory she had or any ranting she needed to get off her chest. And he would give her his honest opinion, whether she wanted to hear it or not. It was what she wanted and what she needed. It was what gave her the confidence to push forward and to brainstorm any crazy idea.

It's what Mike used to do.

Comparing Jack to Mike filled her with guilt that clawed at her stomach and chewed at the back of her brain. She stiffened and took a step back. "Thanks for coming to tell me in person."

Jack's eyebrows drew together, confusion etched on his face. He nodded and pulled his keys from his pocket. "Yeah, sure. I guess you can call me if you need anything."

"I will. Thanks." She turned to her desk and picked up a file folder.

When she heard Jack close the door as he left, she threw the folder down, flopped into her chair, and buried her face in her hands. Pain ripped through her chest and came out in a gut-wrenching sob. *It's never going to be over.*

"Jack told me what happened."

Jo raised her head to see that Lynae had come in. Her friend pulled a chair around, sat down, and put her arm around Jo's shoulders.

Jo wiped her face with the back of her hand. "He wasn't supposed to get the easy way out."

"I know," Lynae whispered.

"It's never going to be over."

"It will. I promise." Lynae pulled a tissue from a box on the desk and handed it to her. "You need to go home and get some sleep. Don't argue with—"

"Yeah, you're right. I do." Jo blew her nose and dropped the tissue in the trash.

Lynae's eyebrows shot up. "I am? I mean, yes, I am."

Jo forced a smile. "I haven't been home in two days. I'm going to go curl up with Mojo and sleep the afternoon away. We have to hit the bowling alley, and evening would be a better time to do that, anyway. You may want to take a break this afternoon yourself."

Lynae slapped her hands on her thighs and stood up. "Don't worry about me."

"Why not? You're always worrying about me." Jo grabbed her bag and keys. She took out her phone and opened the mirror app. Staring at her reflection, she flinched. She couldn't walk through the bull pen with red eyes and a blotchy face. She was supposed to be the badass lieutenant, not the hysterical woman.

Lynae pointed at her bag. "You got sunglasses in there?"

Jo half smiled. "Reading my mind again?"

Lynae winked and opened the door. Jo pulled her sunglasses out, slid them on, then strolled through the bull pen with her head held high.

Chapter 7

Jo reached out from under the covers and grabbed her phone from
the nightstand: *8:43 p.m.* Anger, lack of sleep, and an overwhelm-
ing sense of loss had left her in a state of pure exhaustion. She had
come home and fallen into bed without even taking off the clothes
she'd been wearing for thirty hours. If Mojo hadn't been sprawled
across the bed with her feet pushed firmly in Jo's back, she might have
slept until morning.

While she kicked her way out of the bedspread that had managed to get tangled around her legs and torso, Mojo leapt off the bed
and ran out of the room. Jo sat on the edge of the bed with her head
in her hands.

This isn't going to help. She got up and changed into jogging pants
and a long-sleeve thermal T-shirt. When Jo shuffled into the kitchen,
Mojo was standing by the back door, wagging her tail. Jo pulled on
her running shoes and stocking cap then grabbed the leash from the
hook by the door.

She sent Lynae a text: *Taking Mojo for a quick run, then I'll head
to the bowling alley. I'll take this one alone. No need to interrupt your
night.*

She shoved the phone into a zippered pants pocket and dropped
mace into another. When she opened the door to the cold, inky
blackness of the night, Mojo bolted out, yanking on the leash and almost pulling Jo's feet out from under her. She waited patiently while
the dog sniffed in a frenzy to find the ultimate location to relieve herself, then gave the leash a tug and took off down the sidewalk at a
warm-up stride.

When she rounded the second corner, she picked up the pace. The neighborhood was still, the frigid temperature and early night-fall keeping people indoors. Yellow lights glowed between slits in blind-covered windows, and television screens cast strobe-like images against family room walls.

Drevin Clayburn is dead. He can never tell me what happened in that warehouse.

Mojo's nails clicked on the sidewalk. Jo's feet pounded rhythmically.

Why would he kill himself before his trial? How did he manage it in solitary? It doesn't make sense.

She ran faster. Street signs flashed into focus then became silhouettes as they slid back into the darkness.

I need to know what happened to you, Mike. Why the hell did you rush that building without backup?

She pumped her arms and pushed even harder. Faint puffs of transparent steam rose from her mouth. The cold air burned her lungs.

I can't keep living like this. I have to finish this and let you go.

She rounded the last corner of her neighborhood and kept the punishing pace as she crossed the quiet street into the next subdivision. They made their way to the farthest corner then turned to head back home.

Jo looked down at her faithful friend galloping beside her. Mojo's pink tongue lolled out of the corner of her mouth. "Don't tell me you're tired. We're only half done."

Mojo spared Jo a glance then pulled ahead. Jo's arm shot forward as she struggled to match the collie's pace. "Show-off."

By the time they trotted into the driveway, Jo's legs were burning, and her lungs ached. She let Mojo off the leash then walked around the yard to cool down.

After a few minutes, she pulled out her phone and saw a message from Lynae. *I'm not doing anything. Seems like a good night to go bowling.*

Jo replied: *I'll pick you up in 45 minutes.* She whistled for Mojo. "Come on, girl. Time to get back to work."

JO CIRCLED THE PARKING lot of Kegler's Kove Bowling Alley twice before finding a spot, and she still had to do some creative maneuvering to get into it. Fortunately, she and Lynae were both thin enough to squeeze out of their doors.

When they pulled open the double glass doors at the building's entrance, they were met with thumping music and the thuds of bowling balls hitting hard wood. Round four-person tables surrounded by red pleather chairs covered the concourse. Every surface was littered with clear plastic cups, pitchers of beer, and paper plates holding varying amounts of leftover pizza and chicken strips. Street shoes were scattered under the tables, while coats hung over the backs of every chair.

Jo's stomach grumbled as the smell of greasy bar food—her weakness—wafted over her. "I guess the bowling business is alive and well," she said.

Lynae gawked at the crowd. "Who knew?"

"Let's start there," Jo suggested, pointing to a stool-lined area where the Budweiser horses pranced around a mirror behind four rows of bottled booze.

They made their way through the throng of people and sidled up to the bar. Jo badged the young blonde behind the counter.

The girl gaped at the badge as Jo introduced herself. "I better get my manager," she replied then skirted around the counter and high-tailed it out a door to her left.

While they waited, Jo eyeballed the gaudy carpeting that covered the area and rose two feet up every wall. "Do you suppose there's a company that makes nothing but bowling-alley carpeting?"

"Oh yeah, for sure. And they're totally stoned when they come up with ideas."

"Dude, I know. Let's put colored stars and triangles and shit on it," Jo said in her best stoner voice.

Lynae squinted until her eyes were slits. "Yeah. And let's connect 'em with lines and little circles."

"That would be awesome. Hey, man, you got any more of those Cheetos?"

Jo straightened and nudged Lynae as the young blonde walked back through the door. The girl was followed by a stout man wearing khaki pants and a navy polo with the Kegler's Kove logo embroidered on the left breast. She pointed at Jo and Lynae then resumed her post behind the bar.

The man came around the curved wooden counter. "I'm the manager, Gary Metzlinger."

Jo shook his hand. "Lieutenant Riskin and Detective Parker. We're with the Grand Rapids police. Homicide."

Gary frowned. "Homicide? What can I do for you?"

Jo pulled the driver's license picture of Brad Kramer from her bag and handed it to Gary. "Do you recognize this man?"

The man ran his hand through his thinning brown hair and scratched behind his ear. "Yeah, that's Brad. Can't remember his last name off the top of my head."

"Kramer," Jo offered.

Gary snapped his fingers. "Yep, that's it. Big talker, big spender. Always buys a round or two for the team." He laid the picture on the countertop. "Why are you asking about him?"

"He was murdered, and we believe this was the last place he was seen."

Gary's jaw dropped. "He's dead?"

"I'm afraid so. Did you see him here last Thursday night?"

"I wasn't here Thursday. I usually am, but I took last week off. Julie was working that night."

"Is Julie here now?"

"Yep, I can get her for you." Gary peered up and down the forty-two-lane complex. Several servers in navy-blue shirts carried serving trays. Some had them raised above their heads as they jockeyed for position amongst the patrons. He raised his hand and motioned to a woman holding a tray of shot glasses. She bobbed her head in acknowledgment then continued to sell several more drinks before making her way to the bar.

She grinned at Gary while giving a quick nod to a pile of cash riding the corner of her tray. "Sorry, I was on a roll. Didn't want to give anyone a chance to think twice."

Gary pointed at Jo and Lynae. "Julie, these are detectives from Grand Rapids. They're asking about Brad Kramer."

Sliding the tray onto the counter, she put her hand on her lower back and stretched. "Ugh, Brad. He's a piece of work. What did he do?"

"He's dead," Gary blurted before Jo could answer.

"Oh my God." Julie melted onto a bar stool. "I didn't like the guy, but that's... wow."

Gary walked behind the counter, poured a glass of water, and slid it toward Julie. She took it with a grateful smile and downed half of it.

"This was the last place that anyone saw him," Lynae said. "Do you remember seeing him Thursday?"

"Oh yeah, he was here."

"Did he have an altercation with someone, maybe hit on the wrong woman?"

"Now that you say that, he was all over Cindy."

Jo took out her notebook. "Cindy? Is that another server?"

"No. She's a customer, a regular."

"Do you know her last name?"

"I'll have to look it up." She turned to Gary. "She pays with credit."

"I'll get the receipts," Gary said then hustled through the door behind the bar.

"So you would recognize this Cindy?" Jo asked.

"Sure. She comes every week with some friends. I've never seen her talk to Brad before, but he chatted her up last Thursday, and she let him buy her a couple drinks. He was here until probably one or so."

"Did they leave together?" Lynae asked.

"No, and I think it made him mad, like he had wasted his time on her or something. That's what he's like, though. Or I guess what he *was* like." Julie took another gulp of water. "I remember he threw money on the counter and, you know, gave me the nod and left. He always paid cash, and he tipped really good. That's about the only nice thing I can say about him."

A man who looked to be in his early thirties walked up behind Julie. "Excuse me, Jules." He laid a hand on her shoulder as he reached across the counter to grab a tray. His man-bun and bushy beard screamed hipster.

Julie craned her neck to look over her shoulder. She gave the young man a grim smile. "Hey, Tyler. You know Brad Kramer, right? Bowls Thursday nights. Big talker, big drinker."

"That pretty much sums up every guy here on league nights."

Julie put her hand on Tyler's arm. "These are police detectives."

Lynae gave a curt nod. "Detective Parker. And you are?"

"Tyler Glen," he replied in a shaky voice. His eyes darted nervously between Jo and Lynae.

Lynae picked up the picture from the countertop and held it out for him. "Do you know this man?"

He leaned in for a closer look, his eyes narrowing as he peered at the photo. "Yeah, I know that guy. Why?"

"He was murdered," Jo said bluntly, keeping a close eye on his reaction.

Tyler looked up, wide-eyed. His Adam's apple bobbed twice before he replied, "He's dead?"

"Did you see him Thursday night?" Lynae asked.

"Let me think." His hands shook slightly as he pushed up the sleeves of his cardigan, revealing heavily tattooed arms. He ran his hand through his dark beard. "Not that I remember."

His nervousness set off alarms on Jo's detective radar. *If this guy is someone he barely recognizes, why does his death upset him? He's lying.* "You didn't see him at all on Thursday?" Jo asked.

"I mean... I don't remember specifically. I might have."

Jo leveled him with a practiced, disbelieving cop stare. "You did, or you didn't?"

The blonde cleared her throat. "Um, I saw him leave."

Tyler gaped at the young girl.

Jo shifted around him and stepped up to the counter. "And what's your name?"

The girl released her hair from its ponytail and slid the purple band around her wrist. "April."

Jo reached back and took the picture from Tyler. "And you saw this man leave Thursday night?"

April nodded. "I saw him in the parking lot."

"What time was that?" Jo asked.

"Like, maybe, one fifteen or so."

"What were you doing outside at that time?" Tyler huffed, crossing his arms.

A flush rushing up her neck, April fiddled with the band around her wrist. "I know that's not when I'm supposed to go on break, but it was late, and I needed a cigarette."

"You're supposed to be behind the bar at that time."

"Why don't you let Gary worry about that," Julie said. "I think the important thing right now is to let April talk to the detectives."

Tyler grabbed his drink tray from the counter and propped it on one hip. "Can I go back to work?" he asked sullenly.

Lynae nodded. "Yes. We'll let you know if we need to talk to you again."

Jo watched the hipster dart back into the crowd, his jaw set in a firm line. When a customer stopped him, he transformed into a cheerful, accommodating waiter. *He's pretty good at turning it on and off.*

Jo turned back to April. "Did you see anyone with him?"

April began smoothing her hair back from her face. "Yeah, that's why I remember. He was pretty toasted. There was a guy with him who was helping him to his car."

Julie stopped her water glass halfway to her mouth and frowned. "He didn't seem that drunk when he walked out."

The young girl rolled her eyes as she pulled the band from her wrist and wrapped it around her hair. "Oh yeah, he was bad. The guy had him around the waist, kinda half carrying him."

Jo's pulse quickened. "Do you remember what the man looked like? His size, anything?"

April's face scrunched. "Not really. Our parking lot isn't all that well lit. He was smaller than Brad. I know that. I was kinda laughing, watching him try to help him. His face was all buried in Brad's armpit. Do you think that guy killed him? Like maybe I could have stopped it?"

Lynae shook her head. "We don't know that, and even if he did, you had no way to know."

Jo laid her notebook on the counter and flipped to a blank page. "Could you tell if the man was white, black, Hispanic? What color was his hair?"

April closed her eyes and bit her lip. Her eyeballs moved rapidly under their lids. "I couldn't see anything about his face. He had on a long coat, like an army jacket or something, and a hat. A stocking cap pulled down low. I couldn't see any hair." She opened her eyes and shook her head. "Sorry. I know that doesn't really help."

Jo jotted the description down in her notebook. "Actually, that's very helpful. Did you notice anything distinct about his voice or mannerisms?"

The girl shook her head. "I didn't pay that much attention."

"Do you know what kind of vehicle he was driving?"

"Oh man, let me see." April once again closed her eyes and went through her little memory routine. "It was a big truck. One of those four-door ones. I remember that because he put the drunk guy in the back seat. I think it was dark blue, but it could have been black. I don't know the make or model. I'm sorry. That's all I can remember."

Jo smiled at the young woman. "You've been very helpful."

Gary walked out of the back office and handed Jo a folded piece of paper. "Sorry that took a while, but I found her credit card receipt and made a copy for you."

"Perfect. Thank you." Jo tucked the paper into her notebook. "Can you tell me which lane Brad bowled on?"

"Twenty-four," Julie said. "I know because I take a lot of drinks to his table."

Jo handed each of them a business card. "I appreciate your help. If any of you think of anything else, please give me a call."

On the way out, Jo stopped by the high-top table in front of lane twenty-four. She eyeballed the bar, estimating the distance between the two areas.

"What are we doing?" Lynae asked.

"Brad had it in his head that Cindy was checking him out, enough so that he took the initiative to go talk to her."

"So?"

"You flirt with a lot of guys in bars," Jo said, giving Lynae a sideways glance.

"Hey, now."

Jo shrugged. "Just saying. But how obvious would you have to be to flirt with someone from that bar to this lane?"

Lynae put her hands on her hips and studied the area. "Like blinking-neon-sign obvious."

"Might be that she was just letting the big spender buy her a couple drinks, but the way I see it, someone had to give him the impression that the woman was interested."

"And that someone would have known Brad would follow up on that as soon as he was done bowling. Brad thinks he's gonna get lucky, so he tells the guys to leave without him."

Chewing on her lip, Jo imagined it playing out. "She's a regular and has never given him the time of day before. Suddenly, she's keeping him here later than usual so that he doesn't walk out with the rest of the guys. And that happens to be the night he ends up dead? Seems a little too convenient to me. We need to talk to Cindy, but it will have to wait until tomorrow."

Jo and Lynae headed for the door, past the shoe counter and rows of bowling balls lined up by color. Jo pushed open the glass doors and was mugged by a blast of cold wind. They both tucked their heads down and hustled to the truck.

Lynae dropped into her seat and held out her hand. "I'll make contact with Cindy in the morning."

Jo pulled the paper with the credit card information out of her notebook and handed it to Lynae. "Let's get her down to the station. If she's involved or knows anything, I want her out of her element, maybe a little intimidated."

"Do I get to be good cop or bad cop?"

"I think we'll just stick with one of us having a chat with her for now, but you would definitely be the good cop."

Lynae sighed. "That's what I thought. You have the badass look that I just can't quite pull off."

"It's hard to look badass with all that pretty hair done up in those messy buns. You have to cop it up a little."

Lynae slapped Jo's shoulder. "Aw, you think I have pretty hair."

"Don't make wedding plans right away."

"Wouldn't that make Aunt Trudy happy? She loves me."

"Yes, she does. I'm so glad you happened to be at my house the night she stopped in, or she might have managed to shanghai me into going on that singles cruise."

"Let's not forget that you were the one who introduced me as your partner when I was half-dressed."

Jo threw her head back and laughed. "She hasn't tried to set me up on a single date since she met you."

Lynae rubbed her hands together like a scheming thief. "Mission accomplished."

"You're going to have to come for lunch at my parents' house again soon," Jo said, easing onto a side street in Lynae's neighborhood.

Lynae rubbed her belly. "I think I can make the sacrifice of eating one of your mom's feasts."

"Aunt Trudy keeps asking me why you aren't there. I feel kind of bad making excuses, and I think she's getting suspicious."

Lynae's eyebrows shot up. "That we're not really dating?"

"No, that we're having problems."

"Well, you *have* been seeing a lot of Jack lately." Lynae put on a fake pout. "I'm starting to get a little jealous."

Jo fiddled with the heat knob. "We're just hanging out, catching a drink after work once in a while. Don't worry. You have nothing to be jealous about."

"Uh-huh."

"Don't go there, Nae," Jo said through gritted teeth.

"Come on. You can't tell me you haven't thought about it."

Jo huffed. "All this because I said you need to cop up your hair a bit if you want to be more badass?"

Lynae stared at Jo in the semidarkness of the Ranger. "I'm serious, Jo."

Jo forced herself to concentrate on the road while her brain cycled back through her last two days with Jack: a thoughtful bagel and coffee, an actual date that she didn't run away from, then the bombshell about Mike's killer. She had pushed him away when she wanted to hold on and let him comfort her. And the fact that she wanted to hold on to him scared the hell out of her. She dropped her arm onto the window ledge and unnecessarily adjusted the mirror control, avoiding eye contact with Lynae. "Jack bought tickets to the Garth Brooks concert, and we're going together Friday. It's a date, and I don't know if I'm ready for that, but I'm going."

Lynae gaped at her. "Okay. Wow."

"Yeah, wow."

Lynae turned as far in her seat as her seat belt would allow. "That's a good thing."

"You think? I don't know."

"It's a concert. It's one night out with a guy who's fun and obviously interested in you."

Jo's shoulders slumped. "But Mike—"

"Has been gone for over two years."

"It feels like a betrayal," Jo said, staring straight ahead. She didn't dare to look at her best friend because the tears that were stinging the backs of her eyes and clogging her throat would cut loose.

Lynae laid her hand on Jo's shoulder. "But it's not. You loved him completely when he was alive, and you would love him completely now if he still was. But he's not. You can't betray him by living your life."

"I know, but..."

"It's just a date. For one night, just go and have fun. See how it goes."

As her brain argued both sides of her internal debate, Jo drummed her fingers on the steering wheel. "It *is* Garth Brooks. It's pretty hard to say no. Let's just not talk about it anymore."

"It's hard to say no because it's the ridiculously good-looking Jack Riley, not because it's Garth Brooks."

Jo tried to push Jack's face out of her mind and bring Mike's back. It unnerved her that it was a struggle. She swung the truck into the drive of Lynae's apartment complex. "Oh, look at that. We're back at your place. I guess we'll have to stop talking about my personal life and get back to the fact that someone has been murdered."

"I'll get back to the case if you promise me you'll go to that concert tomorrow and have fun. And give Jack a chance."

Jo stared at her blandly. "Um, no. You'll get back to the case because I'm your lieutenant and I say so."

"You brought it up!"

"And now I'm telling you to let it go. And that's an order."

Lynae raised one eyebrow. "Are you really pulling rank on me right now?"

Jo gave her a stern look, tamping down the guilt that came with knowing she was wrong and being unnecessarily harsh. "Is that what it's going to take for you to get back to work and stop worrying about my personal life?"

Lynae shook her head sadly and reached for the door. "No, ma'am. *Lieutenant.*"

Jo groaned then grabbed Lynae's arm. "I'm sorry."

"It's fine."

"No, it's not. We were having a nice conversation, and I turned bitchy."

"Yeah, you kinda did."

"I'm a mess," Jo said, running her hands through her hair. "I actually felt almost normal for a while. I was even looking forward to going out with Jack. Then that bastard Drevin goes and kills himself, and it's such a slap in the face. It's like I'm starting all over with Mike's death, and I don't know how to deal with it."

"You're my best friend, Jo, and I still feel like I have to tiptoe around certain subjects. It shouldn't be that way."

Jo threw her hands up. "I just don't want to talk about Jack."

"No, you have feelings for Jack, and you don't want to talk about *those*."

"I don't know what I'm feeling for Jack. Part of me wants to find out, but there's a whole other part of me that feels guilt for even thinking about moving on. That part always seems to win."

"There's nothing to feel guilty about."

"That's not—"

Lynae held up her hand. "If you want to keep punishing yourself, I can't stop you. But I'm not just going to sit back and be quiet while you do it."

Jo blew out a resigned sigh. "I know."

"Go get some sleep. I'll see you tomorrow."

Rubbing the pain that had crept into her neck, Jo said, "Actually, I think I'm running on too little sleep. Why don't you deal with Cindy in the morning? I'm going to try to catch up on my Zs."

Lynae opened the door and slid one foot out. "Good plan. You can't have Garth seeing you with those bags under your eyes."

"My thoughts exactly. Not a good way to start a relationship." She tapped the steering wheel. "I'm also going to see if I can talk to anyone at the jail who was there when Drevin died."

Lynae pulled her foot back inside the truck and closed the door. "Will they let you do that? It's not even Kent County. You don't have any pull there. Aren't they doing an internal investigation?"

"I'm sure that their Internal Affairs is on it. I'm just going to call the captain and ask. I don't see what it could hurt."

"Don't you think you should let IA handle it?"

"Do you know how many people have killed themselves in that jail in the last ten years?" When Lynae shook her head, Jo said, "Two."

"Okay."

Jo held up two fingers. "Two in ten years. And a guy who's been cocky all along, yapping that he would beat the rap, suddenly becomes number three? I'm just not buying it."

"Jo, I know it sucks, but don't try to insinuate yourself into that investigation too much. You don't want it to look like you were involved."

"Involved? Why the hell would I be involved?"

Lynae's eyes widened. "He killed your husband! Not everyone thinks like you. Most people would think that his death would make you happy."

Jo shook her head. "They don't understand."

"What if Mike's partner was involved?" Lynae asked quietly. "If someone killed you, I don't know what I would be capable of."

Jo squeezed the bridge of her nose while memories of pointing a gun at Mike's killer, of feeling herself adding pressure to the trigger, flashed like lighting behind her eyes. "You'd be surprised what thoughts actually run through your head."

"Not everyone is as strong as you. Maybe he couldn't deal with being the one who lived."

Jo flopped her head back on the headrest. "I have to find out, even if it's something I don't want to know. I have this constant thought that I'm missing something. It's always been there, tickling the back of my brain, but it's always just out of reach. I used to think it was a clue to the killer, but we found him, and the nagging hasn't gone away. It's stronger now but as elusive as ever." Jo turned her head and looked into Lynae's eyes. "I have to find a way to catch it."

Lynae drummed her fingers on the door handle. "I understand. You're not going to rest until you do this. So whatever I can do to help, you just have to ask."

"Thank you," Jo choked out, her voice thick with emotion.

"Always." Lynae climbed out of the truck and shut the door.

Jo watched until the light in Lynae's apartment came on. Confident that her partner was safely tucked in for the night, she pulled out of the parking lot and drove the quiet, dark streets back to her empty house.

Chapter 8

Jo made a call to the captain first thing in the morning and was given permission to speak with Drevin Clayburn's cellmate as well as the inmate that he'd had the altercation with. She was not given permission to talk with the officer on duty, which came as no surprise. Internal Affairs would want to handle that with no interference.

She drove up the long, winding hill leading to the jail then down the wooded half-mile drive to the parking lot. Inside the plain gray concrete building, she signed in and surrendered her weapon to the desk clerk.

The clerk gave her a retrieval tag, peered over her purple horn-rimmed cheaters, and said, "Captain Brody will be right with you, Lieutenant."

Jo settled into one of the tan plastic chairs along the wall then pulled her yellow legal pad out of her bag and looked over the questions she had jotted down the night before.

After a buzzer broke the silence, a steel door to her left clanged open, and a rigid-looking man marched into the room. His broad shoulders tapered to a trim waist that belied the late middle age that showed on his weathered face. He stopped in front of Jo and leveled her with a steely scowl. "Lieutenant Riskin?"

Jo jumped to her feet and held out her hand. "You must be Captain Brody."

The captain shook Jo's hand firmly, turned abruptly, then walked toward the door he had just come through. "I'll escort you to the interrogation room."

Jo hustled to catch up to him. "I appreciate your giving me this opportunity, Captain."

Without looking at her, he said, "My men followed every procedure down to the wire. We have nothing to hide from you or IA."

"No, sir, I'm sure you don't. I'm more interested in what led up to his solitary confinement than in anything your officers may or may not have done."

Captain Brody led her down a long corridor of beige walls paired with linoleum floor tiles in squares of light beige. Someone had gotten a little wild and thrown a dark-beige square in every other row. *Whoa, slow down there, guys.*

He stopped in front of a metal door with a narrow window. The young officer stationed outside the room straightened. A plaque that read Interrogation Room C flanked the officer's right shoulder.

"Daskin is a high-risk inmate. He'll be cuffed." The captain pointed at the officer, who stood ramrod straight but was still a head shorter than Jo. "But I'm leaving a guard in the room with you."

"That's unnecessary. I would prefer to have the officer stand outside the door."

Captain Brody's eyes slid over her. "Daskin is twice your size, has a hair-trigger temper, and is in here on rape and first-degree murder charges. He battered his victim so severely she was barely recognizable to her own mother. He's got a rap sheet as long as my arm and knows he's going away for good. He has nothing to lose at this point. I strongly suggest you keep the officer in the room with you."

Jo smiled. "All of that is good to know, Captain. But since the inmate will be cuffed to the table, I respectfully decline."

Captain Brody inclined his head. "As you wish, Lieutenant." He turned to the officer. "Cleary, bring Daskin down to speak to the lieutenant then stay on the door."

"Yes, sir." Officer Cleary hightailed it down the hall.

The captain waved at the door to the interrogation room. "Make yourself comfortable, Lieutenant. Officer Cleary will be back shortly." He turned on his heel and marched away before Jo could answer. His shiny county-issued shoes echoed down the empty corridor.

Jo rolled her shoulders and walked into the interrogation room. *Surprise. It's beige.*

She slid into the chair facing the door, took out her notepad and pen, and positioned them on the table in front of her. While she was nervously toying with the curved metal bars that protruded from the top of the table, the door handle clicked.

When the door creaked open, an enormous man in an orange jumpsuit filled the opening. He weighed no fewer than three hundred pounds and stood about six and a half feet tall. His hands were cuffed in front of him and attached to a chain that snaked down his body to the cuffs around his ankles. The tattoos that crept out of his orange jumpsuit and ran up his neck were crudely drawn and hailed his allegiance to the Aryan Brotherhood. She would've bet that he was covered in more hate-filled ink under the jumpsuit.

Officer Cleary held the much larger man by the arm as they shuffled into the room. The officer pushed him, none too gently, into the chair opposite Jo then detached his cuffs from the chain to pull his hands forward and fasten the metal links to the table bracket.

When the prisoner was secured, the officer gave the links a cursory tug then hooked his thumbs under his heavy black belt. "I'll be right outside the door, Lieutenant."

Jo gave him a curt nod. "Thank you, Officer."

After the officer left the room, he positioned himself in front of the narrow window, his sandy-blond hair pressed against the glass.

Jo turned her attention to the inmate and smiled. "Thank you for agreeing to meet with me, Mr. Daskin."

"Didn't sound like I had a choice." His hazel eyes slid over Jo as he took his time to lazily ogle her. "Course, if I knew you were gonna

be so hot, I'd-a been more prepared. You know, put on my dress orange." He grinned and gave her a little wink.

In another life—without the tattoos, greasy hair, and the reason
he was there—he could have been handsome, probably even charming. Jo didn't doubt that he had used that charm to make his victim
feel secure right before he destroyed her world.

She held him in a steady gaze as spiders crawled up and down her
spine. "Well, I don't know about that, but I do appreciate your time."

He scoffed. "Yeah, 'cause I got so many other things I could be
doing right now."

"I just have a few questions about the altercation you had with
Drevin Clayburn in the exercise yard on Wednesday."

"What about it?"

"What started it?"

Daskin slapped the table, and the chains that bound his wrists
clattered against the wooden top. Officer Cleary turned and peered
through the window. Jo discreetly waved him off.

"Little pissant took my cake at lunch the day before."

She raised an eyebrow at the inmate. "Took your cake?"

"Yeah, took my cake." He leaned back in his chair as far as the
cuff chain would allow. "He said he didn't do it, but I know he did."

Jo picked up her notepad and pulled out the pen. "Did someone
tell you he took your cake?"

"Don't matter if somebody told me. It's the only damn good
thing they give us to eat around here, and that little shithead took
mine."

"So you confronted him about the cake?"

He cocked his head. "Yeah, I *confronted* him with my fist."

"You don't look like you've been in a fight."

Daskin snorted. "He tried, but I wouldn't call it a fight."

"So you both got sent to solitary?"

"Yeah. Guess he couldn't handle it." He rolled his eyes.

"Have you ever had an issue with him before this?"

"You mean before he stole my cake?" His tone made it sound more as if Drevin had stolen his wife or his Harley, which Jo envisioned him driving because no other vehicle fit.

She nodded. "Yes, before the cake."

"No, never paid no attention to the guy. Saw him sittin' by himself all the time, but I never had nothing to do with him."

"Then one day this guy that sat by himself and never had anything to do with you just decided to steal your cake?"

"Yeah." Daskin looked doubtful for the first time. "He had two of them. Punk tried to tell me that the dude in the lunch line just gave him two. Nobody ever gets two cakes. And it was kinda funny that mine goes missing and suddenly he has two." Daskin talked himself right back into a clear conviction that the guy who always sat alone, minded his own business, and talked to no one had suddenly decided to steal a precious dinner cake from a monstrous beast.

"Did you ask the man from the lunch line?"

Daskin's bound hands flew up and clattered back to the table. "No, and why should I? I ain't no damn detective, but I think it's pretty obvious. Why do you care so much about this, anyway? I didn't kill the guy. He did that to himself."

"Nobody's trying to pin anything on you. I'm just trying to sort out what happened before he died."

Daskin leaned forward and put his hands flat on the table. "If I'm gonna kill someone, it ain't gonna be a cop killer. We need more of them in the world, you ask me."

Jo mimicked his posture and moved her face closer to his. "Well, I didn't ask you, did I?"

"Oh, now you suddenly don't care what I have to say. Cop gets killed, and everybody thinks it's the end of the world. Nobody gives a shit when one of us gets killed."

"If an inmate gets killed, I give it the same investigation I give any other murder. And the cop he killed was my husband. So yeah, it was the end of the world for me."

Whistling softly, Daskin leaned back. "Shit, I didn't know that."

"Doesn't make any difference, right?" Jo said through gritted teeth. "We need more cop killers in the world." She slid her chair back, walked to the steel door, and rapped on the window.

The officer jolted then turned and opened the door.

Jo pointed at Daskin. "You can take him back to his cell. Then bring Mauricio Duarte in."

The officer unlocked Daskin from the table, took the inmate by the arm, and escorted him out the door. Jo sat back down and closed her eyes.

Drevin Clayburn was set up to get the shit beat out of him by Daskin. But why? He was scheduled for court in less than a month, and he would most likely have been relocated to a maximum-security prison.

Drevin had been quiet and kept to himself. That was surprising. Apparently, the cocky, self-important man she'd arrested wasn't as tough as he had let on.

Then suddenly he decides to take on one of the biggest, nastiest dudes in the joint?

Jo rolled her head and rubbed her neck to work out the tension that had been building all morning. She sat up straight when the doorknob clicked. The steel door again swung open, and Cleary pushed in a wiry Hispanic man as small as Daskin was large. The inmate shuffled over to the table, head down, and dropped into the chair before the officer had a chance to plant him there. Cleary silently completed his routine to secure the inmate to the table then resumed his post outside the door.

Duarte's foot immediately began to tap as he scanned the room, quickly fixating on the large one-way mirror behind Jo. Every prisoner knew what that was.

Jo smiled. "I'm Lieutenant Jo Riskin, Mauricio. Thanks for seeing me."

He looked at her. "Sure, yeah, no problem." He spoke as quickly as his foot moved.

She wondered at what speed his heart must pump blood to keep everything moving at that hummingbird pace. "Drevin Clayburn was your cellmate, right?"

"Yeah, but he offed himself." Mauricio glanced up at the mirror again.

"I understand he was quiet and kept to himself."

"Yeah, he was quiet when he was out of the cell. Pretty chatty when it was just us. He didn't want to get mixed up with anybody. He was getting out and didn't want any trouble."

"How do you know he was getting out?"

Mauricio's foot tapped faster, and his whole body jiggled. "Said he was. Said there was no way the charges were gonna stick."

She pursed her lips. "Pretty confident, huh?"

"Yeah, he said—" Mauricio jolted, his eyes going back to the mirror. His foot tapped frantically.

This guy is a basket case. Jo leaned forward. "What did he say, Mauricio?"

Mauricio stopped tapping and slouched lower in his chair. "I don't know. I forget."

Jo's eyebrows shot up. "You forgot? Just now?"

He glanced at Jo then dropped his gaze to the table. "Yeah, I forgot."

She looked over her shoulder at the mirror. "Mauricio, there's no one behind that mirror."

He frowned as his gaze flicked to the mirror then back to Jo. His eyes clouded over. "Don't matter. I forgot, and I ain't gonna remember."

"Did Drevin talk to you about his case? Did he tell you who else was with him?"

Mauricio's eyes darted to the door then back to the mirror. He licked his lips and shook his head. "He didn't tell me nothin', and I don't know nothin'. I don't want to talk to you no more."

Jo sighed. "Okay. Just remember my name. Lieutenant Riskin. If your memory comes back, you contact me."

"How am I supposed to do that?" He shrugged. "Not that I'm gonna remember anything."

Jo slid a card across the table. "You tell the sergeant you want to talk to me. It's that easy."

Mauricio scoffed but picked up the card. "Yeah, it's that easy. Can I go now?"

After Jo knocked on the door window, Officer Cleary came in, uncuffed the inmate, and pulled him out of the chair. Mauricio looked over his shoulder at Jo before shuffling out the door.

Jo stared at a spot on the wall where the paint had chipped. It had been picked at, probably over a long period of time, by any number of people who sat waiting in the room. One small spot, one defect in the paint, chipped away piece by piece until the ugliness beneath was wholly revealed. *I just chipped away a little bit of the paint from Drevin's death. And I won't quit picking until I find whatever ugliness is hidden underneath.*

Officer Cleary opened the door and poked his head in. "All finished, Lieutenant?"

"Yes, I am." Jo slid her notebook back into her bag and slung it over her shoulder.

"I'm to escort you back to the entrance."

After one more look around the room, she motioned toward the door. "Lead the way."

She retrieved her sidearm from the reception desk, snapped it into the shoulder holster, then slid her coat on over it. As she reached for the outside door, she pulled her hand back as the door swung open and a man stepped in.

Jo's heart plunged to her gut. "Rick."

Rick stopped in his tracks and stood with one hand on the door, his deep-set dark eyes registering surprise. "Jo."

What do I say to Mike's old partner? Why did you let him go into the building alone? Why didn't you follow procedure? Jo hiked her bag up higher on her shoulder. "What brings you here?"

Rick shifted his weight from one foot to the other then leaned against the open door, crossing his beefy arms across his chest. "Just following up on a couple things."

After Mike's death, Jo couldn't bring herself to contact Rick. When the funeral was over, she was bitter that he could go home with his wife and get on with his life, while hers was left in tatters on that warehouse floor where Mike had been gunned down. The guilt of that feeling mixed with her bitterness in a foaming, toxic brew that bubbled to the surface every time she reached for the phone to call him. Eventually, she stopped trying. She didn't know if he had ever tried.

She attempted to push those thoughts into the corner of her brain reserved for late-night guilt trips. It was time to move on. "Sheila good? The kids?"

Rick ran his hand through his thinning brown hair. "They're good. You know, growing like weeds."

Jo's chest constricted. "Well..."

Rick stepped back, pushing the door wider. "Good seeing you, Jo."

Jo forced a smile, aware that it didn't quite reach her eyes. "You too, Rick. Take care." She walked past him then stopped. Keeping her gaze on the parking lot, she said, "Drevin Clayburn, Mike's killer, is dead. Suicide."

"I heard. I'm sorry. I know it's not how you wanted this to end."

"No, it isn't." Jo turned around. "I never wanted to shut you out, either. I just couldn't..."

Rick's eyes softened. "I should have tried harder to reach out to you. I just have so much guilt that I didn't know how."

Jo cocked her head. "Guilt?"

"He was my partner, my friend." Rick shoved his hands into his pockets.

"You were following a lead from a snitch you'd used before. You had no way to know it would take such a horrible turn." She squeezed her eyes shut, trying to block out the image of Mike bleeding alone on a cold warehouse floor. "Can you just tell me one thing?"

"I'll try."

She opened her eyes and looked into his. "Mike was all about procedure. He drilled it into my head. He trained rookies on following procedures, and he would fume for days when someone he trained breached protocol. Why the hell did he break his own rules and go in alone?"

He raised his head to look somewhere over hers. "We thought we had the jump. There were only two of them. Backup was unnecessary."

Her stomach lurched. "I thought you called for backup."

"I did. Mike wanted to get inside and see what was happening, make sure we had eyes on them while the deal was going down."

Jo shook her head. "I just don't understand. He didn't work that way."

"Mike was the best. He just made a bad call."

"Did anyone else know about the sting?"

"No, just us and the captain."

"This isn't how I wanted this to go, you know, talking to you for the first time in so long," Jo said, rubbing her forehead with the tips of her fingers. "I'm sorry to badger you with questions."

Rick kicked a stone with his polished black loafer. "I've thought a thousand times about what to say to you. I just never knew how."

"I know, and it's all right."

"You doing okay?"

Jo shrugged. "One day at a time." She looked over his shoulder at the immense concrete building. "I was better before Drevin took the easy way out. I wanted to see him in a cage for the rest of his life."

Rick sneered. "I don't know. As long as the son of a bitch isn't walking the streets, dead's okay with me."

Maybe Lynae was right and people wouldn't understand that her vengeance would be best served by a daily helping of lost freedom with an occasional side of violence. The silence stretched uncomfortably as Jo tried to think of a reply. Finally, she just said, "I've got to get back. Give my best to Sheila."

"I know she'd like to see you."

Jo smiled sadly. "Sure. Have her call me."

She walked to the parking lot without looking back. After unlocking her truck door, she dropped into the driver's seat, feeling exhausted by the encounter. Her tears fell unchecked as she maneuvered out of the lot and headed back down the scenic driveway. When her vision blurred, she pulled to the side of the road and dug through her purse for a tissue. Her hands shook as she wiped her eyes and blew her nose. "Well, Mike, that was hard."

Talking to Rick was long overdue.

"I know, but it was hard. I don't want to resent him just for living."

You won't always feel that way. And you learned something from talking to him.

"I did?"

You did. Think, Jo.

Jo put the truck back in gear and drove slowly down the winding road, replaying the conversation with Rick over in her head. *Mike said the captain knew about the sting. Montaine wasn't mentioned in any of the investigative reports.*

She slammed on the brakes. Her head jerked forward and almost smacked the steering wheel. She grabbed her phone and scrolled through her contacts with a shaky finger then cleared her throat and took a deep breath before hitting the call button.

"County records, Diane speaking."

"Diane, it's Jo Riskin. How are you?"

"Jo! Girl, it's been so long. I'm doing all right. And you?"

"I'm good. Keeping busy. You know the drill."

"You know I do. I bet you didn't call me out of the blue at work to swap recipes, though, did you? What's up?"

"Well, swapping recipes with me would be a huge mistake." Jo laughed. "But I'm afraid you're right. I need a favor."

"You know all you gotta do is ask."

"Montaine was Mike's captain when he was in Narcotics, but I never heard much about him."

"Not surprising. The lieutenants work the closest with the detectives. I'm sure your team talks more about you than about Captain Quinn."

"I suppose so. And I probably don't want to know what they say."

Diane chortled. "Come on. You know they love you!"

"I don't know about that, but they're stuck with me." Jo moved the phone to her other ear and rested her arm on the windowsill. "What did you think of Montaine?"

"He was okay. Kind of had *his* people, if you know what I mean."

Yeah, Jo knew what she meant, and she wondered who *his* people were. "Is he still the captain of that division?"

"Nope. Brooks came in shortly after..."

Jo recognized the hesitation. Even friends didn't know how to say, "After your husband was murdered." "What happened to Montaine?"

"He moved to the jail."

"That's interesting," Jo said quietly.

"You all right, hon?"

"Yeah. Yeah, I'm fine."

"Hey, it's been a couple months since we had a girls' night out. What do you say we plan one?"

Just the thought of a night out with the girls warmed Jo's heart enough to melt away some of her tension. Nothing was better for the soul than a few drinks, heart-baring conversation, and the kind of raucous laughter that turned heads and left your cheeks aching. "That would be fantastic. You have no idea how much I could use a girls' night."

"I want to go back to that place you took us last summer for Taco Tuesday."

Jo roared with laughter. "The good old Conklin Bar."

"Yes! I'll text the girls and see if we can put something together. I don't have Lynae's number, so add her when you get it. She's a riot."

Jo exited the highway and eased into downtown traffic. "You got it. Thanks for the info on the captain."

"Anytime. See you soon."

Jo disconnected and put her phone back into the console. Her mind was reeling. *The captain, who was the only other person who knew Mike and Rick were pulling a bust the night Mike died, is now in the same jail where Drevin Clayburn just supposedly killed himself?*

That was just a little too convenient. Something was off, and come hell or high water, she would find it.

Chapter 9

Jo parked in her designated spot in the county parking structure and hustled into the station. Digging through her bag for her security card, she strode past the reception desk.

The sultry drawl of the attendant echoed across the tiled room. "That's all right. No need to say hi or anything."

Jo whipped around. "Oh hell, Aneace, I'm sorry."

Aneace broke into a wide grin, her pearly whites gleaming against her candy-apple-red lipstick. "I just like to give you a hard time. You know that."

Jo walked back to the marble counter and leaned her elbows on it. "My day wouldn't be complete without a little harassment from you. How are you today?"

Aneace did a little chair dance. "Oh, you know, I'm fantastic!"

"You really are."

"You have a nice day now, Lieutenant Jo."

Jo slapped the counter then hoisted her bag up farther on her shoulder. "You too, Aneace. Thanks for keeping me in line."

Aneace winked. "Always here to help."

Jo's grin lasted the two flights up to her division. She pushed through the stairwell door and noticed Lynae wasn't at her desk. Without an update from her partner, she decided to dig into some department paperwork that was long overdue. The tediousness of the job would give her time to mull over her conversation with Rick and what, if anything, it meant that the captain was now working at the same jail where Drevin Clayburn just committed suicide.

About an hour later, Lynae appeared in Jo's office doorway with two Bagel Beanery coffee cups. "I figured since I was out, I'd stop and get us cups of the good stuff."

Jo rubbed her eyes and sagged back in her chair. "You look like a coffee-wielding angel right about now."

"Well, I've never been accused of being an angel, but if I was, I hope I would get something better to wield than coffee."

Jo accepted one of the cups and took a sip. She closed her eyes and inhaled the aroma. "I bet more wars have been averted with coffee than with guns."

"They all would be if you were in charge." Lynae dropped into the visitor chair and propped her feet on the edge of Jo's desk.

Jo held up her cup in a salute. "Amen to that."

Lynae took a drink from her steaming cup. "How did it go at the jail?"

"I have more questions than answers at this point."

"Lay it out for me."

Jo set her coffee cup on her desk then steepled her fingers. "The story is that Drevin stole cake from one of the other inmates, an enormous thug that, up until this incident, he had no contact with."

"Then he just randomly decided to steal his cake?"

Jo pointed at Lynae. "Exactly."

"So then the enormous thug kicked the shit out of him, and they both ended up in solitary."

"Convenient, isn't it?"

Lynae watched Jo over the rim of her coffee cup as she took a sip. "That kind of stuff happens in jail all the time."

Jo hopped up and closed her door. "But not usually from the guys that keep to themselves. Or from the guy who just told his cellmate that he's getting out."

"Drevin told his cellmate he was getting out?"

"Yeah. The guy started to say more, but he lost his nerve. He kept looking at the two-way. I couldn't convince him no one was there." Jo returned to her chair.

Lynae dropped her feet to the floor and leaned forward. "He's afraid if he talks, word will get out. It's not unusual for inmates not to trust the guards. Or the police, for that matter."

"Yeah, I know. I may be reading too much into that." Jo absently stared at her cup while she turned it around and around in her hands. "On my way out, I saw Rick."

Lynae's mouth dropped open. "Mike's partner? What did you do?"

Jo looked up and shrugged. "I talked to him. It was awkward, especially at first. You know, we both feel bad for not being better about contacting the other. He said he has a lot of guilt."

"I imagine he does. I would too."

Jo picked at the ribbed cardboard heat guard on her cup. "He mentioned that their captain knew about the bust."

"So? Isn't that pretty standard?"

"A lieutenant knowing would be more standard. And the captain was never mentioned in any of the reports."

Lynae cocked her head. "I think you may be grasping at straws."

"Maybe. I just..."

"I don't want you to get your hopes set on something that isn't there. Something could have happened between when Drevin told his cellmate he was getting out and when he got thrown in solitary, something that woke him up to the fact that he was going to spend the rest of his life in prison. I'd probably think about suicide myself if that's what I was looking at."

"I'll just have to let IAB do their job, I guess." Jo felt defeated. She didn't want to leave it in someone else's hands.

"Any idea when that will happen?"

"I think they get on it quickly. I wouldn't be surprised if they do their initial interviews today, but I don't know. I need to put it away for a while and get back to our case." She pulled the Kramer file out of her open-cases portfolio and dropped it on her desk. "So what did you get from the bar patron?"

"Cindy didn't have much to offer. She was there with some friends and was getting ready to leave when Brad came in and just sat down at her table."

Jo tapped the folder. "Like he thought he had a reason to be there?"

"Exactly. She said it was strange because the two of them had never talked. He'd already ordered her a drink, so she stayed and had one with him. She said he was kind of pushy and didn't take it too well when she told him she was going home alone."

Jo took a sip of coffee, contemplating. "That just plays into what we already thought. Someone tells Brad, 'Hey, that woman in the bar wants you to buy her a drink.' Or maybe he's more explicit than that, and Brad figures he's getting lucky. So he buys a drink, spends some time talking, and expects some payback."

"In the meantime, his friends and probably most of the guys from the other teams leave," Lynae added.

Rolling the scenario around in her head, Jo stared at the murder board. "The killer doesn't really need that long. Just long enough for the guys who are there with him to leave. And they have a habit of doing that relatively early."

Lynae leaned back in her chair and crossed an ankle over her knee. "We're looking for someone who's been watching him and knows his patterns."

Jo thought of Carla Kramer. *Who knows a man's habits better than his wife?* "Or someone like his wife, who knows him all too well."

"It would be pretty strange for a wife to set her husband up by using another woman."

Jo shrugged. She had seen people do some pretty strange things over the years. "Our witness from the bowling alley said he was drunk. What did Cindy say?"

"She said they only had one drink and that he didn't act drunk, just obnoxious."

Jo drummed her fingers on her desk. "Did she see him in the parking lot?"

Lynae shook her head. "He made her nervous. She didn't want to walk out alone, so she called one of her guy friends and asked him to meet her there."

"That Brad must have been a piece of work."

"It makes it hard to feel sorry for him."

Jo raised her eyebrows. "It does, but it doesn't matter how we feel. We work the case the same way."

Lynae's head shot up. "I wouldn't—"

Jo held up her hand. "Sorry. Remnants of a conversation I had with someone else. I know you wouldn't."

"Speaking of that, is Charles okay? He's been acting weird."

"Personal stuff that I can't get into."

"I heard his wife left him."

Jo had hoped that the messiness of Charles's personal life could be kept private, but trying to keep a secret in a station full of detectives was like trying to serve gravy from a colander. "He'll be okay, but that kind of thing can really throw you out of whack."

"Yeah, it can. You're just cruising through life and bam! Something blindsides you, and everything changes."

Jo opened her top desk drawer, reached to the back, and pulled out a KitKat. She held it out and gave Lynae a questioning look.

Lynae blanched. "I shouldn't."

Jo peeled back the wrapper and snapped the bar in half. "Neither of us should, so let's split it."

Lynae's hand shot out, and she grabbed her portion of the chocolate. "I love your logic." She took a bite and moaned as she chewed. "One more thing. Isaac dug up the Kramers' financials, and if Mrs. Kramer was planning to pay someone for taking out her husband, she's not doing it with money. They were barely making ends meet." She broke off another piece and popped it in her mouth.

Jo finished her half of the KitKat and licked a touch of chocolate from her fingers. "What did the life insurance look like?"

"Twenty-five grand. By the time you take out funeral expenses, she's going to be hurting."

"She'd basically have enough left to pay off whoever did this for her."

Lynae slid the last bite into her mouth and washed it down with a swig of coffee. "Then she's rid of the husband, but she loses his child support. If she did do this, it wasn't very good thinking."

"My bet is not on her." Jo popped to her feet and grabbed her coat from the back of her chair. "I think it's time we visit our favorite county coroner."

Lynae followed her out the door. "I hope Kent has something for us, because right now, we're batting zero."

They strode through the bull pen and stopped at the elevator. After they stepped in, Jo pushed the ground-floor button.

"It's early, but Kent always has something for us." Jo shuffled her feet. "I'm going to have to bail shortly after we see him."

Lynae wiggled her eyebrows. "I know. You have a hot date to get to."

"Did you hear anything I said last night?"

"Every word. I'm just choosing to ignore it."

Jo sighed. "Why am I not surprised?"

AT THE COUNTY HEALTH department, Jo and Lynae strode down the long hallway. The chemical smell that pierced Jo's nose and tickled her throat was oddly comforting. It reminded her that, behind the closed doors, doctors and scientists studied hair, tissue, and fiber samples, tested blood and saliva, and performed other miracles that gave Jo and her team the evidence they needed to make arrests. She couldn't say how they did it or how they didn't go mad in the deafening silence of their basement burrow, but she was glad to have them on her side. Even though her job sometimes required wading through blood and often forced her to confront the depths of human depravity, no amount of money in the world could make her work in that dungeon. It took special people, and Kent County had some of the best.

Jo pushed open the extra-wide door that served as the barrier between the world as most people knew it and the world as the coroner knew it, where the gruesome task of opening up a body and removing its organs was all in a day's work. Lynae drew in a deep breath, blew it out loudly, and followed her into the room.

"Never gets any easier for you, does it?" Jo asked over her shoulder as she stepped around the coat rack that held a gray winter coat perfectly styled for an older, conservative man. Black rubber overshoes lay under the stand, and the medical examiner's signature fedora hung lopsided on top.

Lynae scrunched her face. "Nope. I hate this place."

"Well, that's not what a man likes to hear about his domain," Kent Alderink said in the whiskey-smooth baritone that brought classic movies and wingtip shoes to mind. He sat behind his industrial-style desk, a pen poised over a stack of computer paper. The medical examiner had paperwork that rivaled Jo's.

Red crept up Lynae's neck. "Sorry, Kent."

Kent chuckled, opening the creases at the edges of his bright-blue eyes into deep crevasses. "I guess a man with a domain such as mine has to expect such things."

Stainless-steel gurneys and metal instrument trays glared harshly against white cabinets and tile floors. One wall housed twelve steel lockers, their metal handles latched tightly to keep the cold inside where bodies took up temporary residence.

"Oh, I don't know," Jo said. "It seems like a great place to bring your wife on a romantic night out." She had met Kent's wife at a Christmas party years earlier and had learned that the little gray-haired fireball wanted nothing to do with her husband's workplace. Kent had smiled adoringly and teased her about "getting her Italian up" when the feisty woman related an animated story of the first, and only, time she had visited her husband at work. Jo was pretty certain the woman had never sent their children to bring-your-kid-to-work days.

Kent roared. "She loves it about as much as Lynae."

"I deal with it," Lynae replied, glaring at Jo.

That's good. Stubborn and angry are better for the morgue than nervous and nauseous. "Of course you do," Jo said then turned to Kent. "So what's the word?"

Kent peered over the wire-rimmed glasses perched on his nose. "Gehenna."

"A place of torture or suffering," Jo said.

Kent nodded. "That's right."

"I was having a nice day until Jo brought me to Gehenna," Lynae deadpanned.

Jo snorted. Her partner never lost her sense of humor. "You picked an ominous word for the day. Does that have anything to do with our guy?"

Kent pushed his glasses up to his eyes. "I'm afraid it does, but I'll get to that. As Mallory estimated on prelim, time of death is between seventy and seventy-four hours before he was found. Minimal tissue healing on the wounds indicates they were made within forty-eight hours of his death."

"That jibes with what we know so far," Jo said. "He went missing Thursday night. Seventy-two hours puts us at Sunday night. That means he was held somewhere for three days before he was killed."

"So our killer has to have a hidey-hole somewhere," Lynae said.

Jo nodded. "Yeah, he'd have to have someplace secluded to keep him. He's probably single and maybe has a basement room where no one would hear if the vic yelled." She turned back to Kent. "What else?"

He looked over his shoulder at a body on a steel table. "I can tell you that whoever did this wanted him to suffer."

Lynae crossed her arms. "You mean worse than killing him and leaving his body in the woods to be picked at by scavenger animals?"

"There are definitely worse things than death, and this man experienced a few." Kent motioned for them to follow him to the examination table.

The victim lay splayed open from the Y incision made to examine internal organs. Jo positioned herself next to Kent. Lynae took a deep breath through her mouth and let it out slowly through her nose as she walked around to the opposite side of the stainless-steel slab.

Jo caught her eye. "You okay?"

Lynae nodded. "Peachy."

Kent looked from one woman to the other as he pulled on gloves.

Jo nodded. "Go ahead."

He pointed out multiple wounds on the victim's torso. "See these marks? These were all made with a hooked blade approximately two inches long. They're not deep, but the flesh is torn around them."

"We have a witness who saw a man spend a great deal of time sitting in a boat, not fishing, in the area where our vic was found. She mentioned that she saw a gaff in the boat."

"A gaff would, indeed, be consistent with these wounds," Kent said.

"What do these wounds tell us?" Lynae asked.

"He was inflicting wounds that were not likely to kill. Of course, if there were enough of them or in the right locations, they would eventually kill a person. But most likely, the intention here was to cause a great deal of pain without death."

Jo didn't typically disagree with Kent, but she was skeptical. "There's no way our killer didn't mean to kill Mr. Kramer."

"No, that's not what I'm saying." Kent turned to the computer monitor mounted on a stand attached to the table. He tapped a few keys, and an X-ray image appeared on the screen. "Your victim has a fractured hyoid. The cause of death is manual strangulation. His neck is not broken, and the bruising and scratching indicate that he was conscious when he was hanged."

Jo leaned in for a closer look. "We noted the same at the scene. Broken fingernails, blood on the rope. He fought. So what you're saying is our killer didn't push him off the branch for a quick, neck-breaking hang. He lifted him up and left the vic hanging and fighting the rope."

Kent pointed at Jo. "Exactly."

"That would take some strength."

"And some *cojones*," Lynae added.

"Even considering the pulley system a tree branch would form, it would take considerable strength to lift a fighting man of this size off the ground." He winked at Lynae. "The *cojones* are yet to be determined."

"Anything unique about the rope?" Jo asked.

"It's a polyester propylene combination, which would make it very strong and resistant to rot and mildew. It's ideal for marine applications."

"Which goes with our theory that he was brought in on a fishing boat."

Kent nodded. "Yes, that fits."

Lynae frowned. "How does someone get a guy that size, an ex-football player who's awake enough to pull at the rope, into a boat and at least some distance down the river? He would fight like hell and, even bound, would definitely topple a small watercraft."

"Toxicology hasn't come back yet," he responded, "and you know that will take some time, but I'm going to say he was drugged, both to get him into the car at the bar and to get him to the woods in the boat."

"You think maybe the killer slipped something into his drink at the bar?" Lynae asked Jo.

"It's possible, but both our waitress and Cindy"—she looked at Kent—"the woman he was chatting up at the bar, said he didn't act drunk when he left. I'm guessing our perp ambushed him on his way out."

Kent turned the victim's head and pulled up the hair to display the back of the neck. "There's a puncture mark here at the base of his skull with a slight bit of bruising. I'm quite confident that toxicology will verify that he was injected with a drug to make him more cooperative."

"It would have to be a fast-acting drug like Valium or Ativan. There wasn't much time from leaving the bar to putting him in the truck."

Kent nodded. "My guess is he used more than one drug. Ativan would do the trick to make him calm and malleable to get him to the car. To transport him in a boat without the risk of him making any noise, the killer may have used something stronger, like Propofol. It's fast acting, injectable, and is used as a sedative for surgeries and medical procedures. It would put him out without killing him."

"So the killer would need access to drugs." Jo shoved her hands into her front pockets. "He had to have injected Kramer at the bar, or outside, more likely, then he took him somewhere to keep him and inflict those wounds."

Jo looked at Kent. "Gehenna," she muttered, to which he gave a grim nod.

"After he tortured him for a few days, he drugged him again with something stronger, put him in a boat, and took him to the woods," Lynae added.

Jo whistled softly. "Then he waited in the woods for the drugs to wear off so he could watch him fight death? That's cold."

"I'm speculating, Lieutenant. We'll know more when we get the tox report."

Speculation from an expert in the field like Kent was as good as a tox report, so Jo would go on his theory until that report was in her hand. "This was personal, not just some tryst gone wrong."

"Yes, this was personal. These initial wounds"—he gestured at the chest—"were to cause pain. And so was this." Kent held up the arm with the missing hand.

The dried blood and debris had been removed, making the stump look like a slice of raw prime rib. "The amount of blood at the scene would suggest the hand was severed peri-mortem."

"I'm afraid so. He would have bled profusely."

Lynae swallowed hard. "And screamed profusely."

Kent pointed to marks around the victim's mouth. "Fibers in his lungs suggest he was gagged with a cotton cloth. And residue on his lips and around his mouth indicates duct tape."

Jo nodded. "Most likely pulled off after he was too weak to scream or already dead."

"Then there's this." Kent pushed back a flap of skin that had been flayed open with the Y incision, exposing the victim's chest. The numeral 19 was written in bold black.

Jo looked up at Kent. "Nineteen? That's it?"

"That's it."

"Is that a tattoo?" Lynae asked.

Kent took off his glasses and rubbed his eyes. "I thought so at first, but it's actually written in marker. Simple permanent marker."

Jo huffed. "The kind you can buy in absolutely any store. Why couldn't it be some Polynesian artist paint that can only be found in specialty stores?"

Kent pursed his lips. "Murderers can be so unaccommodating."

Jo ran a hand through her hair. "A number can mean so many different things. How many years has he been with his wife? Does nineteen have something to do with that? Did he cheat on her nineteen times? Or with a nineteen-year-old?"

Lynae bit her bottom lip. "Did he do nineteen things to someone, and that's the breaking point? Without more information, it means nothing."

Kent slid his glasses back on and looked at Lynae over the rims. "It means something to the killer."

"Great. I like my killers to be a little more forthcoming." Jo dropped her hands to her hips. "And stupid. I like stupid killers."

"It's very cryptic, I agree," Kent said. "But I have faith in you two. You'll figure it out. I'm afraid this killer does not appear to be stupid."

Jo sighed in frustration. "I'm afraid you're right."

Kent smiled grimly. "Good luck, Lieutenant."

"Thanks, Kent. Always a pleasure." And Jo meant it. No matter what ugliness brought them together, Kent was her Gibraltar: reliable, unchanging, and true.

They left the autopsy room and headed back down the long corridor. The elevator doors opened, and Mallory Wiseman rushed out, staring down at an open notebook in her hands.

Jo sidestepped around her. "Whoa, Mal!"

Mallory's head jerked up. "Oops. Sorry, Jo. There isn't usually anyone in this hallway. Good timing, though. You two are just the people I want to talk to."

"Yeah? You have something for us? A full set of prints and a matching ID in AFIS, maybe?"

Mallory snorted. "Unfortunately, no. The only prints we found belong to our victim."

Lynae scowled. "There's that unaccommodating, not-stupid killer again."

"So what do you have for us?" Jo asked.

Mallory pulled a picture out of the folder she had tucked under her arm. She handed the photo to Jo and leaned in to point. "See this mark? It's a scrape on our victim's lower back."

"Something is sticking out of it," Jo observed. "What is it?"

Mallory nodded. "A sliver of red cedar wood."

Jo's head shot up. "Is that rare?"

"It's a pretty middle-of-the-road option for decking. Not as long lasting as composite or a harder wood but better than pressure-treated materials like pine. It has a decent resistance to moisture, and the heartwood is rot resistant."

Jo bit her lip. "So it could be a good choice for a dock."

"Yes, it would be. People like it for docks and dock decking because it's a softer wood that feels better under their feet."

"And this wood was embedded in his lower back?"

Mallory nodded. "My speculation is he was dragged across the dock by his arms or armpits and his shirt pulled up. Because it's soft, cedar is susceptible to splits and cracks if it's not maintained well."

Jo handed the photo back to Mallory. "That's a pretty solid spec-ulation, especially since we believe he was drugged in order to get him into a boat."

"Well, I hope it helps, because it's all I have at this time."

Jo reached around Lynae and hit the elevator button. "Every piece of the puzzle helps."

Mallory slid the photo back into the manila folder. "I'll send you a copy of this picture and the specs on the wood."

"Thanks, Mal."

When they were back in the elevator, Jo punched the button to send them to the main floor. "We need to get the wife back in here and press her a little."

"I thought we decided the life insurance wasn't big enough to make it worth it for her."

"Sometimes, a little is enough, especially if she wanted out of the marriage. I want another crack at her."

The sun had decided to make an appearance, brightening the previously gloomy day and making the walk to the truck more toler-able.

Jo's phone blared. She pulled it out of her coat pocket and an-swered while starting the truck. "Riskin."

"Hey, can you be at the jail by four o'clock?" Jack's voice was soothing, even when he sounded rushed.

Jo glanced at her watch. "No problem. Why?"

"I called in a favor. You can sit in on the IAB interview with the on-duty officer this afternoon."

Jo gasped. "Seriously? That's fantastic. Damn, first Garth and now the guard? I owe you big."

"Careful. I might make you cook me dinner or something."

Jo grinned. "I'm no Chef Ramsey, but I could probably muster up a decent dinner."

"Considering the kids and I live on mac and cheese and Spaghettios, we would be thrilled with whatever comes out of your kitchen."

"Will you be at the jail?"

"Nope, I've got some things to tie up here. Just ask for Moreland."

"Thanks, Jack. I'll see you tonight." Jo thumbed the phone off and dropped it into its usual place.

Lynae looked over at her. "What's up with Jack that you owe him for?"

Jo grinned. "He called in a favor, so this afternoon, I can sit in on the IAB meeting with the officer on duty the night Drevin died."

"Wow! That doesn't just happen. I mean, the inmates I understand, but the officer? I never thought you'd get in on that."

Jo stopped at a red light. "Neither did I. Apparently, it pays to know people."

"Imagine what you could accomplish if you were sleeping with him."

Jo glared at Lynae. "I'm going to pretend you didn't say that."

"Just sayin'." Lynae shrugged.

Jo pulled into a fifteen-minute loading zone in front of the station. "Unless something breaks, I'll be going home after the meeting at the jail."

"Um, yeah. You can't go to a concert dressed like that."

Jo glanced down at her navy-blue slacks and striped button-down blouse. "I wouldn't be caught dead at a Garth Brooks concert in an outfit like this."

Lynae reached for her bag. "I'll see if I can make contact with Mrs. Kramer this afternoon and get her into the station."

"All right, do that. If anything strikes you, text me, even if it's when I'm at the concert. I'll be right around the corner at VanAndel. I could be at the station in ten minutes."

Lynae's face scrunched. "I'm not pulling you away from your date unless I get a confession. And even then, I can stick her in lockup until morning."

"Press her about the insurance and the separation."

"Yeah, yeah. I've got this."

Jo sighed. "Sorry, I know."

Lynae pulled her coat snug then opened the door and stepped out. She leaned in through the open door and smiled. "Just relax and have fun tonight. And you can tell me everything tomorrow when I call to hound you about it."

Jo rolled her eyes. "I'm sure you will."

Lynae shut the door, waved Jo off, then put her head down and jogged into the station. Jo did a U-turn, cut across two lanes, and jumped onto the highway on-ramp. She didn't know if she would be allowed to ask any questions, but just in case, she mentally ran through her list, trying out different ways of asking to elicit the most honest response.

At the jail, the same receptionist sat behind the bulletproof glass. She pulled back the creaking window, took the sidearm that Jo laid on the counter, and handed her a retrieval tag. She looked over Jo's shoulder. "Lieutenant Moreland, this is Lieutenant Riskin."

Jo swung her head and saw a portly man in a mud-brown suit, sitting in one of the plastic visitor chairs. She pretended to be interested in getting the tag into her pocket as he struggled to haul his considerable weight out of the tight confines of the chair.

He walked over and held out his hand. "Lieutenant, I'm Don Moreland." Beads of sweat had formed on his forehead.

Jo smiled. "Thanks for allowing me to sit in on your interview, Mr. Moreland."

"Please, call me Don. And Jack called in the favor. I knew your husband, by the way. He was a good detective and an even better man."

Jo bobbed her head. "Yes, he was."

Rocking back on his heels, Don shoved his hands in his pockets. He looked at Jo expectantly, but Jo had no idea what he was waiting for.

He cleared his throat. "So, shall we?"

Jo nodded quickly, relieved to break the awkward moment. "Right behind you."

She shortened her stride to keep pace with Don as he huffed down the beige hallway. His pronounced limp clearly made the trek tiresome for him. The yellow legal pad in his right hand swung with each stride.

In a slightly breathy voice, he said, "I'm okay with you asking a question or two, but just know that if I say stop, you have to put an end to that line of questioning."

"Absolutely."

"This is really a formality. We have no reason to believe the officers neglected their duty to the prisoner."

"Have you encountered a time when that did happen?" Jo asked.

"Not in my seventeen years in this location. They run a tight ship here and pride themselves on resolving conflict without violence."

They stopped in front of a nondescript door, and Don pushed it open. He motioned for Jo to go in ahead of him. A chair scraped across the floor, and a man who appeared to be in his midthirties jumped to his feet and stood ramrod straight behind a round Formica-covered table. He stared at a space slightly above Jo's right shoulder.

Don held out his hand. "Officer Finkler, I'm Lieutenant Moreland with Internal Affairs." The officer took his hand and shook it firmly. Don gestured at Jo. "This here is Lieutenant Riskin with the GRPD. She's going to sit in on our meeting."

"How goes the battle, Officer?" Jo said warmly, using her mother's favorite expression.

"Just fine, Lieutenant," Officer Finkler replied in a voice as tightly clipped as his military-style haircut.

Don motioned to the chair the officer had vacated. "Why don't you have a seat? We're just going to have a discussion regarding the death of Drevin Clayburn."

"Yes, sir." The officer's square jaw was set in a firm line as he did what he was told. Somehow, he managed to appear to be at attention even while sitting.

Jo took a seat across the table from him. Don practically collapsed into the cheap plastic chair next to her. She held her breath, waiting for the chair to break, then swallowed her sigh of relief when it held.

Don laid his legal pad on the table. "I'm just trying to piece together the events of the night that Mr. Clayburn died. According to the records, Mr. Clayburn was brought to solitary at 7:17 p.m. Is that your recollection?"

"Yes, sir. I made the file note. It was shortly after I came on duty."

Don adjusted his considerable size, causing the plastic chair to emit a tired groan. "Did Mr. Clayburn appear to be a suicide risk when he was brought in to solitary?"

"No, he did not. He was roughed up from the incident in the yard, but he did not give me any indication that he was suicidal. I checked his file when he was brought down, and he had not given any indication of it prior to his altercation."

"Were you the only person on duty in that wing that night?"

"Yes. The night shift is primarily for doing bed checks. One officer is sufficient."

"When you're the only person on duty, what happens if there's a problem or someone needs medical attention?"

"I call for backup. In the case of an emergency, it takes seconds to get a backup officer to our location."

Don nodded. "And did you have any such emergencies or the need for a backup officer at any point during the night that Drevin Clayburn died?"

If he hadn't been so military precise, Jo might not have noticed the second of hesitation and the slight twitch of his right eye. "There was an unruly inmate in cell S13. He had to be restrained, and I needed one officer for restraint help and one to watch the monitors, which is standard procedure whenever a cell door has to be opened."

"Which officers came to help?"

"Officer Rodriguez helped with the restraint, and Captain Montaine watched the monitors."

Jo looked up from her notebook. "Captain Montaine?"

Officer Finkler shifted in his seat. "Yes, ma'am."

Dan raised his eyebrows at Jo. "Do you have a follow-up question, Lieutenant?"

"Yes. Is it normal for a captain to answer a call for backup?" Jo asked.

The officer hesitated. "There's really no *normal* in our job, Lieutenant."

Jo nodded. "Understood. How long have you worked in solitary?"

"Four years next month."

"And how many times has the captain responded to a routine request for monitor watch?"

The officer sat up straighter in his seat and adjusted his watch. "Never, in my recollection. They were probably short-staffed up front."

"You were short-staffed that night?" Don asked, flipping through his notes.

"I can't say for sure, but that's probably why the captain came back."

Don cocked his head. "Wouldn't that leave the front short?"

The officer's shoulders straightened, and he raised his chin. "I don't know the reason, sir, but the captain is more than capable of monitor watch."

"Of course he is. How long did it take to restrain your prisoner?"

"Approximately fifteen minutes, maybe a little more. He was very confrontational when we entered the cell, and it took a while to get him under control. We restrained him and stayed in the cell until he had calmed to a point that we could remove the restraints and leave him alone until the next check."

Don tapped his pencil on his lips. "When do you do checks?"

"We do block checks every forty minutes."

The IAB officer leaned his elbows on the table and folded his hands. "Did you check on Mr. Clayburn?"

"We do block check every forty minutes, sir." Finkler's volume rose a notch. "That means we check on *every* prisoner."

Don held up his hand. "Relax, Officer. I'm not insinuating that you didn't do your job. I'm just doing mine."

"Yes, sir." The officer folded his hands on the table, and his expression returned to neutral. "At the forty-minute check, if there's no disruption coming from the cell, it's a routine walk-by. I shine a light through the cell windows, but I'm not going to wake the inmates up every forty minutes. That's what I did with the entire ward, except cell S13, for the remainder of the night."

"Who was the disruptive prisoner in cell S13?" Jo asked.

"Gregory Daskin."

"The same Gregory Daskin who had the fight with Mr. Clayburn in the yard?"

"One and the same, Lieutenant."

Don jotted in his notebook. "Not a model prisoner, I take it?"

"Not the worst we have, but he won't be winning any Mr. Congeniality awards."

"Have you had problems with him in the past?"

"A few." Finkler shrugged. "He likes to push his weight around. And I'm sure you noticed his tattoos. He's got a lot of hate in him, and it shows. He'll be transferred to Ionia and will end up a lifer, so he doesn't have a lot to lose."

Jo leaned back in her chair and crossed her legs. *He may not have anything to lose, but did he have something to gain?* "What area does the video surveillance cover?"

"Everything. Hallways, cell doors, entryways, cafeteria, kitchen, library." Officer Finkler counted the areas off on his fingers as he listed them.

Jo wrote the locations in her notebook. "And the surveillance tapes are kept for how long?"

"I don't actually know. I just know that I don't have the authorization to turn them off or delete anything."

"Who has authorization?"

"Just the captains."

"And did you note anything unusual in the video surveillance for the time of Drevin Clayburn's suicide?" Jo asked.

Don cleared his throat. "IAB immediately removed the tape as part of the internal investigation." He turned to the officer. "Where exactly did you find Mr. Clayburn?"

Finkler rubbed his hands up and down his thighs, for the first time showing some anxiety. "He was in his bed, under the covers. His back was to the door. He didn't get up for breakfast, and he didn't respond when I called his name, so I went in there to get him."

Frowning, Don scribbled in his notebook. "So you walked in his cell?"

"Yes. I shook his shoulder, but he still didn't move. So I pulled back the blanket." The officer's Adam's apple bobbed. "There was so much blood." He choked a little on the last word then shook his head.

"Was there blood on the floor?" Don asked.

"No, sir. Just on the bed."

"And you found a weapon?"

"Yes, sir. He had a shiv. The thing is, he didn't pull it during the fight. I don't know where he had it hidden or why he didn't pull it."

"And you heard no noise coming from the cell during the night? No indication that the prisoner was in distress?" Jo asked.

"No, ma'am. Not a sound."

She tapped the push-button end of her pen on her notepad. The story still didn't add up. People didn't slit their wrists then quietly lie down and die. But she had a pretty solid bullshit radar, and it was currently silent. The officer was telling the truth as far as he knew it.

"I believe that's all I have for you, Officer." Don closed his notebook and pushed his chair back. "Lieutenant, do you have any other questions?"

Unable to think of anything else to ask, Jo said, "No, I don't. Thank you for your time, Officer."

The young officer got to his feet. He straightened his back and looked down at Don then Jo. "Our protocol is solid here. None of us wants to lose an inmate, even if he was a cop killer." He nodded curtly, turned on his heel, and left the room.

Don leaned back in his chair. "It appears Officer Finkler followed every protocol. We have pictures of the scene and statements, and we'll review the video. We'll dot every i and cross every t. At this point, there's nothing to indicate this was anything other than a suicide."

Jo ran her hand through her hair. "The scene doesn't make sense the way the officer described it. Clayburn was in his bed, lying on his side with his back to the door. He was covered up with the blanket. That alone is unusual for a suicide. Add to that, his arm would have to have been completely on the bed in order to keep all the blood off the floor. There should have been some panic, some spatter. And even if he didn't panic, his arm would have naturally flopped outward as he was dying. I've worked a lot of crime scenes, and this one doesn't add up."

Don grabbed his notebook from the table and stood. "He was in the room alone, so there's no possibility another inmate killed him. My concern is if our officers followed procedure, if bed checks were done on time, or if the inmate appeared suicidal and was denied help. So far, I have no reason to believe any of those things occurred. There's nothing in his record to indicate a risk. Any suicide is tragic and raises concerns and questions. I'm not finished yet, but ultimately, if procedures were followed and the county is not at risk for liability, that's where my investigation ends."

She stood and shoved her notebook into her bag. "Will you keep me apprised of what you find?"

"Allowing you in on this interview was a favor I owed Jack. Debt paid. But I can't have you interfering in this internal investigation."

"I have no intention of interfering. I just want to know what your findings are."

He started limping down the corridor. "When the official report is released, I'll make sure you have a copy."

Keeping pace with him, Jo responded, "I appreciate that. I'll stay out of your way in the meantime."

He smirked. "Why don't I believe that?"

She stopped in front of the check-in desk and gave Don a crooked grin. "I don't know, but I won't interfere. I want the truth to this mess, and that's all."

He held out his hand. "It's been a pleasure, Jo. I'll send you my report."

Jo took his hand and shook it firmly. "Thank you, Don."

After retrieving her weapon, Jo left the building. Captain Montaine's name had come up twice lately, and she was determined to find out why.

Chapter 10

J o whipped into her garage, killed the engine, and checked her watch. She had given herself just enough time to get ready without too much time to think. Mojo greeted her at the door, squirming and jumping, her tongue lashing out at Jo's face with each leap. Jo dropped her keys in a ceramic bowl on the counter and grabbed a tennis ball out of the same bowl. Then she chucked it into the next room and laughed when Mojo's nails skittered across the floor as she raced to retrieve it. She threw her coat on the dining table and hustled into her bedroom.

Standing in front of her closet, hands on hips, she stared at her wardrobe. *What do I wear? Why didn't I think about this earlier?*

Mojo bounded into the room and dropped the ball at her feet. Jo looked down at the wiggling furball, who stared intently at the ball, her body vibrating with excitement. She bent down to grab the ball, and Mojo licked her across the face.

"Oh come on, that's not fair!" She wiped the slobber from her face and pitched the ball out the bedroom door. Turning back to her closet, she muttered, "Come on, Jo. Don't make this a bigger deal than it is."

She grabbed a blouse off a hanger, something her sister-in-law called "country chic," threw it on over her pink cami, then slid into a pair of low-rise jeans. She rummaged through her collection of footwear and decided on her favorite pair of gray Rocketdog boots.

When Mojo trotted back into the room, Jo gave the ball another toss then hightailed it into the bathroom. She fixed her eyeliner and mascara, added some evening eye shadow, then touched up her foundation. After pulling her hair out of its bun, she bent over and roughly ran her hands through it until it was loose and messy before flipping it back over and lightly patting the ends into place. It was a move she had perfected to quickly change at the station before going out with Mike.

Her heart clenched as her mind was flooded with memories of Mike. She picked up the bottle of Armani Code that still sat on his side of the double vanity and savored his scent. He was everywhere in her house. *Their* house.

What am I doing?

Without giving herself time to think, she grabbed the cologne, his razor, and his toothbrush and shoved them into the back of the bottom drawer of the vanity. Her gut churned as she stared at the empty counter.

Mojo whined and nudged her leg before trotting to the slider leading to the backyard. Jo let her out and paced in front of the door, alternating checking her watch and watching the dog romp in the yard.

Mojo's ears perked up before she bounded out of the backyard and around the front of the house, barking frantically. Jo ran to the front door, whipped it open, and smacked into Jack's chest. "Jack. Mojo..."

Mojo pushed past Jack and planted herself at Jo's feet.

Jack looked down at the growling mutt leaning against Jo's legs. "She's not thrilled to have me here."

She laid her hand on Mojo's head. The dog looked up at her with adoring brown eyes, and her tail thumped. "It's okay, baby." Jo smirked at Jack. "Better stay in line."

He held his hands up. "I'm not moving until you say so."

Jo eased Mojo back with her leg and stepped aside to make room for him to get through the door.

He shoved his hands in his pockets, slid into the entryway, then followed Jo into the kitchen. "Nice place you have here," he said, surveying the room.

She smiled. "Thanks. We spent a lot of time looking for just the right place and neighborhood to raise..." Heat rose up her cheeks. *Way to start the night out by talking about your husband and the kids you don't have.*

He leaned on the kitchen island and smiled. "I get it."

"I know you do. Which reminds me, where are your kids tonight?"

Mojo slumped to the floor with a groan, all the while keeping a close watch on their visitor.

"With a friend of my wife. She has three kids, and mine love it there. She was a big help to me when Laura died." He glanced nervously at Mojo every few seconds while he spoke.

Jo snapped her fingers. Mojo jumped up and trotted to her side. "Do you want a drink?"

He straightened. "Actually, we better get going, or we'll be late."

She checked her watch. "Late for what?"

"We have reservations at The Chop House."

She looked down at her faded jeans. "I'm not exactly dressed for—"

"You're perfect." He cleared his throat. "I mean, you know, your clothes are perfectly fine."

She eyed his snug, faded jeans and black leather lace-up boots—her favorite look on a man. "You dress down pretty well yourself."

"So you won't be embarrassed to have me along when you meet Garth?" He held out his arms and looked down at himself.

Jo grabbed her coat from the back of the kitchen chair, slipped it on, and pulled her hair out of the collar. "Nope, you'll pass." She knelt and took Mojo's face in her hands. "Be good. I'll be home soon." Mojo's tongue shot out and caught her cheek.

"You know she can't understand you, right?"

Jo wiped her cheek with the sleeve of her coat and gave him a flat look. "She understands me better than anyone else does."

She opened the door, set the alarm, and stepped out in front of him. He jogged in front of her and opened the passenger door of his Ford Taurus. Two car seats were buckled into the back. Cheerios and fruit-snack wrappers littered the space between them. A half-full sippy cup sat in the cup holder of the larger one.

He dropped into his seat and grimaced. "I swear I clean it, and the minute I set them in their seats, it's a disaster again."

She climbed in and smiled. "It's perfect."

"How did it go at the jail this afternoon?"

"I have more questions than answers, but I'm glad I was there. Thanks for making it happen."

"Of course. Want to tell me about it?"

As Jack pulled out of the subdivision, she buckled in and gazed out the window. Two women bundled up in heavy coats and stocking caps walked at a brisk pace down the sidewalk, their arms swinging in unison. A small dog trotted along beside them. "Let's talk about it tomorrow. I have just one request for the night."

"Name it."

"I don't want to talk about Drevin Clayburn. Or Mike. I just want to forget it all for one night."

He laid his hand on the console gearshift and glanced at her. "I think that would be great."

"I don't want anything to get in the way of my destiny with Garth."

"Good grief." He rolled his eyes.

WHEN THEY PULLED INTO Jo's driveway at eleven, Jo said, "I just can't get over that concert. Garth was amazing."

"So you've said."

"And so nice. Just like a normal guy!"

"Yep."

"Every song he sang was my favorite. I swear. I would think, 'Oh, this is my favorite song.' Then he would start the next one, and I would go, 'No, wait. This is my favorite.'"

"And you did that all night..."

Pressing her lips together, she squinted at Jack. "I take it I already told you all this."

His lips twitched. "Maybe once or twice."

She cupped her hands over her face, warmth spreading up her neck. "I'm sorry. I'm babbling."

"It's okay. It's cute."

She peered at him over her fingers. "Did you just say *cute?*"

"You don't like being called cute?"

"It's not how many people would normally describe me."

"If only all those criminals whose asses you've kicked could have seen you gushing like a teenager over Garth Brooks tonight."

"I was *not* gushing like a teenager!"

Jack shrugged. "Okay, it's your story. Don't worry. I won't tell anyone that you're not a beautiful badass all the time."

She dropped her hands into her lap and glanced up at her house. A single light glowed from the front porch. She drew in a deep breath. "Do you want to come in for a drink, or do you have to get the kids?"

He cleared his throat. "The kids are spending the night at my friend's house."

She looked over at him and raised an eyebrow. "Just a drink."

"I know." Jack peered out at the house. "You think Mojo will allow it?"

Jo shrugged and opened her door. "It's a crap shoot. You probably should have brought her a treat." She climbed out and headed up the walk.

Jack jumped out of the car and ran around the front to catch up with her. "Why didn't you tell me that before I came?"

"If you thought I was going to make this easy..." Jo pushed her key into the front-door lock.

"Never thought that for a minute."

Mojo whined and scratched on the other side of the door. Jo pushed it open and braced herself as Mojo launched herself at Jo, whining and crying as though they had been apart for months instead of hours.

Jack crept in behind her. Mojo stopped squirming and raised her hackles. Her lip curled as she emitted a low, menacing rumble.

Jo looked over her shoulder. "You really should have thought about that treat."

Jack pressed himself against the wall. "Damn it, Jo. Help me out here."

She snapped her fingers. "Mojo, that's enough."

Mojo gave Jack one last grumble then trotted out of the room. She returned thirty seconds later and dropped a Kong ball at Jo's feet.

Jo tossed the ball into the next room then looked back at Jack, who had unglued himself from the wall. "You can't keep your car clean. I can't resist my dog."

"Is she like that with all your guests, or is it just me?"

"The only guests I have are my family and Lynae, so this is new territory for her." Mojo returned with the ball, and Jo immediately threw it again.

Jack puffed out a breath of relief. "At least she seems to have forgotten about me."

Jo smirked. "We'll see." She went to the fridge and grabbed two bottles of Corona Light. "Why don't we see what we can find on Netflix?"

Chapter 11

What is that noise?

Jo struggled to identify the insistent buzzing. She nestled deeper into the comfort of her warm pillow. *God, I haven't slept this good in years.*

The buzzing stopped then started up again. She rubbed her eyes and attempted to focus. Her gaze landed on a slew of Corona Light bottles covering the coffee table. She blinked and raised her head. Her warm pillow shifted and pulled her closer.

She bolted upright. "Shit, shit, shit!" She shook Jack's shoulder.

He blinked up at her. His shaggy blond hair stood on end. "What's going on?"

"We fell asleep. It's morning. You gotta get out of here."

He scrubbed his hands over his face. "Um... yeah. Okay."

Her phone vibrated, and she snatched it from the end table. "Riskin," she snapped.

"Lieutenant, this is Dispatch. We have a body at 3487 Wilkinson. At the old Crestwood High School."

"Inside the school?"

"On the football field, ma'am."

God, what next? "On my way. Dispatch Detective Parker to the scene."

"Yes, ma'am."

Jo tossed her phone on the end table. "I have to get to a scene."

Collapsing back onto the sofa, Jack closed his eyes. "I'm just going to lie here for a while."

She poked him in the side with one finger. "You can't stay here. You have to go home before anyone sees your car in my driveway."

Jack opened one eye. "You got someone watching the house?"

"No. I just..."

He sat up and ran his hand along the stubble that shadowed his cheek. "Just what? We fell asleep watching a movie. It's not a crime."

"I know." She pinched the bridge of her nose, wondering how she had actually fallen asleep with him there. "It just feels wrong."

He leaned over and kissed her forehead. "You're kind of adorable. And it didn't feel wrong to me. I slept like a baby."

"That's not what I meant." She sighed. "And so did I."

"I'll go. Do you want me to push my car out of the driveway and start it on the next street?"

"You're such a smart-ass."

Jack snickered. He grabbed a few beer bottles from the coffee table and headed toward the kitchen.

She reached out and grabbed his arm. "Thanks for last night. It was the most fun I've had in a long time."

"It was my pleasure. Even if I did have to spend the night competing with Garth Brooks."

"No one competes with Garth Brooks, but you run a pretty close second."

He gave her a smug look. "I can live with that."

She glanced out the window. Dawn had not yet cracked. "I have to get out of here, but go ahead and stick around if you want. No use both of us running on no sleep."

"Thank you." Jack set the bottles down and flopped back onto the couch. He laid his head on the pillow and pulled his long legs up. "It's still warm," he mumbled.

It took every ounce of willpower she had not to crawl back on that warm sofa for just a few more minutes. Instead, she got ready to leave. After grabbing her work bag, she went back into the living room to say goodbye to Jack. He was fast asleep. She pulled a blanket from the hallway closet, draped it over him, then planted a gentle kiss on his cheek.

JO PULLED INTO THE parking lot of the deserted Crestwood High School. Patches of weeds poked through cracks in the asphalt where yellow parking lines were still faintly visible. The sprawling redbrick structure was dilapidated, shattered windows and patches of graffiti the only indications of life. She tracked flashing red and blue lights to the rear of the building, where an ambulance, a fire truck, and two patrol cars were haphazardly parked. When she spotted Lynae backing her Mazda into a corner away from the rest of the vehicles, she swung around and parked next to her.

Lynae unfolded herself from the low-riding vehicle and came around to Jo's door. "This may be the first time I've beaten you to a crime scene."

"Better mark this day down on your *personal best* calendar," Jo said as she stepped out of the Ranger. The crisp air shocked her system and knocked out any remnants of sleepiness. "Although you weren't even parked yet, so I'm not sure that qualifies as beating me."

"Don't be a sore loser." Lynae nudged Jo with an elbow. "Were you late because you had to kick Jack out this morning?"

Ignoring the question, Jo clipped her credentials to her waist and grabbed the rest of her stuff from the passenger seat. She began walking toward the yellow crime scene tape.

Lynae jogged after her. "Why aren't you talking? Was Jack at your place when you took the call? Come on, dish."

"Nothing to dish. The concert was amazing, and we had a really nice night."

Lynae's eyebrows shot up. "And?"

"There's no 'and.' We had a couple drinks, turned on a movie, and fell asleep on the couch."

After Lynae picked her chin up off the ground, she sputtered, "So he *was* still there."

"Yes, but nothing happened." Jo's eyes flicked to her friend. "Except I had the best night of sleep I've had in a couple years."

Lynae's face softened. "Aw."

"Then it was ruined by a phone call."

"You should have taken yourself off the rotation for the weekend."

"I didn't expect it to be a problem." She pointed toward the football field. "Shall we?"

"If you insist."

The officer standing at the perimeter of the crime scene tape gave them a quick once-over. Before Jo could badge him, he said, "Good morning, Lieutenant Riskin."

Jo looked down on the top of his head, which was covered by closely cropped bright-red hair. He couldn't have been over five foot four. *This is the same officer who was at the last scene.* Glancing at the name on his uniform, she asked, "What do we have, Officer Davenport?"

"Another hanging, Lieutenant."

"On a football field? Damn. Is it a high school kid?"

"If he is, he's been in school a long time. It's a little hard to tell, you know, with the hanging and all, but I would put him in his midthirties."

"All right, thanks."

Jo and Lynae walked around a boarded-up concession stand, down a cement handicap-accessible ramp, and through the gate of the fence surrounding the football field. A crowd of people stood in the end zone, staring up at a body dangling from the field goal crossbar. The corpse swayed slightly in the cold morning wind.

Jo drew a pair of nitrile gloves from her bag, snapped them on, then handed a pair to Lynae. "Well, this is a first for me."

Lynae tugged her stocking cap down over her ears, pulled off her warm gloves, and replaced them with the sterile pair. "Why come to a public place to commit suicide?"

Jo approached the body. "Because it's not a suicide."

Lynae scrutinized the area. "We know that already?"

"I'd bet my paycheck on it."

"Well, since I'm sure it's significantly larger than mine, I would love to take it, but I would never bet against you on a crime scene analysis."

"Smart woman."

"Why are we sure it's not a suicide?" Lynae asked.

Jo pointed at the rope secured about five feet up the post to their right. "He would have had to tie the end off first down here."

"Planning ahead." Lynae shrugged. "He didn't want to have to do that part once he got up there and got his nerve together."

Jo held up her hand. "Then he took the other end of the rope, climbed the goalpost—since there's no ladder here—shimmied to the center, wrapped the rope completely around the center post, tied the other end to his neck, and jumped?" She waved at the body. "And since his pants legs are dangling over his feet, he apparently decided to do this barefoot?"

Lynae followed the line of the rope. "It's a winch," she mumbled.

"Indeed it is, my astute partner. He was hoisted up there, then the killer tied the end off at his own level." Jo stepped closer to the body and examined the ground underneath. She pointed to a small dark stain in the grass. "That's going to be blood."

Lynae whistled quietly. "Two hangings in under two weeks."

"Yeah, and I don't like it one bit."

"I bet when we check his hands, we'll find that he fought. At least he *has* two hands."

"That's a pretty small amount of blood under the body."

Lynae turned a full circle, scanning the field. "I bet we'll find a whole lot more blood somewhere else."

Jo wagged a finger at Lynae. "Let's not get ahead of ourselves and assume this is related to the Kramer case. We'll let Forensics do their job then get the body down. Why don't you coordinate that? I want to take a look around."

"I'm on it," Lynae said, snapping off a salute.

Jo walked carefully beneath the body, scanning the ground in the early-morning light. The overgrown grass made the job more difficult, but she spotted what appeared to be drag marks. Following them across the field, she noted streaks and occasional spots of blood. She marked each with a yellow flag from her field kit.

The drag marks ended abruptly behind the bleachers in a dark puddle of congealed blood. On the fence were some old graffiti tags—*Nick Grims is hot*, to which someone had added *NOT* in bold red; *Jerry is a fag*; and *Tracy gives good head*. High school kids could be brutal. The edge of the blood pool was smeared in a random, frantic pattern with drops spattered on either side.

That's too much blood. Lynae's right. Our victim's going to be missing something, and this is where he lost it.

Jo followed the same path back to the body, keeping her eyes down for other possible clues. Two techs in white protective gear squatted under the body, opening their hard-sided silver cases.

Jo recognized Mallory Wiseman beneath one protective facemask. "We gotta quit meeting like this, Mal."

"Agreed," Mallory said, her breath fogging the inside of the mask. "Next time, let me pick the rendezvous location. I'm pretty sure I can do better."

"I sure as hell hope you could." Jo nodded toward the bleachers. "When you're done here, I've got a secondary location under the bleachers. There are a few streaks that follow a drag pattern from here to there, but it looks like our victim was killed and bled out back there and was dragged here to be strung up."

Mallory motioned to the other tech. "Why don't you see what we've got there, and I'll deal with the body."

The tech stood and hoisted his case. "Gotcha." He headed back the way Jo had come.

Mallory snapped on a pair of gloves and smiled at Jo. "I do love my job."

"I guess we're both warped that way."

Sidling up beside Jo, Lynae said, "Let me know when you're ready to take the body down. I've got the firemen ready to move in with their truck on your go-ahead."

Jo turned to Mallory. "We'll leave you to it. Let me know when you're ready."

Jo and Lynae stepped aside to give Mallory room to work. After several minutes of snapping photos from every angle, Mallory pulled her camera strap from her neck and carefully placed the device in her case. She straightened and nodded in their direction. "All right, let's get the rig in here and take the body down."

Lynae trotted to the side of the field to talk with the firemen. Minutes later, the massive fire truck lumbered onto the field, its weight leaving trenches in the moist ground. It parked as close to the body as the vehicle's size would allow.

Two men in long black coats with GRFD in bold red across the back stepped into the articulating boom and closed the metal gate. Jo craned her neck to watch as they were raised to the level of the goalpost.

Mallory stood below it with her hands on her hips. "Be careful with that rope. Cut above the knot. We need it intact."

When they reached the correct height, one fireman held the corpse while the other carefully cut the rope.

One of the men jumped back against the side of the boom as the body slumped into the cage. "Holy crap!"

Jo moved her hand to her sidearm. "What's going on?" she called up to them.

"He doesn't have a foot," the other fireman yelled back.

"Hold that foot up and don't let it touch anything!" Mallory bellowed.

The fireman held the victim's leg up as they lowered the boom. The foot had been crudely severed at the ankle.

"What the hell?" Lynae muttered.

"I have a bad feeling we're going to find a number on this guy," Jo said, shaking her head.

"You think we have a serial killer on our hands?"

"That would be my bet."

"Get that as close as you can," Mallory directed as two EMTs pushed a stretcher toward the aerial lift. She removed a black bag from her kit and unfolded it onto the bed.

As the boom came to a jerky halt, Mallory barraged the firemen with instructions while she unzipped the body bag and held the sides. "Don't let any part of the body touch the ground," she ordered as they slid the corpse into the bag.

Jo and Lynae trotted over. "Hold on a minute. I need to get his shirt open," Jo said.

Mallory's eyebrows shot up. "His shirt?"

"I just want to take a look."

Mallory nodded and pulled the heavy black plastic away from the body. Lynae peered over Mallory's shoulder while Jo reached in, unbuttoned the shirt, and pulled it open.

"Twenty-one," Lynae said.

Jo's heart plummeted. "What does that mean?" she asked her partner.

"Body count?"

Jo cringed. "We have a body from less than a week ago with the number nineteen written in the same place. If it's a body count, that would mean there were eighteen others before the first one."

"And what happened to number twenty? Is there another one that we haven't found that was killed between Kramer and this one?"

Mallory shook her head. "Even finding two bodies in a week is extremely fast. There was barely time to plan between them. Add another victim in between, and it would be almost unheard of." She ran her gloved hand over the number written in black marker. "It appears that you have one killer."

"I need this pushed to top priority, Mal."

"That goes without saying." Mallory zipped up the bag and motioned to the paramedics.

The ambulance driver and his partner pushed the stretcher over to the back of the vehicle. The legs clattered as they met the floor of the ambulance and collapsed underneath the metal gurney. They closed the door and walked around to climb into the cab. There was no need for one to ride in the back.

Jo suddenly felt an intense chill that made the morning's warm start a distant memory. She rubbed her arms. "You think you can get Kent in on a Saturday?"

Mallory cocked her head. "I can hardly get him *out* of the lab on a Saturday."

"Good. I need to nail this down as quickly as possible, or I'm afraid we'll find another body."

Mallory jerked her thumb at the retreating ambulance. "I'm following those guys in, and I'll call Kent on my way. I'll call you as soon as we have an ID."

"Thanks, Mal."

As Jo and Lynae headed back to the parking lot, Lynae asked, "Want me to grab you a coffee on my way in?"

Jo shook her head. "You might as well go home. I'm going to go in and start a board, but until we have an ID, there's nothing else to do."

"I don't have any plans. You can kill some time telling me how things went with the IAB interview." Lynae gave her a hip bump. "And with your date."

Jo opened her truck door. "All right. If I'm going to tell you all that, then I'd love a cup of coffee. I'll meet you there."

Chapter 12

Jo spent an hour telling Lynae about her meetings with the inmates, Officer Finkler, and Don Moreland. She even grudgingly talked about her date with Jack.

Lynae propped her feet on Jo's desk and balanced her coffee cup on her lap. "Damn, woman, you've been busy."

Jo laid her head back on her chair's headrest and closed her eyes. "No kidding."

"If there's something there, you'll find it. You just have to know that there may not be anything there to find."

"I'm so sure of this, Nae, but I'll deal with that possibility if the time comes." Her phone vibrated. She snatched it from her desktop and glanced at the caller ID. "Got something for me, Mal?"

"It was an easy ID. Mr. Matthew L. Wikstrom volunteered at Hillside Youth Center, so his prints were on file. He was reported missing two days ago by his wife. I'm emailing you a clean picture and a copy of his license. The license address is up-to-date."

"Thanks, Mal." Jo disconnected the call and turned to her computer. "We've got an ID," she told Lynae. She opened the email from Mallory and sent the attached pictures to the printer. As the laser printer whirred to life, she slid a new legal pad into her notebook, checked that her pen worked, then dropped a couple of extra pens into her bag for good measure.

Lynae went over and retrieved the printouts. "I'll get a look while you finish your ritual."

Jo pulled her keys out of her bag and hooked them into the front pocket of her pants. Last, she checked to see how much cash was in her wallet then dropped it back into her bag. "Ritual finished."

"He was a good-looking guy," Lynae said as she passed the photo to Jo.

Mr. Wikstrom was a handsome thirty-three-year-old with a thin, angular face and warm brown eyes. Comparing the driver's license photo to the discolored, bloated face on her murder board, and the cleaned-up morgue picture, she found it difficult to reconcile that they were all images of the same man. If at all possible, she would spare Mrs. Wikstrom the pain of seeing those other two pictures. She slid the morgue picture into the back of her notebook and the license one into the front.

With a sigh, Lynae got up and pulled her coat from the back of her chair. "I suppose it's time to go rip someone's heart out."

"Afraid so." Jo opened her office door. "After you, partner."

LYNAE POINTED TO A modern bi-level home. "That's the one."

Jo put on her turn signal and waited as three young women pushing strollers meandered past the driveway. A toddler on a Big Wheel followed, his little legs pumping frantically to keep up. She swung the truck into the driveway and parked beneath a portable basketball hoop with a neon-green bike leaning against it.

The door to the two-stall garage was open. A trailered snowmobile occupied one stall, while a white Dodge Caravan sat in the other. A skateboard lay flipped upside down next to a black resin ramp positioned in front of a pile of leaves.

Jo killed the ignition and pulled the keys. "They have at least one daredevil kid."

Lynae scrubbed her hands over her face. "Let's just get this over with."

As they approached the glass-panel front door, it flew open.

A middle-aged woman rushed onto the concrete porch, eyes wide. "Did you find Matt?"

Jo held up her badge. "Lisa Wikstrom?"

The woman shook her head and wrapped her arms around her ample middle. "I'm Sarah, Lisa's sister. She's in the house. Is this about Matt?"

Jo stepped onto the porch. "We'd like to talk with your sister—"

"Sarah? Who's here?" A younger woman appeared in the doorway, glanced at Jo's badge, then covered her mouth. "Matt," she whispered.

"Mrs. Wikstrom—" Jo began.

The woman's eyes filled with tears. "I know it's bad. I know it. Matt wouldn't just disappear."

Sarah put her arm around her sister's shoulder. "We don't know anything yet, hon."

Lisa pushed away and looked at Jo pleadingly. "Is he in the hospital? Why didn't they call me? I need my purse." She began a feverish search of the entryway.

"Mrs. Wikstrom, your husband isn't in the hospital."

The woman froze then turned slowly, abandoning her search. "So he's not hurt?"

Just get it over with. Jo took a step forward and laid her hands on the other woman's shoulders. "Mrs. Wikstrom, I'm so sorry to have to tell you that your husband is dead. His body was found early this morning."

Lisa blinked rapidly. She shook her head in short, frantic jerks. Her autumn-colored curls bobbed around her glassy eyes.

Jo knew the devastation, the inability to comprehend. Lisa's brain was racing and gaining speed on a dead-end street. Jo gripped the young woman's upper arms, fearing the new widow might faint. "We need to get her to a chair."

Sarah wrapped her arm around her sister's waist and half dragged her to the dining room. She lowered her into a chair then slid into the one next to her.

Dropping her head to the table, Lisa began to sob, an uncontrollable keening emanating from her soul. Her sister draped an arm around her back, leaned in, and spoke quietly.

Lynae found the kitchen and returned with a glass of water. Drinking water didn't do anything, but it gave the person something to focus on, and taking a drink forced a person to breathe.

"Mommy?"

Jo turned and saw a little blonde, sippy cup in hand, dragging a tattered blanket.

"Hey, there," Jo said softly, squatting down to the little girl's level. "What's your name?"

The child eyed Jo cautiously, pulled her blanket up to her cheek, and held out her cup.

"Do you want some milk? Juice?"

"Milk," Mrs. Wikstrom whispered. She held out her arms. "Come here, Lilly."

While Lynae handed a glass of water to her shaking mother, Jo took the cup from the little girl and headed for the kitchen. The fridge was covered with family keepsakes: a fall-colored turkey made from a child's hand, a Kenowa Hills basketball schedule, school pictures, and a wedding invitation, all held firm by brightly colored magnets. A dry-erase board dominated the freezer door, displaying doctor appointments, sports practices, and homework reminders in a rainbow of ink. She pulled out a gallon jug of milk and filled the Disney character cup.

Jo made her way back into the dining room and found the girl curled up on her mother's lap, sleepily wrapping strands of hair around her finger. Her mom stroked her back and cried silently, staring blindly at the empty chair across the table. Jo handed the cup to the toddler, who took it warily.

Cuddling closer, Lilly closed her eyes and sipped on the cup. She let go of her blanket to reach up and stroke her mom's hair.

Sarah held out her hands. "Why don't you let me take her?"

Lisa shook her head and rocked from side to side, humming tunelessly. After only a few minutes, the sippy cup dropped from the child's hand and rolled under the table. Moving mechanically, Lisa stood, hoisted the sleeping child up onto her shoulder, and walked out of the room.

Sarah rubbed her temples then pulled a phone from her back pocket. "If you'll excuse me for a moment, I'm going to call our mom. Lisa's going to need her."

Jo nodded. "Of course."

Sarah punched in a number as she walked to a different room. After a few minutes, Jo stood and glanced down the hallway where Lisa had taken her daughter. The widow was sitting on the floor outside an open bedroom door. She had her head on her knees, which were pulled up to her chest with her arms wrapped around them. Jo walked over and slid down the wall to sit next to her.

"What am I going to do?" Lisa whispered to her knees.

Jo knew the woman was talking to herself, but she answered anyway. "It's going to be hell for a while. Eventually, you'll learn to live with the pain."

Mrs. Wikstrom shook her head. "You don't know."

"Actually, I do."

Lisa rolled her head enough to look at Jo with one caramel-colored eye, black mascara streaking the side. Jo held her gaze without attempting to mask her own pain and saw the moment her words sank in.

"How do you go on?"

"You lean on people who care about you: your sister, your mom, friends. You let yourself grieve. You don't pretend that everything's okay, but you do get up every morning and go through the motions. With time, it eases, and the motions start to feel normal again."

The woman wiped her eyes with the sleeve of her shirt. "We have three kids. What do I say to them?"

"I don't have kids, so I can't pretend to know how to handle that. But there are people who can help." Jo pulled a card from her pocket. She made a point of knowing the counselors in the city and keeping a supply of their business cards. "This is the number for a counselor. She specializes in working with families who have lost a parent. It would be good for all of you."

Lynae came down the hall and leaned against the opposite wall.

Lisa pressed the heels of her hands against her eyes. "I can't wrap my brain around it. He can't be dead. There's been a mistake."

"I'm so sorry, Mrs. Wikstrom. I wish I had magical words to somehow make you feel better, but I don't. I can promise you we'll do everything in our power to find whoever did this."

Lisa turned her head and stared at her. "What do you mean, 'whoever did this'? What happened to him?"

"It's too early to have much information for you," Jo said carefully, "but we have reason to believe your husband was murdered."

Lisa sucked a breath in through her teeth. "What? Who would kill Matt?"

"Probably one of those hoodlums from that center." Sarah was standing at the end of the hallway, arms crossed.

"Not now, Sarah," Lisa said, her voice cracking with emotion.

"Actually, it could be important," Jo said. She turned to Sarah. "Are you referring to the Hillside Youth Center?"

"Yes. That place is full of troubled kids, the kind of kids that would hurt someone without giving two shits about his family."

Lisa shook her head. "Sarah, stop. That place means everything to Matt."

Jo angled her body toward Lisa, effectively blocking her sister. "Was he working there Tuesday night?"

"He's there every Tuesday night." Lisa coughed a little. "Sometimes other nights too. He stays late if someone needs to talk privately. So when it got late, I didn't—" Her voice cracked, and a sob escaped her lips. She covered her mouth, her face contorted in anguish.

Lynae pulled a small packet of Kleenex from her coat pocket and passed it over. Lisa accepted it with a weak smile and used a couple to wipe her eyes and nose.

"What did he do at the center?" Jo asked.

"He was the program director. When people ask him, he says he just plays basketball with the kids, you know, nothing big. But really, he's a role model. He talks to them, lets them know he cares. So many of the kids there don't have a man to look up to. He was someone they could—" Her voice cracked again, and she put her hand over her mouth.

"Any kids in particular that he took an interest in?" Lynae asked.

"He spent a lot of time talking with kids who were just coming out."

"Coming out?"

"Gay, bi, trans. He wanted them to know it was okay... you know, that they were okay. That's why he gets home so late on Tuesdays. There's a group thing, not really counseling but just talking."

"Do you know why he took an interest in that particular group of kids?"

She gave a small shrug. "He just said he knew someone once that he could have helped and didn't, and he always regretted it. He didn't really like to talk about it, but I think it was his way of, you know, atoning or something."

"Did he mention anyone that he had a problem with? Anyone that seemed threatening or that didn't like the extra attention?" Jo didn't want to think that the father who spent his spare time working with kids could have crossed a line, but it wouldn't be the first time.

Sarah huffed. "Those kids are all trouble."

Lisa glared at her sister. "They're mostly just kids who don't have anyone to give them direction. They're not bad kids, just lost. And no, he never said he had a problem with any of them, but he wouldn't have. Even if someone had given him a hard time, he would have just said they were troubled kids and needed help." She pulled another tissue from the pack. "He was a good man. He just wanted to help people."

Jo laid her hand on the other woman's knee. "I'm sure he was. Did your husband know a man by the name of Brad Kramer?"

"I know the name, but I haven't met him. He and Matt go way back, but they haven't been what you'd call real friends for years. Brad got Matt his first job at the Road Commission. But when Matt decided to go back to school to work with kids, Brad kind of turned on him. With Matt, once you're a friend, you're always a friend, so he would talk to Brad once in a while, but they weren't close. Then someone killed Brad, and—" Lisa's head snapped up. "Oh my God. Do you think this has something to do with Brad's murder?"

"We don't know at this time, but there are enough similarities that we're looking at any link between the two."

"But Matt said everybody's sure Brad's wife killed him, and if not her, then one of the women he had on the side. What does that have to do with Matt? He wasn't that kind of guy. Whatever Brad had going on, it didn't have anything to do with Matt."

Jo shifted to fully face the other woman. Sitting on the floor was starting to make her butt numb, but she would sit as long as it took. "We have no reason to believe that Brad Kramer was killed by his wife. At this point, we don't have a solid suspect for his murder. Anything you or Matt may have heard about that is just rumor."

Lisa threw her hands up. "There were so many people who hated Brad, but everybody liked Matt. They didn't have anything to do with each other anymore."

"But you said they go way back?"

"They were friends in high school. But even back then, Matt knew Brad was a jerk. He told me he just never said anything because Brad was such a big deal at the school."

"Then they went to work at the same place?" Lynae asked.

Lisa shoved her hands into the front of her dark hair, resting her forehead on her palms. "Not at first. Matt went to college for a while. That's where we met. But he was going through some stuff, like college kids do, and he quit. Brad had gotten a job with the county right after high school because his uncle worked there. So when Matt came back to Grand Rapids and needed work, Brad got him in. Then Matt got himself together, took night classes to get his degree, and started working at Hillside. I think Brad resented him." Lisa dropped her hands between her knees and leaned her head back against the wall. "I can't think right now."

Jo patted the woman's shoulder. "I'm sorry to have to ask you so many questions right away. We can let this go now and talk more later."

Lisa nodded. "Okay."

Jo climbed to her feet and held out a hand.

Lisa shook her head and laid her head back down on her knees. "I'm just going to sit here a while."

"I don't want to leave you like this."

Lisa raised her head and looked at Jo, tears streaming from her swollen eyes. "I need to sit here a little while. My sister will help." She attempted a smile. "And my mom will be here soon." She swiped a tear from her cheek. "And I guess I have to get used to being alone anyway."

Jo didn't tell her that she would never quite get used to it. She turned and walked back toward the dining room. Lynae followed her.

As they passed Sarah, Jo stopped and gave her a hard look. "She's grieving and needs nothing but your support. Whatever you felt about her husband's job isn't important."

Sarah looked surprised. "I never—"

"If you think you have something that could help our investigation, you bring it to me." Jo pressed a business card into her hand. "To her, you're a shoulder to lean on, someone to talk to and cry with, someone to help her with the kids. You don't lay any blame on her husband for his own death. Understand?"

Sarah squeezed her eyes shut and shook her head. "I didn't mean to blame him."

"I'm sure you didn't, and she needs to know that."

Sarah looked over at her sister still sitting on the floor. She pressed her lips together, nodded, and walked down the hallway. Jo watched as she sat down next to Lisa and wrapped her arm around her shoulders.

Back in the truck, Lynae buckled her seat belt. "Man, that was hard."

Jo glanced up at the front door. A wreath made of artificial leaves in bright fall colors hung in the center. "A happy home makes for a shitty notification."

"Two guys who've known each other for years, who worked at the same place for a while, end up dead within two weeks of each other in very similar fashion. That's no coincidence."

Drumming her fingers on the steering wheel, Jo said, "What were they into that got them in deep enough to be murdered?"

"Not just murdered. Tortured first."

"We need to expand our search on similar crimes."

Lynae turned in her seat and stared intently at Jo. "You think our guy has killed before?"

"These guys could have been running something. Drugs, guns, girls? Hell, we don't know what we're dealing with. But if this is someone's calling card, we need to see if he's left it anywhere else."

"So what's next?" Lynae asked.

"I'll drop you off at the station so you can start running the expanded search in NCIC. I'll go see if Kent has anything for us."

Chapter 13

"Give me something magical, Kent." Jo skipped her usual small talk with her favorite medical examiner. Her experience in the relatively quiet Michigan city had not equipped her for the challenges of a serial killer, and that knowledge weighed heavily on her mind.

Pulling off his wire-rim glasses, Kent stepped to the foot of the stainless-steel table that held the body of the most recent victim. "I took a preliminary look at the ankle. The foot was hacked off very crudely, similar to the way your last victim's hand was severed. The same, or at least a very similar, knife was used in both cases. Soon, I'll be able to tell you exactly what type of blade was used." Kent shook his head. "I can tell you with confidence that the killer isn't a surgeon or medical expert and that he is definitely right-handed."

Jo crossed her arms. "Which doesn't help much since that describes roughly ninety percent of the population. What else have you got?"

"Although the victim has fewer superficial torture wounds than your last one, what he has were made with a weapon of similar size and structure."

"Similar or the same?" At Kent's hesitation, Jo said, "I know you haven't had time for a thorough analysis. I'm not holding you to anything."

"Preliminarily, I would say the wounds all came from the same weapon."

Jo smirked. "Now was that so hard?"

Kent gave her a bland look. "A little. Early analysis of the rope shows that it's of the same material as the one used on the first victim. It's the same color and appears to be approximately the same age."

"I think we can safely assume we're dealing with the same killer in both cases. Maybe we'll get lucky and get some DNA this time."

Kent had been studying the body as she spoke. He suddenly froze, and his eyes narrowed.

Jo's pulse accelerated. She leaned in closer, attempting to get a glimpse of what he was looking at. "What?"

"There's something here." Kent put his glasses back on then reached to the side, never taking his eyes off the body. His fingers fumbled around the silver tray beside the examination table.

"What do you need?"

"Toothed forceps."

Jo scanned the tray helplessly. "I don't know what that is."

"They look like tweezers."

Jo found the tool and placed it in his outstretched hand. She moved closer and looked over his shoulder.

"You're in my light."

He spoke quiet and calmly, but Jo felt sufficiently chastised to duck back to her previous position. She hated waiting and hated it more when she couldn't see what was happening. But she knew her place in Kent's realm, and out of the way was it.

Kent mumbled and coaxed, talking to the ankle as if it were an obstinate child. Jo thought she would burst before he finished.

Kent straightened and stretched his back. "There we go." He opened a drawer on the metal cart beside the exam table and pulled out a small glass vial. After popping the lid, he dropped whatever he had pinched between the tongs into the container.

"What is it?" Jo asked.

"It's a hair. I'll get it right to Mallory."

"I guess that's something."

He labeled the vial and placed it in a clear plastic bag. "Indeed, it could be."

Jo pulled her notebook out of her bag. "Since we're going with the theory that our two vics were killed by the same person, I have Lynae searching NCIC for similar crimes."

"I keep a pretty tight watch on all of the surrounding counties. If anything like this had come up in any of them, I would know about it."

"It's possible he started outside of our area. We'll broaden the search if we don't come up with anything." From her recollection of case studies in her criminal justice classes, most serial killers had a well-defined geographic area of operation. They didn't typically go outside their comfort zone or too far from their nest. But her time in law enforcement had taught her that people were unpredictable.

"I think that would be a good idea, sooner rather than later." Kent used a black permanent marker to label the plastic bag. "Mallory will contact you with the rope and hair analyses. I'll finish here and send you my full report as soon as possible."

"Thanks."

Kent touched her arm. "Don't you want your word of the day, Jo?"

"How could I forget?" She hadn't forgotten, but she didn't have the heart to say, "I have a million things on my mind and don't care."

"Expurgate." At Jo's blank look, Kent gave her a fatherly smile. "Look it up. It's very fitting."

"Sorry, Kent. I'm not in the mood to have to work for it."

Kent inclined his head. "It means to remove parts considered objectionable."

Suddenly chilled, she ran her hands up and down her biceps. "You think our killer considers these body parts objectionable for some reason? That's why he's removing them?"

"You're the expert. I'm just giving you a word to add to your vo-cabulary."

Jo sneered. "Well, I'm going to expurgate the jackass who did this from society."

"I'm sure you will, Lieutenant." Kent chuckled.

I'm in over my head. Serial killers are a whole different breed. They don't play by the same rules as other killers. Their motives aren't neces-sarily about greed, passion, or jealousy, and their victims can be com-pletely random. I'll have to go to the captain and discuss the possibility of bringing in an expert.

Jo had no idea what that entailed. She had never needed outside help. But two homicides in one week by the same killer told her she couldn't let pride get in the way.

Her phone buzzed, and the ID showed Jack's name. "I've got to take this," she told Kent. As she walked out of the morgue, she an-swered, "Hey, Jack."

"Did I get out undetected this morning, or should I expect a call from the press? I'm sure the news is all over town by now."

Jo grinned. "You think you're pretty funny, don't you?"

"As a matter of fact, I do."

Climbing into her truck, she said, "A smart-ass is just what I need after the day I've had."

"Bad day?"

She leaned her arm on the truck windowsill, pressing the back of her already-chilled hand against the cold glass. "I picked up a new case this morning, as you know since you were there."

"Why don't you tell me about it over dinner?"

She checked her watch and realized the day had gotten away from her. Spending time with Jack sounded better than she wanted to admit. "I'd like to, but I really need to get on top of this case. I'm worried that I may have a serial killer on my hands."

Jack let out a low whistle. "Damn. Not much of that in Grand Rapids."

"Yeah, lucky me."

"You'll nail him. Just work it with the pit-bull tenacity you do every case."

"Not sure I like you calling me a pit bull."

"Have I mentioned that pit bulls are my favorite breed?"

Jo snorted as she maneuvered through downtown traffic. "I guess that makes it okay then."

"Go catch a killer, Lieutenant," Jack said before he hung up.

Despite herself, Jo smiled all the way to the station. She marched into the office to find Lynae slumped at her desk with her head in her hands.

Jo perched on the corner of her partner's desk. "That's not the look of someone who's had a breakthrough."

Lynae turned her head to rest it on one hand as she rubbed her droopy-lidded red eyes. "I've got nothing. Abso-freakin-lutely nothing. I've tried everything I can think of, and I've expanded out to surrounding counties. I'm getting zip."

"Why don't you call it a day and let me see what I can find?"

Lynae banged a few keys on her keyboard. "If you find something, I'll refer to you as Your Majesty from this point forward."

"Challenge accepted."

Lynae thrust her chair back and yanked her coat from the back of it. She dug a stocking cap and gloves out of the pockets. "Great. I'm outa here."

"Get some sleep. If I find anything, I'll let you know."

Jo made a fresh pot of coffee then spent the next two hours downing cup after cup as she searched open murder cases, looking for any sliver of a connection that she could pick at. She finally gave up and shut down her computer. The resolve she'd felt after talking to Jack wavered.

She sent a text to Lynae: *You can keep calling me Jo.*

Chapter 14

After a restless night of dreams riddled with swaying nooses, fishing boats, and a stocking-capped man who was always just out of her reach, Jo gave in to Mojo's insistent nudging and rolled out of bed. "All right, girl. Just let me get dressed."

By the time she returned from their morning run, she had to rush to get showered and changed. Sunday morning was for church and a visit with her family. Considering her current case, she would keep the visit short, but she needed that time every week to clear her head. She knew going to church couldn't hurt, and clearing her head could only help. She would take all the help she could get right now.

Her mind slowly eased as she drove through the peaceful countryside. The morning fog was lifting but still settled in the low-lying pockets of open fields. The mostly bare trees stood barren against the emerald-green grass littered with yellow and brown leaves.

She reached across the console and scratched Mojo's back. The dog pulled her nose out of the open window long enough to crane her neck and attempt to lick Jo's face. Jo dodged the tongue and scuffed the top of Mojo's head. Mojo stuck her head back out the window, her ears flopping in the cold wind and her tongue lolling out of the side of her mouth.

Jo pulled into her parents' driveway and opened the truck door. "Go see Grandma."

Mojo bounded out of the truck and bolted onto the porch. Mom opened the front door, waved at Jo, and stepped back to let Mojo in. Jo backed out of the driveway, drove the rest of the way to the church, then parked in the far corner of the lot, close to the cemetery.

She got out of the truck and walked down the center path to the back, where Mike and Little Mike waited for her visit. She stopped in front of the dark stone, picked a few leaves off the base, and clutched them in her hand. The green of the toy tractor she had placed in front of Little Mike's name stood boldly against the stone, no longer hidden by the irises she had tended all summer. Only hay-colored stalks remained, wilted in the pot.

She pulled a tissue from her coat pocket and wiped a smudge from the badge inlaid in the stone. "I sure could use your help right now. I'm in over my head with this new case."

Don't be afraid to ask for help.

"I'm not. I mean, my pride doesn't want to, but I will."

Even with a serial killer, there has to be a reason.

"I know, but I can't find a common link yet. Other than high school and a job from years ago."

People can hold on to things for years before something makes them break.

"What makes a person break this way? How much does a person take before the break happens?"

Some people can take a lifetime of pain, and others aren't strong enough. You're strong enough, Jo.

She blinked away the tears that burned her eyes. "Drevin Clay-burn is dead."

I know. He took the easy way out.

"He wasn't supposed to get that option."

You wanted him dead.

Jo crossed her arms. "I wanted my day in court first. I need answers."

He wasn't going to give you the answers you need.

"We could have made him talk. No way in hell I was going to let him get a deal, but I could have found a way to make him tell me everything."

You can still find a way. You'll find your answers, and you'll get what you need.

Jo rubbed her eyes with the heels of her hands. "I need you back. No one can give me that."

She felt movement behind her and turned to see her mom walking down the path, gazing at the stones as she passed. She stopped beside Jo and put her arm around her shoulders.

Jo laid her head on her mom's shoulder. "I miss him, Mom."

"I know, honey. He was a good man."

Jo nodded as a tear slid down her cheek.

Mom squeezed her arm and kissed her temple. "I'll see you inside."

Jo watched her mom walk back. Vehicles had begun filtering in. People smiled, waved, and greeted each other as the church bells started to chime "Westminster Quarters." The whole scene felt like a different world from where she stood in the solitude of her family's corner of the cemetery.

She squatted and used her finger to follow the lines of Little Mike's name. Then she kissed her hand and laid it on Mike's badge. After wiping away one last tear from her cheek, she picked up the pot of wilted flowers and headed back to her truck to drop it in the bed before joining the rest of the congregation in the vestibule of the church.

Her small-town parish was made up of families and friends who had lived in the same area for generations. Many of the families farmed together, and most saw one another on an almost-daily basis, yet they stood and talked like long-lost friends both before and after Sunday services. Often, the priest would eventually have to shoo at least a few lingerers out the door so he could lock up and go home.

Jo stopped and chatted with a few friends and waved at a couple more before making her way into the church and sitting next to her mom.

Her mind eased as she stood and sang along with the procession-al song then listened to the opening prayers. When the congrega-tion sat, the lector stepped up to the microphone behind the high wooden pulpit. He opened the *Lectionary* and adjusted the micro-phone. "A reading from the book of Deuteronomy: 'If a malicious witness takes the stand to accuse someone of a crime, the two people involved in the dispute must stand in the presence of the Lord before the priests and the judges who are in office at the time. The judges must make a thorough investigation, and if the witness proves to be a liar, giving false testimony against a fellow Israelite, then do to the false witness as that witness intended to do to the other party.'"

Jo propped her feet on the raised kneeler and pressed her hands between her knees. She closed her eyes and let the polished voice of the lector wash over her.

"'You must purge the evil from among you. The rest of the people will hear of this and be afraid, and never again will such an evil thing be done among you. Show no pity: life for life, eye for eye, tooth for tooth, hand for hand, foot for foot.'"

Jo sucked in a quick breath. She dropped her feet from the kneel-er, grabbed a missalette, and flipped pages until she found the day's reading: Deuteronomy 19:19-21.

Nineteen through twenty-one. Hand for hand, foot for foot.

The lector looked up from the oversized book. "The word of the Lord."

It's a Bible verse.

The congregation replied in unison. "Thanks be to God."

He's taking the Bible literally to seek revenge.

Jo stood automatically when the rest of the congregation did. She went through the motions of the rest of the service instinctually, questions buzzing through her mind like bees in a hive. *I have to get to the station and start a search. We aren't looking for a missing hand or foot to find a previous victim. It will be an eye or a tooth or both.*

When the service ended, she slipped out a side door to avoid the people and conversations that an hour earlier she had looked forward to.

Her mom was right behind her. "Joellyn? What's your rush?"

"Sorry, Mom. I'm going to have to skip lunch today. I have to get to the station."

"Why all of a sudden? You have to eat. Take the time to have lunch with your family, *then* go to work."

Jo ran a hand through her hair. "I'm not going to be good company, Mom. My mind is at work. I just had a bit of a revelation."

"Well, I'm glad to hear you had a revelation while in church. But I'm going to guess it wasn't a religious experience."

Jo shrugged sheepishly. "It came from the gospel, if that helps. I was listening. That has to count for something. But I really do have to go to work."

"Come back to the house, and I'll put together a to-go dinner for you. Mojo can stay with me."

"I'll take the food, but Mojo can come to the station with me. She likes to hang out in my office on weekends. Whoever happens to be there always ends up spoiling her rotten."

"Of course they do. Who could resist that mutt?"

Jo hopped into her truck and followed her mom back to the house. Inside, the aromas of chicken and apple pie permeated her senses. Her sister-in-law sat at the dining room table, sipping a glass of red wine, while her niece colored a picture of SpongeBob riding a sea dragon and chattered about her choice of colors. Sprawled out on the kitchen floor, Mojo started thumping her tail madly at the sight of Jo. In the next room, her dad yelled at the television while her brother cheered.

Must be the Lions playing the Bears. Her will to drive to the station and work started to slip. Spending time with her family was exactly what she really needed.

Horrendous images of the latest victims leapt to the front of her mind while the angel on her shoulder reminded her that every minute counted for the next potential victim. Those thoughts steeled her against the comfort of her childhood home. She filled a Tupperware container with a little bit of everything her mom had prepared for lunch, then she cut a piece and a half of pie and slipped it into another one. If she had to spend the afternoon alone in her office, she could do it with a good meal.

She braved the family room chaos long enough to hug her dad and give her regrets for leaving. Mojo trotted beside her from room to room until they finally went out the back door. Even family time had to be trumped occasionally. If she could make a connection, maybe she could stop the next killing.

And she had no doubt there would be another one.

JO STRODE INTO THE office with Mojo. "Isaac! I didn't expect to see you here on a Sunday. Isn't there a game you should be watching?"

Isaac closed the file he had been reading. "I'm frustrated that I haven't pulled anyone in on our drive-by yet, especially since Evans and Mason picked up another one this week. I was going back over the file to see if I missed something." He patted his thigh, and Mojo trotted over to him. She desperately tried to lick his face while he rubbed her neck. "Such a good girl."

"Do you have some secret bacon stash or something? She adores you."

Isaac grabbed Mojo's face and scratched behind her ears while dodging her quick tongue. "We'll never tell. Will we, Mojo?" He leaned back in his chair and gave Jo a quizzical look. "What brings you in?"

"I've got a line on what the numbers printed on my victims mean."

"Can I help? I'm getting nowhere new on this." He gestured at the folder on his desk.

"I don't think so. I'm just going to run some new searches. But on your case, you should pull your witnesses back in one at a time."

Isaac shook his head. "I've already talked to them and gotten nowhere."

"Bring them in here this time. Make them feel important. And safe. Start with the type of car, even if you've been over it before. Work your way to the people in it. Maybe bring in Clark."

"You want me to waste the time of a sketch artist?"

"It may not be a waste of time. Show them you're serious and that you think they have something for you. They think we don't care when something happens in the Slope. Show them they're wrong, that we're pulling out all the stops because we want this solved."

"All right. I'll get Clark lined up then work on getting them in here."

Jo motioned toward the break room. "I'm going to get a pot of coffee going. Walk with me, and I'll fill you in on my case."

Isaac stood up and carefully stepped over Mojo, who had flopped belly-up onto the floor at his feet. She jumped up and trotted over to Jo.

Jo gave her a disgusted look. "Oh, so you're back, my fickle friend?"

Isaac spread his arms wide. "Don't blame her, LT. I'm pretty hard to resist."

"If the love fest is over, let's talk serial killer."

His mouth dropped open. "For real?"

"I'm afraid so." Jo walked into the break room and pulled a coffee filter and vacuum-sealed packet from a drawer. "In church this morning, the lector read those verses about an eye for an eye. You know it?"

"I'm not much of a churchgoer, but even I know that one." He pulled two cups from the cabinet.

"And it's not just eyes. It says, 'Show no pity: life for life, eye for eye, tooth for tooth, hand for hand, foot for foot.' That passage is from Deuteronomy nineteen, verses nineteen through twenty-one." Jo pointed at the cup in Isaac's hand. "I'm not drinking out of that, by the way."

Isaac turned the cup over in his hand, his eyebrows knit in confusion. "Why not?"

"If there are any other options, coffee should not be drunk from a Styrofoam cup."

"Such a snob." Isaac shook his head and put one of the cups back. "Your victims had the numbers nineteen and twenty-one on them."

"And one was missing a hand, while the other was missing a foot."

Isaac raised his eyebrows. "So he's taking that verse literally."

"I think our killer is getting his 'eye for an eye' for something that was done to him."

"Something he deems bad enough that torture and death are appropriate payback."

Jo leaned against the counter. "Call me crazy, but deaths this extreme? I think our victims might have been killers at some point."

"Damn," Isaac whispered. "Have you dealt with a serial killer before?"

"No, I haven't. I'm going to collect as much information as I can then talk to the captain. We may need to call in an expert."

"And you don't have a problem with that? Someone horning in on your case?"

Jo pushed away from the counter. "They're not horning in if I ask for help. And no, I don't have a problem. I want to stop a killer. There's no room for letting pride get in the way."

"You sure there's nothing I can do?"

"Nothing right now. I need to find a tooth and an eye."

Isaac looked at Jo quizzically. "Excuse me?"

"We've got a missing hand and a missing foot. Where are the eye and tooth? Where did our killer start? If I'm right on this, and my gut tells me I am, we've got other victims out there somewhere."

THE FACE OF A DARK-haired, olive-skinned man filled Jo's screen. She scanned the details, and her pulse quickened. *This is our first victim. I'd lay money on it.* She pushed her chair back, rolled away from her desk, and leaned toward her open door. "Hey, Isaac. I think I found victim number one."

Isaac trotted in and came around her desk. He read over her shoulder, "Joseph J. Telknap. Toledo, Ohio. Thirty-two years old. Hanged in an abandoned warehouse."

Jo pointed lower on the screen. "His right eye was removed, and 'Deuteronomy' was written across his chest in black permanent marker."

Isaac whistled. "That's victim number one, all right."

Jo grabbed her phone. "I'm going to leave a message for the lead on that case. Let's hope"—she glanced at the screen for the name—"Detective Jurgens has something solid for us."

"I left someone on hold, so I gotta get back. Let me know what he says, though you'll probably just have to leave a message."

Already dialing the number listed on the site, she nodded absently as Isaac left her office. Jo was pleasantly surprised when the phone was picked up on the second ring.

"Kip Jurgens."

"Detective Jurgens, Lieutenant Jo Riskin, Grand Rapids PD. I'm a little surprised to catch you in the office on a Sunday."

"I'm not in the office, Lieutenant. You called my cell." His deep voice sounded pleasant rather than irritated that she'd called his personal number on a weekend.

"I apologize, Detective. I called the contact number from NCIC."

"No apology needed. I wouldn't list that number if I didn't want it used. So you're in Michigan?"

Jo grinned. "Yes. Your neighbors to the north."

Kip chuckled. "Well, what has you calling me on a Sunday afternoon, neighbor?"

"I've got two homicides in less than two weeks that appear to be related."

"Ouch."

"Exactly. They also appear to be connected to an open case of yours."

"Really? What case?"

She bent down to scratch Mojo's head. "Joseph Telknap."

"Well, I'll be damned. I'll be happy to share what I have, but I'm four months into this investigation and have diddly to show for it. What makes you so sure they're related?"

"I've got two victims who were hanged. One vic is missing a hand, and one is missing a foot. The only pieces of evidence on them are two numbers written in black permanent marker: nineteen and twenty-one. I couldn't make any sense out of those numbers until today."

"What happened today?"

Jo smirked. "I went to church."

"I'm sure your mother would be proud," Kip replied.

"Well, she was there with me, like she is every week." *Why am I telling this guy that?* She cleared her throat. "So anyway, the gospel reading—"

"Was from Deuteronomy."

Jo jabbed her finger in the air. "Bingo."

"And I've got a victim with the same MO, and 'Deuteronomy' was written on his chest. I have that verse in my notes, but with little else to go on, it didn't help."

"Deuteronomy nineteen, verses nineteen through twenty-one, is about an eye for an eye, a tooth for a tooth, and so on." She stood up and walked to her murder board. "So it makes sense."

"Our killer is exacting his interpretation of biblical revenge. That's not the normal everyday shit we see."

She stared at the gruesome pictures of the victims. Once-handsome faces turned grotesquely discolored and disfigured. Bloody stumps left where a hand and a foot had been. "Is anything we see normal and everyday?"

Kip snorted. "Good point. Were your victims found in similar places?"

"Vic one was found in the woods next to the river, vic two at a local high school."

"My vic was left in an abandoned warehouse. We may not have found him for years, but some kids wanted to use it for a haunted house."

"In July?"

He chuckled. "Getting an early start scouting their location. They were planning to make some money, taking people on clandestine tours around Halloween."

"You have to give them credit for their entrepreneurial spirit."

"I didn't nail them on the trespassing. I figured they got enough of a scare from finding a maimed body."

"I did the same with the underage drinkers that found my first vic. According to your report, your vic was missing an eye."

"Yeah, it was removed very crudely. There were a lot of hesitation marks. My coroner decided the perp was someone who hadn't done this before or who was feeling guilty about it."

Jo ran her hand over the picture of Brad Kramer's mutilated wrist. "I've got some pretty badly hacked-off limbs, but my medical examiner didn't see hesitation. So our killer isn't getting better at his craft, but he's getting bolder, like the guilt is gone."

"That's not something we want to happen."

"No, it isn't. Our murderer is writing a message on his victims. They committed a wrongdoing, and this is their just deserts for it. But was it a wrongdoing to him or a wrongdoing to society in general?"

"That's the million-dollar question. I've been working on the assumption that I have a single, unconnected murder. With two more victims, I'll have to go back over my evidence with a different eye."

"There must be another victim that we haven't found yet. You have the eye, and I have the hand and the foot. Where's the tooth?"

"That could be easily overlooked. A missing tooth in an autopsy wouldn't raise any flags like eyes and extremities do."

Jo dropped back into her chair and clicked on the picture of Joseph Telknap. "He should have been before my first victim but after yours, if the killer is following the pattern I think he is. But he could be anywhere. You and I aren't even in the same state. We've got three male victims, so by the laws of serial killers, we should be looking for another man." She hit the print button and heard her printer wake up.

"I'll do some searching on NCIC."

"That's how I found you. I didn't find any other hits, but a new set of eyes on it can't hurt." Jo plucked the picture from her printer, grabbed the tape dispenser from the corner of her desk, and turned to her murder board.

"I have to do something. I feel like I've been pissing into the wind for weeks. Now that I know we may have a serial killer on our hands, I've got different avenues to follow."

Jo pulled Brad Kramer's picture off the board and taped Joseph Telknap's in its place. "You know, I've been trying to wrap my brain around dealing with a serial killer, but this might not actually be what you would call a real serial killer." She left an empty space on the board for the missing victim.

"What do you mean by that?"

She pulled Matthew Wikstrom's picture off and taped Brad Kramer's in that slot. She had to keep them in order so her brain could go through its process. "This may be a limited number of victims that our killer believes deserve to die because of some wrong they've committed against him."

"Do they have a connection?"

Jo taped Matthew's picture in the last space and stepped back to look at her handywork. "My two guys go way back, but they haven't been close in a long time. At this point, their lives don't cross. Different lifestyles, hangouts, outside activities. One's on a bowling league. The other plays on a slow-pitch church softball team. Our first victim was a jackass that most people who knew him wanted to kill. The second was a well-liked, respected family man who worked with troubled youth."

"My vic was originally from Michigan. He left to go to college at Case Western in Cleveland and eventually landed in Toledo."

"He was from Michigan?" Jo gripped her phone tightly. "What high school did he attend?"

"Ah, let me think. I know it was a Grand Rapids city school that's no longer open."

"Crestwood?"

"That's it!"

"Same school as my two victims."

"I think we found our link, Lieutenant," Kip said quietly.

Jo stared at her board. "These guys have been out of school for, what, fifteen years? That's a long time to hold on to something then suddenly go on a killing spree."

"I have a very limited amount of experience with serial killers, but I know that they can lead perfectly normal lives and, one day, just fall off a cliff. It usually takes some life-changing event, something tragic that puts them over that edge."

"So we're all just one tragedy away from being killers?" Jo thought of how much she had wanted to put a bullet in Drevin Clayburn once she was certain he had killed Mike. She had almost convinced herself that she could feel the relief that it would bring. But in the end, she hadn't been able to do it. She just wasn't the kind of person who could put a bullet in the head of an unarmed man, no matter how much hatred she felt.

"I don't think most people are capable of this kind of act against another human being. The trauma has to be deep, and it usually goes way back. Something in childhood leaves such a severe scar that it throws their wiring off a little. They're able to function and live their lives like the rest of us until something triggers that deep-rooted pain and they lose control. We need to find out what happened to drive our killer."

"And knowing more about his childhood could quite possibly lead us to that." Jo sat back down behind her desk. "What did this hodgepodge group do to our killer?"

"Another million-dollar question."

"If we figure this out, we're going to be rich." When he laughed at her joke, she felt a flush of pleasure. She cleared her throat. "I'll get on a deeper background with my two vics and would appreciate anything you can dig up on yours."

"You got it, Lieutenant."

Jo smiled. "It's Jo."

"All right, Jo. I'm only a few hours away. How about I take a little road trip with my file and we put our heads together?"

Jo was surprised by the generous offer. It would help tremendously to get her hands on his evidence and hash the case over with another detective who had already worked part of it. "If you can clear the time, I would appreciate the help."

"I have a lot going on here, but I think it would be a trip worth clearing a day for. This has been at a dead end for too long. Why don't you plan on tomorrow? I'm an early riser, so expect me midmorning."

"I look forward to it."

"See you in the morning, Lieutenant Jo."

She hung up the phone and decided she liked Detective Kip Jurgens—and not just for his sexy voice.

Jo pulled up her email and tapped out a quick message to her team: *Lynae and I will be working with a visiting detective from Ohio tomorrow. Morning briefing will be delayed until he arrives. If this doesn't work with your schedule, please email me an update on your cases.*

Next, she went online and started digging up information on Crestwood School. She found the name and contact information for Betty Purvis, the principal during the time her victims were students. The woman's voicemail picked up, and Jo left her a message requesting a meeting.

She stood up and stretched her back and neck. Mojo popped to her feet, trotted to the door, and looked back at Jo expectantly.

"Yeah, you're right. It's time to go home." She figured she could spend a couple of hours going over the new information she had on Mike's case before calling it a night.

After slipping on her coat, she clipped on Mojo's leash then patted her head while the dog looked up at her adoringly.

"Pretty exciting life we have, isn't it, girl?"

Chapter 15

The next morning, Jo stopped at Sandy's Donuts on her way to work. Her team deserved an occasional treat, and Sandy's had the best donuts in town. When she got to the station, she left the box on the table in the conference room.

At her desk, she listened to a voicemail message from Bonnie Purvis, who said she would be home all morning. Jo gave her a call and arranged an eleven o'clock meeting at the woman's house. She jotted down the address and shoved the note in her pocket.

Through her office door, she saw a tall man step off the elevator. His black hair was long enough to curl over his collar, and his North Face ski jacket pulled tightly across his broad chest. He carried a cardboard evidence box through the bull pen, nodding at people with such ease that they nodded back, even though they probably wondered who he was. Most people walking into a homicide unit appeared guilty, terrified, or in mourning. Jo knew without question it was Kip Jurgens.

She fired off a quick email to her team: *Morning briefing in fifteen minutes.* When she looked up again, Lynae was already greeting their visitor. Kip perched the evidence box on his hip, stretched out his hand, and smiled. Jo couldn't hear what Lynae said, but her words made the handsome detective let out a hearty laugh. When Lynae motioned toward her office, she took the cue and headed out the door to meet him.

After grabbing her case-files notebook and coffee cup, Jo walked over to Lynae's desk. She set down her stuff and held out her hand. "Detective Jurgens, I assume. Jo Riskin."

The detective smiled warmly. "Please call me Kip."

"Thanks for making the trip. Did you have a good drive?"

"My pleasure. It's an easy drive between Toledo and Grand Rapids. The traffic was a little heavier than anticipated, or I would have been here earlier."

Jo glanced at her watch. "You must have left early."

Kip grinned, deep lines creasing the edges of his piercing blue eyes. "I told you I was an early riser. And I'm eager to see what you have."

Jo motioned toward the briefing room. "I'm looking forward to putting our heads together on this too. I waited until you got here to brief my team, so we'll start there."

"Sounds like a good place to start," he replied, hoisting the evidence box onto the corner of Lynae's neat desk.

"I've got a conference room reserved for the day. My office leaves a little to be desired."

"If it's bigger than a standard walk-in closet, you've got me beat."

His voice was like silk, and Jo detected a hint of the South. She lost her train of thought for a second and was saved by her partner.

"I'll show you where the important things are, like coffee," Lynae said, picking up her coffee and notebook.

Kip eased into a beguiling smile. "That would be fantastic."

Jo followed the pair into the break room. Lynae pulled a blue-and-gold GRPD coffee mug out of the overhead cabinet, filled it with coffee, and passed it to Kip.

"Okay. Important task done," Lynae said.

Jo smiled and inclined her head toward the door. "Follow me."

"Lead the way, Lieutenant."

"Only if you call me Jo."

Kip nodded. "Got it."

Jo walked down the hallway then opened the door to the conference room, where her team had already made themselves comfortable. "Take a seat wherever you like," she told Kip.

Kip slid into a chair in the back of the room, while Jo strode to the front and dropped her notebook on the scarred wooden podium. The din of disjointed conversations abruptly stopped, and all eyes turned to Jo.

She pointed at Kip. "We have a guest this morning. Detective Kip Jurgens is here from the Toledo PD to assist Lynae and me on our current case."

Charles crossed his arms. "Assist?"

Jo nodded. "We believe our two cases and his are connected. I'm going to start this morning with the case we picked up Saturday."

"I heard the dude was missing a foot," Charles said.

"I heard clues were written in his blood," Detective Anderson added.

Jo held up her hand. "Yes, our first victim was missing a foot. No, there weren't clues written in blood." She grimaced. "Where does stuff like that even come from?"

"I just heard it." Detective Anderson shrugged and bit off a full third of his donut.

Jo rolled her eyes. "Well, unhear it. It's not true."

After swallowing, the detective asked, "Have you made a connection to your other case with the missing hand?"

Jo nodded. "We're going on the assumption that our cases are related. It turns out all three of our victims attended Crestwood High School here in Grand Rapids, which is where we found our second vic's body."

Charles grabbed his notebook from the table. "Wait a minute." He flipped through the pages, ran his finger down one, then looked up at Jo wide-eyed. "My hooker went to Crestwood."

Lynae sputtered and quickly covered her mouth as coffee ran down her chin. "You gotta warn a person before you say something like that."

Charles snickered. "Normally, I don't kiss and tell, but..."

Lynae's face contorted. "Ewww."

Jo dropped her hands to her hips and stared blandly at the two detectives. "Are you two done?"

"He started it," Lynae mumbled.

Jo looked toward the back of the room and caught Kip's eye. He had his hand over his mouth, casually covering his struggle to contain his laughter.

Pressing her lips together, Jo looked away before she let a laugh escape. She didn't want to encourage those two. "Charles, how many years ago did your vic graduate Crestwood?"

Charles referred to his notes. "Fifteen. We finally got an ID on her. Her name was Shannon VanDorn."

"Graduated the same year as our other vics. Any other indication, besides a common high school, that your case could be related?"

Charles shook his head and puffed out a deep breath. "We don't have a lot to go on at this point with all the damage the vermin and time did to her body."

"Have they determined cause of death?"

"Strangulation."

Isaac tapped the table. "LT, all her teeth were missing."

Jo huffed. "Damn. That has to be our missing vic."

Lynae stopped her coffee cup midway to her mouth. "Missing vic?"

"Sorry, you're a little more out of the loop than you should be." Jo nodded at Kip. "In Detective Jurgens's case, the victim had 'Deuteronomy' written on his chest, and he was missing an eye. The numbers on our two victims and his are part of the Bible verse that talks about an eye for an eye."

Lynae leaned forward and rested her arms on the table. "The victim in Ohio was missing an eye, and our two were missing a hand and a foot. So we needed a tooth."

Jo pointed at Charles. "And we just found one."

"And you think this goes all the way back to some high school grudge from fifteen years ago?"

"I can't make a connection between these people anywhere else, so that's the thread we're pulling right now." Jo held out her hand to Charles. "Why don't I take that file and consider it part of mine."

Charles jumped from his seat and dropped the VanDorn case folder on the podium. "With pleasure, Lieutenant."

Isaac had opened his laptop and was staring at the screen. "Crestwood High School has been closed for seven years, but during the years that our victims would have attended, there were an average of two hundred forty students per grade, so somewhere between nine hundred and a thousand students."

Kip strummed his fingers on the table. "You never know who a group of high schoolers could have tormented."

Jo nodded. "Agreed. I put in a call yesterday to the woman who was the principal at the time. She's available this morning to talk."

"You think she'll remember a few kids from that many years ago?" Lynae asked.

Isaac shuddered. "My experience with teachers and principals is that they never forget anything."

Jo smirked. "A bit of a troublemaker in school, Isaac?"

"I go back for football games sometimes, and I still get the stink eye from a couple of them. It's been twelve years!"

"Well, let's hope Mrs. Purvis has that same kind of memory," Jo replied, opening her caseload binder. "Let's get through the rest of the cases."

Jo listened to the updates on each ongoing investigation, gave input, and doled out assignments. When the last report was given, she slapped her binder closed. "All right, let's get to work."

As the detectives filed out of the conference room, Jo motioned for Lynae to hang back. "We have a few minutes to spare. I'd like to update the murder board with this new information and get you completely up to speed."

"Good idea. I need to get the names and faces straight in my head."

"And the order of death," Jo said grimly. "Kip, let's grab your evidence box so we have everything together. We'll be camped out here for the duration."

"You got it, Lieutenant."

"If you don't start calling me Jo, I'm going to send you back to Ohio."

Kip smirked. "Duly noted."

Once they were settled in the conference room, Jo pulled the most gruesome scene picture from the VanDorn case file, removed Brad Kramer's and Matthew Wikstrom's photos, and shifted them to put the VanDorn one second in line. She pointed at the first picture on the board. "Victim number one, Joseph Telknap, found in an abandoned warehouse in Toledo, Ohio, four months ago. Joseph's eye was removed, and 'Deuteronomy' was written on his chest."

She tapped the newest photo. "Then we have Shannon Van-Dorn, who was recently discovered in an abandoned school in Grand Rapids. According to her autopsy report, she'd been dead for over two months. As we just discovered, she was missing all of her teeth. Due to decay, we don't know if she had a number written on her, but we'll go with the theory that she had a nineteen."

"Why nineteen again?" Lynae asked.

At the top of her murder board, Jo wrote *Deuteronomy 19:19-21*. "That's the full Bible verse." She tapped Brad Kramer's picture then

Matthew Wikstrom's. "And we know about these two. The third and fourth victims, they had the numbers nineteen and twenty-one written on them."

Kip scratched the dark stubble on his cheek. "Shouldn't that be the end of our victims? The killer has completed the verses."

"I don't think so. The verses include eye, tooth, hand, foot, and *life*. I think there will be at least one more."

"So we need to find the connection and try to predict who our next victim will be before he or she turns up dead somewhere," Lynae said. "No pressure, though."

"Yeah, no pressure." Jo checked her watch. "My meeting with the principal is in about thirty minutes, so we should get going."

"Okay, I'll get my stuff."

"I thought I would take Detective Jurgens—"

"Kip," the detective chimed in before turning to dig through his evidence box.

Jo nodded in his direction. "*Kip* with me to talk to her."

Lynae smirked. "All righty then."

"That will give you a chance to catch up on your paperwork," Jo added.

"Oh, goody."

Jo turned to Kip. "Ready to jump right in?"

Kip straightened and winked, his blue eyes twinkling. "Sounds like I better be."

When he smiled, a deep dimple dominated his right cheek. Her throat suddenly dry, Jo took a sip of coffee. *How did I not see that before?*

He swept his hand toward the door. "After you, Lieutenant."

As they stepped into the elevator, Jo's phone signaled a text. She glanced at the display and saw a message from Lynae: *Ditching me for the hottie detective? Aunt Trudy would be so disappointed.*

Jo snorted then responded, *She'll learn to live with it.*

"Everything okay?" Kip asked.

Jo shoved the phone back into her pocket. "Everything's fine."

A PANG OF DISAPPOINTMENT settled in Jo's chest when she pulled onto the street leading to the residence of Bonnie Purvis. She and Kip were having such a nice conversation that she hated to have it end. Not only was he interesting, but he also had a great sense of humor and a killer laugh.

Jo turned into a driveway flanked by a massive walnut tree and two red oaks. At the end of the paved drive, neatly trimmed evergreen bushes and an expansive flower garden embraced a tidy bungalow that sat alone on a lot that spanned at least three acres.

Kip hopped out of the truck and came around to her side. He stood with his shoulders hunched, hands shoved deep in his pockets, while she grabbed her bag from behind her seat and slid her phone into her back pocket. They hustled to the house, taking the wooden steps leading to the wrap-around front porch two at a time.

A hand pulled the curtain covering the door window aside, and an elderly woman's face appeared in the opening. Jo smiled and held up her badge.

Locks clicked, and the door swung open. The woman smiled warmly. "Lieutenant Riskin?"

"Yes, I am. And you're Mrs. Purvis?"

"Bonnie." The woman stepped back. "Please come in."

Jo crossed the threshold ahead of Kip. "This is Detective Jurgens from the Toledo Police Department."

Bonnie's expression turned to surprise. "My, you've come a long way for this."

Kip gave her a full-dimple smile. "Yes, ma'am, I did."

"Well, come on into the living room. I have coffee and homemade cookies."

Kip wiggled his eyebrows. "Coffee *and* cookies. A woman after my own heart."

Bonnie waved her hand in front of her face as a blush crept over her cheeks. "Oh my. Such flattery!"

Jo and Kip followed her ample frame through a small kitchen with tea-kettle wallpaper and into a living room with plush white carpeting and overstuffed furniture.

Bonnie motioned to a coffee decanter and a tray of cookies on an oak coffee table. "Can I pour you some coffee?"

Jo perched on the flowered sofa, close enough to the edge to avoid rearranging the lacy pillows. "Coffee sounds wonderful."

"Thank you. I would love a cup." Kip settled into the green recliner as if he visited the elderly woman on a regular basis.

Mrs. Purvis handed them each a small white china cup delicately lined with pink roses. She took her own to the rocker then pulled on a green cardigan before sitting down. After placing her cup on the end table, she picked up a stack of hardcover books. "After our conversation this morning, I went through my yearbooks and found the years we discussed. I kept a yearbook from every graduating class I was there, forty-six of them."

Jo guessed the principal had started her career as an English teacher. Bookshelves lined every wall in the room. The tomes appeared to be ordered alphabetically within genre. Ian Rankin sat next to J.D. Robb, and Katie MacAlister snuggled next to Debbie Macomber. The yearbooks had their own space on a shelf next to the fireplace. "That's an impressive collection of yearbooks."

"I rarely look at them, but sometimes, I'll hear that someone has died or, more happily, someone has gotten married, had a child, or made it big in their chosen field. I look them up to remind me of who they were."

"Do you usually remember them when you see their faces?" Kip asked.

The woman ran her hand over the red cover of the top book in her hand. "It depends on the student. Plenty of people go through high school trying desperately to make themselves invisible. I tried not to let that happen to my students, but some slipped through. I may look at their face and not remember a thing. It always makes me sad when that happens." There was genuine caring in her dark eyes, and the intelligence behind them had not dimmed with age.

Jo smiled warmly. "You were a good teacher and principal. You cared."

"I certainly did care, and I tried to do justice by every student I encountered. There are those in my profession who do the minimum to collect their paycheck. But most of us want to make a difference."

"The same could be said for my profession." Jo took a sip of coffee from the tiny cup and wondered how Kip was going to handle the delicate china with his big hands.

"Yes, I imagine it could be said for most. It just seems more tragic when, in professions like yours and mine, there's the potential for a real difference in a young life."

Jo thought about Jeron, the ten-year-old kid she had befriended after he turned in evidence that helped her solve a recent homicide. He had the potential to go either way: to a life with the gangs that infested his neighborhood or to a brighter future that his mother so wanted for him. She made a mental note to stop by and see him, to remind him that someone other than his mother cared about his future. "Do you remember Brad Kramer or Matthew Wikstrom?"

"Those two, I didn't even have to look up. There are some kids that stick with you. That whole group did."

"Group?" Jo set her cup on the coffee table and reached into her bag for her notebook.

"There were seven of them. I found a picture of them all together in one of the yearbooks. The year before they graduated." She opened the red book to one of several pages marked with fringed bookmarks and turned it toward Jo.

Kip hopped out of his recliner and planted himself on the sofa next to Jo. He leaned close to look at the picture. A subtle musky scent wafted over her. *Armani Code.* Her heart leapt to her throat. Mike's scent.

"This is Brad Kramer," Bonnie said, pointing at a handsome, smirking blond who had his arm around an equally attractive brunette. "The girl on his arm is Amanda Chatman. If I remember correctly, it's Amanda Reed now."

"They were a couple?" Jo asked.

Bonnie smirked. "It was high school, and they were two of the beautiful people. So yes, at one point, they dated. It didn't take, and oddly enough, they stayed friends."

"You don't hear that very often," Kip said.

"No, but I don't think either of them took it very seriously. At least, I'm sure Brad didn't."

Jo cocked an eyebrow. "A bit of a player?"

"Indeed, he was. I heard he got married quite quickly after high school and had a baby. I had hoped that would tame him a bit."

Jo shook her head. "According to all accounts, it didn't."

Mrs. Purvis shrugged. "Some people just aren't cut out to be tamed."

"You didn't particularly care for him, did you?"

"Does it show?" The woman sighed. "No, I didn't, which feels wrong to say, knowing he's dead. He was one of those kids that had everything that everyone else wanted. That whole group did. But Brad used it to abuse people. He had a mean streak, liked to pick on kids that were different. I had him in my office more times than I can count."

Jo studied the group of kids, arms around each other, smiling faces. "What about the rest?"

"Amanda was a sweet girl. She came from a good family, had a lot of potential. She led a lunchtime Bible study for a while. Back then, that was allowed."

"Doesn't sound like someone who would spend her time with Brad, the way you've described him."

"Brad could be very charming. He was obviously handsome and one of the best athletes the school had seen up to that time. Sometimes, in high school, that's all that matters. But I think that's also why their short romance didn't last."

Jo easily picked out the young Matthew Wikstrom and pointed at his picture. "What about Matthew Wikstrom? Where did he fall in this group?"

The elderly woman ran her hand over the picture. "Matt was a good kid but a bit of a follower. Another good athlete. Not at the caliber of Brad but good. I always thought he was uneasy with his role as one of the school's big shots."

"How so?"

"Just intuition after years working with kids. He always seemed embarrassed by the bullying that Brad dished out. He would laugh and wouldn't stop it, but he never initiated it or really joined in. It clearly made him uncomfortable, but he didn't have the courage to stop it. I was sad to hear about his death."

"He grew up to be a very good man."

Mrs. Purvis smiled. "I'm so glad to hear that. I saw him a few years after he graduated, and he seemed very happy. He was in college—which one escapes me right now—and he had met a girl that he was smitten with."

"He married her and had three kids." Jo's heart clenched as she remembered delivering the news of her husband's death to his wife. "They were happy. And she's in a complete daze right now." Jo wished she had an elixir to cure the pain for the new widow. She would also take it herself.

"Can you show me a picture of Joseph Telknap and Shannon VanDorn? I understand they were also students at the same time as Mr. Kramer and Mr. Wikstrom."

Bonnie's startled eyes shot to Jo's. "Dear God, Lieutenant, are they dead too?"

"I'm afraid so."

The woman's shaking hand went to her heart. "By the same hand?"

"There's no confirmation of that. We're just investigating all possibilities, following all leads, at this point."

Bonnie's eyes narrowed. "But you wouldn't be coming to me, asking me about these kids I knew so many years ago, if you didn't think there was a connection."

"There's no confirmation that their deaths are related, but we are looking into that possibility."

Mrs. Purvis crossed her arms. "That's politi-talk for 'We know this but aren't allowed to say it yet.'"

Jo gave her a half smile. "Are they in this yearbook?"

"They're in this *picture*," Bonnie replied.

So they were all friends. "Why don't we start with Joseph Telknap?"

"This is him," she said, pointing at a boy with dark hair and an olive complexion. He was more serious looking and stood a full head shorter than the other boys. "Joe was another good athlete, but he didn't appear to think it was his future. He had college plans that didn't include football. He took school seriously, where the others considered high school just another extension of their Friday-night lights."

"He was a mechanical engineer and doing very well," Kip said.

"I'm happy to hear that, at least, as sad as this all is," Bonnie replied.

"What about Shannon?" Jo asked.

Bonnie pointed at a pretty brunette wearing too much makeup. She had her arm slung around a boy's neck, her hip cocked jauntily to the side. "Shannon was a handful. She loved the spotlight. She also liked to cut down anyone who thought they could be a part of it. I'm curious where she ended up. I didn't hear anything about her after high school."

"I'm afraid her life didn't go in a positive direction," Jo said carefully.

The older woman ran her finger over the picture. "I'm not surprised."

"Who are the others?" Jo asked.

Bonnie pointed at each of the two remaining students. "Jana Ratliff and Jerry Kader. Jana was gregarious and smart—and very much in love with Brad Kramer. She was wherever he was, doing whatever he was doing."

Jo chuckled as she noted the two names in her notebook. "There's nothing sweeter than teen love. Or more nauseating." She gave in to her complete lack of cookie discipline and slid one of the thick chocolate chip cookies from the tray. When she took a bite, she barely suppressed a moan. "Sweet Jesus, is this legal?"

The older woman beamed. "They're my secret weapon. Keeps the grandkids coming around."

"Will you be my grandma?"

The prim woman let loose with a hearty laugh that surprised Jo and brought a broad grin to Kip's face.

Jo savored another bite then brought herself back to the job. "What about the boy? What did you say his name is?"

"Jerry Kader. He was a sweet boy, quiet and hardworking. I never thought he really fit in with that group. I think Amanda dragged him into it a bit. His death was such a shock to us all. We had counselors brought into the school to help the kids deal with it."

"Jerry Kader died in high school?"

Mrs. Purvis sighed heavily. "Suicide. It was such a tragedy. I don't think there was a single person there who saw it coming. I know none of the teachers did. You talk, you know, afterward, trying to wrap your mind around it. You wrack your brain to think if there was something you missed, something you should have done."

"And no one saw it coming?"

"We knew there was some tension in their little clique, and Jerry was on the outs with many of them the better half of his senior year. But nothing had escalated to a point that we worried about them. If I remember correctly, he was still spending time with Amanda and maybe Jana. It was the end of the year. Everyone was gearing up for finals and graduation. Counselors were frantically working with the kids who had waited until the last minute to decide they wanted to go to college. I'm afraid if there was anything we could have seen, we all missed it."

Jo had dealt with the aftermath of enough suicides to know that far too often the pain was well hidden. "Sometimes there isn't anything to see on the outside."

"You're right, and I know that. But I always wonder."

"Can you tell me how he died?"

The older woman shook her head slowly, gazing at the picture. "He hung himself, apparently in the woods behind their house. His father found him and was never quite the same."

Jo's blood ran cold. *Hung himself. Could there be a correlation? Was it really a suicide, or did our killer start something all those years ago that he's just now finishing?*

Kip leaned forward with his elbows on his knees and his hands clasped together. "Was there any suspicion around his death?"

The woman knitted her eyebrows. "What do you mean?"

"Any reason to believe it wasn't a suicide?"

Bonnie pursed her lips. "None that I ever heard. The police were involved, of course, but as far as I know, it wasn't considered anything other than a suicide."

Kip cocked his head. "Did he leave a note?"

"I don't know. That was a detail that I never found out, and it seemed crass to ask. I wasn't involved in the counseling, as it's not my specialty, so I wasn't privy to the details. I'm afraid I've told you all I know."

Jo had finished the last bite of her cookie while Kip asked his questions, so she took a final sip of her coffee and stood. "You've told us a great deal, and we appreciate your time. You remember those kids remarkably well. It will be my job to get to know the adults. They're in my hands now."

Bonnie stood and reached for Jo's hand. "Take good care of them then, Lieutenant."

"May I borrow the yearbook if I promise to return it to your collection when I'm done?"

Bonnie handed the book to Jo. "Of course." She picked up the plate of cookies. "And here, take a couple of cookies for the road."

Jo grinned. "I was hoping you would say that."

Chapter 16

J o parked the Ranger in the first open space she came to in the station's parking structure. Kip got out, and they met at the front of the truck.

As they walked to the station, Kip shoved his hands in his coat pockets and put his head down. "You never get used to it, do you? The cold, I mean."

Peering at him from under her fur-lined hood, she said, "My brain doesn't allow me to remember from year to year."

"It's even colder here than it is in Ohio," Kip said as he pulled open the heavy glass door of the station entrance.

As the warmth embraced Jo, she pulled her hands out of her pockets and blew on them. "We don't do anything half-assed in Michigan." She waved at Aneace as they walked past the front desk then glared when the receptionist wiggled her eyebrows at Kip's back. She could hear Aneace cackling as the doors closed and had to push back the grin that tried to surface. "I want to check in with Lynae before we get started."

"I'll just meet you in the conference room."

"Great. I'll be there in a few."

Jo jetted through the bull pen and made a beeline for Lynae's desk.

Looking up from her computer, Lynae said, "You look like you're on a mission. Did you get something from the principal?"

"You mean besides orgasmically good chocolate chip cookies? That is, if I remember correctly."

Lynae's jaw dropped. "You got cookies? Why does all the good stuff happen when I'm not there? Did you bring me one?"

"Actually..." Jo pulled the napkin-wrapped cookie out of her coat pocket.

"Oh my God! I love you." Lynae snatched the cookie out of Jo's hand and barely got the napkin unwrapped before taking a bite. "Apparently, you haven't forgotten, because you're dead right," she moaned before breaking off another piece. "It hasn't been that long for me."

"What hasn't been that long?"

Lynae flinched and coughed over the piece of cookie she had just popped into her mouth. Her face lit up as she looked over Jo's shoulder. "Dougie!"

Doug joined them and smiled shyly. "Hey."

"Hi, Doug," Jo said. "How's the detective exam studying going?"

When Doug raised his eyebrows at Lynae, she shrugged. "She figures stuff out. That's why she's the lieutenant."

Jo noticed he had one hand behind his back but decided not to say anything. Instead, she reached over and broke a piece off Lynae's cookie.

Glaring at her, Lynae pulled the cookie out of Jo's reach before turning back to the officer. "What brings you here?"

Doug pulled his hand from behind his back. He held out a package wrapped in bold blue paper with a white bow. "I just wanted to give you this."

Lynae's eyebrows knitted together. "You brought me a present?"

Doug stood with the package held out at arm's length. "Um, yeah. It's just..." Red crept up his neck.

Once she'd set the remainder of her cookie on the corner of her desk, Lynae pointed at Jo. "Don't even think about it." She wiped her hands on her pants then took the package from Doug. After opening the box and pulling back the white tissue paper, she gasped. "I can't believe you did this!"

Doug beamed. "You said you wanted one."

"I know, but..."

Jo peered over Lynae's shoulder. Lying in the box was a gear shifter custom designed with the Grand Valley State University Lakers' logo. "Must be from ShapeShifters. They do a great job with those," Jo said.

Lynae ran her hand over the logo. "Thank you. It's amazing. I don't know what to say."

Shoving his hands into his pockets, Doug said, "Maybe you'll say yes to dinner with me?"

Lynae's eyes softened. "Yeah, I'd like that."

His face lit up. "Really?" He cleared his throat. "I mean, um, cool. How about tonight?"

"Unless something breaks open with this case, tonight would be great."

"Can I pick you up at six?"

"Six? That won't give me much time to get changed."

He frowned. "What could you possibly need to change?"

Lynae shook her head, and a slight blush colored her cheeks. "Six o'clock it is." She laid a hand on his arm and held up the box in her other hand. "Thank you for this."

"You're welcome. I'll see you tonight." Doug walked to the elevator with a noticeable bounce in his step.

Lynae slipped the lid back on the box, set it on her desk, and picked up the remainder of the cookie. She turned around and glared at Jo. "Shut up."

"I didn't say a word," Jo said, holding up her hands.

"It's not a big deal. It's just dinner."

Jo looked pointedly at the box on Lynae's desk. "He's a good guy, Lynae."

"Maybe, maybe not. He won't be around long enough for me to find out."

Jo waved to her left. "Let's talk in my office."

Lynae huffed and followed Jo. Closing the door behind her, she said, "Don't make a big deal out of this."

Jo sat on the edge of her desk. "I'm not making a big deal out of it. But I know how badly you were hurt by your ex, and—"

Lynae stiffened. "I don't want to talk about Adam."

"Just give Doug a chance. Don't let an abusive ex keep you from ever giving another guy a chance to prove he's different."

"That's easy to say when you were married to Mr. Perfect."

"Who I now visit in the cemetery."

"What does—"

Jo held up her hand. "I'm sorry. That was reflex, and it has nothing to do with this. You're right. I haven't been through what you have, so it's easy for me to say. I just want you to give things a chance."

Looking away, Lynae said, "I know, and I will. It's just hard to trust anyone. Especially myself."

"Well, you have me now."

"I had people then too," Lynae mumbled.

"I'm sorry. I didn't mean to put a damper on your day."

"You didn't." Lynae folded her arms and gazed out the window. "I'm pretty good at ruining things all by myself."

Jo jabbed a finger at her. "Stop it. Just go and have dinner with a nice guy, and don't think any further than that. Give him a chance. Give yourself a chance."

"Can we talk about something else? Like what you got from the principal besides the best cookie I've ever eaten?"

Jo walked around her desk and dropped into her chair. "Mrs. Purvis has a phenomenal memory. She also has yearbooks from every year since she started her teaching career. All of our victims hung around together in high school. They were *the* clique."

Lynae slid into the visitor chair. "Damn. So they didn't just go to the same high school. They were friends."

"It gets better. One member of the clique allegedly committed suicide shortly before graduation."

"Let me guess. He hung himself."

"Bingo!"

"Any suspicion that it wasn't suicide?"

"None that the principal knew of." Jo pulled out her notebook and flipped to the page of notes she'd taken at Bonnie Purvis's house. "His name was Jerry Kader. We need to find his family and see if there was more to it than Mrs. Purvis knew."

Lynae held out her hand. "I can do the digging."

Scribbling the name on a sticky note, Jo said, "Find me a name and address, and Kip and I will do the visit. You knock off early to get ready for your date."

Lynae rolled her eyes as she stood. "We'll see." She walked to the door then looked over her shoulder. "I had friends when I dated Adam but not really a *best* friend."

Jo winked. "Now you do."

"Yeah, I do." She slipped out the door.

Jo picked up the picture of her and Mike that sat on her desk. Her arms were wrapped around his neck, her cheek pressed against his. "She deserves someone like you." She sighed and returned the picture to its spot, then she got up and headed for the conference room.

Kip was sitting at the table with his notes spread out in front of him. When he noticed her in the doorway, he said, "Four dead. And two within less than two weeks."

"He's escalating." Anxiety skittered through her belly like roaches. Four victims, three in *her* town. She couldn't let that monster take another one, but with the speed he was going, he probably already had someone.

"He's getting out of control, yet he's not leaving a trail."

"There's always a trail."

"You work your board up in a unique way," Kip commented, leaning back in his chair. He took a tentative sip from his steaming cup of coffee.

"It's how my mind works, which is a little scary to most."

"Can you explain it to me, or will I have nightmares?" Kip grinned, his eyes sparkling.

Cornflower blue. The thought darted across her mind, a habit from years of painting with her mother. She cleared her throat. "I think of a murder as a living organism that needs certain elements to survive. The killer is the nucleus. He's the central element, the control center, but he can't survive as a killer alone. There has to be a victim, there has to be a motive, there has to be a triggering moment, and there has to be background. Any missing element, and the nucleus dies, along with the person's choice to kill."

Kip set his coffee cup on the table. "Interesting. What about opportunity killings?"

"I see you in a dark alley. Victim. I need money, and I believe you have it. Motive." She ticked her points off on her fingers as she spoke. "No one is around, or you look at me wrong, or you take an extra step toward the wall because you don't like the way I look. Any one is a triggering moment."

"What about background?"

"How many people do you see in our line of work that come from wonderful families, were never abused in any way, or didn't get into drugs or gambling?"

"Not many."

"I had one recently, but it's unusual. Everyone has a background, and some will use it as an excuse to kill. Now, I've never dealt with a serial killer, so my board doesn't usually have so many lines from the nucleus. It may not work in this situation. But it's how *I* work. I don't know any other way to put a board together."

"Yeah, it works, but we still need to know the nucleus of our killer."

Jo snapped her fingers. "And we need to know the nucleus of our victims as well, since they're clearly related in some way. What's the common factor that puts them in our killer's path?"

Lynae poked her head through the doorway. "I've got good news and bad news."

"Hit me with the bad news first," Jo said.

"Jerry Kader's mother, Mrs. Eleanor Campbell, passed away six months ago, and the last address on file for his father, Charles Kader, is a long-term men's shelter." She walked in and handed Jo a picture of a gray-haired man with a scruffy, unkempt beard and dull hazel eyes. "I called the shelter, and Kader has been gone for more than two years."

"Living on the streets?"

"Most likely. There's no record of his death or of a change of address after the shelter."

Running a hand through her hair, Jo said, "Shit. We can canvass downtown, show his picture around. Maybe we'll get lucky, and someone will know where he is. What's the good news?"

Lynae handed her another photo. "Jerry Kader's parents were divorced for several years before his death, and his mother remarried. Jerry has a half-brother, Mark Campbell, who lives just outside of town."

Jo tapped the picture. "Here's where we start then."

"According to his employment record, he's an RN and works nights at a med center. This may be a good time of the day to catch him at home." Lynae held up a slip of paper. "I have his address."

Jo turned to Kip. "Would you like to go with us or take the time to go through my files?"

Kip leaned back in his chair. "I'm not up to speed on your victims, so I think it makes more sense for me to stay here."

"All right, we'll compare notes when we get back."

JO TOOK A TREE-LINED exit then drove down three back roads before they came full circle and were once again on the river in front of a coffee-with-cream-colored ranch-style house. She and Lynae took the sidewalk past the now-dying flower bed in front of an enormous picture window. When Jo rang the doorbell, frantic barking broke out inside.

A young man came to the door, wearing nothing but a pair of basketball shorts. He wiped away the sweat rolling down his face with a wadded-up T-shirt in his left hand. Flanking him were a pair of Labrador retrievers, one black and one yellow. Their vigorously wagging tails beat a constant rhythm on the entryway walls.

Jo eyed the dogs cautiously then looked up into the handsome face of their owner. "Mark Campbell?"

The man pushed the dogs away from the door. "Yes. And you are?"

Jo held up her badge. "Lieutenant Jo Riskin." She gestured at Lynae's also-raised badge. "And Detective Lynae Parker with the Grand Rapids Police Department."

Mark glanced at the badges then looked back at Jo. "What can I do for you?"

"We'd like to talk to you about your brother, Jerry."

Mark's face scrunched into a deep frown. "Sure, I guess, but I'm a mess. You caught me in the middle of a workout. Could you give me a minute to throw some clothes on?"

"Of course. Take your time."

Mark stepped back and waved them into the foyer. "Come on in. Never mind the dogs. They're completely useless as watchdogs."

Jo and Lynae moved into the foyer but went no farther. Experience had taught them that "completely useless" watchdogs could turn vicious when strangers wandered around their homes unattended. But the second Mark walked away, the black dog flopped to the floor in front of her and rolled on his back to expose his belly. The yellow one continued to thump her tail against the wall while nudging Lynae's hand with her head.

Chuckling, Jo squatted to give her new friend a belly rub. "These might possibly be the worst watchdogs in history."

"And I thought Mojo was bad," Lynae said, scratching behind the ears of the yellow one.

"Don't kid yourself. Mojo knows you. She'd rip your head off if she didn't."

Lynae snorted. "Okay. If that's your story."

Jo raised an eyebrow. "You should've seen her with Jack the other night. I didn't think she was going to let him in."

Lynae's mouth dropped open. "No way."

Mark Campbell returned, still wearing the same basketball shorts but with the addition of a navy-blue Under Armour hoodie. He stared down at his dogs and crossed his arms. "Seriously, guys? Where's your dignity? Your sense of responsibility?" He shook his head in mock disgust then snapped his fingers.

The dogs jumped to attention and came to his side.

"Go to your rooms," he said firmly with a dismissive wave. Both dogs hung their heads and slunk out of the room.

Jo smiled. "Well, they may not be the best watchdogs in the county, but they're well-behaved."

"They're good company, and that's about it." Mark gestured toward an adjacent room. "We can talk in here." He led the way to a small dining table with four high-back wood chairs. "Please, have a seat."

Jo and Lynae took seats on one side of the table, leaving Mark to slide aside a vase of flowers to face them across the table. Through the other doorway, Jo could see the two dogs in the next room, lying in side-by-side kennels, one happily chewing a rawhide while the other was curled up on a blanket.

"You said you want to talk about my brother? I don't understand. My brother has been dead for fifteen years."

Jo nodded. "I know, and I'm sorry." She could think of no easy way to ask what she needed to know, so she went with the direct approach. "Was there anything suspicious about your brother's death?"

Mark blinked slowly. "My brother committed suicide, Lieutenant. The only thing suspicious about it was that he was a supposedly happy, popular teenager who decided to hang himself."

"That must have been devastating for your family," Lynae said quietly.

Mark folded his hands on the table. "Yes, it was. I was twelve at the time, so a little too young to fully grasp it all, but it was very hard on my mom. I mean, I know it was on his dad, too, but I didn't live with him. I just know my mom never got over it."

"So you had the same mother?" Lynae asked.

"Yes. Our mom divorced his dad when Jerry was a baby. She married my dad when Jerry was five, and I came along shortly after that."

"Do you know Brad Kramer, Matthew Wikstrom, Joseph Telknap, or Shannon VanDorn?"

Chewing the inside of his lip, Mark furrowed his brow. "I remember the names Brad Kramer and Matt Wikstrom. They were good friends of my brother and always at our house. I was little and thought they were so cool. You know, high school guys. Jerry would let me hang out with them sometimes if they were at our house. I don't remember the other names, though. Were they friends of Jerry's too?"

"Yes, they were. They were part of the group your brother hung around with."

Mark shrugged. "Could be. That was a long time ago. But why are you asking questions about friends my brother had back in high school?"

Jo folded her hands on the table. "All four of those people are dead, and the only common link that we can find between them is that they were close friends in high school."

"And you asked if anything was suspicious about my brother's death. Do you think someone killed him? Is that what this is about?"

"At this point, we're just looking at all possibilities. There are links between the cases that we can't overlook."

Mark leaned back in his chair. "It would make more sense than suicide. I know his dad never believed he killed himself. For years, he would come banging around when he was drunk, saying stuff like 'They killed him. Those bastards killed him.'"

"Did he ever say who he thought killed your brother?"

"No, he always just said 'they.' My mom would cry and threaten to call the police." Mark squeezed his eyes shut. "I wasn't sorry when those visits stopped."

"I'm sorry. That must have been very hard on all of you," Jo said softly.

Mark started chewing his fingernail then stopped and slid his hand under his leg. "It was hard, especially on my mom. She never got over it."

"We weren't able to locate an address for your stepfather," Lynae said. "Do you know where we can find him?"

Mark shrugged. "I see him at the mobile methadone clinic where I volunteer sometimes. And once in a while, he stands at the corner of Brookside and Aspen with a sign."

Jo jotted *Brookside and Aspen* in her notebook. "Mr. Kader is homeless?"

"I assume so. He holds a sign that says Homeless Veteran. From what my mom said, he has mental health issues. She never said what they were exactly, but I know everything got worse after Jerry died. Before that, Charlie had a job, paid child support, the whole deal." Mark shrugged. "Maybe he stopped taking his medication or started in with the drugs. I don't know."

Jo pulled a folder out of her bag, took out the picture Lynae had printed of Charles Kader, and slid it across the table. "This is the only photo we have of Jerry's father."

After studying the picture for a few seconds, Mark said, "His hair is longer now, but otherwise, he looks the same. He carries a little dog, usually has it inside his coat with just its head sticking out. He's pretty hard to miss."

"Thank you. That's very helpful." Jo returned the picture back into her bag. "We would also like to speak to *your* father. Is he still in the area?"

"My dad died in a car accident when I was three. I don't even remember him."

"I'm very sorry to hear you recently lost your mother," Lynae said.

Mark closed his eyes and pressed his lips together. "Thank you. She's finally at peace." He opened his eyes and brusquely pushed his chair back. "Is there anything else? I should be getting ready for work." He stood up and stepped behind his chair. The dogs trotted into the room to stand beside their master. Mark dropped a hand on each of their heads without looking down.

Jo got to her feet. "Thank you for your time, Mark."

"You're welcome. I assume if you have any news that involves my brother, you'll be in touch."

Lynae nodded. "Absolutely."

"If you think of anything that may help," Jo said, handing him her card, "please let us know."

Mark took the card. "I can't imagine what that would be, but of course."

"We appreciate it. We'll show ourselves out."

The dogs trotted beside Jo and Lynae as they walked through the foyer. Jo gave each of them a good scratch on the head. Their bodies swayed as their heavy tails swung from side to side.

Jo snorted and shook her head. "You really are the worst watchdogs I've ever met."

When they reached the truck, Lynae glanced over her shoulder before sliding into the passenger seat. "He's watching us through the window."

Jo looked up at the house as she started the engine. The curtain in the front window swayed. "I'm sure we brought up a lot of terrible memories for him."

"I hope he has someone."

As she backed the Ranger out of the driveway, Jo said, "He wasn't wearing a wedding ring, but there were flowers on the table. There's a pretty good chance a guy isn't going to buy flowers unless there's a woman in the house."

"Yeah, good point. Next stop, Charles Kader at Brookside and Aspen?"

Jo checked her watch. "I think we have time to see if he's at his post."

"Plenty of time. And if we have to ask around a bit, I'll just cancel my plans."

"Nope, not happening. You are having your date with Doug."

Lynae rolled her eyes but looked pleased. "Whatever. What if Kader says, 'I killed those people. Arrest me.'?"

"I think I can handle that all by myself. Besides, I have Kip."

Lynae grinned. "And who wouldn't like to have Kip?"

"I was all in after just hearing his sexy voice. Then he walked in, and I saw that face and that body." Jo whistled.

Lynae's mouth dropped open. "You actually noticed?"

"Well, my eyes aren't painted on."

"Don't let Jack see you drooling over our friendly detective."

"Whatever." Jo cranked up the radio. "Let's just listen to Garth."

They spent the fifteen-minute drive back to downtown Grand Rapids singing Garth Brooks songs and talking about the concert. Jo exited the highway, drove down Brookside Street, and parked beside a meter.

Lynae gave her a questioning look. "What are we doing?"

"We're two blocks from Aspen. If he's not there, we're going to have to ask around. It's easier if we're on foot." Jo opened her purse and pulled out her wallet, a handful of receipts, and a pack of Kleenex.

"But it's so cold."

Jo scraped all the change from the bottom of her purse and sorted out six quarters. She dropped the rest back in, along with everything else she had pulled out. "You're such a baby. How did you survive patrol?"

"Lots and lots of coffee," Lynae said, putting on a pink stocking cap.

They got out of the car and walked to the parking meter.

"There's a Biggby's right around the corner. If you stop whining, I'll buy you a cup of coffee on the way back."

Lynae smacked her lips. "I'm feeling kind of hot chocolatey today."

"I'll get you hot chocolate then," Jo mumbled, slipping quarters into the meter.

"I guess I can suck it up then."

Shoving her hands into her coat pockets, Jo said, "It's funny that you think you have a choice."

Lynae huffed and matched Jo's stride as they headed down the sidewalk. They showed Mr. Kader's picture to people on every street corner in an eight-block radius. Most of the sign-wielding patrons recognized him, but no one could tell them where he was. Working their way back to their starting point, they came across a slim man with a full beard standing on the corner two blocks from where they had parked. He held a cardboard sign that read Homeless and Hungry. He stepped up to the window of a dark SUV and accepted a bill someone handed him through the window.

"That guy wasn't there before," Lynae mumbled through the scarf over her mouth. "Think it could be him?"

Jo shook her head. "He's too young, but he might be able to help us."

When they approached, the man backed away. "You're cops. I'm not hurting anyone. I'm just hungry."

Jo smiled. "We're not here to bust you. What's your name?"

The man stopped but continued looking at her warily. "I'm William, but everyone calls me Buddy."

She held out the picture of Charles Kader. "Can you tell me if you've seen this man, Buddy?"

Buddy squinted for a few seconds then nodded. "That's Charlie. He was just here. He got a few bucks and went to get coffee."

"Where does he get his coffee?"

Pointing down the block, Buddy said, "He usually goes to that Sunoco station down there."

"All right. We'll try to connect with him there. If we miss him, do you know where he stays?"

Buddy gestured back toward the highway. "He usually crashes under that bridge. Or sometimes at St. Vincent if there aren't too many people. He doesn't like people much."

Jo knew the underpass he was referring to since it often had a couple of people sleeping there at night. "Good to know."

Buddy held out his hand. "How about a few bucks for the help?"

Jo eyed his sign. "We're not too far from Electric Hero. How about I buy you lunch?"

Buddy folded his cardboard sign and shoved it into the Meijer grocery bag at his feet. "I haven't had a good hot sandwich in a while."

"Well, Electric Hero has the best in town." Jo handed some cash and her car keys to Lynae. "Why don't you and Buddy go get a sandwich. Afterward, you can get the truck and meet me at Sunoco."

Lynae nodded. "You got it."

Jo held out her hand. "Thank you, Buddy. You've been very helpful."

Buddy broke into a wide smile and shook her hand. Jo hoped he would be able to eat a sub with the majority of his upper teeth missing.

The Sunoco station was three blocks away. Jo walked as fast as she could without actually breaking into a jog since she feared scaring Charlie if he saw her running.

She pulled open the wide glass door to the convenience station and immediately zeroed in on a man wearing an army-green jacket and a mud-brown stocking cap. He stood in front of the coffee pots, emptying packets of sugar into a twenty-four-ounce cup. Jo strolled over and grabbed a sixteen-ounce cup. She casually glanced over at the man and saw a brown tuft of hair poking out of the front of his coat. *That's my guy.*

The man caught her look and turned his body away from her.

Jo took a step closer and poured coffee into her cup. "Looks like you've got a little friend here with you."

He lowered his head. "She's not hurting anything being in here."

"Of course she isn't. What's her name?"

He finally turned and looked at Jo. "Maggie."

"I bet Maggie could use a treat. My dog loves the peanut butter dog biscuits they sell at the counter."

Shaking his head, he said, "They cost too much."

"I'd be happy to buy her one."

"Why?"

Jo peered at the little face peeking out of the jacket. "Because I love dogs. I bet you take very good care of her."

The man's face softened. He wrapped his hand protectively around the front of his coat. "I do. She's my only friend."

"Well, in my experience, dogs are much better friends than people. Will you let me buy her a treat?"

He gave an almost imperceptible nod then grabbed his coffee and turned abruptly to walk to the register. Jo slapped a lid on her cup and followed him. She snatched a couple granola bars, a bag of chips, and five dog biscuits from the box on the counter then pulled her debit card out and handed it to the cashier. As soon as the cashier finished bagging the items, Charlie snatched the bag and strode out the door.

Jo quickly grabbed her stuff and trotted out behind him. "Mr. Kader, I'd like to talk to you a minute."

He stopped and spun around to glare at her. "How do you know my name?"

"I'd like to ask you a few questions about your son, Jerry."

Charlie's dark eyes narrowed until they almost disappeared into his cheeks. The paper sack fell from his hand. "Jerry?"

She picked up the sack and held it out to him. "I just have a few questions."

He snatched the bag out of her hand. "Jerry's dead. He's been dead a long time."

"Why don't we sit down?" Jo pointed at a covered bus stop bench.

He nodded but, instead of going to the bench, he sat on the sidewalk with his back against the gas station wall. Jo dropped down beside him and pulled her legs up close to her body in an effort to retain some body heat while sitting on the cold concrete. Charlie pulled one of the dog biscuits out of the sack and unzipped his jacket a few inches. The tiny mutt poked her head out, took a sniff, then snatched the biscuit and hunkered back down inside her cozy coat home. His coat swayed from what must have been her tail attempting to wag in the confined space.

Charlie picked up his coffee cup, held it in his gloved hands, and stared straight ahead. "I don't like to think about Jerry."

"I understand, and I'm sorry that I have to pick at a healed wound."

The man wrapped one hand protectively around his body. "Some wounds never heal."

I was afraid of that. Jo turned slightly toward him. "Can you tell me about Jerry's death?"

"Why are you asking this now? No one wanted to hear what I had to say about it fifteen years ago. Everyone said I was crazy."

"I'm sorry about that. Jerry's brother said you didn't think Jerry killed himself."

"You talked to Mark? I wondered how he's been doing since his mom died. He didn't handle it real well when Jerry died."

"Were Mark and Jerry close?" Jo asked.

"Mark practically worshipped Jerry. You know, the cool older brother. Jerry said he was always tagging along behind him, wanting to hang out with him and his friends. He even tried to come along when I would take Jerry for my weekends."

Jo smiled. "Little brothers have a way of driving their big brothers crazy."

"Jerry loved that kid, though. He was real good with him."

A little black nose poked out from inside Charlie's coat. He reached down and gently rubbed the dog's head. He slid his eyes back to Jo. "You know Mark's dad died."

Jo nodded. "I heard."

"It was real sad. I can admit now that he was a much better dad than I was. He was good to my Jerry. I doubt that Mark remembers him. I think he kind of looked at Jerry like a father as much as a brother."

"It must have been very hard on him when Jerry died. You said he didn't handle it well?"

"I shouldn't have said that. I didn't live with him, so I don't know. I just thought as close as they were, it was strange that he didn't come to Jerry's funeral."

"Funerals can be very hard for kids. Maybe his mom didn't want to put him through it."

Charlie shrugged. "Could be. But if it was in a church, she always wanted the kids to be there."

"Mark said his mom never recovered from Jerry's suicide."

"Suicide," he scoffed.

"You don't believe he committed suicide?"

Charlie threw his hands in the air. "His so-called friends made up lies about him and spread them around. They told everyone he was gay. You ask me, they might as well have put the rope around his neck themselves."

"So they didn't actually—"

He glared at her. "They killed him." He leaned his head against the white cinder-block building and closed his eyes. "They were his friends, and they killed him."

Jo sat silently for a moment, absorbing the new information. When her Ranger pulled into the parking lot, she caught Lynae's eye and shook her head. Lynae turned and parked at the end of the building in a spot where Jo could still see her.

Jo took a sip of her coffee then spoke quietly. "You said they made up lies. You don't believe your son was gay?"

Charlie jumped to his feet. "No son of mine was a queer."

Well, if he was gay, he knew he couldn't count on his dad for support. Lynae jumped out of the truck, so Jo discreetly held up her hand as she got to her feet. "So his friends made up this lie about him. Why would they do that to their friend?"

Holding the dog in place through his coat, Charlie bent down and grabbed the bag and his coffee. "Kids are mean. *People* are mean."

Jo laid a hand on his arm. "Four of the people who you believe killed your son are dead. Murdered."

The man looked down at her hand then shrugged it away. "They deserve whatever they get."

An eye for an eye. "Mr. Kader—"

"I don't have anything else to say." He turned and shuffled toward the bus stop, head lowered against the cold.

Jo walked across the parking lot and slid into the passenger seat of the Ranger. "Mr. Kader was a nice man to talk to until I brought up Jerry's friends. He has an enormous amount of hate built up for our victims."

Lynae started the truck. "Does he still believe they killed his son?"

"In a way. According to him, his friends made up the lie that Jerry was gay and spread it around the school, which drove Jerry to kill himself."

"Why would his friends do that?"

Jo shrugged. "Kids are mean."

Lynae gestured toward Charlie, who had gone over to the bus stop. "He's got motive. Why are you letting him walk away?"

"I don't have anything to arrest him on. He's got plenty of motive, but what about means? How's a homeless man going to get around the way our killer needs to?"

Lynae drummed her hands on the steering wheel as she waited for a GRAM bus to pull over to its stop. "That's a bit of a roadblock, but it would be easy for a homeless man to disappear periodically without anyone noticing."

"That's true. No one really keeps track of the homeless."

Jo looked out the window and watched Mr. Kader climb into the bus. "How much of Grand Rapids does the Metro bus cover?"

"I'm not positive, but I think the greater Grand Rapids area. Why?"

"Mr. Kader just got on it."

Lynae slapped the wheel. "There's your *means*."

"I'm going to look into him. He's anti-social, and his temper flared quickly when the subject of his son's sexuality came up. He could have stewed all these years about those kids making up that *lie* about his son." Jo took a cautious sip from the Sunoco cup, mindful of the steam coming through the small opening. "We need to take a closer look at anyone else in that little clique, the ones who are still alive, anyway. Maybe someone else had motive as well. I got the names from Mrs. Purvis."

"I can do a little research tonight on that group."

Jo smirked. "Nice try. I'll do the research, and I can put Kip or Isaac on it as well. You have plans."

"Just trying to help."

When they reached the station, Jo said, "Don't even come in. You'll get roped into something."

"Yeah, you're probably right. Call me if you find anything tonight. I'll be in early tomorrow."

"Have fun. And tomorrow, you *will* give me all of the details."

Lynae raised her eyebrows. "We'll see about that."

They both got out of the truck, and Jo watched Lynae drive away in her car, just to make sure her partner didn't try to sneak back to work. Then she turned and headed into the station. She found Kip in the conference room, hunched over her files, coffee cup in hand. Two empty bags of potato chips lay crumpled on the table. "How goes the battle, Detective?"

Kip looked over his shoulder, and his face broke into a warm smile. "I've been over every note in your files." He held up a legal pad. "And compared them to mine."

Jo sat down next to him. "You've been busy."

Kip slid his chair closer and pushed the legal pad over in front of her. As she started to read, he slung his arm on the back of her chair. She became intensely aware of how near he was when she felt his breath on her cheek.

"Hey, Jo, I—"

She turned her head and saw Jack jerk to a stop in the doorway. He stared at Kip's arm.

Jo smiled. "Hi."

Kip stood up and extended his hand. "Kip Jurgens, Toledo Homicide."

After a moment of hesitation, Jack gripped Kip's hand and gave it one pump before letting go. "Jack Riley. What brings you to GR, Kip?"

"Kip has a homicide related to our hangings," Jo said. "He came for the day with his case notes so we could put our resources together."

Jack raised an eyebrow. "In Toledo? Interesting. And you're sure they're related?"

"We've only begun the process. It could take a while to prove the connection, but there's no doubt in my mind," Kip said.

"So you drove all the way here to compare notes?"

"I find it usually helps to lay all the evidence out physically." Cocking his head, Kip asked, "Are you a detective, Jack?"

Jack puffed out his chest a little. "Assistant Prosecuting Attorney."

Kip nodded. "So you may not quite understand."

"Oh, I think I do."

Jo started to get irritated at their little male-dominance dance, and she decided to jump in before it escalated into more. "So, Jack, do you have something for me?"

"Oh, yeah. Nothing to do with your case, though. It's personal." He gave Kip a pointed look before turning back to Jo. "Can you give me a call later when you're done with *work*?"

Kip made a show of checking his watch. "You know, it's later than I thought. Why don't I buy you dinner, Jo? We can look over my notes, and you can fill me in on your interview with Mr. Campbell."

Jo snuck a glance at Jack, who was leaning against the wall and making the floor tiles his top priority. "Yeah, okay. Let me get my stuff together."

Jack pushed away from the wall and grabbed the doorknob. "You'll call me when you get home from dinner then?"

Jo nodded and gave him a smile. "Sure."

Jack shot Kip an inscrutable look then walked out the door.

Chapter 17

Jo sipped a cup of coffee while watching the morning news with Mojo sprawled out beside her on the sofa. When her phone rang, she cringed and prayed that it wasn't Dispatch. *Just give me a little more time.*

Grabbing the phone from the end table, she checked the caller ID and heaved a sigh of relief. "Good morning, Jack."

"Good morning."

"Sorry I didn't call you last night. It was pretty late when I got home."

"So I take it you had a good time with Kip?" Jack said the name as if it were poison on his tongue.

"It was a nice dinner. We were able to—"

"Did you go out for drinks?"

She took a sip of coffee and pulled her legs up underneath herself. "He suggested it, but—"

"Of course he did."

"You gonna let me finish a sentence here?"

"What kind of name is Kip, anyway?"

Jo set down her coffee then pulled the phone from her shoulder and eyed the caller ID. *Yep, this is actually Jack acting like this.* "The kind of name his parents gave him."

"Is it short for something, or is it just Kip?"

"I didn't ask him. If you would like to give him a call and discuss his name, I could give you his number." She dropped her hand onto Mojo's head and scratched behind her ear. The furball flopped onto her back and stretched to her full length, exposing her belly. Jo rolled her eyes and gave her a rub.

"You have his number?"

"Of course I do. We're collaborating on a case. What the hell is your problem with Kip?"

"I don't trust him."

She jumped to her feet. "You spent three minutes with him, and you don't trust him? He's not a suspect, Jack. He's a detective helping with my current investigation." Mojo bounded off the sofa and ran from window to window, eager to discover what had her human so agitated.

"I'm well aware."

"You don't trust him about what?" She walked toward her room to gather her things.

"It doesn't matter. He was only here for the day, anyway. Although he took full advantage of that, didn't he?"

"I'm not sure what that's supposed to mean, but if you're referring to our productive talk at dinner, then you're right. He's a good detective who had solid information to add to my case." Storming into the kitchen, she flung her bag onto the counter a little too hard. The canvas tote slid across the Formica and dropped onto the floor, scattering the contents across the tile.

"Fantastic." His voice dripped with sarcasm.

"Did you want to talk to me about something other than Kip and your psychic powers regarding his trustworthiness?" Jo dropped to her knees to pick up the spilled stuff.

"No, I guess that's it."

"What about the *personal something* you came by to see me about?"

"I just wanted to see if you'd had dinner yet or if you had any plans to actually eat something other than a frozen meal and Diet Coke. I know how you get."

"That was nice of you. Why didn't you say so? We could have had dinner together."

"Seems to me you were well taken care of for dinner."

She bristled. "I had a business dinner with a colleague. Was I supposed to get your *permission* first?"

"I didn't say that."

"Well, you're sure acting that way." She sighed. "Look, I don't know what's happening between us, but you acting like this isn't going to work for me."

"I'm not acting like anything. I just called for—"

"For what? To check up on me? To see if I was alone? See if I decided to hop into the sack with the guy I just met yesterday? Because, you know, that's so me." She shoved the papers into her bag. She could hear them crinkle, a sound that would normally have her pulling them back out to straighten them, but at that moment, she didn't care.

"Now you're just being ridiculous."

"Am I? Then what's with the interrogation?" Mojo trotted in and dropped her ball at Jo's feet. Jo picked it up and chucked it hard into the next room. She heard it thud against a door. Mojo's nails skittered across the laminate floor as she ran after her toy.

"I just... never mind."

Jo pinched the bridge of her nose. "I think we need to end this conversation. I'll talk to you later." She disconnected without waiting for an answer then shoved the phone into her pocket.

On the way to work, she tried to focus on the case, but her conversation with Jack kept clawing its way to the surface. She worked in a male-dominated profession, and he had never seemed to have a problem with her having business lunches with any other men. *What's different about Kip that's making Jack act so strange?*

Kip was definitely handsome and engaging, and she enjoyed spending time with him. Their dinner had been not only productive but fun. She felt a pang of disappointment that he had gone back to Ohio, and she intended to keep in touch, at least for the duration of the case.

Am I attracted to him? Does Jack see something that I don't? It was disconcerting that she didn't know the answer, but she didn't have time to dwell on it. She had a case to solve, and her personal life had no business getting in the way.

As she got onto the highway, she forced every thought other than her four homicides to the back of her brain. The case was huge, and it had to be handled with pinpoint focus, not scattered between personal issues.

She parked in her usual spot in the parking garage, and before she could get out of the truck, Lynae pulled in next to her.

Her partner hopped out of her car and jogged over. "Morning, boss lady."

"Well, aren't you chipper this morning," Jo said as she got out of her truck.

Lynae shoved her hands in her pockets and rocked back on her heels. "I don't know what you're talking about."

Cocking an eyebrow, Jo gave her the once-over. "I take it your date with Doug went well."

"Yeah, it was... nice." Lynae skipped down the concrete stairs and rounded the corner to head outside.

Walking beside her in a more sedate fashion, Jo asked, "Where did he take you for dinner?"

"Well, um, his place."

Jo gave Lynae a flat look. "Seriously?"

"It wasn't like that. He made eggplant parmesan and garlic bread. He can really cook. And we took his dog, Morgan, for a walk."

"That does sound nice. Who knew that Doug could cook?"

Lynae's head shot up, a grin spread across her face. "Right? I was shocked."

"What kind of dog does he have?"

Lynae slapped her leg. "The craziest dog you'll ever meet. It's a huge shaggy mutt from the pound. He's obsessed with this hockey puck he carries around all the time, even on walks. Then he drops it and wants you to throw it, but it's covered in slobber, the same slobber that's constantly dripping from the side of his mouth."

Jo laughed. "Sounds like a real charmer. I can see why Doug couldn't resist him."

"I think he felt sorry for him and figured no one else would take him. But honestly, you can't help but like the mutt. He'll drive you crazy, but he's loyal and a lot of fun. He'd probably calm down if he was trained, but Doug's just a big softie."

Jo decided to let the "big softie" comment go and not tease her partner. "And why Morgan? That's an unusual name for a dog."

Lynae shouldered open the station door and motioned for Jo to go ahead. "The name came with him. Doug thinks it was probably Captain Morgan, but who knows?"

"Next time you're there, call him Captain and see if he responds." Jo gave Aneace a wave on the way to the elevator. After they stepped inside, she noticed Lynae had gotten quiet. She leaned over and bumped Lynae's shoulder. "Hey, you still in there?"

Lynae stared at the floor indicator. "Doug asked me to go to a wedding with him next weekend. It's at Rustic Rouge."

"That sounds like fun."

Lynae pulled off her gloves and hat and shoved them into her bag. She smoothed her hair back with her hands and expertly wrapped it into a messy bun secured with a band she pulled from her wrist. "I told him no."

"Why? It sounds like you had a good time."

"I told him I didn't think we should see each other again."

"He's a nice guy, Nae."

When the elevator doors opened, Lynae mumbled, "So was Adam," then marched to her desk.

Jo rushed to catch up to her. "Let's talk in my office."

Lynae flung her coat over the back of her chair then put on a broad smile. "I'm good, Jo. I had a really nice night, and that's enough. You said yourself that I'm chipper this morning."

"Nae—" Jo heard her desk phone ringing.

"Better get that," Lynae said as she flopped into her chair.

"And you call me stubborn," Jo grumbled. She jogged to her office and caught the phone on the last ring. "Riskin."

"Lieutenant Riskin, this is Sergeant Hoskins with Missing Persons."

"What can I do for you, Sergeant?"

"I just took a call from a man whose wife is missing."

Jo walked the rest of the way around her desk and sat down. "I'm Homicide, Sergeant. What's this got to do with me?"

"I understand, Lieutenant, but the call that came in was on a Mrs. Amanda Reed."

"I know that name." She reached into her bag and fumbled through the contents, berating herself for not organizing the mess.

"Her husband called and was freaking out because in the last three weeks, he and his wife have gone to funerals for two of her closest friends from high school, and now she's missing."

Jo pulled out her notebook and flipped to the page marked "Mrs. Purvis – Principal." *Amanda Chatman, now Reed. She was part of that group.* "How long has she been missing?"

"About twelve hours. She was last seen leaving choir practice at St. Andrew's at eight o'clock last night. Apparently, the husband tried to call it in around midnight, but you know how that goes."

"Yeah. Not long enough for a missing adult."

"Right, not even close. He was told he had to wait twenty-four hours, but he called again this morning. When he told me about the funerals, I thought I better take the information and get in touch with you."

"I'm glad you did. What do you know about the wife?"

"Amanda Reed, age thirty-three, married with two kids. Pillar of the community. She volunteers at Our Daily Bread and at her kids' school, and she sings in the church choir. You name it, she does it, as long as it's upstanding and generous. Everybody loves her, and nobody would want to hurt her."

Jo rubbed her forehead. "Any reason to believe she could have just taken off?"

"The husband says no, but most of them say that. A pillar of the community runs off with another pillar after choir practice. Nobody sees it coming. Stranger things have happened, and it wouldn't be the first time."

"Anything is possible, but that would be one huge coincidence. Did anybody see anything unusual?"

"One of the women saw her talking to a man that she didn't recognize, but she said Amanda looked comfortable and even waved as she was leaving. The witness didn't get a great look at the guy because he was wearing a stocking cap pulled low."

Jo sat up straighter. "Medium build, mid-length coat?"

"Exactly."

Jo slammed her hand on the desk. "Shit, shit, shit!"

"We're going to be looking for a body, aren't we?"

"Not if I can help it. I can't start a homicide investigation without a body, but I want to talk to the husband."

"He's on his way in right now."

Jo slapped her notebook closed and dropped it back into her bag. "I'm on my way."

She took the stairs down a flight and jogged to Missing Persons.

Hoskins stood as she approached his desk. "I just got a call from the front desk. Mr. Reed is on his way up."

The elevator doors opened, and a tall, heavyset man stepped out. His eyes darted around the bull pen.

Jo leaned toward Hoskins. "Let's not mention I'm with Homicide."

"Gee, you think?" He pushed away from his desk and strode over to meet the man. "Mr. Reed?"

The man's head bobbed. He twisted a pair of ski gloves between his hands. "My wife. She didn't come home last night."

"I'm Sergeant Hoskins. We spoke on the phone." Hoskins motioned toward the hallway. "Why don't we sit down? Can I get you a cup of coffee or some water?"

"No. Maybe water... coffee. Shit, I don't know. Never mind." He shoved the gloves into the pocket of his down coat.

Hoskins pointed at Jo. "This is Lieutenant Riskin. I made her aware of the case, and she's going to join us."

Mr. Reed glanced over his shoulder and gave Jo a cursory nod. As she followed the two men past the coffee station, she looked longingly at the full pot but didn't stop.

Hoskins stopped at an empty meeting room and flipped on the light. "Have a seat, Mr. Reed."

The big man dropped into one of the small plastic chairs around the white table. "Tom. My name's Tom."

Jo and Sergeant Hoskins took seats next to each other across the table from the anxious man.

Hoskins took out a notebook. "Okay, Tom. Let's get right to it. Your wife didn't come home last night, right?"

Tom rubbed his hands on his thighs. "She had choir practice, just like every Monday night. She usually gets home about eight fifteen, eight thirty. Sometimes, she ends up standing around talking afterward and gets home a little later, but never past nine."

"So what did you do when she wasn't home by nine?"

"I got worried, but you know, she's a big girl. I didn't want to check up on her right away. It was about nine thirty before I tried to call her. Then when she didn't answer, I got more worried."

"Did you try calling her friends or someone else?"

Tom nodded eagerly. "I called all the people in the choir. Mandy has a list of everyone and their phone numbers, and I went right through it and called them all."

"And these people from the choir indicated that she had been at practice that night?"

"Yes, she was there. I tried calling the police after I talked to everyone in the choir, but you guys wouldn't do anything."

"I understand that's frustrating. What about family or other friends?"

Tom ran both hands through his thinning black hair. "After I called the police, I started calling anyone I could think of. Nobody's seen her."

"Has this ever happened before?"

"No, never. Mandy doesn't just not come home."

The sergeant gave him a sympathetic look. "I'm sorry to have to ask, but are the two of you having any problems? Is it possible there's another man involved?"

Tom huffed. "No. We're not having any problems. She didn't just decide not to come home, and there isn't another man. I wouldn't be sitting here if I thought she had left me." His volume rose with each point.

"I'm sure you wouldn't, but most of the time when adults are missing, it's because they choose to be."

Mr. Reed slapped the table. "She didn't *choose* to be gone! Something happened to her." He leaned forward and blinked rapidly as tears flooded his eyes. "You don't know Mandy. She wouldn't do this to me."

Jo laid her hand over the clenched hands of the distraught man. "We have to ask these questions. We'll do everything we can to find your wife."

He swiped at his eyes. "Three people she knows have been murdered in the last month. We figured they were involved in something together, like drugs, maybe. We heard Shannon was a prostitute, so we thought maybe it had something to do with that. But what if that wasn't it? It scares the hell out of me."

"Did Amanda ever mention any other reason someone would target her friends?" Jo asked.

He shook his head. "No. She thought it was odd because Matt was a good guy. She could never see him getting into something illegal, but you know, you don't always know someone like you think you do."

"I don't want to upset you any more than you already are, Tom, but there have actually been four victims. Mr. Telknap, who was also a part of the group your wife hung around with in high school, was murdered almost four months ago."

"Oh my God, this is really happening. You think whoever killed the rest of them has Mandy."

"We don't know that for certain," Jo said gently.

He slammed a hand on the table. "Where the hell else would she be?" He shook his head. "Sorry, that doesn't help."

"It's okay. We understand. Did Amanda ever mention a Jerry Kader?"

Tom's head snapped up. "Oh yeah, I know that name. But he's dead. Mandy takes flowers to his grave every year."

"Really? After all this time?"

Tom nodded. "She feels like she failed him. She never really got over it."

"Failed him how?"

"I don't know the whole story, but from what I remember, one of the guys saw him with a guy, like, you know, *with* a guy. And he told one of the girls, who spread it all over the school. You know how high school is. After that, Jerry's life was hell. All of the guys he hung around with turned on him. Then his dad found out, and that was bad. He ended up hanging himself in the woods behind their house."

"Did Amanda turn on him also?" Hoskins asked.

Tom sighed. "My wife was raised in a very religious household. Her uncle was a priest, and their whole family was super strict. At the time, she believed Jerry would go to hell for being gay. She tried to talk to him about God and how being gay was a sin." He spread his thick hands. "She thought she was helping him. She really did. At the class reunion last year, Mandy collected money to buy some trees to plant around the high school in Jerry's name. All of Jerry's old friends got together and planted them one Saturday."

"That was a nice gesture. Did Jerry's family know they did that?"

"Mandy had someone take a picture of all of them, and she sent it to Jerry's mom with a note."

"Did the news cover it?"

"I don't think so. It was kind of a small event."

"You said it was bad when his father found out Jerry was gay. What happened?"

"I don't know exactly. I wasn't around then. Mandy just said his dad was really bad about it. He was a big, tough guy, and having a gay son just wasn't acceptable for him. The dad always claimed it wasn't true, you know, that Jerry wasn't gay. He said people were spreading lies about him." He rubbed his hands over his face. "Is any of this going to help you find Mandy?"

"I think it will."

"What do we do now?"

Jo nodded at Hoskins. "Sergeant Hoskins and his team will work with my partner and me. We're going to make the assumption that your wife's disappearance may be related to our cases."

Tom dropped his head into his hands. His shoulders shook.

After giving him a minute, Jo said, "I'm going to leave you with the sergeant since he and his team are the Missing Persons experts. When he has everything he needs from you, he'll contact me, and we'll collaborate." She slid her chair back and stood. "Tom, we're going to put every possible resource we have into finding your wife. I promise you none of us will rest until we do." Jo looked up at Hoskins and raised her eyebrows.

Hoskins nodded. "Mr. Reed, let's start with the people in the choir. Did you bring that list with you?"

The man sniffed and pulled a piece of paper from his pocket. Holding it out, he said, "I wrote in some of her other friends' information at the bottom."

"That's great, Tom. This is very helpful." Hoskins took the list and stood. "I'm going to go make a copy of this. I'll be right back." He walked out into the hallway with Jo. "So much for not mentioning homicide," he said.

"I'm sorry, but I believe we're under a serious time constraint. We need anything we can get from him. Let me know if you get anything useful." Without waiting for a response, she turned and strode toward the stairwell.

Chapter 18

J o pulled out her phone and punched in Lynae's number. As soon
as her partner answered, Jo said, "I need a couple people to pick
up Charles Kader. See who's available and have them come see me."

"Will do. What's going on?"

"We have a missing person connected to our vics."

"Shit!"

"My thoughts exactly."

"Did something new come out on Kader?"

Jo rounded a flight of stairs and hit the next one at full speed.
"No, but he's all I've got right now, and I want to press him a little."

"What about the brother?"

"You and I should go see him again this morning. He was young,
but he's a connection. Maybe if we press him, he'll remember something. Shit, I don't know. Meet me in the conference room, and we'll
make out a game plan." She disconnected and slid the phone back into her pocket.

After pushing through the door of the conference room, she
skidded to a stop. Kip was sitting in a chair at the end of the table.

He looked up from the Crestwood High yearbook in his hands.
"Morning, Lieutenant."

"What are you doing here? I thought you were heading home
last night."

"I decided it was too late to make the drive, especially since I'd
had a couple of drinks."

She was oddly comforted by his presence. "Good, I can use you
for another day."

"At your service, ma'am."

She nodded at the yearbook. "Find anything interesting in there?"

"Just a reminder that I didn't particularly love high school."

"Now, I would have thought you ruled your high school."

He snorted. "I was a scrawny little nerd."

Her mouth fell open. "You were not."

"Sure was. I didn't hit my stride 'til college."

"Must have been one hell of a stride."

"Why thank you, Lieutenant."

Feeling heat rise up her neck, Jo turned to the table and shuffled through some paperwork to hide her face.

Kip flipped a few pages in the yearbook. "That reminds me. You have some beautiful flowers on your desk."

Jo scowled. "You were in my office?"

"I stuck my head in there when I got here. I was looking for you."

"I'll check those out later. Lynae should be here any second. We've got a new development."

He sat up straight. The relaxed guest disappeared, and the cop came back. "What development?"

She dropped into the plastic chair next to him. "We've got a Tom Reed working with our Missing Persons detective right now. His wife, Amanda Reed, disappeared last night."

"And you think it's related?"

"Absolutely. She went to the same high school, hung out with the same crowd, has major guilt about how she reacted to Jerry being outed by some supposed friends, and she suddenly turns up missing." She ticked off the points on her fingers.

"Any chance she just left her husband?"

She shook her head. "Husband says no way."

"Well, they all say that, but there really are too many connections for it to be unrelated. How long has she been missing?"

Jo looked at her watch. "Approximately thirteen hours."

"My victim was held somewhere between forty-eight and sixty hours before he was killed."

"So were ours, at least the two we found quick enough."

Lynae strode into the room. Her eyebrows shot up. "Detective Jurgens."

Kip smiled at her. "Detective Parker."

Jo stood. "Lynae and I are going to have another talk with Mark Campbell. Care to join us?"

Lynae held up her hand. "Actually, why don't I stay here and take another crack at Kader? I've got people looking for him right now."

"Not a bad idea, Nae. We don't have any time to waste. Start out just getting an idea of where he's been the last couple days. See if you can make any connections, trip him up on his whereabouts."

Lynae nodded. "Got it."

"And while you're waiting, see if you can find any pictures online of this group planting trees by the old high school. Our missing woman organized a fundraiser to buy and plant trees in Jerry's memory. They took a group picture and sent it to Jerry's mom. The husband didn't say it had any media coverage, but check MLive and any other local news outlets."

"Maybe someone posted something public on a social media page."

Jo snapped her fingers. "Good thinking. If you can see the comments, they could tell us something."

Kip stood and gathered his papers. "Then I'll tag along with you, Lieutenant."

Lynae mouthed, "You're welcome" to Jo before turning to the door.

Glowering at her partner's back, Jo called out, "Notify me the second you get anything worthwhile."

"Right back at ya," Lynae said, flipping a wave over her shoulder.

Jo turned to Kip. "Give me five minutes. I have to get a few things from my office."

"I'll just wait right here."

Jo ran down to her office and stopped in the doorway. A beautiful bouquet of roses stood in a pretty glass vase on her desk. Smiling, she crossed the room and pulled the small card from the plastic fork in the center.

I'm sorry. Let this jealous dumbass buy you dinner?

She chuckled, tucked the note into her pocket, then leaned in to smell the flowers. The fragrance filled her senses and brought to mind sunshine and warm summer days. She moved the vase to the credenza next to her desk then pulled out her phone to call Jack.

"I told you they were beautiful."

She whipped around. "Oh! Kip, you startled me."

Kip broke into a dimpled grin. "Sorry. I can be a bit stealthy."

She laid her hand on her heart. "Well, don't do it again, or I'm likely to spin around and throat punch you."

"Good to know."

"Ready?" she asked as she slid her phone back into her pocket.

He stepped back and performed a courtly bow. "Right behind you, Lieutenant."

After they got into the Ranger, Jo handed her notebook to Kip. "My notes on our first visit with Mark Campbell are in there. They're labeled at the top."

He flipped through the pages and didn't look up until they exited the highway. "So this guy is the brother of the victim that you think started it all?"

"I'm not sure we can call Jerry a *victim*. All indications say he took his own life."

"But you think it's related."

"I do." She shrugged. "I can't put my finger on it exactly, but I keep coming back to it."

"I agree. But how and why now?"

Jo signaled then turned into Mark Campbell's driveway. "That's what I'm hoping to find out."

They strode up the sidewalk to the front door. Jo knocked and heard the loveable lab duo break into raucous barking. "They sound bad, but they're a couple of loveable mutts."

Kip raised his eyebrows. "I never trust the ones that let on that they're loveable."

"I typically feel the same way. But wait until you meet them."

The door opened, and a pretty brunette pushed the two dogs back before asking, "Can I help you?"

Jo held up her badge. "We're here to speak with Mark Campbell."

"I'm sorry. Mark isn't home. Is there something I can help you with?"

"Are you his wife?" Jo asked.

"Yes, I am." She held out her hand. "Rebecca. What can I do for you?"

Jo shook her hand. "Lieutenant Riskin with the Grand Rapids Police. This is Detective Kip Jurgens."

Rebecca's eyes darted between Jo and Kip. "Mark mentioned that the police were asking about Jerry's suicide. I don't understand. That was so long ago."

"We just have some follow-up questions. Do you expect him to be home soon?"

"No, he's at work. At least that's what his calendar says. He worked at the hospital last night, and he's at the clinic today. He has a little break between, but he just sleeps at the hospital."

"That makes for a long day," Kip said.

"It sure does. He used to work first shift at the clinic, but they cut his hours about six months ago. He was able to pick up a part-time position at the hospital. I hate that he has to work two jobs, but also thankful that he does."

Jo strained to peer around the side of the house. "You have a great location here. I bet you have a beautiful view of the river."

"Thank you. We both love the river, so when this house went on the market, we snatched it up." She blew out a quick breath. "Even if it was a little out of our price range."

"Do you and Mark do much fishing?" Jo asked.

"I don't, but Mark loves it. It's how he relaxes." Rebecca stepped off the porch. "You're welcome to take a look."

Jo and Kip followed Rebecca as she walked toward the side of the house.

"My dad and I used to take the boat out quite a bit in the summer to fish," Kip said. "I always thought it would be great to live right on the river."

They rounded the side of the house, and Rebecca stopped at the top of the slope leading to the bank of the river. "Once in a while when Mark was little, Jerry's dad would show up to take Jerry fishing, and he would let Mark tag along. He said they were some of the happiest times he had as a kid. That stopped when Jerry died, of course."

Jo scanned the lawn until she spotted the short silver dock jutting out from the bank. *Metal, not cedar.* She turned back to Rebecca. "It's a great thing for a father and child to do together. Lots of time for talking. It was nice of Jerry's dad to let Mark go with them."

Rebecca smirked. "From what I've heard, Mark was pretty persistent."

"I got that same impression from Jerry's dad." Jo gave her a little wave. "Well, as much as I'd love to sit and look at this view all day, we have to keep moving. We'll try to catch up with Mark later. It was nice to meet you, Rebecca."

"You as well, Lieutenant."

Back in the Ranger, Jo started the engine and stared through the windshield at the Campbells' house. "Mark's got a lot going on with working two jobs and having a house he really can't afford. But it's a nice home, and he has a lovely wife. I hope he can handle it."

"It sounds like he had a pretty tough childhood, but he's doing okay."

She backed out of the driveway then slammed her hand on the steering wheel. "I feel like I'm chasing my fucking tail. I'm no further ahead than I was a week ago. And now Amanda Reed has about thirty-six hours before she ends up our fifth victim."

"We'll get there," Kip said calmly.

"I don't have *time* to get there. If she dies, it's on me." She dropped her elbow onto the windowsill and rubbed her forehead.

"Jo, that's not fair to do to yourself."

She bit the inside of her lip. When her phone rang, she grabbed it from the console and answered brusquely, "Riskin."

"It's Nae. They're bringing Charles Kader in, and I found a couple of pictures of the tree planting. I just sent them to you."

Jo thought about pulling over and checking her email from her phone. Then she decided the few minutes she would save wouldn't make up for the pathetically small screen of her iPhone. *I have got to upgrade.* "I'm almost back at the station. Can you print color copies for me?"

"They're printed."

As she took the downtown exit, Jo said, "You're the best, Nae."

"Yeah, I know."

Jo disconnected and stopped at Michigan Avenue. When she tossed the phone onto the dashboard, it slid across the surface and off the edge on the passenger side. Kip's hand darted out and grabbed it in midair before it hit the floor.

Jo regarded him evenly. "Ever consider baseball?"

"Ever consider giving yourself a break?"

"Nope." She held out her hand, and Kip dropped her phone into it. She gently placed it in the console cup holder. "Better?"

He huffed. "I'm just saying, I've been working on this case for four months, and you've only had it for a couple weeks."

"And in that couple weeks, it's escalated exponentially. You had one body for four months. I've had two in two weeks. Add Shannon VanDorn, and the body count just keeps climbing."

Kip reached out and put his hand over hers. "Two weeks is an incredibly short time to close a case, and you know it. You have to give yourself a break."

"I can't give myself a break right now. A woman's life is hanging on the line, and I have jack shit to—" Her phone rang again. "Damn it. Now what?"

She pulled her hand away from Kip's and grabbed the phone. Checking the screen, she scowled. *Unknown caller.* "Riskin."

"Is this Lieutenant Jo Riskin with the Grand Rapids Police Department?"

"Yes, it is."

"My name is Katie Greenboro. I'm a nurse at Spectrum Hospital." Her voice sounded young and breathy. *She's nervous.*

"What can I do for you, Katie?"

"Well... okay, this is weird for me. I feel like I have to do this, but I'm not sure if it's the right thing to do."

Working to keep the impatience out of her voice, Jo said, "Why don't you go ahead and tell me. If I'm the wrong person to speak with, I'll direct you to the right one."

"I know you're the right person."

Jo swung her truck into the station parking structure. The caller hesitated, leaving a long span of dead air as Jo waited, testing her patience.

The woman exhaled loudly before finally speaking. "There's a man in one of my beds that slipped your card into my hand when I was checking his vitals. He looked at me really... I don't know... pleading like. He's from the jail."

"Is he a prisoner?"

"Yes. There's a guard with him."

Jo clenched the phone tightly. "What's his name?"

"I don't know if I'm supposed to tell you." The nurse sounded as though she was on the verge of tears.

"Did he ask you to contact me?"

"When he gave me your card, he whispered something. It was so quiet, but I think he said, 'Call.' Why else would he look at me that way?"

"I don't want you to do anything against your policies..." Jo trailed off, hoping the woman would fill in the blanks.

"His name's Mauricio Duarte." The sentence came out in a rush, as if the nurse thought saying it fast enough would erase any doubt she had that she was doing the right thing.

A low ringing started in Jo's ears and built momentum until she could hear nothing else. "I need to speak with him. Can you keep him in the hospital until I can get there?"

"I can't do that, Lieutenant. He's complaining of chest pain, so it will depend on the doctor's diagnosis. *They* release the patients, not the nurses."

Jo squeezed her eyes shut. She wanted to scream. She wanted to curse God for his timing. "As long as he's complaining of chest pain, they have to keep him, correct?"

"That's correct." Katie said it like a question.

"Make sure he knows that."

"Okay."

"And make sure he knows that the minute I'm able, I will be there to talk to him."

"I'll try."

"Thank you. You did the right thing by calling." Jo thumbed off the phone and climbed out of the vehicle. Anger raced through her. *Why right now?*

Kip came around the truck to meet her. "Everything okay?"

Jo squeezed the bridge of her nose and concentrated on slowing her breathing down. "That call is related to the most important case of my life, and I can't follow it up right now. It frustrates the hell out of me." Huddling into herself, she jammed her hands into her coat pockets and strode to the station.

Kip followed silently until they were inside and waiting for the elevator. Laying a hand on her shoulder, he said, "Why don't you go and do what you need to do?"

Jo stared at him. "I can't walk out on this case right now. A woman's life is on the line."

"Lynae is working on bringing Mr. Kader in. I can follow up on—"

"This is *my* case, Kip. There's no way in hell I'm walking out on it right now. The other case isn't going anywhere, and no one's life is hanging on it." *Except mine.*

Holding his hands up, palms out, Kip said, "Just trying to help."

"Well, thanks, but I'm good." She punched the button on the elevator.

When they reached the station floor, Kip said, "I'll be in the conference room. And for the record, this is my case too." He stepped out of the elevator and headed left.

Jo walked out behind him and went toward her office.

Lynae popped out of her chair and met Jo halfway across the bull pen to pass her a manila folder. "Here are the pictures of the tree planting from every social media page I could find on Amanda Reed. I've got officers out looking for Kader." When Jo didn't respond, she said, "You look pissed. What's going on?"

"Can't talk about it right now," Jo growled. She stormed into her office and spread the pictures out on her desk. She planted her hands on either side of the glossy images and leaned over to study the beaming faces of four friends standing arm in arm in front of six small weeping cherry trees.

Brad Kramer stood chest out, chin high, one arm slung around Joseph Telknap's shoulders. Joseph grinned mischievously as if he had a secret or had just cracked a joke. Matthew Wikstrom stood on the far right, holding a shovel in his left hand. His right arm was wrapped around the waist of a pretty brunette who smiled shyly. *Amanda Reed.* Shannon VanDorn wasn't in the picture.

Three of those people are dead, and if I don't find the missing piece of this puzzle, one more will be soon. Jo pulled out the second photo. It showed the same four friends, but they were in the process of digging holes. She slid that image to the side and dragged the next one out.

Lynae walked up behind her and looked over her shoulder. "I couldn't find anything on MLive, and these are all that were public on her social media pages. She may have more that are only shown to her friends. I'm sure I could get Mr. Reed to give me access to his wife's accounts if he knows her passwords."

"May need to," Jo mumbled, leaning over the third picture. "Wait a minute." She took it over to the task lamp on the edge of her desk. She held the picture under the light then told Lynae, "I need you to bring this back up on the computer."

"Her page is still open in my browser." Lynae walked back to her desk and dropped into her chair.

Jo followed and squatted down next to her chair. "Bring up the picture where they're planting the trees."

Lynae maximized her browser window. She clicked the tree-planting image, and it filled the screen.

Jo pointed at the left corner of the picture, just outside the main focus. "Zoom in on that."

Lynae magnified the screen and adjusted the image to bring the corner to the middle. Heavily tattooed arms gripped the handle of a shovel, and a foot clad in Doc Martens under rolled-up skinny jeans was propped on the spade. A knit stocking cap sat jauntily on the man's head, blending seamlessly with his bushy beard.

Jo tapped the screen with her index finger. "That's the guy from the bowling alley." She squeezed her eyes shut then snapped her fingers. "Tyler."

Lynae leaned in and examined the image. "Son of a bitch."

"He acted like he didn't know who Brad Kramer was." Jo slammed her hand on Lynae's desk. "Get a couple uniforms to bring him in. I want him in the station, and I want him scared shitless."

"On it," Lynae said, picking up her desk phone.

Jo jogged to the conference room and grabbed the Crestwood High School yearbook from the table.

"What's going on?" Kip asked.

"Remember our interview at the bowling alley? Well, one of the workers just showed up in a picture with all of our victims."

She opened the book to the class photos and skimmed the alphabetical list of seniors. He was in the typical senior pose, leaning against a tree with his arms crossed. His hair was short, and he was minus the beard and tattoos, but it was him. *Tyler Glen.*

She thumbed through the pages, scanning the candid shots: football games, pep rallies, marching band, young lovers walking hand in hand. She stopped when her eye was caught by an image of some familiar faces mugging it up in the cafeteria. Two people sat together at the end of the table, looking at each other instead of the camera. *Jerry Kader and Tyler Glen.*

Got you, you little bastard. She pointed at the picture. "That's our man."

Kip craned his neck to look at the picture. "And why do we like this guy?"

"He failed to mention that he had a history with the victim. He acted like he vaguely knew him from the bowling lanes."

"I'd say it's time to have another chat with him."

"And I'd say you're right. I'm having him picked up as we speak. If he's guilty, I'll know."

"I think I'd like to see you in action."

"You're welcome to watch from the viewing room." She tucked the tree-planting pictures in the back of the book then slapped it closed and made a beeline to Lynae's desk. "What's the word?"

"I called Kegler's Kove," Lynae replied. "Tyler's there. The unis are on their way to pick him up."

"Let's grab something out of vending. It may be our last chance to eat for a while."

Lynae got up and followed Jo. "You ready to tell me why you look like you want to bite someone's head off?"

Jo stopped at the vending machine and rubbed her stomach as she eyed the choices. *How the hell am I going to keep food down?* She looked at Lynae. Tears sprang to the backs of her eyes, and her throat clogged, but she pushed it down. "Drevin Clayburn's cellmate wants to talk to me. Right now."

"That's shit timing. But if he's willing to talk now, he'll talk later, right?"

"I think he faked chest pain to get into the hospital. He slipped my card to the nurse."

"So he doesn't want to talk at the jail."

Jo stared blindly at the vending machine. The bright packaging of the candy, chips, and granola bars blurred and blended together. "That's my take."

Lynae wrapped her arm around Jo's waist and gave her a squeeze. "We'll find a way to talk to him. I promise."

Not trusting her voice, Jo dropped her head on Lynae's shoulder and nodded.

Chapter 19

J o stopped outside the interrogation room where the officers had
left Tyler Glen waiting. "Let's good cop, bad cop him."

"Can I be bad cop?"

Jo looked pointedly at the bun in Lynae's hair. "With that hair?"

Lynae huffed. "Fine. I'll be in the viewing room."

"I'll get him good and worked up. I'm sure you'll know when it's
a good time to come in."

"I wouldn't want to be him by the time I come to the rescue."

When Jo entered the interrogation room, she remained standing
to force Tyler to look up at her. The technique gave the interrogator a
psychological advantage. She kept the Crestwood High School yearbook pressed against her chest with her arms wrapped around it so
he couldn't see the cover. "I appreciate you coming in to speak with
me, Mr. Glen."

Tyler smiled. "Of course. But I don't think I'm going to be able
to help."

"I spoke with Mrs. Purvis, the former principal of Crestwood
High School. Remember her?"

Tyler's smiled faded. He swallowed hard as his eyes dropped to
his feet.

Jo drummed her fingers on the hard red cover of the yearbook.
"I find it very interesting that we came to see you almost two weeks
ago at the bowling alley and asked you about Mr. Kramer's death, but
you never mentioned that you went to high school with him."

His knee began to bounce. "I didn't really know him. I guess I
didn't realize we went to school together."

Jo opened the yearbook to a page she had bookmarked. She laid it on the table in front of the nervous man. "Isn't this a picture of you, Mr. Kramer, and some other friends?"

His leg stopped moving as his eyes flicked to the picture. He nodded almost imperceptibly.

Jo glared at him. "So you *did* know Mr. Kramer?"

"I guess I forgot."

She turned the book back around and studied the picture. "You're sitting at a lunch table with him. If I remember anything about high school, it's that a person's spot in the lunch room defined his friends."

Tyler slouched in his chair. His fingers picked nervously at the hem of his V-neck sweater. "Okay, so I knew him."

She put both hands on the table and leaned forward. "Yet when we show up with his picture, you act like you've just seen him around the bowling alley. I find that very unusual, Mr. Glen."

"We haven't talked since halfway through our senior year."

"What happened? Why would you stop talking with a good friend during your senior year of high school?"

Anger flashed in his eyes. "I found out what a horrible person he was."

"Why was he horrible?"

Jaw clenched, he crossed his arms and looked away.

She pointed at the young Jerry Kader smiling broadly at Tyler. "You were close to Jerry Kader."

Tyler glanced at the picture then looked away, blinking rapidly. He chewed his bottom lip.

"His death must have been hard on you," Jo said.

He sniffed then took a deep quivering breath. A tear ran down his cheek. "Me and Jerry, we were a couple, but no one knew." He shook his head and sighed. "Until they did."

"How did they find out?"

He wiped his nose with his sweater sleeve. "Some guys from my old school that I still hung around with used to have parties at this old warehouse. Me and Jerry would go sometimes. Those guys knew I was gay and didn't care, so we could be ourselves there. One night, Joe was at the party and saw us holding hands."

"Do you mean Joseph Telknap?"

Tyler nodded. "Yeah. I don't even know why he was there. Jerry kind of froze when he saw him, and then we left right away. Anyway, Joe told Shannon all about it. She had a big mouth and told everybody."

"And your friends gave you a hard time about it."

"Gave us a hard time? That's..." He shook his head, causing the loose bun on top to bounce. "It was hell for both of us but worse for Jerry."

"Why was it worse for him?"

He shrugged. "Those guys weren't really my friends. I was only there because of Jerry. And I was okay with who I was. But not Jerry." He glanced at Jo then dropped his eyes back to the table. "They killed him as much as the rope did."

"So in your opinion, Jerry's friends were responsible for his death?"

Tyler's eyes narrowed. "That's not my *opinion*. That's a fact. If just one of them had been nice..." He pressed his lips together and turned his head.

"From what I've gathered, Brad was the ringleader of the group that drove your boyfriend to kill himself. It's interesting that the last place Brad was seen was at your place of business."

Tyler's eyes fluttered. "So?"

"You have to see why this puts you pretty high on my suspect list."

"Suspect list?"

Placing her hands on the table, she leaned forward. "You've been hanging on to a lot of anger for a long time, Tyler. Brad and his cohorts killed Jerry, so you killed them."

Tyler jumped out of his chair. "What? No!"

"Those guys ruined your life. You said so yourself."

"I'm not sorry they're dead, but that doesn't mean I killed them!"

No, it doesn't. Jo stared into the frantic eyes of the young man across the table. "But you know something that you're not telling me. And I suggest you sit down and start talking because it's not looking good for you."

"I don't know any—"

Jo slammed her palms on the table. The sound reverberated through the small room. "I've got four dead bodies. If you know something—"

His mouth fell open. "Four?" He dropped back into his chair.

She pulled the pictures of Matthew Wikstrom, Joseph Telknap, and Shannon VanDorn from the back of her notebook and laid them out across the table.

Tyler's hand flew to his mouth. "Oh my God!"

"Tell me what you know."

"I don't know anything!"

"I don't believe that for a minute. Tell me what you know, Tyler. I don't have time for this."

His eyes glistened with tears. "I got a phone call."

"A phone call from who?"

His face crumpled. "I don't know."

"So you get a phone call from some unknown person, and you just decide to help him kill a man?"

Tears streaked his cheeks, and his nose ran unchecked. He leaned his elbows on the table, gripped his hair with both hands, and rocked back and forth.

She bent over and asked, "Who called you, Tyler?"

He continued to rock. "I don't know. Oh God, I don't know."

The door opened, and Lynae slipped in, carrying a box of Kleenex. She went over and laid her hand on Tyler's shoulder. When he looked up at her, she smiled and put the box in front of him. He grabbed a tissue and wiped his nose.

In a compassionate tone, Lynae asked, "Do you need something to drink?"

He nodded. "I could use some water."

Jo straightened. "I'll get it. I'm about done with this guy."

"Thanks, Lieutenant," Lynae said as she slid into the chair next to Tyler.

Jo walked out of the room, told Isaac to get her a glass of water, then slipped into the observation room next door. Kip looked up when she entered.

She grinned. "I think he's a little nervous."

Kip returned a look of unabashed approval. "You're a force to be reckoned with, Lieutenant."

"Now watch Lynae smooth his rumpled feathers," she said, turning to the window.

Lynae's voice crackled through the speaker. "The lieutenant will be back in a few minutes with some water."

Tyler stared nervously at the closed door. "She's pretty scary."

Jo snorted.

"She can get a little worked up," Lynae said, "but it's just because she cares."

"I don't know what she wants from me."

"You just need to be honest and tell us what you know. Can you do that?" Lynae pulled her chair closer to Tyler. "Do you know who called you?"

"I really don't. I swear."

"Was it a man? What did the caller say?"

"Yes, it was a man. He said he knew Jerry, and he knew that Brad and his friends killed him." He sniffed and reached for another tissue.

"You know Jerry killed himself, though."

Tyler's lip quivered, and he blinked rapidly. "He wouldn't have if his friends hadn't turned on him. He just needed a friend."

"He had you," Lynae said quietly.

"It wasn't enough for me to tell him he was okay. Jerry needed people to like him, and he thought no one ever would again."

Jo stared through the glass and watched through her own reflection as Tyler grabbed yet another tissue. Her heart ached for the teenager Jerry had been.

Kip shifted his weight. "Poor kid."

Jo nodded. "I was just thinking the same thing."

The door opened, and Isaac walked in with a bottle of water.

Jo tipped her head toward the glass. "Lynae's on a roll. Why don't you take that in? Tell them I got a call."

Isaac gave a quick nod and backed out of the door.

Lynae's voice came through the speaker again. "I'm so sorry, Tyler."

Tyler gave her a sad smile through quivering lips. "He was my first love."

Lynae leaned forward and folded her hands on the table. "I can see why you would feel the people responsible for his death should pay."

Tyler's eyes widened. "I told you I didn't kill him."

Isaac walked into the interrogation room. He handed the water to Tyler then turned to Lynae. "The lieutenant had to take a call. She'll be back with you soon."

Lynae smiled. "Thanks." When the door closed behind Isaac, she turned back to Tyler. "Who called you, Tyler?"

"I told you I don't know."

Lynae sighed. "The lieutenant's not going to want to hear that."

Tyler's leg began to bounce. "All the guy said was that he wanted to tell Brad that he ruined his life."

"Did he say how Brad ruined his life?"

"No."

"And you didn't think that was strange?"

Tyler's eyes narrowed. "He ruined my life, too. After Jerry, I went back into the closet for years because I was afraid."

"I'm sorry. That must have been hard for you."

"Yeah." Tyler pushed back a strand of hair that had fallen out of the bun. "Anyway, I was just supposed to find a way to keep Brad at the bowling alley after his friends left." He shrugged. "It was easy."

"So you told him Cindy had been asking about him."

"How do you know?"

Lynae gave him a bland look. "It wasn't too hard to figure out."

"Brad was always hitting on someone. I knew he would stay and buy her a drink."

"So you weren't curious about who called or what he was going to do to Brad?"

"I was going to follow Brad out and see who talked to him, but all of a sudden, he was just gone. I went out to the parking lot, but he wasn't there." He rubbed his eyes with the heels of his hands. "I guess I thought the guy might rough Brad up a little or something, and I know that's wrong, but I never thought he would kill him. I swear I didn't know."

Lynae glanced up at the one-way. "I think you should tell the lieutenant what you told me."

Jo looked up at Kip and wiggled her eyebrows. "Time to recon with that force again."

He winked. "Wouldn't want to be him."

"Nope, me either." Jo left and went back into the interrogation room.

Tyler jumped when she entered.

Jo dropped a legal pad and a pen on the table in front of him. "Why don't you write down everything you just told Detective Parker?"

Tyler gave Lynae a betrayed look. Lynae just looked blankly back at him.

He swallowed hard and picked up the pen. "Am I in trouble?"

"You're an accessory to murder," Jo said.

"But—"

She held up her hand. "If you cooperate fully, we can see about lessening the charges." She tapped the legal pad. "Full cooperation."

Tyler nodded and began to write. Jo sat in the chair across from him and watched as his pen flew over the pad. He filled almost two pages while chewing a fingernail on his left hand down to the quick.

After fifteen minutes, he laid the pen down. "That's everything."

"You said you were called? Did he call your cell phone?" Jo asked.

He nodded. "It's the only phone I have."

Jo held out her hand. "We're going to need it."

Tyler pulled the phone out of his coat pocket and handed it to her. "The code is 3578. He called me the night before... before the bowling alley thing... at like nine o'clock or so."

"Your phone will be taken into evidence. I don't know when you'll get it back."

"What's going to happen now?"

Jo nodded toward Lynae. "Detective Parker will take you down to booking."

"Booking?"

"You're being charged with a crime, Mr. Glen."

He pressed his fingers to his eyes. "I can't believe this is happening."

Jo picked up the high school annual. *Take it easy on him. This isn't our man.* "We appreciate your cooperation. You'll have to go through the booking process and post bail. You won't be locked up for very long, but your day in court will come." She plucked the legal pad from the table and held it up. "If this helps us find the killer, we'll remember your cooperation when it comes time for sentencing."

Tyler heaved a shaky breath. "Okay."

Lynae led him out the door.

As soon as they were gone, Jo tapped the code into Tyler's phone. She thumbed through Tyler's phone calls and stopped when she reached the day before Brad Kramer disappeared. One call after nine o'clock came up without an associated contact name. "Gotcha."

She jumped out of the chair and jogged to the bull pen. "Isaac, can you do a phone number search for me?"

Isaac turned to his computer and hit a few keys. "All right, hit me."

Jo rattled off the number. Kip came over and stood beside her.

Isaac said, "That number is registered to a Mrs. Eleanor Campbell at 69230 Biltmore Drive."

"Son of a bitch. That's Jerry Kader's mother."

"You think his mother did this?" Kip asked.

Jo shook her head. "His mother has been dead for six months. Someone else is using her house." She thought through the possibilities and kept coming back to the same one. "Does the Metro bus go as far as that address?"

Isaac pulled up the Metro website and zoomed in on a map. "The closest bus stop to that address is two blocks south."

"That's easily walkable." Jo chewed the inside of her lip. "What about Brad Kramer's and Matt Wikstrom's houses? Are they on the route?"

Isaac grabbed the file from the corner of his desk and flipped through the pages to find the addresses. He zoomed in on the map for each one. "Both addresses are within a couple blocks of a bus stop."

Jo turned to Kip. "We need to get into that house." She grabbed her phone and dialed Jack's number.

He picked up on the first ring. "Are we back to talking?"

After signaling for Kip to wait there, Jo hurried to her office. "I need a search warrant, and I need it now."

"On what grounds?" Jack's voice went all business.

She grabbed her coat from the hook on the back of her door. "I've got a man in custody who received a phone call from someone asking him to delay Brad Kramer the night he disappeared. We traced that number, and it belongs to Eleanor Campbell. She's the mother of Jerry Kader, who committed suicide in high school and was a friend of each of our victims."

"And you're sure that's where the call came from?"

"The phone that was used is a landline from that address." She picked her bag up from the floor. "And I've got a missing woman who doesn't have much time left."

"You had me at landline. I'll contact Judge Franklin."

"Thanks. Meet us at 69230 Biltmore Drive. We'll go in as soon as we have it in hand."

"Consider it done."

After disconnecting the call, she went back to Isaac's desk. "I need you to go down to booking and relieve Nae. Tell her to meet me in the parking garage." As he raced away, she turned to Kip. "You want to ride with us?"

"Hell, yes."

Chapter 20

Jo, Lynae, and Kip sat in Jo's truck across the road from the house registered to Eleanor Campbell. The faded-gray bungalow was nestled among oak trees with the river at its back. The waning light of the afternoon sun cast long shadows across the mud-colored leaves that lay thick and wet over the yellowing fall grass.

Jo drummed her fingers on the steering wheel. "What's taking him so long?"

Lynae gave her a bewildered look. "He had to write up the warrant, contact a judge, get it signed, and get here. That's going to take slightly longer than it took us to walk to the truck and drive here."

"We don't have time to just sit here," Jo huffed.

"We can't go in without that warrant."

Jo flopped her head back onto the headrest. "I know, I know." She checked the rearview mirror for the dozenth time then straightened. "That's Jack's car." She hopped out and walked back to the white county van parked behind her Ranger. Leaning her head in the open driver's window, she said, "No one should be living here, but stay in the van until we have the place cleared."

The driver nodded. "We'll be right here, Lieutenant."

Jack had pulled up behind the van. She met him as he was getting out of his car.

Dropping a manila envelope into her outstretched hand, he said, "Signed, sealed, and delivered."

"You're awesome."

Jack winked. "Try not to forget it."

"Try not to make it so easy sometimes."

Jack leaned in and kissed her forehead. "I'll try."

Jo stepped back and glanced over her shoulder. "Jesus, this is not the time for that."

"Damn, blew it already." He shoved his hands into his pockets and shrugged sheepishly.

"No, just..." She slapped the envelope on her hand. "I gotta go kick some ass."

Jack grinned. "Got it." He rattled his keys in his pocket. "Did you like your flowers?"

"They're beautiful. I started to call you, but I got distracted."

"Sorry, I'm afraid I might have been that distraction," Kip said from behind her.

Jo whipped around just in time to see Kip's smug smile. Beside him, Lynae pressed her lips together and became intensely interested in her fingernails.

Jo pointed at Kip. "You cover the back. I don't want anyone going out while Lynae and I go through the front."

Kip gave a curt nod and jogged toward the house.

Jo turned back around. "Jack—" He was sliding into his car. *Shit. I don't have time for this.*

Lynae sidled up beside her. "We're definitely talking about that later."

"Nothing to talk about." Jo pulled her weapon out of the harness and released the safety. "Ready?"

Lynae had her gun out and held down at her side. "Right beside you, partner."

Jo kept an eye on the windows as she approached the house. She leapt up the three steps leading onto the small concrete porch. Lynae trotted behind her then got into position beside the front door.

Jo knocked and listened for any noise coming from inside. When she heard nothing, she banged harder. "This is the police. Open up."

Lynae leaned to the side and peered through one of the dust-covered windows. "I don't see any movement inside."

Jo knocked again. "This is the police. We have a warrant to search the premises!" She tried the knob. "It's locked. Stand back."

Lynae's eyebrows shot up. "You're going to kick it in?"

Jo glared at her. "Don't sound so surprised. I've kicked in a door or two. Besides, the wood is rotting in the frame. It should be easy."

Jo squared off, balanced her weight on her left leg, then pulled her right leg up and drove it into the door just below the knob. The door bowed, and the frame cracked, but it held. She backed up, positioned herself again, and slammed her foot into the same spot. The frame splintered with a loud crack. The door swung in and thudded against the inside wall. Jo went through the opening high and left. Lynae pivoted in low and right.

"This is the police. We have a search warrant," Jo called out into the murky room.

"There's no one here," Lynae said.

Holding her gun out at eye level, Jo scanned the area as they picked their way across the open room. "Keep that gun out. You never know."

They moved quietly past a living room with brown shag carpeting. An oversized crucifix hung over the mantel.

They made their way to the back door, securing the kitchen and dining room as they went. Jo opened the door for Kip.

"You get to kick the door in while I wait?" he whispered.

Jo leveled him with her deadliest glare. "Serves you right."

Kip gave her a lopsided grin then nodded toward a set of descending stairs to their right. "I'll check the basement."

Jo turned to walk down a hallway lined with doors. Lynae followed, weapon raised.

"What is that?" Lynae whispered, pointing at a small plastic bowl attached to a cross hanging next to the first door.

"Holy water," Jo said, looking down the hallway. "They're on every doorway."

Shivering, Lynae said, "Creepy."

Jo opened the first door and swung in on the right with Lynae behind her to enter on the left. The still room held only a double bed and a dresser.

Jo pointed above the bed at a framed print of *The Last Judgement*. "Now *that's* creepy."

Lynae stared wide-eyed at the image of tortured souls in multiple levels of hell. She shook her head slowly and backed out of the room.

They secured the next two rooms.

When they finished the last one, Jo flipped the safety on her weapon and slid it into the holster. "I think we've covered the whole place."

Lynae followed suit. "This looks like a kid's room."

"Complete with clothes on the floor." Jo picked up a T-shirt and held it up to herself. "But this is a man's size."

Lynae walked over to the pressed-wood dresser. She leaned over and blew the dust off a baseball trophy perched on top. "'Jerry Kader. Most Valuable Player.'"

Jo nodded. "This is Jerry's room. I'll start here."

Lynae strode toward the door. "I'll go get the forensic team."

"I saw a phone on the kitchen counter. Have someone swab it. Check on Kip in the basement before you go out."

"No need. It's clear," Kip said, stepping into the open doorway. "I'll start searching through the rubble, but I need a pair of gloves."

Lynae pulled a pair from her bag and handed them to him. Both headed back down the hallway.

Jo retrieved a pair of nitrile gloves from her GRPD jacket and snapped them on. The bed was unmade with the blankets wadded at the foot. A dinner plate and a glass sat on a nightstand next to the head of the bed. She leaned over and peered into the glass. A gob of black muck was caked on the bottom.

Floorboards creaked, and the mumble of Lynae's voice came from another room. Another female voice replied.

Dust, disrupted from its long-settled home, floated in the air as Jo pulled open each dresser drawer. She sifted through T-shirts, socks, underwear, blue jeans, and sweatpants. In the back of the top drawer, a brown leather wallet was shoved beneath an American flag bandana. She pulled it out and opened it. The smiling face of a handsome young man peered out from a driver's license tucked into the plastic on the left side. She thumbed through the cash neatly pressed into the center pocket.

Lynae returned. "Find anything interesting?"

"This room is a shrine. I'm guessing it hasn't been touched since Jerry died. There's a pretty interesting science experiment going on in a cup over there."

Lynae scrunched her nose. "Gross."

Jo tossed her the wallet. "That's Jerry's. Complete with thirty-seven dollars."

"So they literally touched nothing?"

"So far, it appears that way." Jo pushed the last dresser drawer closed and bent over to reach under and behind the dresser. She pulled out a handful of old receipts, a candy wrapper, and a photo of a smirking Jerry with his arm around a beaming brunette. "Jerry and Amanda Reed."

"I'll get going on the bedroom next door. Forensics is starting with the kitchen and living room area."

Jo straightened. "I don't think anyone spent any time in this room recently, but I'm going to finish it up, anyway."

She rifled through shoe boxes and clothes in the closet. Under the bed, she found a plastic baggie that held the remains of what was probably marijuana. The nightstand drawer contained the same yearbook she had gotten from Mrs. Purvis, a Grisham novel, and a deck of cards bound with a rubber band.

Feeling despondent, Jo left the room and poked her head into the next one. Lynae lay sprawled on the floor, shining a light under the bed.

"Find anything in here?" Jo asked.

Lynae picked her head up and pushed her hair away from her face. "Not a thing. This appears to be a spare bedroom. Probably Mark's at one time, but it's pretty sterile now."

"Okay, I'm going to the master bedroom."

"Have fun with that creepy picture of hell hanging over your head."

Standing in the doorway of the master bedroom, Jo surveyed the space before beginning her search. The room was immaculately clean and Franciscan Friar bare.

Well, this shouldn't take long.

She quickly made her way through the mostly empty closet then rifled through neatly folded shirts and polyester pants in a five-drawer chest. Across the room stood a dark-wood dresser with a round mirror. Taped to the mirror was the prayer card from Jerry's funeral. The drawers housed socks and underwear on one side, and a pile of pamphlets filled the other. Each cover was emblazoned with Church of the Forsaken above a sun held in cupped hands that dripped blood. Inside was a scripture verse followed by its relevance to the world. She leafed through a few of the booklets and noted a common doomsday theme. No doubt one of those lessons related to an eye for an eye.

After pulling out a large evidence bag, she slid the stack of pamphlets inside then opened the next drawer. Inside were two Bibles and a spiral-bound notebook with Economics written on the front. The notebook was out of place amongst the rest of the religious articles. She flipped through it and noted that it was filled with small, precise handwriting. *Football practice was a bitch today. It's so hot, and the coaches are such dicks.*

The pages were worn and loose. Someone had read them over and over. Her heart pounded in her ears. *This isn't a school notebook. It's a diary.*

She skimmed a few of the pages, touching as little paper as possible, looking for something other than typical teen drama. Toward the back she found several dog-eared pages that were more worn than the rest. She read the first marked page. *Nothing is ever going to be okay again. Everyone laughs when I walk by. They talk behind my back and call me fag to my face. I can't do this anymore.*

Carefully turning the pages, she found each of her victims' names highlighted on the worn paper. She pulled out her phone and took pictures of each of the marked pages, working her way backward through the journal. Her heart ached for the distraught boy, who hadn't gotten the chance to become a man.

Lynae appeared in the doorway. "My room's clean. Did you find anything?"

Jo held up the notebook. "Jerry's diary. Not only has someone been reading it, but they've also marked pages referring to each of our vics." Running her hand over the worn page, she could almost feel the pain emanating from the paper. "It's heartbreaking."

Lynae leaned against the doorframe and crossed her arms. "Do you really think someone would kill him because he was gay?"

"This was fifteen years ago. We've come a long way, but even today, it happens. But no, I don't think someone killed him."

"Why not?"

Jo turned the book around and held it out at arm's length. "Read the last entry."

Lynae stepped closer and peered at the page. "Wow, that *is* heartbreaking. His friends might not have put the rope around his neck, but they still helped kill him."

"That's the same thing Jerry's dad said."

Lynae cringed. "They haven't located him yet."

"If we don't find him and Amanda dies, it's on me."

Lynae glared at her. "What are you talking about?"

"I let him go."

"You didn't have anything to hold him on. We have laws about that, as you're well aware."

"He practically handed me his motive on a silver platter. Mark said he was mentally unstable." Jo held up the notebook. "If he saw this, it would have put him right over the edge. I could have found a reason to bring him in and have him searched."

"It would have been pretty shaky ground. Yes, he's got motive, but he doesn't have anything in the way of means or opportunity that we can prove."

"Every victim's house is within easy walking distance from the bus line. That's the means. We need to find him and find him fast." Jo stormed out of the room and down the hallway. She walked over to a young man on the forensic team and held up the notebook. "Can I get this dusted for prints right away?"

"Of course, Lieutenant." He pulled a brush and powder kit from the silver hard-sided case that sat open next to him.

After laying the book in his outstretched hand, she reached into his case and took out an evidence bag then signed and dated the bag and passed it to him.

Kip came around the corner. He held an army-green coat, a brown stocking cap, and a pair of cowboy boots. "These were lying on a chair in the basement. At our scene, my forensic team found size-ten-and-a-half boot prints."

"Mine, too, at the first scene."

Kip signed the items over to the same tech who was working on the notebook. "The basement is mostly empty, except for some old stuff in boxes, but I'll see what else I can find down there."

When he left again, Jo called out, "Nae, let's see what's outside."

Lynae walked out of Jerry's room. "I took another look around in there, but I didn't find anything else."

"Since our killer used a boat to transport Brad Kramer, I think we ought to have a look in the back." She walked to the rear of the house and opened the sliding door that led to a massive tri-level deck overlooking the backyard. Ancient oak and pine trees surrounded the property to the north and south. The river lay to the west.

They stepped out and closed the door behind them.

Pointing toward a clump of trees bordering the river, Lynae said, "I think I see a boathouse beyond those trees, off that dock."

As they walked toward the boat, Jo scanned the area. "There aren't any close neighbors. He could easily drag someone across this yard without being seen."

"And that boathouse would be a perfect place to keep someone. Even if someone did come by the main house, they wouldn't find him."

They pushed through the line of trees and down the fishing dock. The wood planks shook as they crossed.

The boathouse's red door was ajar. Jo pulled out her gun and switched off the safety then booted the door the rest of the way open and swung in, gun first. Lynae pivoted in behind her.

The room was filled with buckets, fishing poles, and nets. A wood workbench that ran along one side was littered with fishing line, tools, and various types of artificial bait.

Jo pointed at the boat that floated in the middle of the boathouse. "Green Lund fishing boat. We're going to want Forensics out here."

Lynae pulled out her radio and called for a Forensics team. She pulled her coat over her nose. "God, it stinks in here."

"Gasoline, oil, and fish guts." Jo slid her gun into the holster. "Check the boat for rope we can compare to what we have in the lab.

We'll let Forensics do the rest. I'll go through the shit on this work-bench." She began sifting through the mess.

"Hey, Jo." Lynae held up a metal pole with a two-pronged hook on the end. "This looks like what Mrs. Schoen said she saw in the boat that night."

"She called it a gaff, and that definitely could have made the wounds on Brad Kramer,"

Jo said then heard the techs coming down the dock. She stepped out of the boathouse and motioned to one of them. "Hey, Stacy, we need this swabbed."

Stacy nodded and came in, lugging her forensic kit. Lynae hand-ed the gaff to her.

Jo opened a set of wooden cabinets that hung off-kilter from the unfinished wall then glanced over her shoulder. "Any rope in that boat, Nae?"

Holding up a mesh basket, Lynae said, "Just what's attached to this."

"Damn." Jo dropped to her knees to look under the bench. A coil of rope was tucked behind two oversized plaid dog beds. "Found some rope." She pulled the length out and studied one end. "Defi-nitely cut with a sharp knife."

"And since it's clean, I'd say it was cut quite recently," Lynae added.

Jo reached into Stacy's case and pulled out a large evidence bag. She dropped the rope into it and scribbled her name on the outside. "We need to get some skin samples from it. A cut fishing rope doesn't mean squat unless there are some matching fibers."

Lynae stepped out of the boat. "None of this is helping us find Amanda."

"Damn it. No, it isn't. Let's get the team together at the station and go over what we found and hope that APB pulls Mr. Kader in off the street. If I can grill him, I can get him to tell me where she is."

She turned to Stacy. "I'll leave this in your capable hands. Our victim was in that boat, so I want it gone over with a fine-toothed comb."

"You got it, Lieutenant."

Jo started toward the door then stopped. "Two dog beds."

Lynae gave her a puzzled look. "Huh?"

Jo pointed at the space below the workbench. "*Two* dog beds. And both are too big for Kader's little dog."

Lynae's eyes widened, and she nodded. "But not too big for two overly friendly labs."

"Maybe we shouldn't be looking for Jerry's dad. We should be looking for his brother." She pulled out her phone and punched in Isaac's number.

His deep voice came on after one ring. "Breuker."

"Isaac, I need Mark Campbell's work address and phone number."

"Got it." Isaac rattled off the information.

Jo repeated it out loud while Lynae tapped it into her phone.

"You need me to do something, LT?" Isaac asked.

"Stay close to the phone and that magic computer of yours. We're following a new lead and may need your help."

Shoving her phone into her pocket, Jo turned to Lynae. "Let's get back up to the house."

Once back inside, they found Kip still searching through the basement junk.

Jo walked over to him. "Kip, I think we should talk to Mark Campbell again."

"What did you find?"

"The boathouse has what looks like could be the weapon used to torture our victims. And someone's been hanging out in that boathouse with a couple of dogs."

"You think it's those terrible watchdogs of Mark's?" Kip looked at her skeptically. "That's pretty tenuous, Jo."

She nodded. "I know, but *this* is where the phone call came from. Mark has access to this house."

"And with the bus route, so does Jerry's dad," Kip countered.

"I know, and I've been leaning heavily toward him. I figured he's been carrying around that hatred for those kids all these years and finally cracked."

"And now you don't think that?"

"We found the journal in the mom's bedroom. Divorced or not, she would have shared something like that with Jerry's dad. But I don't think it's something a parent would share with a child."

"So Mark never knew why his brother, whom he practically worshipped, killed himself."

Jo spread her hands wide. "Then at a point in his life when everything has gone to hell, while he's cleaning out his dead mother's house, he finds out that it's because his friends turned on him."

"It was the last straw," Kip said.

"It gave him somewhere to turn his anger," Lynae added.

Jo nodded. "And it's something that he can control. I want to talk to him again and take a different approach. Lynae and I are going to the clinic where he works to bring him in for questioning."

Kip hooked his thumbs into the front belt loops of his jeans. "Seems like you're leaving me with the busywork."

"Mark has met both Lynae and me. If he is our guy, I'm afraid bringing in a new face could alert him and make him panic. I want to get him out of the clinic without any problems."

Rocking back on his heels, Kip regarded Jo skeptically. "All right, I'll meet you back at the station."

"I want a couple of people—make it Anderson and Madison—to stay here in case he comes back. Can you take care of that?"

"Of course. Be careful."

"Always am," Jo said over her shoulder as she went up the stairs.

Lynae slapped her arm as they strode out the door. "It's cute how many men around here are worrying about you."

Jo smirked. "And they're both so damn good-looking."

"I'm having a hard time getting used to you noticing," Lynae said as she walked around the front of the truck and hopped in.

After climbing in and starting the truck, Jo answered, "It's getting harder and harder *not* to notice. Now tell me where I'm going."

Chapter 21

At the clinic, Jo badged the receptionist. "I need to speak to Mark Campbell. It's urgent."

The young woman swiveled her chair and asked a middle-aged woman in a white coat, "Dr. Jeffries, Mark isn't here today, is he?"

The doctor's chin stayed pinned to her chest as she peered over the black-and-gold cat-eye glasses perched on her nose. "He was *supposed* to be here, but he called in sick... again."

"Has that been a habit?" Lynae asked.

The woman nodded. "I'm afraid it has been recently. Is he in some kind of trouble?"

"We just need to speak with him right away." Jo pulled a card out of her pocket. "If he calls or stops in, please call me immediately."

Her brown eyes bulging, the receptionist nodded as she took the card.

The doctor peered over the young woman's shoulder. "I have patients here, Lieutenant. If he's a danger..."

"There's no reason to think you or your patients are in immediate danger," Jo said, "but if he does come here, try not to behave differently. Just call me."

The doctor nodded. "We can do that."

Jo smiled thinly. "Thank you."

Back in the truck, Jo said, "I think we should go back to Mark's house. He may have circled back home after we left."

"Or maybe he was home all along, and his wife was covering for him."

"I hate to think that's possible, but I don't put anything past people anymore."

Jo was lost in thought as they drove back to Mark and Rebecca's house. *If Mark was their killer, what would make him seek revenge all these years later?*

As they pulled into the drive, Jo saw the curtain in the oversized picture window slide back.

Rebecca met them at the door. "Is something wrong, Lieutenant? Is Mark okay?"

"He didn't come home?"

"No, but I don't expect him to." Rebecca wrung her hands. "What's going on?"

"May we come in?" Jo asked.

Rebecca searched Jo's eyes, clearly confused by the return visit. She stepped back and opened the door. "Of course."

They followed Rebecca to the dining room, where she motioned to the table. "Do you want to sit down?"

Jo slid into a chair, while Lynae stayed on her feet, her eyes inconspicuously scanning the surrounding rooms. The two dogs whined from their locked kennels, their eyes alert and ears perked.

Rebecca sat across from Jo. "Why are you looking for Mark again? I told you earlier he's at work."

"We tried the clinic. He isn't there today."

Rebecca's face fell. "What? But... he said he was going to work."

"He's been missing a lot of work recently."

"No, he..." Rebecca pressed her fingers against her eyes. "He's gone all the time. Maybe I got his schedule wrong."

Sliding into the chair next to Jo, Lynae asked, "He's gone all the time because he has two jobs?"

"That, and he's been cleaning out his mom's house so we can sell it. She died six months ago, and he's the only one left to take care of it."

"Have you gone with him to his mother's house?"

"I did at first, but then he didn't want me to anymore." Rebecca shrugged. "I think it might be a little therapeutic for him."

"Does he spend a lot of time there?" Lynae asked.

"He has been lately. He takes the dogs, and sometimes he even spends the night."

Alarm bells sounded in Jo's head. A couple days alone in the house were exactly what her killer would have needed. "I remember you said he lost his job about six months ago also."

"Yes, he did. This year has been hell for us."

"This may seem like an odd question, but is Mark a religious man?"

Rebecca gave Jo a puzzled look. "It's kind of funny you ask, because he wasn't until recently. His childhood kind of turned him off it."

Jo cocked her head. "How so?"

"When he was little, they went to church. I don't remember what religion, but I guess it doesn't matter. When Jerry died, I guess his mom went off the deep end, and church was her life jacket. I didn't know her then, of course, but Mark said the church they had always gone to wasn't godly enough—her words—so she joined this weird fringe religion."

Church of the Forsaken.

"It's one those fire-and-brimstone churches where everybody is going to hell except the chosen few. It totally freaked Mark out. I mean, he was just a kid! As soon as he was old enough, he stopped going with her."

"So Mark never went as an adult?"

"Never." She dropped her eyes to the table. "Not until Theo died," she said quietly.

"Theo?"

"Theo was our son. He was born premature, twenty-seven weeks." Looking up at Jo with watery eyes, she said, "He lived for three months, but his little lungs just couldn't do it. He died almost nine months ago."

"I'm so sorry," Jo said quietly.

Rebecca wiped away a tear. "Mark was lost. Then he was angry."

"I imagine he was."

"Out of the blue one Sunday, he decided he was going to go to church with his mom. I didn't want him to. It's such a..." She raised her shoulders in a helpless gesture.

"Did you ever go with him?"

Rebecca shook her head. "He wanted me to after he started going regularly, but it just wasn't my thing."

Leaning forward, Jo folded her hands on the table. "Rebecca, do you know where Mark is right now? It's quite urgent that we speak to him."

"No, I thought he was at work. What is this about? Is he in danger?"

"At this point, we're not sure. Can you think of any place that he would go instead of work?"

Rebecca narrowed her eyes and bit her lip. Finally, her shoulders fell. "I really can't. He spends all of his time between work and his mom's house."

"If he comes home, it's imperative that you contact us. Can you do that?"

"Can I call him?"

Jo considered. "I don't think that's a good idea right now. It would be better if you wait and talk to him when he comes home." She pushed back her chair and stood.

Lynae reached out and squeezed Rebecca's hand. "Thank you. We'll show ourselves out."

Rebecca pressed her lips together and nodded.

As Lynae buckled into her seat, she said, "She's going to call him, isn't she?"

"Most likely. I hate to leave her alone and anxious, but we can't worry about that right now."

"Maybe it will work to our advantage and he'll come home. It would look more suspicious if he didn't."

"That would be ideal." While Jo drove out of the neighborhood, she called in an APB for Mark Campbell then assigned two officers to keep an eye on the Campbells' house in case Mark returned. She hung up the phone and turned to Lynae. "He lost his son and his mother within two months, then his hours got cut back."

"Can you imagine the medical bills from having a child in the NICU for four months? Losing those hours must have been devastating."

"So he turned to the religion he hated as a child?"

Lynae shrugged. "Maybe deep down inside, it made him feel safe or something."

"I get it to an extent. My church was salve for my wounds when Mike died. Then when I lost the baby... I don't know, I guess I felt better knowing they were together."

"Maybe that's what Mark was trying to find."

"But the church he's going to is on the fringe. It doesn't sound like they comfort people. More like they *scare* them into conforming. It's a shame he didn't go back to the church they attended before Jerry died. That might have really helped."

"So you definitely think Mark is our guy?" Lynae asked.

Jo nodded. "I definitely do now. I think he was lost and angry after his son died, then his mom died, and he had his hours cut practically at the same time."

"Add stress and maybe more anger over the job, and you have a pot of boiling oil. But why, after all these years, would he go after kids that his brother went to high school with?"

"He's been cleaning out his mom's house. *Someone* has been reading that diary. What if it was him, and right in the middle of all of this stress and anger, he discovers that the brother that he looked up to so much was pushed over the edge—pushed into committing suicide—by his so-called friends? Now you've dumped cold water into that pot of boiling oil."

Lynae mimicked an explosion with her hands. Jo nodded grimly.

"So now what?" Lynae asked.

"Let's get back to the station and go through the evidence with new eyes. We know who our killer is, and we know he has Amanda Reed."

"We have to find her. She doesn't have much time."

"I was too late for Matt. I'll be damned if I'll be too late for Amanda."

Lynae cocked her head, regarding Jo thoughtfully. "I thought we were a team."

Jo shot her a confused glance. "What? Of course we are."

"Then why is it *you* let Kader go, and *you* were too late for Matt Wikstrom? Why not *we*?"

Rubbing her forehead, Jo asked, "You want me to blame you?"

"You always give credit to your team when we do something right, but you take all the weight when things go wrong."

"I'm the lieutenant. The buck stops with me."

"And I'm your partner, so I'd like to think we share the buck."

Jo smirked. "Is that a thing? Sharing the buck?"

"You know what I mean."

"I'm sorry. I do know what you mean. What can I say? It's a personality flaw, the weight of the world and all that jazz."

Lynae crossed her arms. "Well, quit it. No one is to blame for any of this except our killer. We didn't have the evidence we needed to piece this together before Matt Wikstrom was killed. Now we do. So stop the blame game and put your mind to figuring out where we can find Mark Campbell."

Jo did a mock salute. "Yes, ma'am."

Slouching in her seat, Lynae said, "Just sayin."

"Okay, I'll totally blame you for everything from now on, partner."

"I'll believe it when I see it."

Jo rolled her eyes. "Sometimes I wonder about you. And I'm starting to think we shouldn't ride together anymore. Seems like every time we do, we either spill our guts or get into a tiff."

"Yeah, we keep returning to the scene of the crime."

Jo handed Lynae her phone. "Speaking of crime scenes, why don't you go through the pictures I took of the journal pages. Look for any mention of our victims. We need to put all our heads together and figure out where we can find Amanda Reed before it's too late."

Lynae glanced at her watch. "It's getting late. Do you think anyone will still be at the station?"

"I hope so. I think at least Kip will be there."

Lynae took the phone and spent the rest of the ride in silence other than the occasional sigh or mumble as she read through the last days of Jerry Kader's life.

When they got back to the station, Jo was relieved to see that Isaac and Charles were still there, so she rounded them up to join them. The elevator dinged, and Jo glanced over and saw Kip step out, a Coke in one hand and a sub sandwich in the other.

She gave him a quick wave. "Perfect timing. We're meeting in the conference room."

Once they were all gathered in the conference room, Jo stood in front of her murder board and wrote, *An eye for an eye, a tooth for a tooth, a hand for a hand, a foot for a foot, a life for a life*, at the top. "Deuteronomy nineteen, verses nineteen through twenty-one. We know that our killer is using these verses as his reason to kill. We believe our killer is Mark Campbell and that he's exacting revenge on the people he believes killed his brother."

"So you're not looking at his dad any longer?" Charles asked.

"Nothing is off the table right now, but according to his wife, Mark has been spending a great deal of time cleaning out his mother's house. He's even been spending some nights there."

"And we know the call that went to Tyler at the bowling alley came from that house," Lynae added.

"Do we have motive?" Kip asked.

"We do." Jo ran through the events of Mark Campbell's life and her interviews with Jerry's father and Mark's wife.

"Wow, I almost feel sorry for him," Isaac said.

Jo pointed to the murder board. "It doesn't matter what drove him to it. This is what he did."

Isaac nodded as his eyes skimmed over the gruesome pictures on the board.

"The big news is that we recovered a journal kept by Jerry Kader while he was in high school. His mother kept his room as a kind of shrine. Nothing appeared to have been touched except the journal. It's been logged in as evidence, but I took pictures of the pages." Jo waved at her partner. "Lynae marked the passages that mention our victims."

Lynae cleared her throat. "To make a long story short, Jerry Kader was gay, and when his friends—our victims—found out, they turned into assholes. According to everything we've learned, that's why he killed himself. Every one of our victims is mentioned in the last few months of the journal." She slid her finger across the phone screen and read aloud, "'Joe saw me and Tyler dancing at Coop's party. He looked at me like I was shit on his shoe. Why was he even there? Everyone will know now. How can I go back to school?'"

Jo grabbed a dry-erase marker from the table and wrote, *Saw at party*, above Joseph's picture. "During his interrogation, Tyler also told us about this party. Apparently, they had parties in a warehouse that someone's dad owned. They were with Tyler's friends from his old school, and they never expected to see Joseph, or anyone else from *their* school, there."

"So suddenly he's outed during his senior year in high school," Isaac said.

Jo nodded. "Right."

Lynae slid to the next picture on the phone. "This next one's from a week later. 'Someone wrote "faggot" on my locker in lipstick. At lunch, Shannon took out her lipstick and looked right at me while she put it on. Brad laughed like it was the funniest thing in the world. Matt wouldn't look at me.'"

Jo added, "And according to Amanda Reed's husband, Shannon was the one who blabbed it around the school." She wrote, *Lipstick, Blabbed,* over Shannon VanDorn's photo. "What do we have relating to Brad Kramer?"

After scrolling through a few screens, Lynae said, "This one mentions him. 'Went to a bonfire at Seven Mile. Brad grabbed me and Tyler and shoved our faces together. He tried to get us to kiss. He wouldn't let us go until Amanda finally told him to stop.'"

Jo wrote, *Grabbed, embarrassed at party*, above Brad's name.

"The next one mentions Matt Wikstrom. 'Before the game today, Brad said maybe I should go play for the other team since that's my thing. Everyone laughed and walked away. Even Matt.'"

"Everyone else did something to embarrass Jerry. Matt just doesn't feel like he fits," Kip said.

Lynae shrugged. "He was a nice guy who just didn't have the balls to stand up for his friend. Walked away when Jerry needed him."

"I guess in this guy's mind, that's enough."

Jo nodded toward Lynae. "Nae, can you read us what the entry says about Amanda?"

"It's one of the last entries. It says, 'Amanda wants me to go to her church with her. She told me about some parts of the Bible that say God doesn't want us to be gay. She wants to help me change so I can go to heaven. I can't change. My friends hate me and now even God wants me to change? What's the point?'"

Jo wrote, *God*, above Amanda's picture. "Okay, we have the who, the what, and the why. Now we need the where." She pointed to Amanda's picture. "We need to find Amanda Reed, and we need to find her now."

Lynae looked up at the clock that hung above the door. "We have less than twenty-four hours."

"At least we *think* we have twenty-four hours," Charles added. "But if Mark gets spooked at all, that could narrow our time frame."

"Matt Wikstrom and Shannon VanDorn were both found either in or by a school," Isaac pointed out.

Jo nodded. "This all happened while Jerry was in high school. Maybe that's a key. Why don't you see if there are other closed schools in the greater Grand Rapids area."

"On it," Isaac said, turning to his laptop.

Kip ran his hand over his five-o'clock shadow. "He definitely prefers hidden or abandoned places. The warehouse where we found Joseph Telknap had been empty for years."

Jo scrutinized the picture of Joseph lying on a concrete warehouse floor. He had outed his friend when he was young and immature and paid all those years later. *If he hadn't gone to that party, none of this would have happened.* "He's not looking to get caught. He feels compelled to do this. The warehouse probably seemed safe." *Just like the party seemed safe back in high school.* She cocked her head. "It's interesting that the party that started all this was in a warehouse, and Mark left Joseph's body in a warehouse."

"You know, I was just thinking the same thing," Kip said.

"I had a case quite a while back where the victim was found at Seven Mile. It's a clearing in the woods on the west side of Seven Mile Road." Jo tapped Brad Kramer's picture with her knuckle. "Brad embarrassed Jerry at a party in the woods, and he was found in the woods at a spot that's known to be a party place."

Charles pointed at the picture of Shannon VanDorn. "It may be a stretch, but Shannon was found in a school, and you could connect that to her spreading the rumor around the school."

Jo pictured the brassy teenager whispering to anyone who would give her the attention, trying to destroy her so-called friend. She stared at the remains of her once-pretty face and had a momentary image of her whispering with her now-toothless mouth. She looked back at the picture of Joseph Telknap with his missing eye. Her gaze moved to the words above his picture and focused on "saw."

She grabbed her marker and circled the word then followed it with a line and circled the hole where Joseph's eye should have been. She did the same with "blabbed" over Shannon's name and drew the line to her mouth. Following the now-obvious pattern, she circled each word and drew the connection to the missing body part.

"Holy shit," Lynae mumbled.

Jo stepped back and scrutinized her work. "He gave this a lot of thought. It explains why he traveled to Ohio for his first victim."

"He had to do it in order," Kip said.

"Does this help us find Amanda?" Charles asked.

Jo shook her head. "I don't give a damn what's going on in his warped mind about the why. We need to know the where. Considering how methodical this is, there will be a pattern."

Tapping Matthew Wikstrom's picture, she said, "Matt was found on a football field. Does that make sense?"

Lynae thumbed through the photos on Jo's phone. "The journal just says, 'at the game.' It doesn't say what kind of game. But it happened in the spring, and that's not football season."

"They played football together," Kip said. "Maybe it's just related to the game and them being teammates. The goalposts could have just been the easiest place to hang a body."

"There wouldn't be an easy place to do that on a baseball diamond. Regardless of his reasoning, he's definitely returning them to the scene of the crime. Leaving them in locations that fit their crime against his brother."

"Or in his mind, their sin," Lynae said.

Jo shrugged. "It's a theory and a pretty good one." She studied Amanda Reed's picture. "Amanda tried to save Jerry's soul. She's the only one that didn't intentionally hurt him. According to her husband, she thought she was helping him."

Charles stifled a yawn. "It's a little ironic that her so-called crime was religion, and now Jerry's brother is using religion against her."

Using religion against her. Jo snapped her fingers. "We're going to find her in a church."

Kip nodded. "It makes sense. And it's the only thing, really, that does."

Jo turned to Isaac. "Cancel that school search and start looking for old churches. Since we're in West Michigan, I'm sure there are a lot of them."

Isaac rubbed the heels of his hands into his eyes then dropped them back to the keyboard.

After checking her watch, Jo realized her team had been at work for too many hours. "On second thought, let me do it. Why don't you all take a few hours of down time, try to get a little sleep."

Kip's blue eyes narrowed as he knit his eyebrows. "Do we have time for that?"

"If we're going to search churches, doing it in the daylight will help. But more importantly, I don't want us all going out on the streets and potentially into a dangerous situation without all our faculties."

"What about you?"

"I'll run the search then take some downtime. I'm not much of a sleeper, anyway."

"I'll stay here with Jo," Lynae said.

Jo shook her head. "Go. I need you at your best."

Lynae stood and stretched. "All right, if you insist. I'll take a few hours and be back by six."

Checking her watch, Jo nodded. "That's reasonable. We'll be ready to go before daylight. I'll see you all then."

After her team headed out, Jo started a search for closed churches that had not been bought or restored. While she waited, she searched bibleverses.com and printed out a list of every place an eye for an eye was mentioned in the Bible. Then for good measure, she searched for other verses about revenge.

When her search finished, she scanned the surprisingly long list of locations for anything close to Eleanor Campbell's house. She wasn't surprised to find that no church had stayed empty near the river. She broke the list down by location and split it so they could go out in teams and cover more ground.

With the search ready, Jo turned to the Bible verses to see if she could glean anything new.

Chapter 22

J o felt a light pressure on her back as the rich aroma of coffee wafted over her. Her arms were stiff, and her shoulders ached.

Amanda Reed.

She bolted upright, knocking to the floor the papers her head
had been resting on.

"It's okay. It's early," Lynae said, holding out a cup of steaming
coffee. "We all just got here."

Jo squeezed the back of her neck and rolled her head, the Rice-
Krispies sound of her cartilage reminding her why she rarely slept at
her desk. She took the cup and held it in both hands, deeply breathing in the smell of morning.

Lynae bent down and picked up the papers. "I think the rest of
us may be better rested than you."

"How did the search go?" Kip asked from the doorway.

Jo waved a hand at the papers Lynae held. "I've got two lists that
I split up by location. There are more than I anticipated."

"We're ready to get started," Kip said, jerking a thumb over his
shoulder at Charles and Isaac.

"Give me a few minutes to splash some water on my face, and I'll
be ready."

Jo reached under her desk and pulled out her emergency bag
then went to the restroom to freshen up. After ten minutes, some
cold water, a toothbrush, and hair spray, she felt semi-human again
and headed back to her office.

Handing one list to Charles and keeping the other, she said, "You
have the south and east sides of town, and we have north and west.

Isaac, I want you to stay here and stay on your computer. Keep digging. If we strike out, be ready to give us somewhere else to go."

"I'll be ready," Isaac said, pulling off his coat.

Kip looked over Jo's shoulder at the list. "I assume you'll want to drive since I don't know the city."

Jo pulled her clutch piece from the holster around her ankle. She checked the clip and safety, slid the gun back into place, then slipped an extra clip into her pocket. "You'll be going with Charles. I go through every door with Nae."

Charles slapped Kip on the back. "Sorry to disappoint."

Jo pulled her Kevlar vest from its post next to her coat hook, shrugged into it, then wrestled her coat on over it. "And everybody get your Kevlar and wear it. Kip, you can use Isaac's."

Lynae groaned. "No. I hate wearing Kevlar."

Jo gave her a curt look and shook her head. She pulled a stocking cap from her coat pocket, pulled it on, then checked her sidearm before shoving it back into the holster. Next, she clipped a police radio to her belt. "Keep in close contact with us, and call for backup when you need it." She pointed at Charles. "No cowboys—understand?"

Charles gave her a quick salute. "Aye, aye, Captain."

She nodded toward Kip. "And on the way, fill Detective Jurgens in on SOP according to Lieutenant Jo."

When Lynae and Charles hustled to their desks, Kip crossed his arms and spread his legs into a fighting stance. "You think I can't handle myself, Lieutenant?"

"I'm sure you can handle yourself just fine, Detective, but right now, I can't be worrying about an unknown."

"I hardly think I'm an unknown at this point."

"It's nothing personal, Kip. In a potentially dangerous situation, I like everybody following the same rules. *My* rules. These are *my* people on the line."

"Understood." An easy grin formed on his face. "I can play by your rules."

"You're a wise man."

Kip reached out and grabbed her hand. "Be careful."

Jo winked. "I told you I always am." She squeezed his hand then pulled away and stepped out of her office and into the bull pen. "All right, let's go."

AFTER STRIKING OUT at four locations, Jo and Lynae pulled into the parking lot of St. Agatha's. The cream-colored brick was obscured by bright splashes of graffiti. Trash littered the bushes and grass surrounding the cathedral-style church. Weeds turned to stalk, and overgrown brown grass burst from cracked sidewalks. Four vehicles sat in the lot, one with a flat tire and two pulled up close to the surrounding houses. The fourth, a Chevy four by four, sat close to the back door of the church. Jo parked near the truck and glanced inside. Heavy camouflage gloves lay in the passenger seat along with a black stocking cap.

Charles's voice crackled across the radio. "Checking in, LT."

Jo pulled the radio from her belt and pressed the talk button. "Go ahead."

"We've hit all our locations, and still no sign of life."

She rubbed the back of her neck. "All right, check in with Isaac and see if he has anything else for you."

"On that."

Jo checked her watch. They were down to twelve hours. If they had to go back to the drawing board, Amanda Reed would die. She pushed back the doubt and fear of failing the woman and walked around the truck, straining to see into the back seat. Rubber boots and a coiled-up rope the same color and texture as they'd found on their victims lay on the floor. She pulled out her phone and dialed Isaac's number while walking to the back of the truck.

"Breuker."

"Isaac, I need you to run a plate." She rattled off the plate number.

"Give me just a few minutes, LT."

Lynae waved her over to the back door. Jo trotted over, keeping away from basement windows. A busted padlock hung from the heavy wooden door. Jo pulled out her gun and clicked the safety off, and Lynae nodded and did the same. Jo spoke quietly into the phone. "Text me when you have that run. We're going in."

"That's not a good idea, LT."

"Just hurry up." Jo shoved the phone into her back pocket, put her radio on silent, and slowly pulled open the door. The old hinges groaned. She cringed and stopped moving, listening for any noise inside the old building. Looking over her shoulder at Lynae, she shook her head then squeezed into the small opening without pushing the door any further open. Lynae followed her through the small space.

Jo held her gun out in front of her as her eyes adjusted to the dim light. The room was silent. Watching each other's backs, they moved slowly forward. The carpeted hall gave way to an expansive place of worship. Chunks of dirt and debris were scattered across the gray-tiled room. Mosaic stained-glass windows lined the side aisles, though some were broken and had shards of brightly colored glass sprinkled beneath them. Dark-wood pews sat facing a chipped white-marble altar. A large wooden crucifix hung morosely over the scene.

Jo's heart thundered as they silently moved as one through the sanctuary, entering each open space gun first. Dust stung her eyes and tickled the back of her throat. Each breath brought the smell of neglect and forgotten promises. She leaned back and whispered into Lynae's ear, "Let's check the basement."

Lynae nodded and motioned to the back. Jo relaxed her gun arm and turned around to face the back of the church. When her phone vibrated, she reached into her pocket and hit the power button to silence it then pulled it out and read the message. *Plate registered to Eleanor Campbell.*

Jo held the phone out for Lynae to read then tapped out, *Send backup.*

A muffled whimper echoed through the room, and something solid hit the balcony floor. Jo jerked her head up while swinging her gun toward the balcony.

A man's voice echoed across the expanse. "Hello there, Amanda." The voice was pleasant—too pleasant.

"I hope you're comfortable," the man cooed.

Jo reached out and grabbed Lynae's arm. She pointed to a noose loosely wrapped around the railing then flung over a rafter. The end disappeared somewhere in the dark recesses of the balcony.

"Where am I?" a woman slurred.

Lynae motioned to the stairs along the right side of the long aisle.

"It doesn't matter. You will know it only as hell," the man growled.

An outside door slammed, and Jo's gaze snapped in the direction of the noise. *Shit, the wind.*

A chair scraped across the floor of the balcony. "What the fuck?"

A woman slammed into the railing. Her hair was disheveled, and black streaks ran down her face. Her shoulders were pressed tightly back, her arms pulled behind her. Dark blotches stained the front of her shirt. A gun was pressed to her temple, and only the hand of the gunman could be seen.

"Don't move, or I'll blow her brains out," he rumbled.

Jo kept her gun trained on the woman. *Give me an inch, you bastard.* "Mark, you have nowhere to go."

The young face that Jo had once considered handsome peered around the head of the bound woman. "I'm going to hell, Lieutenant. And I'm taking this woman with me."

Jo scanned the vestibule. *How the hell are we going to get up there?* "You don't want to do that, Mark."

"How do you know what I want?" he screamed through clenched teeth.

Amanda squeezed her eyes closed. "Mark, I'm sorry."

"Sorry? You're sorry?"

She nodded frantically. "Yes. Yes, I'm sorry."

Mark pressed his face against Amanda's head. "You throw that out pretty casually, don't you, Amanda. Why should I believe you?"

"I wouldn't hurt anyone on purpose, especially not Jerry," Amanda blubbered.

Lynae held her gun in both hands and kept it trained on the balcony as she slowly eased away from Jo.

"Oh, good. So you didn't kill my brother on purpose. I guess that makes everything okay," Mark spat. "You hear that, Lieutenant? She didn't *mean* to kill my brother. My mistake."

Amanda's face contorted. "I didn't kill—"

He cracked the gun across Amanda's cheek, and the crunch of metal on bone echoed through the church. "Shut up!"

Amanda's head jerked to the side then snapped back. A thick bubble of dark blood formed under her right eye then oozed down her cheek.

Jo used the time to slide farther to the side. Out of the corner of her eye, she saw Lynae do the same.

Mark's gun swung over the top of the balcony railing. "Stop moving! I know what you're doing."

Jo froze. "Mark, put the gun down, and we can talk about this. We know that Jerry's friends turned on him. We know you loved your brother, and you want to blame someone for his death, but this won't change anything."

Mark grabbed Amanda's hair and pulled her head back. He put his mouth next to her ear. "I blamed him. But now I know it was you. You killed my brother."

Amanda shook her head frantically. "No, Jerry was my friend."

Mark screamed, "He was your *friend*? He. Was. Your. Friend?"

She squeezed her eyes closed and tried to pull her head away.

A door latch clicked to Jo's left. *Backup.* "Mark, Amanda didn't kill your brother. Put the gun down and—"

Mark's hand shook as he pressed the gun to her head. "It's all in his journal. She told him he would go to hell for being gay. You killed him!" he screamed in Amanda's ear.

"No, I didn't say that!"

"It's right there in black and white, Amanda. He decided if even God couldn't love him, what was the point?"

Tears ran down Amanda's face. "I was trying to help him."

"Help? You were trying to help?"

Amanda's head bobbed up and down.

Mark pressed the gun tighter against her temple. "You killed him. All of you did!"

"We didn't mean to," Amanda sobbed.

Mark yanked her head back and turned her face toward him. "Look at me."

Amanda sniffed, her eyes still squeezed shut.

"Look at me!" Mark shrieked. Veins bulged in his neck.

Amanda's eyes popped open. She tried to pull her head back.

Mark leaned in close and spoke through gritted teeth. "You killed my brother. My dad was already dead, and when my brother died, my mom never looked up from her Bible again. She didn't care about me. She only cared about my eternal soul. And my soul was never good enough. It was never gonna be. You made my life hell."

"I didn't mean to. I'm so sorry," Amanda sobbed.

"It's too late for sorry, Amanda." Mark reached to his right and grabbed the rope slung around the balcony, exposing half his body.

Lynae fired off a shot then bolted for the stairway. A second boom reverberated through the expansive room. Lynae jerked and dropped between two pews.

"Nae!" When Lynae didn't answer, Jo grabbed her radio from her belt. "Shots fired! Officer down!" Her voice cracked. "Officer down at 4692 Twenty-Second Avenue. Get an ambulance here now!"

Get up, Nae.

She crouched low and scuttled across the length of the pew. Wood splintered from the seat back in front of her before she heard the crack of another gunshot. She dropped to the floor and crawled to the end of the row. Lynae lay motionless on the tile floor across the aisle.

Another shot rang out, chipping the marble floor inches from where she crouched. She swung her gun above the pew and stole a glance at the balcony. Mark stood behind Amanda, his arm wrapped around her neck. *Damn, I can't take a shot.*

"Nae, say something," Jo hissed across the aisle.

Lynae remained still.

Jo took a deep breath, bounded to her feet, and covered the distance of the center aisle in two long strides. A bullet splintered the wood seat as she dove for the cover of the pew and scrambled to reach Lynae.

Footsteps pounded up the stairs, and she heard people yelling commands. The thundering of her heart in her ears drowned out the other sounds. She felt as if she were underwater and they were yelling from a boat. Her breath came out in short, hissing gasps.

She dropped to the floor next to her motionless partner. "No, no, no." Her hands shook as she slid them under Lynae's head, feeling for blood.

Bile rose in her throat. "Oh God, please."

Where did he hit her? She ripped open the front of Lynae's jacket.

Lynae moaned. "Damn, woman. At least buy me a drink first," she mumbled.

Choking out a sob, Jo dropped her head onto Lynae's chest. She felt the solid form of her bulletproof vest.

Lynae's head flopped to the side. "I now love Kevlar."

Jo wiped her eyes with the heels of her hands. "Are you okay?"

"Did I get him?" Lynae mumbled.

Jo snorted and looked over her shoulder. "I don't know. All hell broke loose when he shot you."

"What are you doing down here then?"

Jo's mouth dropped open. "I kind of had more important things on my mind, like whether or not my best friend was alive."

Lynae tried to sit up, flinched, and dropped her head back to the marble floor. "If I were dead, it wouldn't hurt this much. Now get up there."

Jo grabbed Lynae's hand. "You sure you're okay?"

"Go."

"Don't you dare move. Stay down and out of range. Understand?"

Lynae nodded before Jo jumped to her feet and ran to the stairs. She scurried up them silently, keeping her head down. Two officers were stationed where the stairs met a safety rail. Their guns were held at eye level, trained on the assailant, who was backed into the corner of the balcony.

"Is Lynae okay?" one of the officers whispered.

Jo crouched down beside him. "Yes. Thank God for Kevlar. What's happening?"

"He's got the rope around her neck and the gun to her head. He's behind her, completely covered. We can't get a shot."

Jo peered around the corner of the stairs to assess the situation. Amanda Reed's whole body shook as she cowered in front of the railing. A purple line streaked across her left cheek, the swelling pushing her eye closed. Mark had an arm snaked around her neck, clutching the end of a white rope, and his other hand held a pistol against her temple. The rest of him was hidden from view, tucked into the corner of the balcony.

"They're too close to the edge. He could fling her over before we get a shot off."

"As soon as he pushes, we put him down."

Jo eyed the rope thrown over the rafter. It was just out of reach of the balcony. If Amanda went over the railing, there would be no way to get to her fast enough to save her. She followed the line of the rope to where it coiled under Mark's feet. "The rope isn't tied off. You put him down, and Amanda Reed falls onto the wooden pews and tile floor below."

"Not ideal, but the odds of her living are better with a fall than with a close-range bullet," the officer whispered.

Jo chewed her bottom lip. "I don't like the odds either way."

The officer motioned with his gun. "I've got someone at every corner. He just has to give us an inch."

Jo reached into her back pocket and took out the Bible verses she had printed out. She skimmed the text and zeroed in on a few key phrases then shoved the paper back into her pocket, took a deep breath, and put her hands in the air, her gun dangling from her pointer finger.

The officer scowled at her. "What are you doing?" he stage-whispered.

"Giving you an inch."

"Mark, I'm going to drop my weapon in your sight," she said calmly.

"I'm not letting her go."

Jo gingerly stood up, keeping her hands above her head, and took a couple steps toward Mark and Amanda.

Mark pointed his gun at her then back at Amanda's head. "I'll kill her."

Amanda whimpered. Blood stained her shirt and the waist of her khaki pants.

"I know you will."

Keeping her eyes on him, she bent slowly at the knees, laid her gun on the floor, and kicked it to the side. "I'm unarmed."

Mark jerked his gun in the direction of the stairs then quickly brought it back to Jo. "They're not."

She took a step toward him. "Don't worry about them. Talk to me."

"Nothing to talk about. Stay back."

Jo kept her hands at shoulder height, palms out. "I know that you've had more to bear this year than anyone could handle. I know about Theo."

Mark peered around Amanda's head, revealing only one eye behind her dark hair. "How do you know that?"

"I talked to Rebecca. She's worried about you."

"She'll be better off without me," he said through clenched teeth.

Jo took another step. The distance between them seemed like a mile. "You felt helpless when Theo was sick. You couldn't protect him. It was out of your control."

"I can't protect anyone."

"You couldn't protect Jerry." Jo slid her foot forward.

Mark's hand tightened on the rope pulled taut around Amanda's neck. Amanda's eyes pleaded with Jo as tears ran down her cheeks.

Jo took another step. *Almost in diving distance.* "You were just a child."

Through the balcony railing, Jo saw Lynae scoot across the side aisle and press herself against the wall. *Damn it, Nae, I told you to stay down.*

"He was my brother," Mark whispered.

Jo nodded and slid a step forward. "I know you looked up to him. Jerry was almost like a brother *and* a dad, wasn't he?"

"He had a dad, and I kind of did, too, until he died. Then his dad just forgot about me."

"I'm sorry for everything your family went through. And I'm sorry that you've gone through so much this year. But killing Amanda won't bring your brother back."

"I know he's not coming back, because he's in hell, and now I'm sending all of his friends to spend their eternity there with him."

"You want his friends to pay. I understand, but—"

"No, you don't understand! Someone has to pay for killing him. For killing my whole family," Mark hissed.

"Jerry killed *himself*, Mark." She took a full step forward.

Mark's face contorted. His hand shook. "No! That's what they wanted us to think, but it wasn't his fault. I blamed *him* for ruining my life. I hated him!"

"Then you found his diary," Jo said quietly as she sidestepped to the left.

Mark pulled on the rope around Amanda's neck and pressed the gun hard against her head. "I hated *him*." His voice cracked on a sob. "When all along I should have hated *them*. They killed him. The Bible says—"

"An eye for an eye," Jo finished.

Mark's eyes lit up. "Yes! You see? Mom always said all the answers are in the Bible. I didn't believe her. I walked away, but I came back. I understand now."

Jo kept her eyes trained on Mark, her hands still raised in full view. She pictured the verses printed on the paper crumpled in her back pocket. "Repay no one evil for evil."

Mark's brow furrowed. "What?"

"That's also in the Bible. So is 'forgive and you will be forgiven.'"

The gun shook in Mark's hand. "I'll never forgive them. They ruined my whole life."

Forcing a composed voice over the sound of her hammering heart, Jo said, "Love your enemies and pray for those who persecute you." *Is that right?*

"Shut up!" Mark screamed. Amanda jolted and squeezed her eyes shut.

Jo froze in place. "Let's just stay calm."

"You're trying to confuse me. I read the Bible. I'm doing God's work."

"Mark, God wants us to forgive, not take revenge. That's for him to sort out in the end." Jo slid her foot forward. She was within reach. *Will my vest withstand a bullet from this close?*

"Stop moving! I gave them what they deserved, an eye for an eye." He pressed the gun against Amanda's head. "And now it's her turn."

The church doors flew open. Mark's head snapped toward the sound, and his hand lost its grip on the rope. Jo lunged forward, grabbed Amanda by the shoulders, and pulled her to the floor, rolling on top of her body in one motion. The coil of the loose rope pressed between them.

A shot rang out. Jo braced for the impact to pummel her vest.

Metal clattered on tile, and footsteps pounded across the floor.

"Don't move! Put your hands up."

Jo pulled her clutch piece from its ankle holster as she rolled off Amanda. She swung her gun around and pointed it at where Mark had been standing. The young man sat slouched against the railing, his hand pressed against his right shoulder. Blood seeped between his fingers.

After holstering her weapon, she kicked his gun away from his reach then scrambled to him and checked for other weapons. She pulled a knife from his waistband and handed it to an officer behind her then yelled over the railing, "All clear."

Lynae stood with her legs braced, gun still trained on the balcony.

Jo grinned. "Nice shot, partner."

Relaxing her arms, Lynae slid the gun into the shoulder holster. "I don't miss twice."

Jo leaned over Mark and pressed her hands firmly against his wound. As the EMTs hustled toward them, Mark grabbed the front of her jacket. "Just let me die."

"Not today," she replied as she released the pressure and turned him over to one of the waiting EMTs.

Jo motioned to an officer standing next to the stretcher. "Cuff him to the bed and ride with them. Make sure he's secured at all times during the transfer and in the hospital. If he has to go into surgery right away, you go with him."

"Yes, ma'am." The officer pulled his cuffs from his belt and secured one end to Mark's wrist.

Jo eyed the paramedics sternly. "He's not to be uncuffed for any reason."

The older of the two paramedics looked at the officer. "We'll keep him alive. You keep him secure."

Jo backed out of their way, holding her bloody hands away from her body. *Thank God it's his blood and not Nae's or Amanda's.* She gazed above the balcony at the stained-glass window portraying open hands and a dove in flight. "Thank you," she whispered.

Jo took a towel from the outstretched hand of an officer and scrubbed at the blood as she walked back to Amanda Reed, who sat slumped on the floor. A paramedic was crouched in front of her, gently examining her increasingly swelling cheek. The rope lay beside her, and a red burn discolored her neck. The EMT reached into his bag, took out an icepack, popped it to life, and handed it to Amanda. "We're going to need an X-ray of that, ma'am."

Amanda took it and gingerly held it to her face. She gazed at him, a stunned look of incomprehension on her face.

Jo waited as he did a quick examination of her other wounds then sidled up behind him. "How is she?"

He looked over his shoulder then stood to face Jo. "Her cheekbone may be broken. We'll need an X-ray to know for sure. She has several knife wounds on her abdomen. Most appear to be superficial, but I think we'll need to stitch one of them." He lowered his voice. "And I'm a little concerned about shock. We'll take care of her." He glanced at the EMTs hoisting Mark onto the stretcher and watched the officer clasp the other end of the handcuffs to a bar on the side. "We have two vehicles. She won't be transported with him."

Jo walked over to the dazed woman and dropped down beside her. "Are you okay?" she asked quietly.

Amanda shook her head. Her lip quivered, and she pulled her legs close to her body, wrapping her free hand around her knees. Her body rocked rhythmically. "When Jerry died, I had so much guilt."

"You didn't kill him, Amanda."

Amanda held the ice against the side of her face. Tears streamed down the other cheek. "I didn't help him, either."

Jo squeezed her hand. "It's time to put away the guilt. You can't go back. You can only move forward."

Amanda gazed at the EMTs hoisting the gurney that carried Mark Campbell down the stairs. "I feel sorry for him."

"He killed four people and would have killed you. There's no room for sorry."

Amanda sniffed and nodded, wincing at the sudden movement.

"I'll have to get a full statement from you, but for now, let's get you to the hospital. I'll get in touch with your husband so he can meet you there. He's frantic."

Amanda smiled through the tears. "He's a good man."

Jo stood, helped the other woman to her feet, and wrapped an arm around her.

Blinking rapidly, Amanda pressed her lips together then hugged Jo. "Thank you."

The EMT helped ease her onto a stretcher then motioned for help from his partner.

Lynae walked around the corner of the balcony stairs. She rubbed her side and winced.

Jo bit her lower lip. Her eyes burned. In three long-legged strides, she reached her friend and wrapped her in a hug. "I didn't think you had your vest on," she choked out.

Lynae hugged her tight. "My boss is a stickler for rules."

"I love your boss."

"So do I." Lynae pulled back and draped her arm around Jo's shoulder. "I can catch a ride home. You have to get to the hospital and talk to Mr. Duarte."

Jo wrapped her arm around Lynae's waist and gave her a squeeze. "I appreciate it, but I imagine Kip is chomping at the bit to find out what happened here. This is his case too. Besides, you need to have a doctor give you the once-over."

"I'm fine, but I know I have to go. Department policy, blah, blah. Speaking of which..." She unholstered her gun, checked the safety, then held it out to Jo.

Eyeing the weapon, Jo fought an internal battle. Every cell of her being screamed that taking Nae's weapon was wrong.

Lynae nudged Jo's hand with the handle of the gun. "Take it, Jo. I've never been through it, but I know the drill for an officer-involved shooting."

"I don't want to put you on suspension. I need my partner."

"Trust me, no one hates the idea more than me."

Jo huffed then motioned for an officer. "We need to take Lynae's gun as evidence. As her partner, I'm going to stay hands-off."

Nodding, the officer said, "I'll take care of it, Lieutenant."

"We also need to get this whole area taped off. I'll ask the Michigan State Police to investigate the officer-involved shooting, so we're not going to touch this scene until I've made that contact."

"Yes, ma'am." He dug a leather glove out of his pocket, slid it on, then held out his hand to Lynae. "Sorry, Parker."

Lynae laid the gun in his hand then started to unclip her badge from her belt. Jo held up a hand. "You don't have to turn in your badge for a temporary suspension. If fact, you'll have to stop by the station in the morning so I can issue you a new weapon."

"I'm sure I'll need that sitting at home, twiddling my thumbs while you wrap up our investigation. And fair warning, I'll probably be a miserable bitch to live with until this is all over."

Jo snorted. "Duly noted."

Footsteps pounded up the balcony stairs. A bald head followed by enormous shoulders rounded the landing. Officer Doug Jacobs came to a halt then grabbed Lynae by the shoulders and crushed her against his chest. "You're okay."

Lynae leaned into his broad chest for a moment then pulled back. "Doug, what are you doing here?"

"I heard the lieutenant's call come across the radio. I know her voice, and as frantic as she sounded, I knew it was you."

"I wasn't frantic," Jo grumbled.

Lynae cocked her head. "So you came here?"

"I was worried." The big man shuffled his feet.

"But I told you we weren't going out again."

Doug's face fell, and his arms dropped to his sides. "I know, but we're friends, right? Maybe I shouldn't have—"

Lynae popped onto her tiptoes and kissed him on the cheek. "Yeah, you should have."

Jo cleared her throat. "Officer Jacobs, could you give Nae a ride to the hospital for me?"

Doug grinned down at Lynae. "Yeah, I think I can do that. Come on, Nae."

Jo gasped.

Lynae stopped dead in her tracks. "What did you call me?"

Shaking her head slowly, Jo patted the big man on the shoulder. "And you were doing so well."

Doug's confusion was written all over his face. "Isn't that your nickname?"

Crossing her arms, Lynae said, "Only Jo calls me that."

Doug held up his hands. "I didn't know."

"I'll let it go this time. But *only* this time," Lynae said.

Jo squeezed Lynae's shoulder. "I gotta go, *Nae*." She winked at Doug then went down the stairs and to her truck.

Chapter 23

Kip paced in front of the reception desk. His head jerked up when Jo came through the door. "What the hell happened? Are you okay?"

Jo halted just inside the door and looked down at her blood-stained jacket.

Kip stepped over to her and put his hands on both of her shoulders. "Jo?"

"It's not mine," she said absently. *And it's not Nae's.* "It's Mark Campbell's. We got to them in time."

Kip broke into a wide grin. "That's fantastic news. I hated sitting on the sidelines."

"I know it sucks. Could have just as easily been in one of your churches and me sitting."

The door opened behind her. Kip's eyes rose to the door then back to Jo. He reached out and gently ran his thumb across her cheek. "As long as you're okay."

Aneace cleared her throat. "Good afternoon, Mr. Riley."

Jo jerked and looked over her shoulder. Jack stood stock-still in the doorway, his hand still on the handle.

Jo took a step away from Kip. "Jack, you're just in time."

Jack glared at Kip. "It appears so."

"We found Amanda Reed and arrested Mark Campbell. Lynae shot him, but it was a clean shot. He'll live. She's at the hospital."

Jack's eyes settled on Jo. "That's great news." His eyes darted to Kip. "I guess that means you'll be heading back to Ohio."

Kip straightened his shoulders. "Yes, I suppose it does. We'll have to continue to work together throughout the trial."

"I imagine that can be done via email," Jack replied.

Kip hooked his thumbs in his front pockets and rocked back on his heels. "We'll see."

"You've been a tremendous help. I'm glad we could work together," Jo said.

"It's been my pleasure."

Jo checked her watch. "I need to get a statement from Amanda. Mark Campbell will be in surgery, and we'll have to wait until the doctors give us the okay to interrogate him. It could be a couple days. You could still make it home tonight. You already stayed longer than planned."

"I'm actually going to give my lieutenant a call. I'd like to stick around for the interview with the suspect if she'll approve it."

"Of course. If she doesn't approve—"

"Why don't we talk about the plan over dinner?" Kip interrupted. He held Jo's gaze and eased into his oh-so-sexy smile.

Jo felt a dim pulse of electricity.

Jack spread his legs in a defensive stance and worked his jaw.

Jo caught his eye. Her pulse spiked, blood surging to her heart. She spread her arms and looked down at herself. "I'm going to clean up then head to the hospital. After I talk to Amanda, I have a personal matter to take care of."

Kip cocked his head with a slight bow. "Another time, then."

Jo gave him an unencouraging smile. "Another time."

Jack twirled his keys around his index finger and strolled to the elevator. "I've got a meeting to get to. Congratulations on the bust."

Jo and Kip stepped onto the elevator behind him.

"Thanks. It's a huge relief to have Amanda safely back," Jo replied.

"And to have a madman off the streets," Kip added.

Jo leaned against the elevator wall. "Madman, yes, but also a guy with a messed-up childhood who had everything in his life fall apart."

Jack nudged her shoulder with his. "You're not getting soft, are you, Lieutenant?"

Jo pushed down any thoughts of feeling sorry for Mark Campbell. A lot of people had messed-up childhoods. And even more people had lives that fell apart. But that didn't give them a free ticket to kill. She gave Jack a scornful look. "Hell, no. Son of a bitch shot Nae."

Jack snorted. "That's more like it. Wait... what? Is she okay?"

"She was wearing a vest. She'll be bruised, but she's okay." Jo jabbed him with her elbow. "You think I'd be here chatting if she wasn't?"

"Yeah, I wasn't thinking."

Jo turned to Kip. "I have to make a call to the state police and get cleaned up, but then I can help you get your box packed back up before I go."

"Already done. I had nervous time to kill while you were making my bust," he replied.

Jo cocked an eyebrow and glared at him. "Your bust?"

Kip shrugged. "Just sayin'."

The elevator stopped, and the doors slid open. Jo headed to her office while Kip broke off to the conference room. *His bust?*

She opened the side drawer of her credenza, pulled out a neatly folded white button-up that she kept for emergencies, then headed for the restroom. After cleaning up, she threw her coat back on, grabbed her bag, and left.

AFTER TAKING THE SHORT drive to Spectrum Hospital, Jo parked in the massive visitor parking structure then pulled off her police jacket, grabbed her plaid ski jacket from the back, and wrangled it on. After pulling her hair out of the tight ponytail, she ran her hand through it then pulled down the visor and looked in the mirror. *Shit, there's blood on my face.* She riffled through her bag, found an antiseptic wipe, and cleaned it off before hopping out of the truck.

After crossing the skywalk to the main building, she headed to the emergency room. Badging the triage nurse at the front desk, she said, "Amanda Reed."

The nurse led her to a room and poked her head in the door before holding it open and stepping aside. Amanda lay on her side, facing her husband, who had pulled a chair close to the bed.

Mr. Reed looked up and jumped to his feet. "You're the detective who... I don't... I don't know how to thank you."

Jo smiled. "Having your wife here safe and sound is all the thanks I need." Walking farther into the dimly lit room, she peered at Amanda. "How's she doing?"

"All stitched up and sleeping."

"Not sleeping," Amanda mumbled.

Tom sat back down and took his wife's hand. "You should be."

"I'll talk to the lieutenant first," she said as she struggled to roll over.

Scooting around the bed, Jo said, "Don't move. You're fine right there."

"Why does it hurt more now than it did a couple hours ago?"

"Adrenaline. You had bigger things to worry about then."

Tom stood and motioned for Jo to take his chair. "I'm going to go call my parents and check on the kids. I'll be right back."

After he left the room, Amanda rolled her eyes. "He probably won't leave my side for months."

Jo chuckled. "I have a feeling you're right. And I can't say I blame him."

"Yeah, this isn't something I'm going to get over right away."

Jo slid into the chair and pulled a notebook out of her bag. "When you're feeling better, I'm going to ask you to walk me through everything you remember from beginning to end."

"Okay, but I have some blank spots. Like I remember meeting him in the parking lot at church. He told me who he was. He was smiling and friendly." Amanda's eyebrows furrowed as her eyes shifted from side to side. "Then I don't remember anything until I woke up in this bedroom with crosses and this weird painting."

"Were you bound?" Jo asked.

Amanda squeezed her eyes shut and nodded. "I thought he was going to..."

"Did he sexually assault you?"

"No, nothing like that. Mostly, he paced the floor, mumbling to himself. He had these pamphlets that he kept reading from. It was weird stuff."

Jo jotted a note in her book then asked, "Were the pamphlets religious?"

"Yeah, but not a religion like I've ever heard. He had a knife, and he would cut me while he was reading from them. He said he wanted me to suffer like I made Jerry suffer. He kept saying, 'He bled for our sins. You'll bleed for yours.'" Amanda reached her hand out and gripped Jo's arm. "I never meant to hurt Jerry. I wasn't trying to use religion *against* him. I was trying to help. My faith makes me feel secure and loved. I wanted to give him that too. But I was young, and I didn't know how to handle it. I did it all wrong."

Jo set her notebook and pen in her lap then laid her hand over Amanda's. "You've spent a lot of years blaming yourself. It's time to forgive yourself. I think that's what Jerry would want."

Amanda pulled her hand away and wiped her eyes. "I'm sure he would. He was a sweet guy."

After dropping her notebook into her bag, Jo stood and laid her hand on Amanda's shoulder. "Why don't you get some sleep. I'll come by your house and talk to you again when you're up to it."

Nodding, Amanda closed her eyes. "Thank you, Lieutenant."

Jo left the room and waved at Tom, who waited outside the door, then headed back to the front desk, where she was told that elevator C would get her to the heart center.

Once in the elevator, she shuffled from foot to foot as the doors closed. She yanked up the strap of her bag, fidgeted with the snap, and stared at the floor indicator as the elevator rose.

An elderly woman leaning on a three-legged cane with tennis balls attached to the feet reached out and patted Jo's hand. "It will all be okay, dear."

Jo looked down at the pale, gnarled hand. "I sure hope you're right."

The elevator dinged, and the doors opened. Jo stepped to the side and held her hand in front of the door to keep it from closing.

The woman looked up, her cloudy brown eyes filled with wisdom. "Things have a way of working out the way they're supposed to. Whatever that way is."

Jo half smiled and laid her hand on the old woman's bony shoulder. "Thank you. I needed to hear that."

The woman nodded then made her way painstakingly slowly out the door. Jo watched her toddle down the long corridor then checked the directory and went the other way. She approached the nurses' station and leaned on the counter.

A pretty young nurse smiled up at her. "Can I help you?"

Jo glanced at the photo ID that hung on a clip from her blue uniform. "You're Katie Greenboro?"

The young woman's eyes grew wide. "Are you Lieutenant Riskin?"

"Yes, I am. Is Mauricio Duarte still here?"

Katie smirked. "Those darn chest pains just won't go away." Her smile faded as she quickly glanced around. "But they're going to have to before they order more invasive testing. Right now, we're just monitoring."

Jo leaned in. "Thank you. If you could take me to his room, I'll find out what he wanted to talk to me about. He may feel better after he gets whatever it is off his chest. Pun intended."

Katie giggled and jerked her head in the opposite direction of where Jo had come from. "He's this way."

Jo followed the girl, who walked faster than her tiny frame should have allowed, to the end of the cool green hallway, then they turned left.

The nurse gave a door a cursory knock then poked her head in. "Mr. Duarte? You have a visitor."

Jo jutted her chin at the officer sitting in the visitor chair. He inclined his head stiffly back.

Jo unzipped her jacket and pulled it back enough to reveal her badge then reached her hand out to the officer. "Lieutenant Riskin, GRPD."

Jo's head slowly eased back as the man stood to his full height. He shook Jo's hand in a viselike grip. "Tanner Wilson."

Tanner released Jo's hand, and she fought not to wiggle her fingers. "Can you give me a few minutes with your prisoner, Tanner?"

Tanner shook his head. "I'm responsible for him. I have to stay with him at all times."

Jo nodded. "I understand and appreciate that." She gave Mauricio an intentionally thorough look. "He's cuffed to the bed, and I'm armed. I'll take responsibility for him inside this room. If you stand right outside the door, he can't go anywhere. I think that covers us."

The officer assessed the situation and the prisoner. His square jaw worked as he considered Jo. "My ass is on the line..."

"And will be covered by me. I'm a superior officer. If anyone questions your decision, you can tell them I gave you a direct order."

Tanner craned his neck to the right until it cracked. He looked over Jo's head at Mauricio and pointed, his bicep straining the seams of his uniform shirt. "The lieutenant is in charge, but I'm right outside that door."

Nodding nervously, Mauricio darted his eyes from the officer to Jo. Tanner swaggered to the door and yanked it open. Jo waited for the door to close fully then turned to the bed. Mauricio had pulled the white sheet up to his chest, one corner balled up in his clenched fist.

As she eased into the chair next to the bed, Jo said, "I understand you want to talk to me."

Mauricio's eyes darted to the door. "I can't go back there. He's gonna kill me."

Jo's heartbeat quickened. "Who's going to kill you?"

"I hadda get outta there. I couldn't talk to you there," he whispered. His leg bounced compulsively.

"Who's going to kill you, Mauricio?"

His eyes again shot to the door then back to Jo. "The same guy that killed Drevin."

"Drevin Clayburn killed himself," Jo said calmly over the thundering sound of her rushing blood.

Mauricio licked his lips and shook his head frantically. "No, he didn't. He said he was gettin' out. He didn't off hisself. He killed him. And he knows I know."

"Who is *he*?" Jo asked.

The man's leg bounced harder. He balled up the sheet, let go and pressed it out, then balled it up again. "I don't know his name. The guy that came and talked to Drevin right before he died."

"Would you know him if you saw him again?"

Mauricio's eyes grew wide, and his head jerked to the door. "See him? Is he here?"

Shaking her head, Jo laid a hand on the man's forearm. "No. No one is going to hurt you here." She pulled her bag off her shoulder then took out a blue file folder and pulled a picture from inside it. She gazed at Mike's laughing face as he and Rick stood on either side of their captain in a group picture taken at the last division golf outing Mike ever attended. Jo's gaze went to the captain's crooked grin. The group was reacting to some joke no one would remember. Her blood boiled. *If you betrayed him...*

She turned the picture around and held it in front of Mauricio. "Is that man in this picture?"

Mauricio's eyes scanned the picture. His eyes locked in then shot up to Jo's. "Yeah."

She struggled to control her breathing and keep her hands steady. *His own captain. What could be worse?* She took a steadying breath through her nose. "Can you point to him?"

"Are you gonna protect me?"

"Which one?" Jo said again through clenched teeth.

Mauricio's hand snaked out from beneath the sheet. His finger tapped the picture. "That one."

Jo shook her head. The picture dropped from her hand. She sucked in an unsteady breath. "Are you sure?"

Mauricio nodded. "You gotta protect me."

Jo dropped to her knees and picked the picture up from the floor. Her eyes locked onto where Mauricio had pointed. Bile burned in the back of her throat.

Rick. Oh Mike, your own partner. Your best friend. Her heart ached for the betrayal her husband would have felt in those last moments. The thought of Mike's best friend, the person he trusted to always have his back, the best man in their wedding, betraying him so horribly shook Jo to her core. She thought of Lynae and the trust she had in her partner—the confidence to go through any door with Lynae at her back—and what it would be like to know Lynae had set her up to be shot in the line. Mike knew he had been set up. He had tried to tell her, but she couldn't see it through her grief. Her mind had told her she was looking for a drug dealer, and she had been blinded by her trust in Rick.

Not anymore, you son of a bitch.

Mauricio eyed her cautiously. "Who is that guy?"

Jo cleared her throat. "You're telling me that's the guy that you saw talking to Drevin Clayburn before he died."

Mauricio nodded. "That's the guy. And Drevin, he came back all cocky, said he told him where the bear shits in the woods. He had a recording of that guy telling him to off that cop. That was when he told me he was gettin' out."

Jo's stomach churned as she tried to wrap her mind around Rick's betrayal. She held up the picture and pointed at Rick. "And it was this man. After talking to *this* man, Drevin was sure he was getting out."

Mauricio's head bobbed. "Yeah, that guy got him the gun and told him to switch plates with a random car so he wouldn't get caught. He told me all about it. And now he's dead. And that guy in the picture, he knows I know. He's gonna kill me too."

"How do you know he knows about you?" Jo asked.

Mauricio licked his lips, and his hand tapped compulsively on the bedrail. The handcuff chain rattled against the metal. "He was there. The day you came and asked me questions? He was there again." Mauricio's eyes grew wide. "Did you tell him you were talking to me? I didn't tell you anything."

Jo laid her hand on the mattress for support. Her world was spinning. "I haven't spoken with anyone about our meeting. And you're right. You didn't tell me anything. Did he speak to you that day?"

The man shook his head. "He walked by my cell. Ran his hand along the bars. But he didn't talk to me."

"What makes you afraid for your life? He could have been there for any number of reasons."

"The guard, he came by later, and he said, 'Keep your head on a swivel, Duarte. Lewis has eyes everywhere.'"

Jo's heart lurched. "Which guard? What's his name?"

Mauricio pushed his hand against the mattress and hoisted his body up farther in the bed. His bound arm pulled against the cuff. "Conti. He's cool, you know, treats us good. He was warning me. I don't know no more than that, but I think Drevin told that cop that he told me. You know, like I'm his backup or somethin'." His eyes grew wide in a pleading expression. "I got a family, and I'm goin' clean when I get out. I swear. You gotta help me."

Jo's mind reeled. Images flashed behind her eyes in rapid succession: their wedding; Rick's toast; fantasy football draft day as they sat around their dining room table with Rick harassing Mike on every pick; golf outings; fishing trips; poker games; and Jo and Rick's wife, Sheila, rolling their eyes at their husbands' obvious man crush on each other. The betrayal cut so deep Jo felt it slice through her bones.

Officer Wilson poked his head in the door. "Everything all right in here, Lieutenant?"

Mauricio's head swiveled to the door, and his foot bounced.

Jo put on a blank mask. "Everything's fine, Officer. We're almost finished."

The officer nodded, pulled his head back, and let the door close.

Jo turned back to Mauricio. "Are your chest pains real?"

The man blinked rapidly, his lips pinched together.

Jo nodded faintly. "Understood. Listen, I can't encourage you to stay here pretending to have medical issues. Eventually, the tests they run will be more invasive, and any unnecessary procedure runs a risk."

The man's eyes shot to Jo's. "It's better than being dead."

Jo tapped her fingers on her thigh rhythmically. "Let me try to pull some strings. They won't do anything more today."

Mauricio grabbed her hand. "Are you gonna help me?"

Jo put her hand on top of his. "Yes, I am," she said, looking him in the eye.

"How do I know? You could just be saying that."

"Two weeks ago, I went to court to speak on behalf of the man that led us to Drevin Clayburn. For two years, he withheld information that I needed. As angry as that made me, I gave him my word that I would go to bat for him if he helped me. And I did." Jo gave Mauricio a level stare. "You have my word."

The man's eyes scanned the room, his jaw clenched. His head bobbed in a rapid nod.

Jo stood, looked one more time at the group picture, then slid it into her bag. "I'll be back."

She turned on her heel, flung the door open, and stormed out of the room. The officer jolted out of his position slouched against the wall next to the door.

Jo flung her hand toward the door. "He's all yours." *Don't know if I can trust you, either, Officer. Don't want to look like I'm satisfied with my meeting.*

Jo left the hospital and walked back to her truck. She ripped the door open, dropped into her seat, and covered her face with her hands. A sob erupted from deep in her throat. "Oh God, Mike. I'm so sorry."

The tears came, and she let them then rubbed her burning eyes and dug through her purse for a Kleenex. Then the anger set in. *His best friend. His partner. For what? Money? Self-preservation? What would make you kill your friend?*

She knew the temptation was there for some—drug money there for the taking before it was documented, or the payoffs to look the other way, miss the bust, take the information from the informants, and use it to steer your team in the wrong direction. It would be so easy. Every cop knew some would take that temptation, but they were few and far between. And she'd never thought she knew any of them. Not in her worst nightmare was it Rick.

But it was.

She gazed at the photo-booth-picture strip she kept tucked in her dashboard. Mike grinned mischievously as Jo kissed his cheek. It was such a happy moment.

"How did I miss it for so long, Mike?"

Grief is blinding.

"I knew you wouldn't just crash into that warehouse unprepared. You were too good for that. Nae questioned it immediately."

You trusted Rick and took him at his word. So did I.

"Why didn't Madison catch it? He was the damn investigator. He had the file, did the interviews, and had the full resources of his department. Was he involved? Did Rick pay him off?" Jo's mind dug into a smorgasbord of possibilities.

Slow down, Jo. One step at a time. First, you have to prove it. Be careful. You're dealing with a detective. He'll know if you're sniffing around.

Jo dropped her head back onto the headrest. "I've already been sniffing around.

You were looking for a drug dealer, not a dirty cop. Look at the evidence again but with new eyes.

"I wish you were here."

I am here, Jo. I'll always be here. But it's time to move on.

"What?" She jerked to sit upright. "No."

She knew she was talking to her subconscious. She knew Mike's words were her own thoughts lingering in the back of her mind, too afraid or stubborn to come out on their own.

She wiped her eyes and started the truck. "I know you're gone, but I'm never going to stop wishing you weren't."

LOST IN HER THOUGHTS, she drove home. Rick had set Mike up that night. He went into that bust knowing his partner was going to die, and in those last moments, Mike knew it. He had tried to tell her.

Why did he do it? Had he been dirty for a while and Mike found out?

Drevin Clayburn knew why and had probably threatened to turn State's evidence against him. Now he was dead, and Mauricio Duarte feared for his life. One vicious act led to another. It had to end somewhere.

It ends here and now.

She pulled into her driveway and sat in the truck, staring at her house. She wanted to scream and cry. She wanted to barge into Rick's house and tell him she knew what he'd done to his partner, to the man who considered him his best friend. To her love.

But giving away her hand and quite possibly doing something she would live to regret wasn't going to help. She needed a voice of reason. She grabbed her phone from the truck console and dialed Jack's number.

His smooth baritone filled the line. "Hey, Jo."

The sound of his voice broke another dam, and Jo could only squeak out a few words. "I need you."

"Where are you? Are you hurt?"

"Home. Not hurt," she managed.

"I'll be there."

She threw the phone onto the passenger seat and laid her head back. She couldn't put one foot in front of the other to get out of the truck and walk into her house, so she sat there, stuffing down her emotions and putting her guards back up.

Jack's car swung into her driveway, and he parked behind her truck. Jo got out of the truck and met him between their vehicles.

He searched her eyes, worry and compassion playing across his face. "What's going on?"

Her guards fell, and her emotions rocketed back to the surface. She covered her face and collapsed into his arms. "It was Rick."

He wrapped his arms tightly around her, his cheek pressed against the top of her head. "What was Rick? Who's Rick?"

"Rick Lewis was Mike's partner. He set him up," she mumbled against his chest.

He stepped back, both hands on Jo's shoulders. "God, I'm sorry, Jo. How do you know?"

She pulled a Kleenex out of her pocket and wiped her nose. "Drevin told his cellmate. That was why he was so sure he was getting out."

"So Mike told the paramedics, 'set up,' not 'sit up,'" he said quietly.

She pinched the bridge of her nose. The paramedics had told her Mike kept saying, "sit up" and "Jo." He had been trying to tell her. "I was too close to it. All this time, it was right under my nose, and I didn't see it."

Jack folded her back into his arms. "Don't blame yourself. Someone not so close to it should have caught it. Are you sure about this?"

"I'm sure, but I don't have any proof. Why don't you come in the house. I'll tell you what I found out."

He looked over his shoulder at his car. "Well..."

Jo jerked her head to look at his car. "Is someone with you?"

Is he on a date? She felt as if she'd been punched.

"Yeah."

She stepped back. "Why didn't you say so? I didn't mean to interrupt your night."

"You interrupted me making grilled cheese sandwiches while the kids watched *Bubble Guppies* on Nick Junior."

The kids. Of course. Her relief was palpable. "I'm sorry. I didn't even think."

Jack closed the gap between them and took her hand. "I don't want you to think before you call me."

She squeezed his hand. "Bring them in. I make a mean grilled cheese."

"Mojo?"

"She loves kids. The worst she'll do is lick their faces. I'll go in and get her calmed down first, though. She's probably about crazy by now with me sitting out here all this time."

"I'll get the kids, then," Jack said.

Jo dug her keys out of her pocket while walking to the garage. As soon as she approached the service door, she could hear Mojo whining on the other side. She opened it and braced herself for the onslaught from her wiggling, slobbering furball. Instead, Mojo bolted through the door and ran to the driveway, barking frantically. Jo raced behind her.

Jack froze at his car, one child on his hip, the other holding his hand. "Hi, Mojo," he said calmly.

Mojo's bark turned to an excited whine as her tail wagged her whole body. The little girl holding Jack's hand squealed, let go of his grip, and ran toward the dog, blond curls bouncing. Jo dropped down beside Mojo and took her collar. The excited dog strained her neck forward, her tongue making desperate attempts to connect with the little girl's face.

"Be gentle, Maddie," Jack warned.

Jo smiled. "It's okay. She won't hurt you."

Maddie stroked the dog's head with her mittened hand. Mojo's quick tongue landed a slobbery kiss on the little girl's cheek. She scrunched her face and backed away. When Mojo dropped to the ground and rolled onto her back, Maddie giggled and sat down to rub the dog's belly.

The little boy in Jack's arms reached out and squirmed toward Mojo. Jack squatted down next to the dog, set the boy on the ground between his legs, and guided his hand to gently pet the dog.

"Don't pet her hard, Logan," Maddie said sternly.

Jack winked at Jo and mouthed, "Little mom."

Jo's heart clenched. It all felt so right and normal. She leaned toward Maddie and said quietly, "You know what Mojo really loves?"

Maddie shook her head shyly.

"Watch." Jo raised her voice. "Mojo, where's your ball?"

Mojo's head popped up. She scrambled to her feet and raced into the yard, nose to the ground. In less than a minute, she trotted back with a yellow tennis ball in her mouth, dropped it next to Jo, stepped back, and barked. Jo flung the ball into the air. Mojo took off at a dead run and caught the ball in midair. Maddie giggled, and Logan clapped his chubby hands.

Mojo trotted back proudly and plopped the ball at Jo's feet.

Jo wiped the slobber-covered ball on her pants and held it out to Maddie. "You want to give it a try?"

Mojo watched the exchange as the girl took the ball, and her eyes never left the prize. Maddie threw the ball as far as her young arm could then squealed with delight when Mojo bolted after it. The dog came back, dropped it at Jo's feet, and quivered in anticipation.

Jo picked it up and wiped it off then raised her eyebrows at Jack. "Why don't we take this to the backyard."

"Right behind you." He scooped up Logan and swung him easily onto his shoulders.

The toddler beamed and grabbed Jack's hair in both dimpled fists.

Jo snapped her fingers. "In the house, Mojo."

The dog raced through the garage service door. Jo winked as Maddie looked up at her, wide-eyed. "She's pretty smart."

Inside the house, she thumbed on the floodlights for the backyard. "Why don't you take the kids and Mojo out to the backyard while I make the sandwiches," she said as she opened the fridge and took out the fixings for grilled cheese.

Jack slid his hand under her chin and lifted her head. "Then we'll talk."

"Yeah," she breathed.

Jack kissed her forehead then turned around and gestured grandly. "Come on, crew. Let's take this outside." He opened the slider to the backyard and led the kids out.

Mojo stood in the doorway, wagging her tail and looking at Jo.

"Go on," Jo said. The words were barely out of her mouth when the dog scampered through the door and into the yard.

As she grilled the sandwiches and put them on plates with potato chips and pickles, Jo realized she was humming. The giggles and squeals from the backyard warmed her heart, and she stopped more than once to watch them through the window. She set the plates on the table then stuck her head out the slider door. "Dinner's ready."

"Yay, grilled cheese," Jack yelled, throwing his hands in the air.

The kids giggled and ran for the door with the dog on their heels. Jo helped Jack strip off their boots, coats, hats, and mittens then he herded them into the bathroom to wash their hands while she set down food and water for Mojo. The dog flopped on the floor with a groan, tongue lolling out the side of her mouth.

"They're busy, aren't they, old girl?" Jo chuckled, patting her head.

Dinner was a whirlwind of chattering kids, spilled milk, and dropped food. Mojo quickly learned that the most advantageous place for her to lie was under the table, where she vacuumed up every crumb that fell. When they were finished and the kids were settled into the living room to watch a cartoon, Jack came back to the table to help clean up. "Bet you didn't know two kids could wreak such havoc in such a short amount of time."

Jo surveyed the table. "It *is* impressive. Next time, bring sippy cups." *Did I just say next time?*

He handed Jo her water glass. "I was in a bit of a hurry."

"Thanks for dropping everything and coming."

He pulled out a chair and gestured for her to take it. "That cartoon will keep them entertained for a while. Tell me what happened today."

Jo slid into the chair and leaned her elbows on the table then scrubbed her face with her hands and rubbed her temples. "You know, for a few minutes, I actually forgot about it."

"Kids will do that," Jack said then took her hand. "Now talk to me."

She took a deep breath then launched into a full account of her conversation with Mauricio Duarte. Jack was quiet through the whole speech, interjecting only the occasional exclamation or question.

Finally, Jo got up, went to the kitchen, and pulled the picture of Mike, Rick, and the captain out of her bag. She brought it back to the table and dropped it in front of Jack. "I showed Mauricio this picture and asked him if the person Drevin talked to was in it." She squeezed her eyes shut, took a few deep breaths through her nose, and worked her jaw to keep the tears at bay. "I thought it was the captain. But it was Rick." She covered her face with her hands. Her voice cracked. "His own partner."

Jack scooted his chair closer and wrapped his arm around her shoulders. "I hate to ask, but are you sure this source is reliable?"

Jo pulled away and rubbed her eyes. "He's afraid for his life enough that he's faking heart pain to stay in the hospital. He's sure if he goes back, he'll end up 'committing suicide' like Drevin."

"That's a serious accusation. You're going to need some evidence."

Jo threw her hands up. "Don't you think I know that?" It came out louder than she meant it to. She looked over her shoulder at the kids, but they sat oblivious to anything other than the dancing characters on the television. "Sorry, I didn't mean... I know you're just trying to help."

He gave her a half smile. "I'm thinking like a prosecutor. Which is what I think you need. You can't go off half-cocked and start throwing accusations out against another cop."

"I know. Do you know what it took for me to not drive to Rick's house and kick his door in? I want to corner him and shake him down."

"Jo—"

She held up her hand. "I know I can't. I know I have to play dumb." She pushed to her feet and gave her chair a shove. "Which should be easy since I've been dumb for the last two years."

"Knock it off," Jack snapped.

Jo raised her eyebrows at his tone.

Jack crossed his arms. "I mean it. Stop beating yourself up."

She pressed her lips together and squeezed her eyes shut. "You're right. It won't help. I have to find a way to protect Mauricio long enough to nail Rick."

"Even if he is worried about this Mauricio guy, he isn't going to kill him. It would be pretty obvious if two cellmates ended up dead within a short time frame."

Jo walked to the window and gazed out at the backyard, which an hour earlier had held so much fun. Now it was just cold and empty. "He's scared. He'll make a mistake. Drevin threatened to turn on him, and he took a dangerous chance going to the jail."

"He must have a partner."

"The captain. He took the call to cover in solitary. They must have set the whole thing up. I have nothing but gut on that one, but I know it now like I know my own life story."

Leaning back in his chair, Jack crossed an ankle over the other knee. His pant leg pulled up to reveal tiny snowmen on his socks. "There has to be video. That place is on tight surveillance."

Jo nodded. "Internal Affairs took it immediately. I'm sure they won't let me see it, but I'll call Don Moreland, the IA officer who's handling the case. He's looking at suicide, but he'll be thorough. I'll just hint at a blip of missing time he should keep his eye open for. I'm sure he'll be thrilled to have me chime in with advice," she said sarcastically.

"Why don't you let me call him?"

"And what legitimate reason could you possibly have for even asking about the case?"

Jack opened then closed his mouth and smiled sheepishly. "Yeah, you're right."

"He knows my interest and won't question my pursuing it. I don't want to tip my hand to Rick." She could hardly say his name without grimacing. The taste of deceit and betrayal felt bitter on her tongue. "He saw me at the jail. I ran into him as I was leaving."

Jack's face fell. "Did you tell him why you were there?"

She searched her memory. The encounter had left her feeling better until she made the connection with the captain. "I don't think I did."

"If he knew why you were there, you could be in danger."

"He wouldn't come after me. I know I asked him why they went in without backup." She crumpled onto the sill of the picture window. "I did the same thing today. I told them to send backup then went in without it."

"You were just—"

"I almost got Nae killed," Jo interrupted.

Jack pushed to his feet and in two strides was in front of Jo. He took her by the shoulders. "It's not the same thing, Jo. You went in to save a life."

"I know, but—"

"No buts. Lynae is okay. Yes, you made a mistake. And I'll feel a whole lot better if you learn from it and never make that mistake again. But you weren't going in with the intention of hurting your partner."

"God, no. She's my best friend." Jo smirked. "You should have seen Jacobs. He came plowing in there and just about crushed Nae. He heard my call and knew it was her."

Jack cocked his head. "Are they a thing?"

Jo shrugged. "No, but it could happen. I can see it."

"If you say so. Look, it's been a hell of a day. Why don't you make it an early night?"

Jo pushed away from the window. Cartoon noises and kid giggles came from the next room. *It's going to be so quiet when they leave.* "Why don't you stay for a bit. I haven't watched cartoons in a while."

Jack snorted. "Oh, gee, you poor thing. No dancing animals or terrible child actors? How do you manage?"

"It's a struggle." She grabbed their glasses of water and led the way to the family room.

Jack sat on the sofa, and she dropped down beside him, propping her feet on the end table and leaning against his shoulder. Little Logan toddled over, and Jack lifted him onto his lap. Before long, Maddie crawled onto Jo's lap. Jo pulled a blanket from the back of the sofa, wrapped it around her tiny frame, and snuggled her close.

Two hours later, when Jack decided it was time to get the kids home and into bed, Jo's heart ached to keep them all there. She helped him carry the sleeping kids to the car and buckled in, then snuck a kiss on Maddie's forehead before slipping out of the car.

Jack leaned against the driver's door. "I've been thinking."

"Scary."

He gave her a flat look. "I'm worried that Rick may realize you're on to something. He's a dangerous man."

She cocked her head. "Trying to find a way to stay and protect me?"

He raised an eyebrow. "Well, there *is* that picnic we never had."

Jo rolled her eyes and raised her hand to smack his shoulder, but she stopped mid-smack. "Maybe we should *let* Rick know we're on to him."

"What do you mean?"

"If Rick gets nervous, that's when he'll make a mistake. He should know we're on to something. I need to piece it together, but I have an idea brewing."

He crossed his arms. "You won't go off and do something on your own, right?"

She put her left hand on her heart and raised her right hand as she backed toward her house. Jack sighed, got into his car, and started to back slowly down the driveway.

Jo could see the silhouette of the car seats and little sleeping heads in the back seat and could smell Jack's cologne in her hair. She ran to the car and caught him at the end of the drive.

He rolled the window down. "Did I forget something?"

Jo leaned in and kissed him softly.

When she drew back, he wore his lazy smile. "Did I forget anything else?"

She slid her hand into his hair and kissed him again. That time, she didn't hold back. The jolt it sent through her took her by surprise. She hadn't thought she would ever feel that jolt again. She pulled back and pressed her forehead against his.

"If I keep asking, will you keep answering the same way?" he asked.

She smiled and leaned in for one last quick kiss then stepped back. "You have to get the kids into bed, and I have a plan to put together."

Jack leaned his head against the headrest. "You're killing me. Call me in the morning."

"I will," she promised. She gave a quick wave then went back into the house. She would be up all night again, but she wouldn't be poring over the details of Mike's murder. She would be putting a plan into action to catch the man responsible for it.

Chapter 24

When Lynae stepped out of the elevator at seven forty-five, Jo was waiting at her desk. "The coffee's hot. Grab a cup and come to my office."

Lynae pulled her coat off and dropped it into her chair then unwound the striped GVSU Lakers scarf that she had wrapped around her neck and dropped it on top of her coat. "You look wired. How long have you been up? And how much coffee have you had?"

"What day is it? And I lost track a couple pots ago."

Lynae closed her eyes. "Oh boy."

"I'll be in my office."

After a few minutes, Lynae came in with her hands wrapped around a cup of coffee and propped herself on the side of Jo's desk. She took a sip of the steaming coffee. "Okay, what's going on?"

"First things first," Jo said, holding out a firearm. "Your replacement weapon. You'll get yours back when this is all settled. I spoke with the Michigan State Police, and they will be doing the investigation. I'm sure they'll be contacting you today."

"I'll just be sitting at home, knitting or something." Lynae took the gun and slid it into the empty holster clipped to her belt. "I know he's a serial killer and all, but I'm really glad I didn't kill him. That's the first time I've actually had to discharge my weapon at a scene."

"Shooting a person is never something to take lightly, but in this case, you probably saved a life. And it very well could have been mine, so thank you."

"I got your six, partner."

Picking up her coffee cup, Jo noticed a distinct shake in her hand. Apparently, there *was* such a thing as too much coffee. She took a sip, anyway. "Mark Campbell had surgery last night to remove the bullet that you so nicely placed into his shoulder. He's secure—cuffed and guarded. He isn't going anywhere, so I'll wait until tomorrow to interrogate him."

Lynae set her cup down on Jo's desk. "I wish I could do that with you."

"Me, too, partner."

"But since we caught him with our victim and he confessed to the murders, it's pretty much a formality."

Jo shook her head. "I want intent. I don't want him to get off on an insanity plea. This took planning and plenty of it. It was premeditated and drawn out over a significant period of time. I want a full time frame, why he chose the victims and locations, and how he carried out the plan."

"What about Amanda Reed? Were you able to interview her?"

"I was, but it was short. She didn't tell me much that I didn't already know. Since she was awake and coherent inside the house, she'll be able to identify it. I think it's as we suspected. Messed-up childhood and then one thing after another going wrong in his life in a short period of time. He just snapped. Finding out about Jerry was the straw that broke the camel's back."

"And he used religion to justify his revenge."

On a shrug, Jo said, "It's sad how badly people can warp something that's meant to be sacred and comforting."

"That's messed up, but this isn't why you were up all night, drinking pots of coffee."

Jo took another sip of coffee. She was pretty sure her blood-to-coffee level was well above the legal limit. "No, it isn't. I'm going to fill you in quickly, but then you have to go home. As bad as it sucks, you shouldn't be here for anything more than your weapon."

"I know." Lynae sighed.

Jo laid out the story of her encounter with Mauricio in all its detail. When she choked out the part where Mauricio picked Rick out of the picture, Lynae gasped and covered her mouth.

"Oh no, no, no. Not his partner."

"Yeah, his partner. Which brings me to today. I have a plan to take down Rick. I want to lay it out for you before I bring in the whole team, but..."

"I know, I have to get out of here. Suspension and stuff." As Lynae reached for her coffee cup, she winced and absently rubbed her side. "I just don't understand how someone could betray their partner like that."

Jo laid a hand on Lynae's arm. "Have I mentioned how sorry I am that I dragged you into that church without backup?"

"Jo, don't. You didn't drag me anywhere. In fact, I believe I was the one who found the open door."

Jo dropped her hand and concentrated on the floor tiles as they swam beneath her moist eyes. "I'm the lieutenant. I'm responsible."

"Didn't we already have this conversation?"

"Nae, if I ever lost you, I don't know what I would do."

Holding up her hand, Lynae said, "Stop. Other than a healthy bruise, I'm fine. And I'm not going anywhere. But why didn't you call me last night after you found out about Rick?"

Jo smirked. "You left with Doug."

Lynae clenched her jaw and glared at Jo. "So what? You shouldn't have been alone."

"I wasn't."

Lynae grabbed her arm. "What? And you waited this long to tell me?"

"I called Jack. He came over... with the kids."

"Oh, with the kids." Lynae groaned.

"They played in the backyard with Mojo, and we ate grilled cheese and watched cartoons. Maddie sat on my lap and fell asleep."

Lynae's expression softened. "That sounds nice."

"It was exactly what I needed," Jo whispered. She pushed away from her desk. "Now what I need is to set up this sting so I can fry the ass of the bastard who killed my husband."

"And... she's back. Who are you going to bring in on it?"

"Charles. He's great at spotting holes in a plan." Jo eyeballed the bull pen. "And it looks like he's here."

Once she'd zipped up her coat and grabbed her coffee cup, Lynae backed toward the door. "On my way out, I'll tell him you want to talk to him."

"Thanks. I'll call you as soon as this is done. We'll grab a beer, and I'll tell you everything."

"I'll be dying a slow death until then." Lynae left the office, and within a minute, Charles was at her door.

"Lynae said you want to see me?"

"Have a seat," Jo said then launched into the same story she had just finished telling Lynae.

When she stopped to take a breath, Charles said, "How do we fry the bastard, and how soon can we do it?"

"How quickly can you put together a surveillance team with audio?"

"Probably as quickly as you can brief whoever we're wiring. Wait—it isn't you, is it? Because I don't think that's a good plan."

Jo shook her head. "No, I thought about that, but it would never work. My plan is to use Jack as bait and have Mauricio wired."

"How can Jack be bait?"

"He'll call Rick and tell him he's got a prisoner that has solid information that could lead to more arrests on Mike's murder. He can be vague, tell him he doesn't know any more than that but that since Rick was Mike's partner, he wanted to keep him informed."

"Rick will be in a panic, knowing the only information this prisoner could have is against him," Charles said.

"Exactly. Jack will give him a short time frame to act. He won't be able to put together much of a plan other than threats."

"Audio surveillance will be easy, but video would be a nice boost."

Jo hesitated. Video would be ideal, but this had to be done quickly. "Do you think you can manage that fast enough? I want to do this today before there's any chance of the hospital releasing Mauricio or Rick getting any ideas without our team there to protect him."

"It shouldn't be a problem." Charles leaned forward and rested his forearms on his thighs. "Okay, what are your concerns with your plan?"

"My main concern, other than just the general fear of this blowing up in my face, is security and safety in the hospital. We have to be able to take him quietly or outside the building."

"Why don't we lay out the logistics and see what we can come up with."

For the next hour, they went over the plan that Jo had spent the whole night formulating, then together they picked people to complete each part of the puzzle.

When they had it laid out, Charles stepped back and surveyed the board with their notes. "This is going to work."

Jo stared at the board, her hands wrapped around her now-empty coffee cup. "The biggest piece is Don Moreland. I have to give him a call this morning and first tell him what I know then convince him this is going to work."

"I don't know him at all, so I have no opinion on what he'll think, but it's a good plan. Does it worry you, wondering who we can trust?"

"I've given that some thought. But I truly believe... I have to be-lieve... that this is isolated. I couldn't do my job if I didn't believe that law enforcement are the good guys. The bad ones like Rick are the rare exception. There are bad people in any job. They just have to be dealt with."

"Yeah, you're right. And it is time to deal with this one."

"Wish me luck." Jo snatched her phone from her back pocket and looked up Don Moreland's number. She punched it in and paced in front of her desk while it rang.

"Don Moreland."

"Don, this is Jo Riskin," Jo began.

"What can I do for you, Lieutenant?"

Jo thought she heard a hint of annoyance in his voice but chose to ignore it and plow right in. "I had an unexpected conversation with Mauricio Duarte, Drevin Clayburn's cellmate, last night, and—"

"How do you have an *unexpected* conversation with an inmate?"

"I got a call from the hospital where he was brought in with chest pain. He gave my card to the nurse and asked her to call me."

"And you didn't think getting me involved would be a good idea?"

Jo had no doubt about his annoyance that time. She sat down and leaned her elbows on her desk and squeezed the back of her neck, where tension was beginning to build. They weren't off to a good start. "I didn't know why he wanted to talk to me, but from what I got from the nurse, he was afraid and asked for me specifical-ly."

"And what did Mr. Duarte have to say that he didn't already tell me in his interview?"

"He identified Mike's partner, Rick Lewis, as the person Drevin met with shortly before he died. Drevin was confident he was getting out after that meeting. He told Mauricio that he was the cop that got him the gun and told him where to be. He also told him that he was working with Rick and that Mike was on to them. Drevin was blackmailing Rick."

"That's a pretty strong assumption."

"Rick told me the only people who knew about the bust that night were him, Mike, and their captain. The same captain who watched the monitors the night Drevin died. And the captain was never mentioned before. I think seeing me threw Rick off, and he slipped."

The other end of the line went silent. Jo waited then pulled the phone away to be certain she still had a connection. "Don?"

"We found two short blips on the surveillance video from that night."

"Blips? What does that mean?"

"A very short loss of time. Nothing in that area changes during that time, so we missed it the first time through. I've been bothered by the timing and went back through the video several times. There's a three-second blip, and twelve minutes later, there's another one. It bothered me because it's too short for anything to happen."

"Except someone slipping past the camera. It's not too short if it's well planned." Jo's heart raced, and her stomach churned. *His partner and his captain?*

"Lieutenant, we've had our eye on Mr. Lewis for a while now."

Jo's heart plunged. "You have? Why didn't I know?"

"You know very well that our department doesn't discuss our investigations with other officers. But I believe we need to work together at this point. However, we have nothing to indicate that the captain was involved. And I'm not about to jump into an accusation like that without proof."

Jo's eyes narrowed, her mind focused. "The inmate who caused the disruption had to be involved. We can lean on him. And if we nail Rick, he'll turn on the captain. I guarantee it. He's a coward. Hear me out."

She laid out the plan that she and Charles had put together. Don interjected with questions and suggestions until they had a new, improved plan.

"I'll deal with the hospital and surveillance," Don said. "You deal with getting the prosecutor on board."

Jo grinned. "Jack will help us. I'm sure of it. This is going to work, Don."

"I hope so. I'll be at your station as soon as I have my team put together."

DON MORELAND BRIEFED his team and Jo's on the operation. They laid out each player's role, covered a map of the hospital floor, and fielded questions. When everyone was confident, they headed to the hospital. On the seventh-floor cardiac unit, Charles stopped to talk to Katie Greenboro while Jo and Don went straight to Mauricio's room. They excused the officer on duty and dropped into chairs next to the man's bed. Don motioned for Jo to take the lead.

She leaned forward and rested her elbows on her knees. "All right, Mr. Duarte, we're both going to get what we want here, but I need your cooperation to make it happen."

The inmate licked his lips. His eyes darted to Detective Moreland. "If I cooperate with you, he's going to kill me."

Jo shook her head. "No one is going to kill you. You're in a hospital. You're guarded. He's a detective and knows it would be impossible to hurt you here without being caught. Now, if you go back to jail..."

Mauricio shook his head vehemently. "I can't go back there."

"I can't keep you from going back to jail. But if you help us catch the man that you're afraid of, he won't be a threat to you anymore.

And I'll be sure to let the judge know you cooperated with us. How soon are you getting out?"

"Not soon enough."

Don sat back and crossed his arms. "You cooperate, and maybe I can make it happen sooner. At the very least, I can get you relocated for the duration of your sentence."

Mauricio shifted his weight. The cuff around his wrist rattled against the metal bedrail. "What do I have to do?"

"If all goes as planned, Detective Lewis will pay you a visit this afternoon," Jo said.

Mauricio's eyes bulged. "No!"

Don held up his hand. "We'll have eyes and ears on you, and officers in the next room. You won't be hurt."

Mauricio's leg bounced violently, and he rubbed his free hand up and down his thigh. "I guess I don't got a choice."

Jo said a silent prayer of thanks. "All I need you to do is tell Mr. Lewis what you know. Be honest, and don't try to make anything up. He'll catch on to that."

Mauricio nodded. "Okay, I can do that."

"I know you can. Don't tell him you've already talked to me. Tell him you're going to talk to a Mr. Riley. Can you remember that?"

Mauricio frowned and looked from Jo to Don. "Mr. Riley. Who's he?"

"He's the county prosecutor. Mr. Lewis will know who he is, so you don't have to remember that. You just have to remember his name."

"And I just tell him Drevin told me everything?" Mauricio asked.

Don nodded. "That's right. Don't make anything up. Just tell him the truth."

"And he's not going to kill me?" The man's voice cracked. He shifted his small frame nervously.

"We'll be watching," Jo said. "If he makes a move toward you, we'll be in your room in seconds."

Mauricio bit his lip. He reached up with his free hand and toyed with a gold crucifix that hung around his neck. "Okay, I'll do it."

Jo wanted to hug the little man. Instead, she stood and gave him a brief nod. "Thank you, Mr. Duarte. My team will be coming in to prep your room."

Don opened the door and stood back to let Jo go through. She motioned to the officer standing guard at the door, and he slipped back into the room.

Nudging her with his elbow, Don said, "Nice work."

Jo beamed. "You too."

"Let's get the team on this."

Jo caught Charles's eye and did a quick fist pump.

He excused himself from the young nurse and strode over to Jo. "He's in?"

"He's in."

Pointing at a uniformed officer who was leaning against the counter of the nurses' station, Charles said, "I've got the officer's replacement here."

Jo looked the officer over. "Perfect. You'll change shifts with the current guard at three o'clock." She turned to Don. "How quickly can you get eyes and ears in that room?"

"They gave us a room down the hall. Well, actually, I think it's a janitor's closet, but we'll be able to cram in there and make it work. The real work happens in that room. It will only take us a half hour to get the equipment set up in the witness's room."

"I don't suppose you have room for Charles and me in that janitor's closet?"

Don gave her a derisive look. "Not a chance. I can barely fit my guys and the equipment in there. Besides, I don't even want you in the building. He could take an unexpected detour. He sees you, it's all over. The guys on my squad have never met Rick, so there's no chance they'll be made."

"I appreciate that, and I expected you'd kick me out. We'll have a car outside." Jo surveyed the surroundings as her mind played through the operation step-by-step. "We stay out until three. As soon as they change guards, you get in and out. I don't know the current guard, so let's keep him out of it. The fewer people involved, the better. I'll have Jack make the call at the same time."

Don nodded. "That's how I would play it."

Jo held her hand up. "And I want ears."

"Of course. I need you out of sight but not out of the loop."

"Appreciate it."

Don bent and picked up one of the heavy silver cases filled with tech gear. "Let's get to it."

Two plainclothes officers gathered the rest of the gear and followed Detective Moreland down the hall to the room they had been assigned. He seemed to have lost his limp. His strut told Jo he was right in his element.

She checked her notes to make sure she wasn't forgetting anything on her list. One misstep, and she could show her hand. Not only would the whole operation be a bust, but they also might never have what they needed to prove Rick's guilt. That thought churned her stomach and left a bitter taste in her mouth.

With two items left on her list, she tagged Charles to handle the first. "Will you advise the nurse and Mauricio's doctor not to engage in conversation when Rick comes in? He'll try to slip in unnoticed. If they see him, they should act as if they don't."

Charles nodded. "I'll talk to them."

She checked her watch. "We've got about two hours. I'm going to get out of here and talk to Jack. He's a key player, so I sure hope he can act." Jo took a shaky breath. She had to rely on her team. Though she trusted Charles with every fiber of her being, she wished that Nae were there to watch her back. "I'll need you to get my ears from the techs then get the hell out of here. I have an unmarked sitting on the street outside Emergency. I'll meet you there."

Charles gave her a quick salute. "We've got this."

"I know you do." She checked her notes one last time and marched to the elevator. *The only thing left is to make the call.*

Chapter 25

Jo paused outside Jack's office, debating how to act. *Come on, Jo, you're acting like a teenager. This is work.* She rapped on the door and leaned forward to listen for a response.

"Come in."

She poked her head in the door.

Jack looked up from the papers spread out on his desk, his face set in a scowl, but his eyes softened when he saw her. "Hey."

Stepping into the expansive office, she said, "We're ready for you to make the call."

Jack pushed the spread-out papers together and stacked them on the corner of his heavy oak desk then dropped his pen into a wood pencil holder with the Kent County seal emblazoned in gold plating on the front. "Tell me again why we're leading Rick right to our only witness?"

Jo lifted her hands to her hips. Her fingers dug into her sides. *He is not going to muck this up now.* "We've already had this conversation. He's not going to just come out and admit that he set Mike up and is responsible for the death of the one man who can finger him. He has to believe he's going to silence a witness."

Jack crossed his arms over his chest. His black suit jacket bunched around his turquoise shirt. "I don't want to play a part in setting up a man to get hurt. That sets the city, and me personally, up for a lawsuit."

Jo leaned on his desk, her fingers splayed. "He's not going to walk into the hospital and kill him. He's not stupid. He's going to attempt to shut him up. He'll threaten him, he'll pull out all kinds of stops, but he won't hurt him."

"How do you know?"

"He's a detective, Jack! He knows that there's a guard right outside the door. He knows that there are cameras and all kinds of potential witnesses. All he's going to do is tell him he needs to keep his mouth shut. He's going to slip in and out as quietly as possible."

Jack picked at nonexistent lint on his jacket then brushed his pants legs. "If he knows he's guarded, he may not come at all."

She seethed at his nonchalance. "He has to. As far as he'll be concerned, this will be his only chance. Once Mauricio talks to you, all bets are off, so he'll take the chance. He's been working Narcotics for years. He's been in plenty of dangerous, unpredictable situations, and he's good at thinking on his feet. He'll make up a good excuse to be in that room and figure the guard won't even question it."

"Which, of course, he won't, because he's your guy."

Jo gave him a feral grin. "Exactly. And when that goes well, he'll feel even more confident."

Resting his arms on his desk, Jack stared at his folded hands and worked his jaw.

"Jack, I've got the whole team set up and ready to go," Jo said through gritted teeth.

He sighed. "All right, where's my script?"

Slapping her hands on his desk, she said, "That's what I wanted to hear." She pulled a yellow legal pad from her bag and handed it to him.

He picked up the pad, leaned back in his chair, and propped his ankle on his knee. His socks were navy blue and covered in snowflakes.

"Do you actually like winter?" Jo asked, scowling at the socks.

Jack's puzzled gaze followed hers, and his face brightened. "Oh yeah, I love it!"

She narrowed her eyes. "You're dead to me."

"But it's—"

Jo held her hand up. "Nope, don't want to hear it." She pointed at the notepad. "Learn your lines."

"Bossy," Jack mumbled. He pulled a pair of black plastic-framed glasses from his jacket pocket, slid them on, then settled back in his chair to read Jo's notes.

Jo wandered to a light-maple bookshelf. Two framed pictures sat among the legal tomes, both beaming photos of Jack with a beautiful brunette, the first on a beach, her mass of curly hair blowing in the wind, Jack's eyes mischievous, and the second next to a hospital bed with a newborn swaddled in a white blanket with pink and blue stripes. The woman was gaunt, her face pale and thin. A blond curly-headed toddler was curled up next to her mom. *Maddie and baby Logan. That couldn't have been long before his wife died.*

Jack scooted his chair forward and tossed the notebook down. "So basically, I'm calling Rick and telling him that I have an informant who's telling me Mike was set up to be killed on the bust, and he's going to tell me who it is in exchange for a commuted sentence, yadda yadda. I'll say that I thought since he was Mike's partner and he was there that night, he may want to sit in and hear what this guy has to say. Courtesy call and all that. I can't be there until six o'clock because I have a meeting." He rubbed his hands over his face and scratched his cheek. "I think I'll say I have a deposition. That way, I can say it will be around six, but you know, these things can go a little late. I may not be there right at six."

"Not your first rodeo, is it?"

"Nope." Jack checked his watch. "Now get the hell out of here so I can make this call."

Jo scowled. "Why do I have to leave?"

Jack waved his hand toward the door. "I can't have you in here distracting me."

"How am I distracting you?"

"You just are." Jack pointed at the door. "Go get settled with Charles. I'll let you know when I get in touch with him."

Jo glanced at the Oldsmobile Scramble golf clock behind his head. "You have fifteen minutes. Don't call him before three o'clock."

Jack saluted. "Yes, ma'am, Lieutenant. Now go."

Jo rolled her eyes and walked out.

JO PARKED ACROSS THE street and a block down from the hospital, careful to avoid any hospital parking structure where Rick might recognize her truck, then walked to the car where Charles waited, reclined in the driver's seat with his notebook in his lap.

Sliding into the passenger seat, Jo said, "And now we wait. I feel like every damn time something is going on with Mike's case, I'm sitting in a car."

Charles pulled his seat to an upright position and tossed the notebook into the back seat. "Yeah, it sucks just sitting here."

Jo pulled out her phone. *Six minutes after three.* She dropped the phone into the console, leaned her head back, and closed her eyes. "Jack should be on the phone with Rick by now."

"How long do you think it will take him to get here?" Charles asked.

"He'll know he has about three hours before Jack will get here, but I think he'll come as soon as he can get away. He won't want to cut it too close."

Jo took the two-way radio from the dashboard and pressed the talk button. "This is Lieutenant Riskin. Is everyone in place? Eyes and ears planted?"

A male voice crackled over the line. Jo recognized it as Don Moreland's. "Eyes and ears are currently being planted. Everything is under control. Stay out of sight."

Jo looked at Charles and rolled her eyes. She held the two-way up to her mouth and pressed the button. "We're well out of sight and will stay that way." Tossing the radio back onto the dash, she said, "I hate this."

Her phone toned, indicating a text message. She grabbed it from the console and dropped it between the seats. "Damn it!" She frantically dug between the seats, only serving to lodge the phone down farther.

Charles laid a hand over Jo's. "Relax. Let me help." He reached over to the front of Jo's seat and pulled back the seat release. The seat slid back, and her phone dropped to the floor.

Jo grimaced. "Thanks. I'm a little rattled."

"That's what I'm here for."

Jo opened the text message from Jack. *Call made. He fell for it hook, line, and sinker.*

Nice work. I owe you.

I like the sound of that. Need any other favors?

Jo could feel the smile spread slowly across her face.

Jo turned her body away from Charles and tapped out, *You can handle only one favor for me at a time,* then slid her phone into her back pocket. She scooted down in her seat then pulled her case notebook out of her bag and scanned the notes of each open case, glancing at the clock periodically. The radio crackled occasionally, sending a rush of adrenaline pumping through her veins each time, but it was always idle chat or equipment tests between techs. When her notes were updated, she slapped the notebook shut. She missed Lynae and the constant chatter that filled the time on stakeouts. She wanted to talk about Mike, maybe even about Jack. The quiet wait was torture. She turned to Charles, who was silently scrolling through screens on his phone. "How are things going with you and Lisa?"

He shrugged. "Pretty much the same. I've been calling her every night. Sometimes she talks to me. Sometimes she doesn't."

"What about the kids?"

"I talk to them every night." His face brightened. "I'm going to see them this weekend. I think I'll take them to Dave and Buster's to play some video games."

"That would be fun for all of you."

"Yeah, I probably like video games more than a guy my age should."

She chuckled. "Well, it's good to have that in common with them, anyway."

"Whatever happens with me and Lisa, I'm gonna take care of those two. I mean, I know I'm a lousy husband, but I'm not a lousy dad."

"You never have been," Jo said sincerely. "Just give them your time. That's all they really need."

Hanging his head, he said, "I'm sorry I copped an attitude. This has been pretty hard to handle, and I was just being a jerk. I would never let it affect my work. I hope you know that."

"You know how I feel about getting justice for every victim. I probably came down on you a little harder than I had to. Just don't do it again, and we can forget it ever happened."

Charles smirked. "Deal."

Jo checked her watch for the umpteenth time then flopped her head back against the headrest. "This is taking forever. Maybe he's not coming."

"He may have been in the middle of something. He wouldn't want to look suspicious bailing out."

"I know. He's too smart for that. Maybe he's too smart for our plan."

"No, it's a good plan. Maybe he wants to make it look like he just got there a little early."

"That makes sense. He wouldn't get here too early. Then what? Leave and come back? That's way more suspicious. Getting here just a little early would be much smarter."

Charles gave her a smug look. "Yeah, well, I'm pretty damn smart."

"And so humble." Jo settled back into her seat. "Why, oh why, didn't I bring coffee? It's like it's my first stakeout or something."

"Sorry, I never thought about coffee."

"Lynae would have brought some." When Charles gave her a blank look, she shrugged. "Just sayin'."

"I've got some Coke back there," he said, jerking his head toward the back seat.

"I guess that'll have to do." When she turned around, she found a cooler on the floor of the back seat and retrieved a twenty-ounce Diet Coke. She unscrewed the top and took a long, satisfying drink.

The two-way crackled. "Subject has entered the room."

Jo jerked and spilled pop on her lap. She wiped a hand across her pants, screwed the top back on the bottle, then threw it into the back seat. After grabbing the two-way from the dashboard, she turned up the volume then punched the talk button. "Patch us in."

"WHAT ARE YOU DOING here?" Mauricio's voice quivered.

"I got a call from Mr. Riley at the prosecutor's office. He asked me to meet him here," Rick replied smoothly. The sound of his voice made Jo's gut quiver.

"He told you?"

"Yes, he told me you have some news relating to the murder of my old partner."

"I... um..."

"He called me as a courtesy." Jo heard a chair scrape across the floor. "I hope you're not expecting him to cut you a deal."

"He's going to help me get out early."

"No, he's not. You'll be right back in your cell as soon as you talk. Won't that be nice?"

"He said..." Mauricio's voice trailed off.

Jo snapped her head to look at Charles. "He's confusing him."

He held up his hand. "Give him a chance."

The bed squeaked. *Mauricio shifting his weight or Rick leaning on the bed?* "I've got good information. Right from Drevin Clayburn."

"And what exactly do you think you know?" Rick asked.

"I should wait till Mr. Riley gets here." Mauricio's voice cracked, nerves clearly playing with his mind.

Jo shook her head. "No, you shouldn't!"

"I think what you should do is tell me what you know," Rick said.

"Then what?" Mauricio squeaked.

"I guess that depends on what you tell me," Rick replied in his smooth, calm voice.

"Drevin told me everything. He told me he was getting out and it's because you were gonna fix it," Mauricio's voice finally crackled over the radio.

"Now why in the world would I do that, Mauricio? Drevin Clayburn killed my partner."

"He told me—"

"Drevin was a liar." Jo could hear the sneer in Rick's voice. She pictured him leaning over Mauricio's bed.

"Then how come he had a recording of you telling him to off that cop?"

The silence lasted so long Jo thought they had lost their connection. She picked up the two-way, smacked it with the palm of her hand, then fiddled with the volume button. She heard a chain rattle. Mauricio was fidgeting.

"What do you want?" Rick spit out.

"I want to get out," Mauricio said so quietly Jo barely heard. She turned the volume button all the way to full.

"I can get you out faster than some prick prosecutor."

Jo sat up straight and stared at the two-way, willing Rick to say more.

"Mr. Riley said he can help me. If I tell him what I know, he'll help me."

"No, he won't!" Rick roared, followed by more silence. "No, he won't," he said more calmly. "You keep your mouth shut, and I'll get you out. I have connections."

"I don't trust you. You killed your partner for drug money."

Jo raised an eyebrow at Charles. "The little man has some balls after all."

Something banged on the floor. "Listen, you pissant, you never say that again."

"Drevin told me. You gave him the gun, said it was unregistered. You told him to go to the grocery store to get a car because they don't have cameras. He told me everything. You looked the other way for the payout, but your partner was catching on."

"You keep your mouth shut, or you'll end up just like your good friend Drevin."

"He said your partner would never look the other way. He was gonna take you down so you had to off him."

Jo squeezed her eyes shut. Her jaw clenched so tight her teeth ached. *Poor Mike. He knew Rick was dirty. A little more time, and he would have taken him down. Why didn't he tell me?* She knew the answer before her mind had even asked it. He was protecting her.

"I said shut your mouth," Rick spat. "One word of this... One fucking word, and you'll be sorry. You won't get off as easily as your cellmate did. I'll make you wish you were dead first."

"What am I supposed to do? I told Mr. Riley I got something for him," Mauricio pleaded.

"You're gonna tell him that you don't know nothin'. You're gonna tell him you made it up so you could get out."

"Okay, I won't tell him," Mauricio squeaked. "But you gotta help me out."

"I'll help you as soon as you tell me where that recording is."

"No. That's all I got. I give you that, then I got nothing."

"You *don't* give me that, and you're gonna suddenly find yourself suicidal just like your friend did."

Jo heard rustling and the squeak of bedsprings. Mauricio was fidgeting. "Okay, but he's gonna be here soon. What do I do?"

"You tell him you lied. I'm gonna be all in your face, telling you how you gotta give it up because Mike was my partner. But don't say one word."

Jo pounded her fist on the dashboard. Tears choked the back of her throat and spilled down her cheeks. "Son of a bitch! Listen to him. He didn't give one damn about Mike."

Charles looked at her with a cocky grin. "No, he didn't, but he's done, and you have your answers. You nailed him, Jo."

Jo heard a door slam. "Don't move, Rick." Don's voice had an air of command Jo hadn't heard before.

"What the hell?"

"You're under arrest for the murder of Detective Mike Riskin and inmate Drevin Clayburn. You have the right to remain silent."

"Don—"

"Anything you say can and will be held against you in a court of law."

"I know my damn rights."

"You have the right—"

Jo shut off the two-way and flopped her head back on the headrest. "Hell, yeah, we did." She took a minute to let it sink in then flung the door open and jumped out. *His partner. His best friend.* The betrayal was immeasurable. Her gut scorched with anger so intense it seared through the pain.

Charles trotted up beside her. "Where are you going?"

"I need to see him," she seethed.

He grabbed her shoulder and pulled. "That's a bad idea right now."

Jo jerked away and stomped to the side door of the hospital, where the police cars waited. A uniformed officer pushed through the door. Rick followed, hands bound and head down. Don held one arm and had the other hand firmly on his shoulder.

Jo stormed up to the group. "How could you?" she spat.

Rick's head jerked up, his eyes intense. "Jo, I—"

"You were his best friend. His partner. He trusted you."

"I didn't mean for it to go this far."

"Save it for the jury."

Rick's eyebrows shot up. His face was smug. "It'll never get to a jury."

Jo dug her fingernails into her palms. "You son of a bitch," she fumed. Her arm shot back.

Grabbing her fist and forearm, Charles said, "Don't give him the satisfaction."

Jo yanked her arm away and straightened her jacket then lifted her chin. "Get him out of here."

Jo watched Don push Rick into the back seat of the waiting patrol car then climb into the front passenger seat. As the car drove off, she turned to Charles. "What the hell?"

"Jo, you couldn't—"

"Of all people, I never thought *you* would stop me from decking him."

Charles shrugged. "The high road sucks, but you had to take it."

Laying her hand on Charles's arm, she said, "Thanks for forcing me onto it. I wanted to pummel the hell out of him."

"Don't we all."

The anger seethed, and the pain burned. "This *will* make it to court," she said through clenched teeth.

"Yes, it will. He can talk all the smack he wants, but he hung himself, and he'll pay."

Jo smiled at the thought. "You know, other than a deficit in small talk and a lack of reading my mind, you make a pretty good temporary partner."

"I'm gonna tell Lynae you said that."

"Emphasis on temporary," Jo said then gave him a wave as he veered off toward the car.

As she walked back to her truck, Jo dialed Lynae's number. When her partner answered, she let the tears come. "We got him, Nae."

"Oh my God, Jo, finally. That's the best news I've heard since... well, ever."

Jo wiped her face on the sleeve of her coat. "I wish you could have been here."

"Me too. I've been sitting here dying. I want to hear every single word of what happened, every move that was made. Everything."

Jo slid into the driver's seat of her truck. "That could take a while. I'll be home in twenty minutes. I've got cold beer in the fridge."

"I'm on my way."

Chapter 27

"We did it, Mike. We took Rick down." Jo sat in front of the dark gravestone. The half-frozen ground was numbing.

I knew you would.

"He'll pay for the rest of his life. It's not enough, and it won't bring you back, but at least it's something."

It is good enough, Jo. It has to be.

Jo pulled her legs up and wrapped her arms around them. "I'm sorry you had to go through that alone. I wish you had talked to me."

Rick was dangerous. I didn't want to get you involved.

"I was pregnant. You were protecting me."

Always.

She pulled her coat tightly around her body. A light snow fell, the flakes melting as they touched the ground. Water drizzled down the tombstone. She reached out and brushed it from Mike's name then pulled her sleeve over her hand and also wiped Little Mike's. The snow kept falling and obscuring the words.

No matter how hard or how many times I wipe it away, I'll never be able to keep up. Maybe it's time to just let it be.

She scooted to her knees and rearranged the golf balls and toy truck she had placed on the ledge of the gravestone. She kissed her hand and pressed it to Mike's name then did the same with Little Mike's. "I love you guys, and I always will."

After getting to her feet, Jo walked slowly out of the cemetery. She pulled out her phone and dialed Jack's number. "Want to take the kids to the children's museum?"

"You bet. When can you be ready?"

She looked back at the dark stone of Mike's grave and took a deep breath as it blurred behind unshed tears. "I'm ready now."

Acknowledgments

Writing a book is an experience in which you genuinely find out who your friends are. I'm humbled and grateful beyond words for the outpouring of support by family, friends, and coworkers. To include the name of each person who encouraged and supported me is impossible. You know who you are, and I truly appreciate each and every one of you.

I would be remiss if I didn't include a special note for a few people who went above and beyond.

The professionals at Streetlight Graphics for creating my amazing book cover.

The editors and proofreaders at Red Adept Publishing, especially Lynn McNamee and Susie Driver, for pushing me, at times while I kicked and screamed, to take my characters and story to the next level. I'm in awe of your knowledge and professionalism and thankful for your patience and friendship.

Kurt Delia, CEO of Delia Tactical International LLC, for your willingness to school an old friend on police procedures in officer-involved shootings. You're the nicest scary, kick-ass dude I know, and I'm glad you're on my side.

Diane Butts and Kim May for throwing me one heck of a book-signing party for *Warped Ambition*! That's going to be hard to top, but I'm willing to try!

Stacy Hubert for meetings to discuss plot lines, "what if" text messages, your early read (even if I don't love all the red), and your honest opinion. Your friendship means the world to me.

My parents and sisters for all the love and support that anyone could hope for. I'm more grateful for your encouragement and determination to support and promote me than I could ever put into words.

My kids, without whom none of this would matter. Dream big and fight with all you have for those dreams. There's no part of me that doubts you will. I'm proud every day to call you mine.

John—like everything else in my life, this dream is possible because of your love, fierce loyalty, and unfailing belief in me. Thanks for sharing the joy when I succeed and the tears when I don't. Successes and failures come and go, but you will always be my constant, my rock, my love.

Also by Debbie S. TenBrink

A Jo Riskin Mystery
Warped Ambition
Warped Passage

Watch for more at debbietenbrink.wixsite.com/author.

About the Author

Debbie TenBrink grew up on a farm in West Michigan, where her family has lived for over 150 years. She still lives within five miles of her childhood home with her husband, four children, and dog, Mojo (who is the only real-life character in her book). She has a Master's degree in career and technical education, and she taught computer classes in two local colleges before beginning her current career as a software specialist for a law firm.

In her free time, Debbie enjoys camping, hiking, sports, and any other activity she can use as an excuse to spend time in the great outdoors. Other hobbies include reading (of course), having long conversations with the characters living in her head, and an almost frightening interest in true crime TV shows.

Her passion for writing began in childhood with short stories and poetry, and she can't remember a time when she didn't know that she would someday write a novel.

Read more at debbietenbrink.wixsite.com/author.

About the Publisher

Dear Reader,

We hope you enjoyed this book. Please consider leaving a review on your favorite book site.

Visit https://RedAdeptPublishing.com to see our entire catalogue.

Don't forget to subscribe to our monthly newsletter to be notified of future releases and special sales.